Heaven Scent

By Sasha Wagstaff

Changing Grooms
Wicked Games
Heaven Scent

Heaven Scent

SASHA WAGSTAFF

headline
review

First published in 2011 by HEADLINE REVIEW
An imprint of HEADLINE PUBLISHING GROUP

1

Cataloguing in Publication Data is available from the British Library

ISBN 978 07553 7814 2

Typeset in Garamond by Avon DataSet Ltd,
Bidford-on-Avon, Warwickshire

Printed and bound in Great Britain by
Clays Ltd, St Ives plc

Headline's policy is to use papers that are natural, renewable and
recyclable products and made from wood grown in sustainable forests.
The logging and manufacturing processes are expected to conform
to the environmental regulations of the country of origin.

HEADLINE PUBLISHING GROUP
An Hachette UK Company
338 Euston Road
London NW1 3BH

www.headline.co.uk
www.hachette.co.uk

For Mum and Dad,
for all those summers spent in France and much more

Prologue

It was true that the French loved a good funeral, Guy Ducasse thought as he stared out of the window at the newly dug grave. He raked a shaking hand through his sleek silver hair, leaving it uncharacteristically dishevelled. It was almost June and brilliant sunshine played on the new gravestone, seemingly unaware of the mourners' preference for a more appropriately dismal, grey sky.

Guy glanced at his elder son Xavier. Wearing a charcoal-grey suit with a discreet black Yves St Laurent tie, Xavier appeared outwardly poised, glamorous, even. His chocolate-brown eyes were impenetrable, as usual, but behind the suave exterior, Guy knew Xavier to be passionate and headstrong, just like his late mother.

'First your mother . . . and now Olivier,' Guy said in a hoarse voice. 'It's too much, Xav.'

Xavier turned away and glanced at the private garden-cum-graveyard attached to La Fleurie, the Ducasse family's beautiful Provence estate. The walled-off garden was as neat as a pin but, Xavier thought grimly, it was far more crowded than it should have been. Moss-covered gravestones marked the resting places of Aunt Paulette and Uncle Henri, of Xavier's own mother and now, with a suitably stylish slab of pristine black marble, Olivier had joined them.

Death by jet ski, Xavier mused. His cousin Oliver had been a hugely likeable playboy who, during his brief but explosive twenty-six years on the planet, had somehow

1

managed to clock up an astonishing number of wrong-doings. And as much as Xavier had adored his cousin, he had to admit that 'unruly, spoilt and irresponsible' would perhaps have been a more fitting epitaph for his headstone than the flowery, poetic prose Leoni had insisted upon. But, of course, no one liked to speak ill of the dead.

'What the hell was he doing in St Tropez, anyway?' Leoni asked, joining Xavier.

'I know . . . Plage de Tahiti, of all places.' Xavier smiled at Olivier's elder sister. The nudist beach just south of St Tropez had been made famous by Brigitte Bardot back in the 1950s but even now it boasted its fair share of hardcore exhibitionists. Still, as wild and self-indulgent as Olivier had been, it was an unlikely holiday destination for the eligible young bachelor.

Leoni tried to smile back. Clutching a cup of hot coffee, she wore a chic black couture dress that gave her an air of composure but Xavier, noting her shaking hands and pale complexion, knew his cousin was distraught at losing her brother. With her glossy brown hair cut in a sharp, chin-length bob and her brown eyes hidden behind glasses, Leoni resembled the consummate businesswoman, even on a day like this. Fiercely independent, she had been brought up to hide her emotions, just like everyone else in the family, but inside, she was vulnerable and feeling terribly alone.

Xavier snaked an arm round Leoni's shivering body as she slumped against him, slopping her coffee on the exquisite, period flooring.

'How could he do this to me, Xav?' Leoni sobbed as she allowed him to gently remove the coffee cup from her hands. 'He was my brother . . . he was all I had left . . .'

'I know,' Xavier soothed as her tears soaked his shoulder. Suddenly she twisted away from him and headed to a quiet corner to try to pull herself together.

Xavier felt a reassuring hand on his shoulder. 'Ashton,'

he said, turning to find a familiar face. 'So glad you could make it.'

'Sorry I missed the service,' Ashton said in English, his attempts at French atrocious at the best of times. Worriedly, he shot a glance at Leoni. 'I got here as quickly as I could . . . terrible delays, of course.'

Xavier gave him a warm smile. Ashton Lyfield was a family friend, a school pen pal from England who had been taken under Olivier's hedonistic wing one summer a decade or more ago. Ashton and Olivier had become firm friends – rather surprisingly considering Olivier had always been flamboyant and charmingly insincere, whereas Ashton, with his very blue eyes and sandy blond hair, was honest and engaging. More than that, Ashton was most emphatically British although he harboured a love of all things French. These days, he worked as an architect in Paris but spent all of his spare time at La Fleurie with the Ducasse family – a semi-permanent but very welcome house guest.

'God, I'm going to miss Oliver.' Ashton grinned but it was tinged with obvious sadness. 'Strange, really. He was such an unpredictable, unreliable bastard, never where he was supposed to be and always up to no good. But I couldn't help thinking the world of the crazy, bloody idiot, you know?'

He frowned. 'Where are the twins?'

'I sent them back to the house after the service,' Xavier answered. 'Seraphina was a mess and Max . . . well, you know how out of control he's been since our mother died.' He grimaced. 'Their private college has given them compassionate leave but I still think someone needs to keep a close eye on them.'

Ashton nodded, looking up as a tall, soignée woman entered the room. Trailing distinctive wafts of the classic Rose-Nymphea perfume she always wore, Xavier's grandmother Delphine leant heavily on her mahogany cane as she paused before the family. Everyone jumped to their feet, and no

3

wonder – Delphine was a force to be reckoned with; a veritable backbone of steel disguised in a vintage Chanel suit and topped with a chignon of deceptively soft-looking snow-white hair.

'Mother,' Guy said respectfully, taking Delphine's arm as her keen, hazel eyes surveyed the family.

'We must be strong,' she said, frowning at Leoni who was struggling to control herself in the corner. How inappropriate. Clearly, they were all upset about Olivier's death, but there were practicalities to deal with and sobbing into a tissue wasn't going to do anyone any good. 'Pascal is here,' Delphine announced as an unassuming, bespectacled man in his sixties joined them. 'I assume everything is in order, Pascal?'

Never failing to be intimidated by Delphine whenever she made the trip from her home in Toulouse, the family solicitor nonetheless found himself duty bound to deliver some bad news. 'I'm afraid not,' he answered solemnly, producing a huge batch of paperwork tied up with neat ribbons. 'I have discovered something about Olivier that is rather . . . unfortunate.'

'What does that mean?' Leoni asked nervously. 'Is it gambling debts? I mean, we all know Olivier had a problem but surely that sort of thing can be brushed under the carpet?'

'There *are* a few debts to settle at various casinos,' Pascal offered, 'but that's not the problem. It's his share of the family business that's become an issue, you see.'

Guy frowned. 'Surely it just gets divided up and redistributed? Each member of the family is a shareholder . . . it's how we've always done things.'

Pascal sighed. 'I know, Guy. Look, I'm sorry to tell you this at such a sad time but it seems Olivier wasn't just on holiday in St Tropez.' Looking worried, he bit the bullet. 'By all accounts, Olivier was . . . well, he was on his honeymoon.'

'What?' Delphine was stunned. 'Married . . . *Olivier?* No, I don't believe it . . . that can't be true.'

4

Xavier quickly examined the paperwork. 'It *is* true,' he confirmed. Christ, only Olivier could deliver such a surprise after his untimely demise. 'According to this, Olivier married an English girl called Cat Hayes three weeks before his accident. The sly fox. He got hitched without telling us, then died a few weeks later. What are the odds?' Xavier instantly regretted his flippancy when Leoni, her face white and pinched, abruptly sat down.

Ashton, struggling to keep up with the high-speed French conversation that was going on around him, finally worked out what Xavier had said. His mouth fell open. This was outrageous, even for Olivier!

Delphine was pale. An English girl? Meeting Guy's eyes, she acknowledged that this wasn't the first time an English girl had married into the Ducasse family. But Elizabeth, Guy's deceased and much beloved wife, had been a different case entirely. This girl was an unknown . . . an intruder.

'Who is she?' Leoni asked, her voice shrill. 'She must be some sort of gold digger!'

A tight-lipped Delphine agreed. 'She must be dealt with . . . immediately. I will move back here until this is sorted out, Guy.'

Leoni's eyes widened in horror.

Delphine ignored her and appealed to Guy. 'There is so much at stake, Guy. The business . . . Olivier's share is worth – well, it's priceless.'

Groaning inwardly at the thought of untangling such a mess, Guy took the marriage certificate from Xavier. How could Olivier have been so stupid? To marry a girl he most likely barely knew . . . it was imprudent, even for his nephew! He turned to Pascal. 'Where is Cat Hayes now? Back in England, I assume.'

Pascal consulted his notes. 'It would seem so.'

Seeing Leoni trembling, Ashton reached out and put a hand on her shoulder. 'Maybe this girl . . . this Cat . . . didn't know

5

who Olivier was?' he suggested. 'Isn't it possible she met him in good faith and just . . . fell in love?'

Leoni shrugged off his hand. 'You're just saying that because she's English!' she spat then instantly regretted it. 'I'm sorry, Ashton. You forget that not everyone is as "proper" as you are.'

Xavier shot Ashton a warning glance; no one could reason with Leoni in her current mood. Diplomatically, Ashton retreated; the last thing he wanted to do was upset his friend further.

'Look, we don't know who Olivier's wife is or what she knows,' Guy cut in sensibly. 'I think we should invite her to La Fleurie and find out what her intentions are.'

'Welcome her with open arms, you mean?' Leoni exploded. 'Over my dead body.' She flushed, casting her eyes to the ground. 'Sorry, bad joke.'

'We will give her a chance,' Guy admonished. 'That's all I'm saying. Pascal, please prepare a letter asking this girl . . . this woman . . . to join us here in Provence.' He rubbed his chin ruefully. 'God, we don't even know how old she is!'

'I'll also prepare a legal document,' Pascal said, sliding his eyes to Delphine's for approval. 'Something formal, something that makes the feelings of the family absolutely clear.'

Delphine nodded. 'Very good, Pascal. Nothing is more important than the business. Or the family, naturally.'

Leoni eyed her grandmother. 'Ah yes, business and family,' she repeated with more than a hint of sarcasm. 'What, Grandmother, could *possibly* be more important?'

Smacking the floor sharply with her cane, Delphine limped out of the room with her back erect and her shoulders square.

Xavier surveyed the effect of Olivier's bombshell. His cousin would be rolling around in his grave with glee if he knew the commotion he'd caused. However, for the rest of them, it presented a very real and very complicated dilemma. Was

Olivier's wife . . . or widow, as she was now, genuine? Had she known who Olivier was and how much he was worth when she married him?

Xavier shrugged the thought aside. Whatever the truth, this Cat Hayes was in for a rough ride. Unless she had seriously done her homework, she would have no idea how tight-knit and loyal the Ducasse family were. And if his grandmother had anything to do with it, Olivier's widow would find herself unceremoniously ejected from La Fleurie within the space of a few days, even if they did have to pay her off.

But then, Xavier thought philosophically as he watched his dysfunctional relatives bristling at the possibility of a battle, what family wouldn't want to protect a multi-million-euro perfume empire? Grabbing his cigarettes with a shrug, Xavier left them to it.

Chapter One

Staring out of the window, Cat numbly poured herself a glass of white wine. She glanced at the box on the table. It contained a neat stack of framed family photographs and a couple of awards she had won at work and the sight of it made her spirits plummet despairingly. As if things weren't bad enough . . .

The past seven months had been the toughest of her life. Even the usually raucous Christmas season had passed by in a dismal, uneventful blur, failing to lift her spirits and making her all the more aware of her solitary status. The one thing Cat had always been able to rely on – the one thing that had kept her going – had been her job with one of the most high-profile branding agencies in London. It had fired her up with passion and enthusiasm on a daily basis. Until today, at any rate.

Cat pushed her dark blond hair out of her eyes and groaned. Six or seven months ago, she had been a fun-loving, carefree girl with a good job, her own flat and nothing more taxing to worry about than where to go with her friends on a Friday night. What a difference a few months could make, she thought, biting her lip. Recklessly romantic at the best of times, she had well and truly thrown caution to the wind this time. While on holiday with her best friend Bella and a few other girls in glitzy St Tropez, Cat had fallen head over heels in love. A heady tryst with a gorgeous Frenchman had unexpectedly led to a simple but romantic marriage ceremony on a beach with a Provençal sunset shimmering in the background.

'There you are!' said Bella, bursting into the flat, a letter clutched in her hand. 'What are you doing here? Why aren't you in your own flat? I've been banging on the door for ages.'

Cat looked up vaguely. 'Sorry . . . I let myself in with your spare key because I knew you'd be home early today.' She gave her best friend a watery smile. 'I don't know how much longer I'll be in my flat, you see. And . . . I-I didn't want to be on my own.'

'Why aren't you at work?'

'Ah, work,' Cat said in a flat voice. She raised her wine glass in a mock salute and realized it was empty. 'I'm afraid I've just joined the ranks of the unemployed. Brian fired me this afternoon.'

'No way!' Bella slipped the letter into her pocket and slumped down next to Cat. 'How could he? You're the best in the business. And after everything you've been through too.'

'Brian doesn't care about that,' Cat informed her. 'He was furious with me for going on holiday, let alone for extending it for my honeymoon.' She winced as she said the word 'honeymoon'. Too emotionally spent to cry, she squashed it down and continued. 'Brian kept me on to finish the Neon Flash campaign then this afternoon, right after the deliriously happy client left, he fired me, telling me I'd let him down because I took a month off. I mean, seriously, Bel, I took a holiday for the first time in three years!'

'Bastard,' breathed Bella.

Neon Flash, a make-up brand developed by a skeletal pop star obsessed with eighties neon, had been an absolute nightmare, the most challenging of Cat's career. It had involved working twenty-hour days and Cat had dedicated herself to it without complaint both before and after her holiday. It had been gruelling but a welcome distraction from her grief. Now, she had nothing and all she could think about was Olivier.

Tall, with dark, mischievous eyes and hair the colour of glossy hazelnuts, Olivier had been one of the waiters who worked along the beachfront. He was penniless but happy, he said, and he possessed that indolent, sexy charm only the French can pull off. But that wasn't the only reason Cat had been attracted to him. Olivier was also hugely likeable; he worked hard and had a down-to-earth attitude to life. He had told her that he had been brought up in a dilapidated house in a Provençal village and his parents, like hers, had died when he was young. It had bonded them, giving them a connection Cat had never felt with anyone else. Her heart clenched as she thought about how happy she'd been, how carefree . . .

'And I've lost my flat,' she added in a small voice. 'It's going up for sale and I had to put an offer in by the end of the week. I can't do that without a job, can I?'

'Oh, Cat.' Bella squeezed her hand. Cat had been her best and most loyal friend since school and Bella couldn't bear to see the pain and anguish in her eyes. Until a few months ago when Olivier had died, Cat had been so full of life and laughter, and now she had suffered yet another crushing blow. Bella thought worriedly of the letter in her pocket but she knew she had to tell Cat.

'Sorry to dump this on you but . . . you know Serena in number ten?' Cat barely responded and Bella pushed ahead. 'She's been away in South Africa visiting that millionaire boyfriend of hers. Anyway, she came back on Sunday and she had this mountain of post and when she finally opened it all, she found this.' Bella pulled the letter out. 'It had been posted through her letter box accidentally. It's from some solicitor in France . . . Provence, to be exact.' Bella paused. 'The letter didn't make any sense to Serena but then she saw your name at the top so she gave it to me to pass on.'

Cat took it listlessly. 'I guess it's something to do with Olivier.'

'It is. Olivier *Ducasse*.'

'Who?' Cat asked, confused. Her Olivier went by the surname Laroque.

'That's what I'd like to know,' Bella responded. 'Because this letter is all about Olivier's death in St Tropez . . . and it's from his family.'

'His *what*? Olivier doesn't have any family. He said his parents died and he was all alone . . .' Cat stared at the letter, her eyes skimming over the polite words and formal English phrases, barely taking them in. They could have written it in French, Cat thought randomly; after all, she was fluent in the language thanks to the time she had spent in France with her parents as a child. But she guessed they didn't know that. Bewildered, she read some phrases aloud. '. . . *offer our most heartfelt condolences . . . hope you have recovered from Olivier's untimely death . . . please join us at our house in Provence to discuss some business . . .*' Cat met Bella's eyes. 'Business? What business?'

'I have no idea. Hang on . . . Ducasse . . . Ducasse . . .' Bella shook her head. 'Nah, it can't be them. Forget it.'

Not really listening, Cat reread the letter. 'Why would he lie about having a family?'

Bella shrugged. 'Maybe he's ashamed of them. Maybe they're a bunch of nutters and he didn't want you to be put off. Or . . .' Triumphantly, she threw another idea out. 'Perhaps he just fell out with them at some point and didn't want to talk about it. That sounds reasonable, doesn't it?'

Cat nodded slowly. 'I guess so. But I wish he'd confided in me about them, Bella. Maybe I could have done something . . . helped him mend whatever went wrong . . .'

Bella said nothing; now was not the right time. Still, when *was* the right time? She had tried once before to voice her concerns about Olivier not being who he said he was and

12

Cat had blown up spectacularly. There was a lot about Olivier that hadn't added up, such as his claiming to be penniless but somehow managing to afford a beachfront apartment in one of the swankiest areas in St Tropez, his phone constantly ringing, even though he claimed not to have any responsibilities elsewhere, his penchant for gambling and vintage champagne . . .

Maybe a rich friend had paid for the apartment, as he said, and for the champagne and the gambling. It was perfectly possible that Olivier had had rich friends who funded his holiday; he had been charming and charismatic enough to attract, well, anybody. But Bella had never managed to quite believe it.

'You should go,' she said brightly.

Cat lifted her head. 'Go? Go where?'

'To Provence.' Bella tapped the letter. 'I mean, you were his wife, you have a right to meet his family, don't you? Those officials treated you like dirt when Olivier died.'

Cat grimaced at the memory. It was true. When Olivier had been pronounced dead, she had been treated like some silly bimbo who should back off and let those in charge get on with their job. When she had tried to protest that she wasn't Olivier's girlfriend, she was his wife, the officials had shrugged dismissively and told her to go home. She'd been in no state to do anything but flee back to England to the security of her job and her friends.

'They must want to meet you,' Bella went on. 'Why else would they have sent you this letter asking you to join them in Provence?'

Cat shrugged. 'I just don't know if I can face it . . . it's been so hard . . .' Fiercely, she dashed her tears away.

Bella looked contrite. 'I can't even offer you a room in my flat,' she confessed. 'That guy I've been seeing for a while, Ben? I asked him if he wanted to move in at the weekend and he said yes . . .' She winced. 'I'm so sorry, Cat. I can tell him it's not possible if you need to stay here.'

Cat's head snapped up. What was she doing, sitting here being miserable? What would that achieve? She might be a jobless, homeless twenty-six-year-old widow, but life went on, she just had to take charge of it.

'All right, I'll go to Provence,' she said resolutely. 'I'll book a flight and go.'

Bella grinned. 'That's the Cat I've been missing for the last few months,' she said with some relief. 'I was beginning to think that crazy, reckless girl I used to be best mates with had gone for good.'

Cat held her wine glass out for a top-up. 'As if.'

Bella started to make plans. 'I can look for jobs for you while you're out there. Ben has some good contacts in the advertising business, he used to do IT for Brian's competitor. I'm sure we'll come up with something.' She chinked her glass against Cat's. 'By the time you've sorted out whatever business you need to in Provence, you'll have a brilliant new job and life will be back on track.'

'God, Bel, I hope you're right.' Cat gulped her wine. 'I just can't help worrying that Olivier's family might not like me as much as he did.'

'Why on earth wouldn't they?' Bella told her loyally. 'You're fabulous and I bet this trip will be just what you need to, you know, get some closure, or whatever they call it.' She pulled a face at the empty bottle. 'I just hope Olivier's family have a big enough supply of wine for your visit . . .'

Sitting in her office at the warehouse that packaged up Ducasse-Fleurie perfumes, Leoni gritted her teeth. She pushed her glasses further up her nose and sketched out yet another idea for the new line she was working on, scribbling rapidly for a good ten minutes without pausing. Finally she sat back and surveyed her handiwork. It was no good, she simply couldn't concentrate. Just like her other efforts this morning, her latest

14

one was terrible. Leoni screwed it up and threw it in the bin to join the pile of other scrunched-up, angry-looking balls of paper. Her ideas, usually so clear and precise, were muddled and chaotic this morning. Nothing was flowing and nothing made sense.

She stood up and surveyed the thousand-strong workforce that supported the Ducasse empire. They all seemed so laid-back. Where was the spark? Where was the passion? It was all very well being cosy and family orientated but she couldn't help thinking the business needed a vigorous shake-up. The fact was, Ducasse-Fleurie was flagging. No one wanted to admit to it but the figures spoke for themselves. Sales were down and the once well-respected Ducasse-Fleurie name was fading into the background as trendier, younger and fresher perfumes hit the market.

Ducasse-Fleurie had been resting on its laurels for too long, Leoni mused. No new fragrances had been created for years. Their bestselling classics, Rose-Nymphea and L'Air Sensuel, formed the mainstay of the business, but they were seen as the older woman's perfumes. Which made the product, and somehow the company itself, seem dated and out of touch. Ducasse-Fleurie still made money, vast quantities of it, comparatively speaking, but it was on the wane.

Leoni smoothed her chic black Roland Mouret dress and marched downstairs into the warehouse. If only she could create a new perfume – or 'juice' as it was known to insiders – herself because then she could take control and mastermind a company revamp. But since Aunt Elizabeth, their master 'nose' or scent creator, had died two years ago, there was no one to conceive a new fragrance.

Actually, that wasn't true, Leoni reminded herself as she sternly narrowed her eyes at a gossiping employee who quailed and hurriedly returned to work. Xavier had inherited his mother's rare and much sought after gift for blending aromas and was more than capable of taking over the creative arm of

Ducasse-Fleurie. He just didn't want to. Or maybe he had reasons none of them knew about, Leoni acknowledged more charitably. Xavier had fallen apart after Elizabeth had died and he had hung up his lab coat, apparently for good.

Leoni headed outside for some air. She wanted to develop a new fragrance, two even . . . a home fragrance line . . . a store in Paris . . . Ducasse-Fleurie had been conceived as a 'fragrance only' line like Fragonard, Annick Goutal and Pierre Bourdin, and for several decades it had outsold some of the most popular household names. The ongoing obsession with celebrity had saturated the fragrance market in the same way it had the publishing world, and classical perfume lines had been hit hard, with celebrity scents stealing most of the coveted top ten spots each summer. Leoni sighed and got into her navy sports car, the most sedate-looking car the Ducasse family owned. Since Olivier had died, nothing seemed right, Leoni thought. Her private life seemed stark and empty, and professionally she felt equally dissatisfied. She needed something, anything, to give her a new lease of life.

God, she missed Olivier so much it hurt! The grief she had barely allowed herself to acknowledge rose to the surface and threatened to suffocate her. And some other emotion was hovering nearby – fury. Leoni was so angry with Olivier, she could barely see straight. How dare he leave her like this, she raged as she activated the security gates and headed up La Fleurie's vast driveway. Didn't Olivier know how lost she would be without him? Didn't he realise the vulnerable position she would be in? Olivier might have been an irresponsible playboy but he had been her rock, the only one who ever took her work ideas seriously. Without him, working in the family business would be harder than ever.

How could he marry some stupid English girl and then get himself killed, the stupid idiot, Leoni thought tearfully. And on top of everything, her twenty-ninth birthday was only a few days away and a huge party had been planned, which was the last thing she wanted. She couldn't even summon up the enthusiasm to comment on colour schemes or food ideas.

Leoni came to a halt in the driveway just as another car smoothly pulled up next to her. With a sinking heart she realised it was her grandmother's bullet-grey limousine. The matriarch of the family was back, she thought gloomily, and that could mean only one thing. Aside from rocking her already unstable position in the family business and making a grand entrance before her birthday party, Delphine's arrival signified something Leoni had been absolutely dreading. After an inexplicable eight-month silence, Olivier's widow must be on her way. Maybe the strikes the French airport staff had promised would keep her away, Leoni thought hopefully. Or maybe they wouldn't. Leoni slammed her hand on the steering wheel. She couldn't bear it, she really couldn't. Wasn't it bad enough that Olivier had spent the last few weeks of his life with someone they didn't even know? And now this girl was actually going to be staying at La Fleurie with them; they would have to speak to her, eat with her even. It was nothing less than intolerable.

Feeling panicked, Leoni took out her mobile phone.

'Ashton?' she turned on her car engine. Remembering how terrible his French was, she spoke in English. 'I need a drink right now. Do you want . . . La Belle Vie is fine. I'll meet you there in five.'

'Should we disturb him?' Seraphina fretted as they loitered outside Guy's office. She fiddled nervously with the long white-blond plait that hung over one shoulder. 'I really want to spend some time with him before we go back to that horrible college again.'

Max shrugged, looking sullen. 'He'll be too busy. He always is.' He folded his arms across his chest, the gesture unconsciously defensive.

Seraphina sighed. Max was sensitive but the barriers he erected around himself made him quite unpleasant to be around at times.

Seeing Seraphina's nut-brown eyes cloud over with disappointment, Max relented.

'Fine, let's try.' But don't say I didn't warn you, his expression said as he moved closer to the door, his arms still folded and his chin tilted angrily.

Seraphina knocked on the door of their father's office.

'Come in!' came the rather curt response.

Seraphina unconsciously squared her shoulders. She glanced around the office, noting how disorganised it was. Cardboard boxes containing sample perfume bottles were stacked under the window, paperwork to be signed sat in a neglected pile on the desk and reams of the lilac ribbon Ducasse-Fleurie was famous for spilled down from the shelves. The air was infused with a rich, heady aroma from tester tabs and open bottles belonging to other perfume houses.

Guy looked up irritably. 'Yes?'

'We wondered if you wanted to do something,' Seraphina ventured timidly.

'Do something?'

Seraphina cringed, mortified by her father's slightly withering expression. 'Er . . . together, you know. You, me and Max.'

Guy suppressed a sigh and with obvious reluctance put the disappointing spreadsheets he was deciphering to one side. What was it about the twins that irked him so much? he asked himself.

Max was as tall as all the Ducasse men, with tousled dark hair and moody, liquid-brown eyes. But he had a chip on his shoulder the size of Paris and he wore a permanent scowl. He was wildly out of control and under constant threat of expulsion from his expensive college. Hardly the model son. And then there was Seraphina. She was the very image of his beloved Elizabeth with her fragile, luminous beauty and her dreamy, idealistic approach to life. She was wearing tight black jodhpurs and a red silk shirt, a disturbing combination of schoolgirl innocence and womanly maturity.

Guy stared at them, conscious of the inexplicable pain in his heart. He knew he couldn't deal with them right now. 'I . . . have too much work to do,' he stated, averting his eyes. 'I'm sorry,' he added inadequately, not looking up.

Max's lip curled. It was just as it had been for the last two years.

'Come on,' he said to Seraphina, taking her arm. 'We're clearly wasting our time here.' Ignoring his father's tense shoulders, Max shot him a contemptuous look before leaving.

Seraphina allowed herself to be pulled from the room and followed Max to the stables behind La Fleurie. Nothing seemed to please their father these days, she thought miserably, least of all his children.

Max saddled up his favourite horse, a fine dappled grey named Le Fantome. Some people said greys were unlucky but Max adored his horse. Even after what had happened to his mother, he trusted Le Fantome with his life. He pulled the worn, navy cashmere jumper he always wore out riding over his dark hair and breathed in the stable's pungent aroma of straw, manure and excited horses. It cleared his head and calmed him, the way it always did. He had found other ways to relieve his stress over the past couple of years but this was legal and far safer than his other hobbies.

'What do you think Olivier's wife will be like?' Seraphina wondered aloud, hoping to distract Max's dark mood. She smiled as her horse Coco, named after her heroine Coco Chanel, came to the stable door and nuzzled her hand.

Max shrugged, his mouth twisting scornfully. 'Who cares? She's probably just some bimbo who found out how much Olivier was worth and made him marry her somehow.' Inserting a foot into a stirrup, he smoothly mounted his horse.

Seraphina looked unconvinced as she hoisted a saddle on to Coco's back and quickly did up the straps. 'I can't imagine how anyone could have persuaded Olivier to do anything he didn't want to do.' She couldn't help feeling sorry for Olivier's bride; not only had she lost her new husband within weeks of marrying him, she now had the Ducasse family to contend with. And they were a force to be reckoned with, Seraphina thought grimly. The ones that were left, anyway. Suddenly overcome with sadness, she cast her eyes to the ground to hide her tears.

Max slipped off his horse and put his hand on her shoulder. 'Stop that, will you? You can't let this get to you . . . you just can't.'

'I know, I know. I'm trying to be strong.' Seraphina's shoulders shook as tears slid down her cheeks. 'It's just . . . losing Mother . . . and now Olivier . . . it's too much.'

Max felt despair wash over him. What did she want from him? Why did she keep crying like this? Max felt sorry for his sister but he didn't know how to deal with her unhappiness.

'Let's ride,' he said roughly, pushing her towards her horse. He remounted his and kicked his heels against Le Fantome's flanks. 'Catch me up!' he shouted as he cantered towards the Ducasse family lavender fields.

Quickly wiping her tears away, Seraphina jumped up on to Coco's back and headed after her twin. If Max could cope with Olivier's death without shedding a tear, then so must she.

With the assurance of a seasoned player, Xavier tossed his remaining poker chips on to the table and flipped his hand over. It was a royal flush, with spades – the perfect hand. There was a ripple of applause from the watching crowds but Xavier shook his head modestly. He might be a good bluffer but he couldn't take credit for the luck of the cards. Thank God he didn't have Olivier's penchant for gambling; as fun as it was, everyone knew the house always won in the end so it was a mug's game unless it was a casual pastime.

Rather like relationships, Xavier thought ironically. Fun was paramount – these days, anyway. He had long since given up serious dating. Just like gambling, it was only for the self-deluded, in his opinion. Catching the eye of a slinky brunette he had dated a few times, Xavier gave her an appraising once-over, wondering how on earth her low-cut satin dress was managing to contain her impressive breasts.

'You are a better poker player than your cousin, Monsieur Ducasse,' Gaston, the owner of the casino, said in a discreet aside. He nodded at the croupier to pay out, standing beside Xavier with his hands behind his back. 'Olivier's death is undoubtedly a great loss. My bottom line will suffer enormously in the long run.' He smiled genially.

'I think we both know you'll be far better off without Olivier wrecking the joint every Friday night, Gaston,' Xavier commented.

Gaston inclined his head politely. Olivier had rarely left the establishment quietly and usually it had been with the assistance of the casino's security staff. Xavier Ducasse, however, was a gentleman, known for good play, large tips and impeccable manners. He also boosted the number of female players, who seemed to have inside knowledge about Xavier's movements, turning up whenever he did, dressed to kill in sexy gowns. They were like groupies around a pop star, simpering and posturing in the desperate hope of being noticed, but Xavier seemed mostly oblivious to their presence.

'Olivier was reckless,' Xavier added, 'in all aspects of his life.' He scooped up his chips and deftly slipped a hefty one into the top pocket of Gaston's rather shiny suit. He headed to the bar, accompanied by Gaston. 'I trust my cheque covered all my cousin's outstanding debts.'

'It did. Thank you. You are indeed a gentleman.' Gaston

was aware that Xavier had paid Olivier's debts out of his own bank account rather than the family account.

'Ah well, it's easy to be a gentleman when you have money.' Xavier ordered a Scotch on the rocks.

'I disagree,' Gaston said politely. 'Your cousin had plenty of money too but he was short on both manners and decorum, if you don't mind me saying so.' He flushed. 'Not that I should speak ill of the dead.'

Xavier sipped his drink, glancing across the bar. The brunette he had spotted at the table was giving him the eye and he smiled at her.

'I heard Olivier got married before he died. Is this true? Olivier wasn't the marrying type, surely.'

'News travels fast around here.' Xavier stood up and smoothed the front of his well-cut Dior suit jacket. 'You heard correctly. Olivier's young widow is due at La Fleurie any day. Our solicitor's letter arrived at the wrong address, by all accounts, hence the long wait.'

'She is, perhaps, after the Ducasse fortune,' Gaston said lightly.

Xavier glanced down at the brunette who had shimmied to his side. 'Who knows?' He casually tucked the girl's hand through his arm, racking his brain to recall her name.

'Will you get involved in the business again one day?' Gaston asked hopefully. His mother was a huge fan of Ducasse Perfumes but having worn Rose-Nymphea for years, she yearned for something different – something 'fresh but timeless' was how she put it.

Xavier's chocolate-brown eyes had become distant, and Gaston thought he might have put his foot in it.

'Oh, I doubt I'll work at Ducasse-Fleurie again,' Xavier answered smoothly, guiding the brunette towards the exit. *Monique*, he thought triumphantly, that was her name. 'We have much better things to do, don't we, Monique?'

*

Miles away on a film set in Paris, Angelique Bodart was posing for her final scene, wearing a black silk negligée and high heels, her artfully coloured hair reaching almost to the cleft of her bottom. She pouted and slipped the negligée from her shoulders. It slithered to the ground, revealing very full breasts and creamy skin. She stood facing the camera full frontal, picked up a dagger and traced the tip down her naked body. The script called for her to stab herself because her lover had left her for another man. With several breathy moans, she fell to the ground and rolled into her final position. She turned her head to one side, buried her hand in her bush and faked death in the throes of a violent orgasm for all she was worth.

'And . . . CUT!' the director shouted frenziedly.

Angelique lay prostrate for a moment before sitting up gracefully and acknowledging the round of applause she received from the appreciative onlookers. She slipped her negligée back on loosely and strode to the director's chair where she inspected the rushes over his shoulder. Satisfied she looked her best and had given her most accomplished performance, Angelique took a seat at the back.

At once her assistant Celine was at her side.

'Newspapers,' Angelique demanded.

Celine hurriedly placed a number of crisp newspapers on Angelique's lap. 'Your favourite society pages are in the middle,' she stammered.

Angelique gave her an icy stare and flapped her hand in dismissal. Adoration was one thing but endless fawning became so boring after a while.

She flipped through the papers with little interest until she reached the society pages, where she spotted a picture of Xavier Ducasse with a glossy brunette on his arm. Angelique sucked in her breath. Xavier Ducasse, handsome, rich and sexy, always stylishly dressed and eminently beddable, as she knew first hand.

Angelique read the caption. 'Xavier Ducasse attending a charity ball with Monique Rouman, a model and aspiring actress, on his arm . . . they've been dating for a few weeks – could it be serious?' Angelique's stomach tightened with jealousy.

As she read the article beneath, her eyes widened in disbelief. It appeared that Olivier Ducasse hadn't died single, as was first supposed. It now transpired that he had married someone shortly before his accident, which meant that his inheritance – in other words, a sizeable slice of the family perfume empire – now belonged to his young English widow. Angelique read on, shocked to discover that Olivier's wife was a girl he had met in St Tropez last year.

Well, well, well. Angelique sat back, a smile playing across her lips. What an interesting turn of events. She would have enjoyed witnessing Delphine Ducasse's reaction to learning that Olivier had left a widow. If Angelique knew Delphine as well as she thought she did, the family matriarch would be fighting tooth and nail to make sure this unknown English woman didn't manage to get her hands on a single Ducasse euro or bottle of scent.

And what about Xavier, what did he think about it all? Xavier . . . the one that got away . . . the one man who had rendered her putty in his hands. At the time, their relationship had been private – not even the press had got wind of it, which was exactly how Angelique had liked it – and it might prove advantageous now, she thought.

She tossed the newspapers to one side, her blue eyes sparkling with anticipation. All she had to do was think of a way to be accepted into the Ducasse family fold once more. But would they welcome her back? She had tentatively tried to re-enter their circle a few times before but it had been tricky; the Ducasse family were a difficult clan to infiltrate, especially when it had been achieved once already.

Xavier, La Fleurie, the Ducasse family – everything about

them represented what Angelique so desperately wanted from life. The respect that came with old money, the lavish yet somehow discreet way they enjoyed the privileges their long-established name brought them . . . Angelique looked at the newspapers again. This news changed everything. She knew that now was the time to make a move. All she needed was a legitimate way in . . .

Chapter Two

Mystified, Cat leant forward and tapped the driver on the shoulder. 'I'm sorry, I think there must be some mistake,' she said in rapid French. 'We're going the wrong way, we must be.'

She sighed as the driver ignored her. Her French might be a little rusty but it was perfectly competent. The driver must have understood her but for some reason he wasn't responding.

Cat glanced out of the car window again. The sky was darkening as evening descended and they were heading south of a pretty village at the foot of Mont Ventoux. Cat was sure they must be lost but she was so tired after her terrible journey, she wasn't sure she was up to having a full-scale row with her driver. She was surprised he had even turned up. After being delayed for days at both Gatwick and Nice due to strikes by French airport staff, she had half-heartedly dialled the number given in the letter, not really expecting anyone to answer. She had been taken aback when a voice informed her that a driver would be with her in quarter of an hour. And, give or take a few minutes, he was.

Now Cat was beginning to think she should have made her own way to Olivier's parental home because after passing between two enormous security gates that had magically and soundlessly opened as they had approached, the car was heading down a long driveway overhung with trees. Occasional lamps marked the side of the gravel and bright lights flitted in and out of sight in the distance but it was impossible to see too far ahead.

'I'm looking for . . . for La Fleurie,' Cat repeated in French, glancing down at the address on the crumpled letter. What did La Fleurie mean? She racked her brains. Flowery? Full of flowers? 'It's probably very small . . . I'm sorry but we must have taken a wrong turning somewhere.'

'We are going the right way,' the driver assured her in accented English. He liked her cascade of messy, butterscotch-coloured hair and sexy, almost athletic body and wondered if this was Olivier's much-debated widow. He decided she must be; after all, who hadn't heard of the Ducasse estate around here? And she was English, as the rumours had suggested, even though she spoke decent French with a reasonable accent. In his opinion, she didn't look much like the gold digger everyone in the village said she was, but then what did he know?

Cat scratched her head. Where on earth were they going? Olivier said his family – what was left of them – lived in a tiny, rundown house in a little-known village. Even in the disappearing light, it was clear that this vista was far too grand. Cat sat back tiredly, wondering if the driver thought she was on holiday and in need of a flashy hotel to stay in.

Cat wished this was the case. She felt tense and anxious at the thought of meeting the Ducasse family – petrified, in fact. And this hapless driver going off course on to what looked like a millionaire's private grounds wasn't exactly helping.

The car swept round the final neat curve of the driveway and Cat gasped.

'La Fleurie,' the driver announced grandly as the car slid to a halt.

'It can't be,' Cat whispered in utter disbelief as she stared at what was a bona fide French château. It had three floors, with beautiful duck-egg blue shutters and a grand, double doorway flanked by lion statues. It was breathtaking.

As Cat climbed out of the car, she was hit by a rich, earthy scent. Looking up, she guessed it must be coming from the abundance of bright yellow blossoms that grew in a graceful arc across the front of the house.

'Le mimosa,' the driver explained helpfully. 'They . . . 'ow you say . . . bloom very early 'ere.' He nodded, giving her a wink. 'Useful for the *parfum, oui*?'

'Er . . . *oui*,' Cat agreed, nonplussed. Why on earth was he talking about perfume? Too stressed to think about it, she glanced down at her outfit, suddenly conscious that her black skinny jeans, dove-grey sweater and low-heeled boots might not be appropriate attire in a grand old château. Especially one that France's answer to royalty might reside in.

'The Ducasse family . . . they are very well respected in France,' the driver informed her. 'They have history . . . they are old money, you know?'

'Right.' Cat was feeling more anxious by the second. Old money? Well respected?

'Good luck!' the driver said with a grin after he had heaved her luggage out of the car. He waved away her attempts to pay him or even give him a tip. 'Guy Ducasse has taken care of everything.' Realising belatedly that he'd forgotten to advise the Ducasse family of Cat's arrival, he took the decision not to mention this to his passenger. 'You no longer need to worry about money, eh?' he added in rapid French.

Before Cat could ask him what he meant, he was back in his car and heading down the driveway, his mobile phone glued to his ear. Cat swallowed. Time to get on with it. She rang the doorbell at the front of the château but there was no response, so she headed round the side, dragging her bags behind her. She could hear classical music in the distance and she soon found herself in beautifully kept gardens lit by spotlights.

A sound to her right made her squint into the darkness. There was silence for a moment but then the noise came again – a distressingly pitiful sob. Dumping her luggage, Cat headed towards the sound and stumbled upon a small alcove, covered by a pretty tangle of roses. Inside the alcove was a young girl curled up in a foetal position, her long platinum-blond hair obscuring her face as she wept unrestrainedly.

Cat faltered, unsure whether she should intrude on the girl's distress. She could only be about fifteen.

Abruptly, the girl stood up, pushed back her blond hair and quickly wiped her eyes. Wearing an ivory silk dress that made the most of her porcelain skin she was astonishingly beautiful close up. Not noticing Cat standing in the shadows, she slipped out of the alcove and headed towards the château.

Cat gulped. She now knew for a fact that she was underdressed; judging by the girl's outfit, there was some sort of party going on inside the château. Forgetting about her luggage and taking the same path as the girl, Cat found herself staring up at the back of the château which was just as beautiful as the front, with balconies, shutters and outside lighting. About to go inside, she caught sight of a young boy, no older than the sobbing girl, reclining on a wrought-iron chaise longue. He had dark hair and chiselled cheekbones and he was smoking the most enormous spliff. An older-looking girl sat next to him, giggling uncontrollably. Spotting her, the boy held the joint out.

'*Vous fumez?*' he asked, his eyes slightly glazed.

'Er, no, I don't smoke,' Cat said, backing away. In her confusion, she took a path that headed back into the gardens and with the crazed laughter of the teenagers ringing in her ears, she found herself at the edge of a shimmering pool. Hearing splashing sounds, Cat froze. Nearby, there was a heated Jacuzzi tub, steam rising out of it. Two people were in it, a redhead who looked suspiciously as if she might be naked beneath the water, and a man with sleek, dark hair and broad shoulders.

As the man let out a throaty laugh and turned round,

Cat saw an arrogant nose, a wide mouth and sexy, sleepy-looking brown eyes. She caught her breath. For a moment, she was transported straight back to St Tropez, where a grinning Olivier had scooped her up in his arms in the glittering blue sea, his grin infectious as he leant in for a lingering kiss. Swallowing, Cat pushed the painful vision away, desperate not to make a fool of herself by allowing agonising memories to take over. She couldn't think about Olivier right now.

Scrutinising the man in the pool again, Cat realised that he actually looked nothing like Olivier. He was in his early thirties, he had broad shoulders and he was very handsome but that was where the similarity ended. His hands wandered cheekily to the girl's breasts, and as if he sensed Cat's scrutiny, he turned and faced her. Cat backed away and with renewed determination headed for the château. Olivier's family – if that was who she had just encountered – were not what she had been expecting at all.

Heading back the way she had come and entering through ornate double doors, Cat found herself in a stunning lemon-yellow sitting room full of antiques and tasteful ornaments. The classical music she had heard outside was now louder, as though a full string quartet were at work, and there was a murmur of voices and muted laughter coming from one of the other rooms. Mustering up some courage, she opened the door and went in.

As the final bars of the classical piece died out and silence fell, Cat found herself facing a crowd of people holding champagne flutes, the men in black tie and the women in exquisite evening gowns of silk, satin and lace. They were all staring at her in bemusement, clearly wondering who she was and why on earth she was there. Waiters and waitresses were unobtrusively circling the room with trays of Bellinis and canapés but even they were goggling at Cat as if she were a national exhibit.

Feeling absurdly scruffy in her jumper and jeans, Cat took in the room in astonishment, dazedly noting high ceilings, apricot walls and heavy, expensive-looking curtains at the windows. Period furniture, stunning paintings . . . My God, she thought, was that an original Monet? Her father had adored Impressionist painters and Monet's water-lily series, glorious studies in rose-pinks, powdery blues and distinctive, cool greens, had been his favourite. The painting, small but striking, had to be the real thing; along with everything else in the room, it looked authentic and priceless.

So much for Olivier's 'humble' upbringing, Cat thought, totally lost for words.

'You must be Cat Hayes,' said a good-looking man with sleek silver hair and an amiable smile. His English was flawless. He stepped forward and grasped her hand warmly. 'I'm Guy Ducasse, Olivier's uncle.'

Cat looked at him. He was in his fifties, she thought as he gripped her hand, and there was a hint of sadness in his otherwise friendly brown eyes. She realised he was saying something about not expecting her until tomorrow and she hurried to explain herself.

'They . . . they laid on an extra flight,' she stammered, wondering at his almost accentless English. Olivier had spoken English with a heavy French accent.

Guy smiled, half guessing what she was thinking. 'My late wife was English and the children have had many English nannies over the years.'

Even more confused about Olivier's heavy accent, Cat caught sight of the girl she had seen sobbing earlier. It was hard to believe this was the same person. She seemed self-assured and poised, her brown eyes remarkably clear, if rather frosty.

'This is my daughter, Seraphina,' Guy said, still speaking in English. He stared at Cat. This was not the tarty young bimbo he had envisaged Olivier's widow to be. She looked to be in her mid-twenties and she was very pretty. He caught a waft of Jo Malone's Lime, Basil and Mandarin and raised his eyebrows approvingly. A radiant, citrus scent with floral tones – a good choice, in his opinion, it suited her looks perfectly. He couldn't help warming to her, despite his mother's instructions for all of them to keep their distance. Most of them were in fact doing just that, albeit accidentally, he realised; Xavier, Max and Delphine were all absent.

Someone came into the room and Guy flexed his shoulders as though he was expecting trouble. 'Ah, this is Leoni. She's—'

'Olivier's sister,' Cat breathed. Leoni was the spitting image of Olivier with her glossy dark hair and the deep brown eyes – somewhat masked by the unattractive glasses she wore. Even her chin was the same – small with the faintest cleft. Wearing a chic black column dress, Leoni wasn't a pretty girl but she had presence.

'How dare you come here like this?' Leoni hissed in English, her face turning pale. 'It's my birthday party. You have no right to turn up and make yourself at home!'

Appalled, Guy touched his niece's arm. 'Leoni! Remember your manners.'

Leoni shook her head vehemently. 'No, Uncle!' she snapped in French. 'She's not welcome and I won't pretend that she is.' She turned furious eyes to Cat and continued in French. 'You are not family, do you understand me? And you never will be.' Her lip quivered. 'Just because you married Olivier doesn't mean you belong here. Whatever you think you're entitled to, you can forget it, do you hear?'

Cat recoiled and the crowd of people gasped collectively. The look in Leoni's eyes was one of utter hatred. Cat flushed. What had she done, apart from marry the man she had fallen in love with? She wanted to hit back at Leoni but she stopped herself; it wouldn't be a good idea, not when the atmosphere seemed so volatile. She wondered if Leoni assumed she did not understand French.

Guy swiftly cut in. 'They laid on an extra flight and I've only just had word from my driver, Leoni. He should have called me at the airport and then we would have had more warning.'

'Pah!' Leoni was incensed. 'It is disrespectful to Olivier's memory to burst in on a family party.' She turned her back on Cat.

Guy ushered Cat to one side. 'Leoni is still struggling to come to terms with Olivier's death,' he explained in a low voice. 'Please forgive her. Er . . . where is your luggage?'

Still reeling from Leoni's onslaught, Cat had to think for a second. 'It's outside in the garden.' She winced, knowing she must sound crazy.

'I'll get the staff to collect it for you.' Guy led her towards the door and nodded at the quartet to start up again. 'But for now, I will show you to your room. You must be in need of a bed or, at the very least, a hot shower.'

Cat blinked. The staff? She followed Guy out of the room and heard the conversation resume loudly as soon as they left.

'You have caused quite a stir.' Guy smiled as he led the way into a spacious hallway and up a sweeping, marble staircase edged with an elaborate wrought-iron banister. 'I would show you around the house but it's too dark now. The stables are located at the back of the house by the lavender fields, and there is a graveyard just in front of them. Olivier is buried there. You may wish to visit his place of rest while you're here.'

Suddenly exhausted, Cat felt tears pricking her eyelids. This was so much harder than she'd imagined. In some ways, Olivier's death felt like a lifetime ago but being here, with his family, made it all seem very real and very recent. Embarrassed, Cat wiped her eyes. Guy pretended not to notice. He showed her into a pale room with raspberry-coloured curtains, an ornate four-poster bed and what looked like immaculately preserved Louis Quinze furniture.

'You should sleep, perhaps,' Guy suggested kindly, thinking how vulnerable she looked with her red-rimmed eyes and pale face. 'Feel free to join us downstairs if you wish but if you're too tired, we'll understand.'

Cat shook her head and sank down on to the four-poster bed. 'Sleep sounds good.' She didn't want to say it out loud, but nothing short of near-death could have persuaded her to go back to the party. Something occurred to her.

'Are . . . are Olivier's parents here?' She asked. It was suddenly important to know that the only thing Olivier had lied about was his upbringing. The death of his parents had been key to their relationship, it had been what had bonded them so deeply and she had to know for sure that Olivier had been genuine about the terrible riding accident that had snatched his parents from him at a young age.

Guy looked puzzled. 'Olivier's parents are dead. I'm so sorry, I assumed you knew. They died some years ago.'

Cat let out a ragged breath. All at once she felt better. She listened tiredly as Guy told her where to go for breakfast in the morning and she was hazily aware of him mentioning a meeting in a few days' time in a boardroom. Shortly afterwards, he left the room.

Cat sent Bella a text to tell her she'd finally arrived, then lay down on the bed fully clothed. She barely stirred when someone quietly brought in her luggage. Soon she fell into a deep sleep.

Outside, Xavier was climbing out of the jacuzzi tub stark naked. Rubbing his dark hair with a towel and shivering slightly in the chilly night air, he stared up at the house thoughtfully. So that was Olivier's wife, he thought, looking round for his boxer shorts. *Widow*, he corrected himself. Therese, the girlfriend who had recently replaced Monique, emerged from the tub. Running towards him with her shaven privates on full display, she whipped the towel from his shoulders and made a show of drying her hair with it, her breasts jiggling provocatively.

Xavier retrieved his boxer shorts from a nearby plant pot and pulled them on, slightly unnerved by Cat's arrival. He hadn't expected her to be so beautiful, that was for sure – Olivier's previous girlfriends had been pretty enough but this girl was different, not what he had expected at all. Perhaps she was less dazzling close up. Xavier shrugged and lit a cigarette to get warm. Why did he even care? Olivier dying so suddenly had revealed the extent of his sordid misdemeanours and Xavier had spent the past few months settling tabs with various bar and hotel managers and scaring off drug dealers he had found skulking around the grounds of La Fleurie. Olivier's widow was most assuredly not his problem. Olivier had had more vices than any of them had guessed and Xavier had resolved to keep most of the details to himself. Leoni was in no fit state to hear any more negative press about her dead brother and there was nothing to be gained from antagonising his grandmother, who already thought Olivier was an impetuous, irresponsible playboy.

Impulsiveness was a family trait; hell, pretty much all of them made recklessness seem like a national sport, but, Xavier thought reasonably as he pulled his white dress shirt over his head, Olivier had pushed the boundaries further than any of them.

'Oooh, it's so cold,' giggled Therese, putting his hand on a breast covered in goose bumps.

Xavier smiled distractedly.

'What's wrong, cheri?' Therese asked, pouting when she saw his serious expression.

'Just thinking about Olivier's widow,' Xavier said, removing his hand from her breast and flipping his Zippo lighter open and shut edgily. He wondered if Cat Hayes knew how out of control Olivier had been. Probably not. She'd only known him a few weeks. No sane person married someone they hardly knew, did they? Marriage was something to be respected, not something to indulge in impulsively, just because you were in the first throes of lust. No, Cat Hayes either had to be a gold digger or she was insane, as far as he was concerned.

Realising he had ten minutes before they were due inside for Leoni's cake and speeches, Xavier tipped Therese back into the Jacuzzi and slipped in after her.

'Can you *believe* she just turned up like that and burst into my party?'

The following morning, Leoni was still fuming. Her party had been ruined by the impromptu arrival of Cat Hayes; her guests had talked of nothing else from that point on. Even when her grandmother and uncle had gone to bed and the more boisterous guests had ended up in the pool, Leoni had still found herself fending off impertinent questions about Olivier's stupid widow.

Leoni had drunk far too much champagne in an effort to block Cat Hayes's existence out of her head and she now had a terrible hangover that a pint of cold water and four aspirin hadn't been able to shift. So she'd called up Ashton and joined him at the house he was working on for a client. Situated on the hilltop village of medieval Mougins, near Cannes, the veranda afforded them magnificent views of Grasse, which was all very well, but Leoni would have preferred a strong, hot coffee because that was the only thing she felt might revive her.

'I just wish she hadn't turned up unannounced,' Leoni added sulkily as she threw herself into a padded chair next to him.

'Well, she couldn't have known it was your birthday party,'

Ashton pointed out, as he unrolled his architect's plans. Sensing Leoni bristling with resentment, he hid a smile and continued. 'And frankly, I can't see you turning down a lift after being delayed in an airport for two days. You'd have done exactly what she did.'

Leoni stared straight ahead moodily. 'Oh, whatever. And who leaves their luggage in the garden, for heaven's sake? The girl is clearly deranged.'

Ashton pinned his plans down with an ashtray and glanced at Leoni. Wearing a black crepe shift dress, she looked professional and ready for work but there were dark shadows under her eyes and her shoulders were hunched with tension. Ashton sighed; if only Leoni were more approachable, he would have given her a good hug.

'So, how are you really bearing up?' he asked, going for the easier option. 'I do realise it must have been hard for you to come face to face with Olivier's widow like that.'

Pushing her glasses up on to the bridge of her nose, Leoni almost smiled. 'Bearing up' – how very English. But then that was Ashton; he was such a gentleman. She felt glad she had him as a friend because she felt so *safe* with him. Their friendship was uncomplicated, almost replicating the brother-sister rapport she had had with Olivier. 'I'm . . . angry,' Leoni answered truthfully. 'No, I am more than angry, I am *livid*.' She spun round to face him, forgetting to speak English. 'We are supposed to welcome this widow with open arms,' she spluttered. 'I cannot . . . I *will* not do such a thing! It's undignified and unreasonable and under no circumstances will I lower myself to play nicely with this, this . . . bimbo!' She stood up and paced the veranda.

'Leoni, Cat Hayes was *asked* to come to La Fleurie. She didn't turn up unannounced or uninvited, she responded to a letter she was sent, the one that went astray for so many months, and she did as she was told and booked a flight here.' Ashton held his hands up in defence, his pencil in the air.

'And before you accuse me, I'm not just saying that because she's English, all right?'

About to blast him, Leoni closed her mouth. He was right; Olivier's widow had simply responded to the invitation to La Fleurie. It wasn't her fault the letter had gone missing and she had made the effort to visit as soon as she had received it. Was that a good thing or a bad thing? Leoni didn't know any more because her head was in a mess. The arrival of Cat Hayes had sent her spiralling all over the place and the drama of last night was affecting her ability to think clearly. She choked down a sob, feeling desolate.

Ashton watched her, wishing he could do something to help but he knew she would tense up and reject his offer of comfort. He busied himself with his plans, knowing she hated being seen to be weak or emotional in any way.

Leoni looked at him. Ashton would never know but many years ago, when they were teenagers, she had developed the biggest crush on him. It had lasted for years, a painful, unrequited crush that no one had known about until the day a young Ashton had been chatted up by the curvaceous redheaded sister of one of Olivier's friends. Her brother had caught her agonised glance and, characteristically amused, a youthful and rather wicked Olivier had told his older sister that she clearly wasn't Ashton's type and that she should stop trotting around after him like a lapdog. Excruciatingly embarrassed, Leoni had resigned herself to being no more than Ashton's friend from that point onwards. Unrequited love was a hideous thing and if she wasn't his type, then so be it. It had taken time – too much time – but Leoni was finally over him.

Dabbing her eyes and pulling herself together, she forgot about the past and retreated into the safety of business. 'Did I tell you about my plans? I have so many ideas. Obviously, if I could persuade Xavier, I'd get him to create a few new scents, of course, but if not, I'm going to try and convince the family to branch out and develop a home fragrance line. You know, candles and linen sprays.' Her brown eyes lit up. 'Some of my favourite British perfumers do this – Miller Harris, Jo Malone. I really think we need to get involved.'

'It's genius!' Ashton smiled supportively. 'Sorry, I mean it's a great idea.'

'Do you think so?' Leoni brightened. 'I already have a contact that makes wonderful candles – Jerard something or other. And I also want to open a store in Paris but Uncle Guy is sure to dismiss the idea.' Her eyes narrowed. 'And if he doesn't, my beloved grandmother will definitely step in and veto my plans.'

Ashton waved a hand. 'If anyone can convince her, you can, L,' he said, unthinkingly using his pet name for her. 'If you're serious about this idea, you could always join me when I next head home to visit my family. You could do some research there and visit Jo Malone and Miller whatsit while we're there.'

Leoni's mouth twitched. 'Miller Harris.' She thought for a moment. 'That's a great idea. Thank you, I will.' She caught a waft of his aftershave as he stood up. Dunhill London, with its crisp scent of apple, followed by the rose heart note and the winey patchouli base tones. It was modern and British. And so very Ashton.

'I feel much better,' Leoni said, standing up and giving him a brief kiss on the cheek. 'You always manage to do that.'

'Do I?'

'Always.' Leoni smiled. 'Even my hangover seems to have lifted. It's almost like having Olivier here again.' Her voice cracked but she was in control. 'Have fun with this house,' she said, jerking her thumb in the direction of the sitting room inside. 'Please don't tell me they're going to install a Jacuzzi tub out here?'

Ashton grinned. 'I talked them out of that so they've settled for one in the games room instead.' His eyes alighted on the slender curve of Leoni's neck as she headed inside with a wave, and he reminded himself that he had a job to do. With an effort, he refocused on his plans.

Chapter Three

Having spent a restless night sleeping in the four-poster bed while the party downstairs became increasingly raucous, Cat woke late with a pounding headache. Feeling groggy, she threw back the white linen sheets she'd slept in, surprised to find that a raspberry-coloured silk floss duvet had been added during the night for warmth.

A 'guilt' duvet, Cat thought with a flash of humour as she headed into an ensuite bathroom with walls the colour of cherry blossom and pristine white fittings. It had a free-standing bath, an enormous shower and two sinks, which were surrounded by small, expensive-looking toiletries. It was like being in a luxurious hotel, Cat mused. A hotel without the usual welcoming reception. Guy had been polite and friendly but that had been about it.

Cat turned the shower on, jumping as hot water immediately shot out of several jets in the walls. She was still upset about Leoni's reaction to her arrival but she hoped it was just a knee-jerk reaction. Didn't Leoni realise she was just as devastated about Olivier's death? As odd as the situation was, they actually had something in common: they had both loved Olivier and they both missed him terribly.

Cat peered into the bathroom mirror, shocked at how pasty she looked. A bad night's sleep on top of her airport delays had left her looking ill and fragile – and crying into her pillow hadn't exactly helped, she thought ruefully. She was furious with herself for feeling so emotional after so many months had passed but being here made her feel closer to Olivier somehow, even if coming face to face with evidence of his privileged upbringing had shocked her to the core.

What she needed to do now was find out why Olivier had lied to her about them. Cat determined to do some digging and learn more about her late husband while she was here. He must have had a good reason to hide his family from her, she told herself firmly; it was just a matter of finding out what was behind it all.

As she dried herself, Cat noticed a silver monogram in the corner of the white towel. The letter 'D' entwined with the letter 'F'. She frowned. 'D' for Ducasse, obviously, but what did the 'F' stand for? She put on some make-up in an attempt to look more human – plenty of blusher and a smear of pink lipstick. Bypassing a bright green dress that looked far too jaunty for a widow to wear, she decided on a more sombre black one. It was short but it would have to do, and she added a long cream sweater to keep the morning chill at bay – it was January and even though it was much warmer than in the UK, it wasn't sunbathing weather, by any means.

In the room, she found a formal invitation that must have been delivered while she was in the shower. Handwritten but on a stiff white card with silver edging, it requested her presence at a meeting in the boardroom the following day. Cat assumed this must be the 'business' the letter had outlined and taking her unexpectedly sumptuous surroundings into account, she was beginning to realise there could be legal implications to her marriage to Olivier. They must be suspicious of her, at the very least.

She went downstairs and left the house, wrapping her arms around her protectively as she braced herself for bumping into a member of the Ducasse family. Finding herself by the oval pool, which looked just as impressive in the cold light of day, Cat remembered the couple frolicking in the nearby hot tub and wondered who they were. Sure she wouldn't be able to eat a thing, she avoided the salon Guy had told her breakfast was served in, not least because she couldn't bear the thought of running into Leoni. The last thing Cat needed right now was a fracas with Olivier's formidable sister over the Bonne Maman preserves.

Staff were milling about discreetly, wearing white and maroon uniforms with the same swirly monograms on their lapels as the towel upstairs. Cat watched them, open mouthed. She'd assumed that the staff she'd seen last night had been hired for the party but apparently not. What looked like maids, gardeners and footmen were cleaning up debris from the party and ensuring that the château was put back to its immaculate best. One maid rescued what looked suspiciously like a pair of knickers from behind a pool lounger, discreetly stuffing them into her pocket without missing a beat, as if such things were an everyday occurrence.

Bemused at just how rich the Ducasse family were, Cat was about to head towards the graveyard Guy had mentioned when she realised she wasn't alone. Turning apprehensively, she found Guy's daughter, the girl she'd seen sobbing, staring at her with slanting, feline eyes. She was wearing a pair of tight jeans that made her legs look endless, and a pink Lacoste sweatshirt. She appeared taller than she had the night before and she was clutching a small photo album. Her expression was haughty and Cat bristled, realising it wasn't just Leoni who resented her presence.

'What are you doing?' Seraphina asked in perfect English, her tone as chilly as her gaze.

'Just . . . looking around,' Cat responded lamely, not wanting to admit she had been about to visit Olivier's grave.

'Wondering how much it's all worth?' Seraphina returned.

Taken aback, Cat shook her head. So she was right about the Ducasse family being wary of her and her motives.

'I saw you admiring the Monet last night,' Seraphina commented, watching Cat carefully.

43

'The Monet? God, yes . . . it's absolutely stunning.' Cat couldn't help laughing. 'It's not every day you get to see a real one, is it? At least, it might be for you but it most certainly isn't for me – or for most people.' Seeing Seraphina's unchanged expression, Cat decided on a more open approach. 'My dad loved Monet, especially the water-lily series. Seeing the Monet reminded me of him . . . he'd have keeled over if he'd seen that last night. So if I seemed a bit dumbstruck, the honest truth is that I was.'

Not sure if the story about her Monet-loving father was true or not, Seraphina gestured to a sun lounger and took a seat on one nearby. Cat sat down, wondering why the girl wanted to talk to her. The comment about the Monet made her sigh and, glancing up at the château, she felt perturbed. What did they think she wanted – to be given part of the house, or something? It was too silly for words.

'You don't look much like a widow,' Seraphina said in an unfriendly tone.

'Really?' Cat wasn't sure what a widow should look like. She glanced down at her outfit. 'Is it the dress? It's too short, isn't it?'

Seraphina shrugged and didn't comment. 'The family have been discussing you non-stop since Olivier died,' she informed Cat, almost as if she was assessing her reaction. 'We didn't know if you were ever going to make an appearance.'

Cat quickly explained the missing solicitor's letter. 'I didn't know if I should come,' she admitted, 'especially since so many months had passed since Olivier died.' She looked away. 'But then I decided I had nothing to lose. I didn't even know any of you existed until I received the letter.'

Seraphina raised her eyebrows disbelievingly. 'Really? How odd.'

'I know.' Cat had an idea Seraphina was being sarcastic and that made her feel uneasy. She paused, not sure how to word her question but she had to know why Olivier had pretended his family didn't exist. 'Was Olivier estranged from his family?' she asked. 'Had there been some sort of big argument?'

'No!' Seraphina looked astonished. 'I mean, he and Grandmother never saw eye to eye, but there was no big argument, to my knowledge. Why would you think that?'

Cat bit her lip. Surely it was inappropriate to reveal that Olivier had pretended he was penniless and that he didn't even have a family to speak of. 'He . . . gave me the impression his life was . . . not as lavish as all this.' Cat gestured to the pool and the extensive grounds of the château.

'*C'est bien de lui*!' Seraphina exclaimed. 'How like Olivier . . . you know, to lie to you like that,' she translated for Cat's benefit, unaware that Cat had understood her. 'Olivier was *un farceur* . . . a prankster,' she explained. 'He would often pretend he was poor because it amused him.'

'Did he? Did he really?' Cat immediately felt better; so she had been right to believe Olivier wasn't a phoney. She still couldn't understand why he would have played such a prank on her, especially after they were married, but she guessed perhaps she didn't know him as well as she'd thought she did. That's what happened when you fell head over heels and married someone you barely knew, she thought wryly. Impulsiveness was all very well but it had its down sides.

Something occurred to Seraphina. 'Did Olivier use the name Laroque or did he tell you he was a Ducasse?'

'He used the name Laroque,' Cat replied, wondering why Seraphina had asked this. Before she had a chance to question her, Seraphina caught her off guard.

'Did you love him?' she asked bluntly. Her feline eyes demanded the truth.

The question hit Cat like a body blow. She *had* loved Olivier, very much, but clearly the family doubted her feelings. Cat understood why they had misgivings about her – they'd never met her before now, for a start – but still, the fact that

Seraphina was even asking her that question filled her with sadness.

'I fell head over heels in love with him,' she confessed frankly. 'He was handsome but he was so kind and funny too.' Cat paused. 'The holiday . . . it was so romantic and even though I knew it was crazy, when Olivier proposed, I had to say yes. I mean, I wanted to do it, I would never have married him if I hadn't had deep feelings. It just felt right to live for the moment.' She turned to Seraphina. 'You must believe me. Who would do something as serious as getting married if they weren't in love?'

Seraphina let out a short laugh. 'You'd be surprised, especially where my family are involved.' She studied Cat, trying to work out if she was genuine. She seemed it – her aquamarine-blue eyes seemed honest and everything about her behaviour and manner appeared sincere. Seraphina put down the photo album and pulled the sleeves of her sweat-shirt over her hands. She wanted to trust Cat, she really wanted to believe Olivier's widow wasn't a gold digger, but having grown up around adults who mistrusted people's motives where money was concerned, Seraphina felt the need to be cautious.

'Leoni seems very upset about Olivier's death,' Cat commented, wondering why Seraphina was scrutinising her as though she were a fascinating artefact in a museum. 'Understandably so,' she added, in case she sounded unsympathetic.

Seraphina sat back and said nothing, her expression impassive.

Cat couldn't help wondering why Seraphina appeared so sanguine; aside from the tears she had witnessed last night, she couldn't see any evidence of grief over Olivier.

'We . . . we lost our mother two years ago,' Seraphina said suddenly in a soft voice, as if she'd guessed what Cat was thinking. 'And Olivier's parents, our aunt and uncle, died too but that was a very long time ago.' She picked at the sleeve of her pink sweatshirt distractedly, her eyes downcast. 'We are used to loss, I suppose.'

'Does anyone ever get used to it?' Cat said, staring past her.

Seraphina looked up. It sounded as though Cat knew what she was feeling but that was impossible because no one understood. 'We . . . we're not supposed to show emotion,' she said in halting tones, not sure why she was confiding in Cat. 'Not in public. Grandmother frowns on it.'

So that was why Seraphina had needed a private place to weep. Clearly, betraying emotion was unacceptable in this family. 'That's a shame,' Cat responded as tactfully as possible. 'Sometimes having a good cry or just opening up to someone can make all the difference.'

'No one knows what it feels like,' Seraphina blurted out, tears clouding her vision. 'When you lose someone, I mean.'

Full of compassion, Cat nodded. Having lost her own parents at Seraphina's age, she knew how difficult it was to accept such an unfair situation. 'It's like the rug's been pulled out from under you, isn't it?' she commented, thinking aloud. 'No, worse than that. It's as though there's this big hole in your heart that can never be filled again. People think they understand what it's like to lose a parent but they don't. You feel so abandoned . . . so alone.'

Seraphina stared at Cat. No one had ever described it like that to her before but the words summed up her feelings perfectly. Realising she had found a kindred spirit in Cat, Seraphina felt the urge to open up to her more. She was starved of female companionship because all her friends were at college and career-obsessed Leoni and her austere grandmother were hardly ideal confidantes.

'I don't actually know what I'm doing here,' Cat said, sitting up and hugging her knees. 'I mean, I was invited and the letter mentioned something about business but, I don't know, I thought perhaps the Ducasse family wanted to meet me.' She laughed. 'Get to know me, or something.' Remembering Leoni's horrified expression, Cat's eyes became sober. 'I think I've made a huge mistake.'

Seraphina felt a flash of guilt. If Olivier's young widow was as genuine as she appeared, she must be feeling bewildered and hurt by the hostile reception she had received. Seraphina tried to make amends.

'You must meet the rest of the family,' she said in a warmer tone. 'My brother Max – he's my twin but he's dark and, just to warn you, he can be very moody. Boys.' She rolled her eyes. 'My older brother Xavier is gorgeous and the best person to be around, but he's a bit preoccupied with his new girlfriend, Therese. She's a redhead and bit of a slut, between you and me. But I'm biased. I always think Xavier deserves better because he's had such a hard . . .' Seraphina stopped, as if she felt she had said too much. She stood up. 'Anyway, he's lovely. I'm sure you'll meet him soon. How long do you think you'll be here?'

Cat shrugged. 'I expect I'll fly back at the weekend after this meeting. I haven't a clue what it's about but I hope it gets sorted quickly. I have a life back in England.' She grimaced. 'Not a great one, admittedly, but still.'

Seraphina picked up the photo album and thrust it into Cat's hands. 'Here are some photos of Olivier. I thought you might like to see them.' Seraphina didn't want to admit she had an ulterior motive for showing Cat the photos: she wanted to gauge her reaction and check if any tears that appeared were crocodile ones or real ones.

Touched, Cat took the album and opened it. She gasped as Olivier's grinning face stared back up at her. The hazelnut eyes met hers and Cat traced a finger round his tanned jaw. 'Do you know, I'd almost forgotten what he looked like,' she murmured, her voice unsteady. 'I only had a few photos on my phone and I kept looking at them but somehow I couldn't quite see Olivier . . . not like this.' Overcome, she turned the pages of the album, barely able to keep back the tears when she found a photo of Olivier as a small boy, his shoulders already broad and his grin cheeky and appealing.

Seraphina had all the evidence she needed; Cat's reaction was totally genuine, she was sure of it. 'Keep them,' she offered generously. 'We have plenty of photographs. No one will mind. Look, I'm off for a ride so I'll see you later, all right?'

'Thank you . . . this means . . . thanks.'

Cat sat back clutching the album. She flicked through the pages again, feeling sad and alone. Then she jumped up and headed to Olivier's grave, not even looking over her shoulder to check if anyone was watching her. She found his pristine black gravestone and fell to her knees in front of it.

'Olivier,' Cat whispered, her heart clenching. 'God, I miss you so much.' She put her head in her hands, utterly distraught but glad finally to be able to say goodbye, something the French officials had denied her. 'I'm so sorry . . . you said one of the things you admired about me was my zest for life.' She sniffed, almost breaking into a smile. 'Not much of that going on at the moment. I've done nothing but cry and make a fool of myself since you've gone . . . you'd be telling me off for snivelling all over the place if you could see me.'

Staring at the photographs again, Cat remembered exactly why she had fallen in love with Olivier. And reaching out to touch the words engraved into his headstone, she opened up and told him everything, all the things she'd wanted to say since he'd died. At the end, Cat let out a huge sigh and pulled herself together. She had cried enough. It was time now to do whatever his family needed her to do so she could go home and get on with her life. Clutching the photo album, Cat left the graveyard and headed back to her room.

Upstairs, leaning heavily on her cane because her arthritic hip was causing her pain, Delphine watched with pursed lips. A convincing, heartfelt performance; Cat Hayes made a pretty little widow. Delphine snorted. The sooner she and Guy confronted her, the better, she thought, picking up the phone.

'Bonsoir, Monsieur Gregoire!' Ashton called to his neighbour who was struggling with some parcels outside his apartment. Ashton entered his own apartment with the same sense of pleasure he always felt when he came back to Paris after a trip away.

Just a few steps away from the famous Avenue des Champs-Élysées, the Parisian apartment was Ashton's pride and joy. He had heard about it from his former boss three years ago and had only managed to secure it by selling everything he owned of any value, including his house in England, and a vintage car that had been his pride and joy. He had also been forced to accept a generous payment from his parents which basically meant he had nothing left to fall back on; he had effectively already spent any inheritance that would have been due to him.

The purchase had left him severely out of pocket (he was still struggling to claw back his day-to-day expenses) and without a single luxury item to his name, but Ashton didn't care because this was the kind of apartment he had read about and hankered after for years. Boasting period features, elegant fittings and a traditional *balcon* with a stunning vista of the Place de L'Etoile, the apartment was, quite simply, an architect's dream.

Ashton collected up his post and listened to his answerphone messages. There was a message from Jeanette, a gorgeous Parisian girl he had been out with a few times.

'*Appele-moi*,' her message said breathily. Call me. '*Tu me manques*, Ashton . . .'

Hearing that Jeanette missed him and wanted him to call her, Ashton scratched his head and wondered what to do. She was a lovely girl but something was missing between them, though he couldn't put his finger on what it was. Maybe it was because he spent much of his life in Provence with the Ducasse family . . .

Recognising the writing on an envelope as that of his friend Herve, Ashton forgot about Jeanette and tore it open. Herve was an architect he had studied with who often let him know about sensational buildings that were coming up for sale. He had impeccable taste as well as knowing exactly the kind of buildings that sent Ashton's heart rate soaring with enthusiasm. Feasting his eyes on the grainy photograph of an astonishingly beautiful building with a sign saying '*A Vendre*' next to it, Ashton felt the familiar buzz that shot through him when he looked at something he would kill to work on. It wasn't just that the building appeared to be a perfect example of late eighteenth-century, Rococo-style architecture, it looked as though it might be just the right property for Leoni's Paris shop.

Ashton grabbed his keys. If this place was for sale, he wanted it. He checked the directions and headed to the building on foot. This was why he'd become an architect, he thought to himself, as he darted between chattering tourists and busy shoppers browsing along the majestic streets of the Champs-Élysées. It was this buzz, the thrill of discovering something old and beautiful that could look spectacular when it was developed.

Coming from humble beginnings in Oxfordshire where he discovered a talent for freehand drawing and a love of old buildings, Ashton had decided early on that he wanted to be an architect. He had paid his way through five years of study, plus two stints in professional studios in London and Paris, and had now made a name for himself – a good one. He was very much in demand with high-end clients and the majority of his commissions were split between Paris and the south of France.

Ashton made his way to the Right Bank in the ninth arrondissement, not far from Galeries Lafayette, the glittering department store. He turned into a pretty street off the main boulevard and was soon standing in front of the property. It was on the small side but it was perfect for a perfume shop. It had a wide window at the front and an ornate but welcoming door to the right. It would look beautiful lit up from the inside, maybe with some small chandeliers, Ashton decided. The shop came with a room at the back as well as a flat above it, a tiny space little bigger than a one-bedroomed studio but ideal for a storeroom or small office. Leoni was going to love it, Ashton thought. She would want it instantly, he was sure of it. It was crying out to be filled with discreet lighting and elegant packages with lilac ribbons for people to take away in stiff, white, monogrammed bags.

Ashton noticed an attractive woman standing near the property, making notes in an expensive-looking leather journal. She looked to be in her forties and she had a glamorous coil of russet hair at the nape of her neck. She wore a black trench coat, belted at the waist, and sheer black stockings. Feeling his eyes on her, she threw him a seductive smile, her eyes full of mischief.

Ashton reddened slightly and turned away, he was ridiculously shy and her stare was provocative. Hearing the woman's heels clicking on the pavement, he looked up to see her sashaying away, her hips swinging sexily and unapologetically as she made her way down the street. Ashton hoped she wasn't as interested in the building as he was, because he was going to do whatever he had to in order to secure it.

Delphine was feeling very out of sorts as she sat in a café waiting for a friend. Cat Hayes' arrival had unsettled her. She hadn't met her personally, so far, but she had been unnerved to see Seraphina chatting to her for so long. Cat Hayes had no airs and graces, according to Guy, and if she was a gold digger, she was hiding it well, by all accounts.

Not that it mattered, Delphine reasoned, sipping her

espresso. Cat Hayes could be beautiful, she could be ugly, she could be pleasant or she could be shallow; it was unimportant in the scheme of things. Whatever she was like as a person, Delphine could only imagine one outcome for Cat Hayes: being sent packing on the first suitable flight home with no claim whatsoever to the Ducasse-Fleurie fortune.

'So.' Cybille Thibault took a seat opposite her good friend. She ordered an espresso for herself and leant forward, her eyes sparkling with interest. 'What's she like?'

Delphine took a moment to formulate her answer. Cybille was a coiffed, chain-smoking dragon who had lived off her billionaire husband's inheritance since his well-publicised debacle with two underage sisters but she was also an important member of Delphine's inner circle. Cybille was a gossip but a discreet one and she wielded great power. Somehow, she had survived her husband's recent scandal unscathed and her opinions mattered greatly. She was also a good friend of the editor of one of France's best-selling society magazines, which was probably one of the reasons she had emerged apparently untouched from her husband's shame.

'Well?' Cybille frowned impatiently, playing with her cigarettes.

'I haven't met her properly yet. But I saw her from a distance and she seemed . . . very normal.'

'Normal?' Cybille put her coffee cup down with a clatter. 'What does that mean?'

Delphine shrugged vaguely. 'She didn't look remarkable in any way.'

Cybille sat back and narrowed her eyes. 'Was she pretty?'

'She was . . . passable.'

Cybille smiled triumphantly. 'So she *was* pretty. I thought so.' She lit a cigarette, daring the staff in the café to tell her off. 'The thing to remember about Olivier is that he was a playboy – he played the field and he had his pick of women. Now, did she seem flashy or cheap?'

Delphine sipped her coffee. 'I couldn't say. Her clothes weren't of any note and neither was she.'

Cybille delicately puffed smoke out of her nostrils, somehow managing to make it look classy. 'You really are being most ambiguous, Delphine! How am I supposed to help you if I don't have any information?'

'Help me?' Delphine raised her pencil-thin white eyebrows.

Cybille considered her. 'Delphine. How do you think I survived my husband's disgraceful scandal?'

Delphine patted her chignon with slight distaste. 'Good connections?' she offered, not sure what else to say.

Cybille looked smug. 'Well, yes, that helps, of course. But when cornered, we women need to be smart, we need to be one step ahead of our adversaries.'

'And how, pray tell, do I get one step ahead of Olivier's widow?' Delphine moved her coffee cup to one side as Cybille discreetly pushed a business card across the table. 'Yves Giraud', it said in bold, black lettering.

'A private detective?' Delphine's voice rose to a squeak.

Cybille shot her an indignant look, glancing over her sholder to see if Delphine's raised voice had attracted attention. 'What are you trying to do, ruin my reputation?' She looked affronted. 'I'm telling you about Yves because you are my good friend and because I care about you.'

Delphine inclined her head. 'Sorry. I just don't understand why I would need a private detective. I can see why you did – forgive me, I am only speaking the truth here, Cybille – but how does this apply to my situation?'

Cybille lit a cigarette with the dying embers of her other one, giving Delphine a shrewd glance. 'What do you know about this girl? What do you really know about her? I suspect not a great deal. And why should you? You haven't even met her yet and all you know is that for some strange reason she married Olivier last year on holiday.' She grimaced. 'Talk about "marry in haste, repent at leisure", or whatever that expression is. Anyway, once you confront her, you may find you have absolutely nothing to worry about. Perhaps she will simply accept your pay-off – you *are* intending to pay her off, I take it?'

Uncomfortably, Delphine nodded. She detested discussing such vulgarities in a café.

'Absolutely the best course of action,' Cybille assured her. 'And if all goes according to plan, she will be on a flight home in no time. But should she refuse to sign the paperwork or throw something else your way, you need a plan B.' Cybille tapped the business card with a fingernail painted a garish shade of pink. 'Yves Giraud is plan B. He's an excellent investigator and if there is something to find, he will find it. Perhaps Miss Hayes has something to hide? Perhaps Yves might unearth something unsavoury about her she wouldn't want revealed?'

'Blackmail?' Delphine could barely say the word out loud.

Cybille waved her cigarette in the air. 'Such an ugly word! I prefer to call it insurance. Sometimes, if a situation becomes unpleasant, one has to fight dirty, especially when it comes to family.'

She had said the magic words as far as Delphine was concerned. When it came to family, she would stop at nothing to protect her own.

'You make a good point, Cybille,' she said, smoothly sliding the business card off the edge of the table and into her Chanel handbag. She got to her feet, picking up the bill – it was the least she could do. 'Thank you. I'll keep you up to date with developments.'

Cybille nodded sagely. 'You do that,' she said, reaching for another cigarette.

Xavier strode to the stables restlessly, wondering whether he should give Therese a call back. She'd been badgering him all day and he was about to give in when he discovered his younger brother Max standing next to the dormant lavender fields that would burst into a riot of violet and indigo in June. He was staring down into the rocky valley below, transfixed. Xavier put his phone away. He had been meaning to speak to Max since the party and now seemed as good a time as any.

'Hey,' he said, reaching Max's side. He glanced down at the valley, realising Max was doing what he himself often did, visiting the place their mother had lost her life over two years ago. It might seem maudlin to others but it was strangely comforting.

'Hey,' Max returned, glancing at him moodily.

Knowing he smoked, Xavier handed him a cigarette. 'Do you want to be on your own?'

Max shook his head and accepted Xavier's lighter. 'Not really. Did you enjoy the party?'

Frowning as his phone beeped loudly at him, Xavier ignored yet another phone call from Therese.

'She's getting clingy,' Max observed slyly, knowing how much Xavier hated it when girls did that.

'Why do I always pick women who need me to reassure them day and night?' Xavier groaned.

Max blew smoke into the air. 'Because you play the field.' He shrugged. 'If you change girlfriends more than you change your underwear, they tend to need reassurance that you're still interested in them.'

'When did you get so wise about women?' Xavier laughed, giving him a brotherly shove. He supposed Max was right; like Olivier, he chased women indiscriminately, at least that's what he'd done for the past two years or so. Before that, he had been optimistic about love. No, he had been *in love* with the whole idea of love, prepared to settle down and be grown up and responsible.

Xavier gritted his teeth, hating what he had become. He had changed beyond recognition. Before *her*, he hadn't been remotely cynical, but these days he went after women with cold detachment – anything to avoid making the same mistake twice. Xavier's eyes darkened as he lit a cigarette. Everyone thought he was screwed up over his mother's death because he had refused to take part in the family perfume business since then, but there was far more to it than that.

'Women,' Max said, knowing Xavier was contemplating the past. He knew exactly what had happened to his brother two years ago but he wouldn't ever tell a soul, one, because it was way too private, and two, because one sniff of it would have the press setting up camp outside the château.

Xavier nodded in agreement. 'I'm always honest about my intentions,' he said, his sense of humour returning. 'But what good does it do me? They still want me to commit in some way. If anything, me saying I don't want a relationship encourages them.'

Max laughed. 'It's a bit like the business, Xav,' he commented. 'The more you say you don't want to get involved, the more everyone gets on your case to do it.'

It was true. Since his mother's death, Xavier felt that everyone was relying on him, waiting and expecting him to take up the reins and carry on where she left off. Being a 'nose', a scent creator, was an exceptional and much envied talent, Xavier knew that. He was invaluable to the family business because he understood the brand and he was the only one who could create something new to breathe life into the company. If only he could find it in himself to care. Once upon a time, his life had revolved around whether *iris poudre* and blackberry blended well and whether 'gourmand' scents featuring edible or dessert-like qualities really did bring about a sense of well-being. But these days, such things barely touched his radar.

'Did you meet Olivier's widow last night?' Xavier asked, blowing smoke into the air.

Max's expression was guarded. He was fairly sure it was Cat Hayes he had offered his spliff to but he was hoping to God she didn't grass him up. 'Not really.' He shrugged.

'Me neither. At least, she caught me with Therese, skinny-dipping, but we didn't exactly have a chat.' Xavier grinned. He probably looked like a spoilt playboy, splashing around naked in the hot tub, but what did he care? The opinion of Olivier's widow hardly mattered.

'Enough about me,' he said to Max, turning to face his brother. 'Where were you last night?'

Max looked evasive. 'I was . . . around,' he said, scowling slightly. 'What are you getting at?'

Xavier met his eyes sternly. 'You know exactly what I'm getting at. Were you doing drugs again?'

Max threw his cigarette into the valley aggressively. 'You can't ask me that!'

'I can ask you anything I damned well like and you'd be better telling me than our father. He'll go mad if he finds out you're doing drugs, you know that.' He noted the shock in his brother's eyes. 'Oh, come on, Max! I know all the signs. Olivier was just as bad. You're on a dangerous path right now and you don't want to end up the way he did.'

'Olivier had a great life,' Max said flippantly. 'And I don't do jet skis, so there's no danger there.'

Xavier gripped his arm. 'Olivier is dead, remember?' he howled angrily. 'He's buried in the ground and we're still picking up the pieces – at least, I am. The last thing I want to do is clear up after my baby brother too.'

Max shook his hand off. 'Sorry, I didn't realise I was such a burden to you, Xavier. Don't worry, I'll be fine, you won't need to "clear up" after me, all right?' He stormed off, his dark head down and his hands shoved into his pockets.

Xavier sighed; he hadn't handled that well. He hadn't meant to make Max feel as though he was a burden, he was just trying to get the silly kid to make more sensible decisions. Xavier cursed under his breath, knowing he had probably made matters worse. Turning, he saw his father approaching. Xavier's heart sank. He wasn't in the mood for a confrontation and that was all his father seemed to want from him right now.

'There you are,' Guy said. 'I've been looking for you everywhere.' He couldn't bear the sight of the valley that had taken his beloved wife from him but, strangely, his children seemed drawn to it. Perhaps they felt closer to Elizabeth here but he found staring at her place of death traumatic. 'We're going to speak to Olivier's widow tomorrow morning. Do you want to be there?'

Xavier shook his head. 'No thanks. I'm sure it will be tedious and unpleasant.' He noticed the deep lines etched down his father's cheeks, marks that had only appeared in the past year or so.

Guy shook his head, raking his silver hair back with an impatient hand. He reminded himself to stay calm. Xavier had a temper and getting cross with him would achieve nothing. 'She's a very beautiful girl, you know. She may not be the gold digger we all assumed she was.'

'What, because she's beautiful?' Xavier scowled. 'Olivier had relatively good taste in women, so his widow wasn't likely to be ugly. But it doesn't mean her intentions are pure, does it? She has to be slightly mental, at least. If she wasn't after Olivier's money, she's crazy for marrying someone she barely knew.' He shrugged. 'Who cares, anyway?'

'Xavier!' Guy roared, his good intentions to stay calm evaporating. 'This is important to the family, you need to step up and get involved!'

Xavier's fiery temper flared up just as quickly. He turned on his father. 'Why do I need to? Because it suits you?' He lifted his chin angrily, his dark eyes flashing. 'All you care about is the business! You can't stand the fact that I'm not interested in the money or in perfume. You think my life should be ruled by it like yours is. I don't care, all right? Not any more.' Xavier stormed back to La Fleurie looking just like his brother Max a few minutes ago.

59

Despairingly, Guy stared after him, ignoring the uncomfortable feeling that Xavier might have a point about his life being ruled by the family business. But someone had to care – didn't they?

Chapter Four

The next day, feeling deeply apprehensive, Leoni ventured back to La Fleurie. There was a family meeting to attend after the weekend and there was no way she was missing that.

Maybe Olivier's gold-digging widow had already left, Leoni thought hopefully as she strolled outside into the watery sunshine. She flexed her shoulders; it felt surprisingly good to be back at La Fleurie, where she still had an office. Having moved into a nearby apartment a few years ago, Leoni split her time between the perfume warehouse and La Fleurie, crashing out in her apartment when she needed sleep or privacy. Work was manic at the moment and at least when she was in the family home, she could be herself and let go of the tough façade she put on at the warehouse. Well, Leoni thought, it wasn't all a façade; she supposed she was tough in many ways and she was certainly more focused on work than the rest of her family.

Leoni's moment of relaxation was short-lived. Catching sight of a mane of butterscotch-blond hair in the pool house, she realised Olivier's widow was indeed still around. Turning puce and not even stopping to think, Leoni marched in and confronted Cat.

'What are you doing here?' she blurted out brusquely in French.

Startled, Cat simply stared at Leoni. She was wearing a conservative navy dress that, whilst chic, made her look far older than she was. Her severe expression intimidated Cat but the eyes were so like Olivier's, the jawline identical too . . .

Leoni looked pained. Not only did Olivier's silly widow have the most appalling dress sense, the girl couldn't even understand basic French. Why else would she be staring at her so gormlessly? Feeling irritable, she opened her mouth to ask the question again in English.

'God, but you look like Olivier!' Cat declared, before she could stop herself. Then she repeated the statement in French.

Leoni flinched, clearly taken aback. Belatedly, it occurred to her that Cat may well have understood every word of the spiteful speech she'd delivered at her party. Leoni felt a pang of regret. It had been a nasty moment, one fuelled by too much champagne and raw grief, but it was out there now.

Defensively, she responded, her next words more loaded with sarcasm than she intended them to be. 'Well, I hope me looking like Olivier doesn't make you feel awkward.'

'Not at all. In fact, it's . . . it's actually oddly comforting.' It was. It was like seeing Olivier again in some ways, although obviously Leoni was her own person and didn't appear to share many personality traits with her brother. Olivier had been so hedonistic and funny, and Leoni . . . well, Leoni seemed far more serious. And very angry. But maybe Olivier's death had done that to her – death rarely brought out the best in people.

Cat immediately felt contrite. Leoni was Olivier's sister and the last thing she wanted to do was provoke her further. 'I'm so sorry, it must be such a shock meeting me like this. I know I'd find it hard. But please don't worry too much. I reckon I'll be leaving soon and you can all get on with your lives again.' She gave Leoni a warm smile, to show there were no hard feelings.

Disarmed by Cat's honesty, Leoni felt wrong footed. She tried to look at Cat the way Olivier might have done; after all, with all the women at his disposal, he had chosen to marry Cat, so there had to be something special about her. Grudgingly,

Leoni admitted she had a certain appeal. Aside from the crumpled white top and jeans, Cat was really pretty, not at all the brassy tart they'd been expecting. She had a hesitant but friendly smile, and a lovely figure, slightly too curvy to suit French couture but still, Leoni supposed she could see the attraction.

'Have you met my grandmother yet?' she asked Cat.

Cat shook her head. 'Not yet. There's a meeting later today . . . in the boardroom, apparently.' She paused and glanced up at the château. 'I know this place is huge but I didn't realise it had a boardroom.'

'On the top floor.' Leoni nodded, wondering if Cat knew what she was in for later. She was disappointed she hadn't been invited – put out, even. Olivier's business was her business, surely. But, as usual, she wasn't deemed important enough for an invite. Leoni felt riled all over again.

'I have no idea what the meeting's about,' Cat ventured, more to fill the awkward silence than anything else. As soon as the words were out, she realised she'd put her foot in it in some way. Leoni's face darkened and her expression became closed again.

'Really? You expect me to believe that?'

The venom in Leoni's voice was unmistakable. Wondering what the hell she'd said that had been so inflammatory, Cat was beginning to feel quite antagonistic herself. What was *wrong* with this family? Obviously she had guessed that the family might want to protect their finances, but she was still none the wiser about the details.

'Yes, I really expect you to believe that,' Cat fired back.

'Pah!' Leoni could barely contain herself. Cat might look innocent enough but she found it impossible to believe the girl was completely in the dark about Olivier's wealth and his involvement in the perfume business. The vast château with its incredible grounds must have given it away, surely! How did Cat think the family had amassed such a fortune? Granted, the Ducasse family had been privileged to begin with, but the stables, the horses, the cars . . . such opulence was rarely sustained on inheritance alone.

'What did you even have in common?' Leoni demanded, her gunshot delivery making an already fraught Cat recoil again. 'You and my brother, how well can you possibly have known each other? Are you in the habit of marrying people you've known for five minutes?'

Cat squared up to Leoni. 'It may sound crazy to you but we fell in love. It was as simple as that. And no, I'm not in the bloody habit of marrying people I barely know! I'm not a . . . a serial widow or something, I haven't left dead husbands littered all over the world, for God's sake.' Pausing for breath, Cat realised her shoulders were shaking. 'Olivier asked me to marry him and I said yes. I knew it was madness but I loved him.'

'How touching,' sneered Leoni, feeling a bolt of something very much like jealousy shooting through her. She pushed it to one side. She hadn't been expecting Cat to hit back the way she had; Olivier's widow clearly had more backbone than she'd thought.

Cat bit her lip furiously. She didn't want to let rip at Leoni but she wasn't sure she could take much more of her contemptuous dismissal of the one meaningful relationship she'd ever had with a man. Brief, yes . . . reckless, maybe, but it had still been meaningful.

'Yes, we fell in love,' she said again. 'We shared a bond because we both lost our parents at a young age. Is that so difficult to believe?'

Leoni faltered. 'You lost your parents too?'

Cat nodded. 'In a skiing accident when I was fifteen. It affected me deeply . . . the way it did when it happened to Olivier . . . and you too, I assume.'

Leoni raised her eyebrows sceptically. Their parents' death had barely seemed to register on Olivier's radar at the time. If anything, he seemed to use it to justify his irresponsible behaviour. Leoni could recall many a time when Olivier had held his lack of parental guidance up as an excuse for his increasingly debauched actions and, if she remembered rightly, it had been a favourite chat-up line of his to con girls into feeling sorry for him.

Was that the case with Cat? she wondered.

'Incidentally was Olivier drunk when he proposed to you?' she asked laconically. 'Because my brother was drunk quite a lot of the time, you know. He had a bit of a problem, in all honesty, but we all ignored it.'

Cat swallowed. 'Was he . . . *drunk* when he proposed to me?' What sort of question was that?! 'I think this conversation is over,' she said stiffly, her heart crashing in her chest. 'I appreciate that Olivier was your brother and that you can't bear the thought of him marrying anyone, least of all me. But I can't listen to any more of this.'

Cat stalked away from the pool house with her head down.

Leoni flushed. She couldn't seem to stop herself from trying to hurt Cat and prove that her marriage to Olivier was a sham. But, in all honesty, she didn't feel very proud of herself right now.

Scuffing his feet on the gravel path outside La Fleurie, Max lit another spliff. Life at home was becoming so intolerable, he was almost tempted to go back to his horrendous college early, just to get away. He was thoroughly fed up with all the drama.

Bloody family, he thought crossly. All they did was fuss and moan and ask him what he was up to all the time. Even Seraphina was doing his head in being all concerned and caring, and the last thing he wanted to do was yell at her so he had slipped away to be by himself.

Sometimes, being wealthy was shit, Max decided grumpily as he glanced over his shoulder at La Fleurie. It should be fun but most of the time it was rubbish. *Poor little rich boy,* he mocked himself, knowing how pathetic he sounded. Who wouldn't envy him his lifestyle? His family owned one of the most beautiful and luxurious houses in Provence and he wanted for nothing. Well, almost nothing.

Angrily, Max ground his spliff underfoot. Everything had gone wrong since his mother died, everything. He was so furious with his father, he didn't know what to do with himself, but he knew he wouldn't know what to say to him even if there was the remotest chance he could spend five minutes alone with him.

Looking up warily, Max caught sight of a girl he knew from his boarding school. A nondescript girl with long brown hair and pretty eyes, Madeleine was the daughter of Clare and Phillipe Lombard who were friends of the family. Clare had been a close friend of his mother's so Max felt obliged to be vaguely polite to Madeleine, even though he really wasn't in the mood to talk. He settled for a smile that he hoped wasn't a grimace.

'How are you?' she asked. Wearing jeans with a black velvet jacket and a cream scarf knotted round her neck, she looked as though she should be cantering around on a pony. Randomly, Max wondered if she ever rode but he couldn't be bothered to ask.

'I'm home for the weekend but I'll be back at college on Monday,' Madeleine went on when Max didn't respond. 'Do you know when you'll be back?'

Max shrugged. He was being rude, he knew that, but he just couldn't find it in himself to make small talk. He realised everyone in the town must be talking about Olivier's sudden death and about his widow's arrival and it made his blood boil. Couldn't they find something else to talk about?

Madeleine's green eyes were full of compassion. 'It must be so hard losing Olivier after everything you've been through.' She tentatively touched his arm. 'If you ever want to talk . . .'

Barely listening, Max gave her a careless nod. He could hear the roar of approaching motorbikes. Three of them shot down the path and skidded to a halt next to Max and Madeleine. Pierre and Thierry, two of the older kids from college, tore off their helmets. Veronique, a sexy-looking sixteen-year-old was on the third bike, her black hair spilling out across her shoulders. She had been at Leoni's party the other night but she wasn't officially Max's girlfriend. Giving Madeleine a withering look, Vero fixed her eyes on Max with intent.

'Want a ride?' she drawled seductively, revving up her bike.

Max didn't need asking twice. Leaping on behind Vero, he snapped on the spare helmet she offered him and wrapped his arms round her waist. He let out a whoop as the bike shot off at high speed. A dismayed Madeleine stood in a cloud of dust, her black velvet jacket ruined. Max felt a momentary pang of guilt, but then he pushed it aside and tightened his grip round Vero's narrow waist as they sped off into the distance.

Later that day, Leoni headed into the kitchen to make herself a black coffee. The staff had been given the afternoon off and she was glad; Leoni couldn't face small talk right now.

Finding the espresso machine up and running, Leoni helped herself to a strong, black coffee. She couldn't stop thinking about her altercation with Cat. Either she was a very good actress, or the girl had genuinely been in love with Olivier. The thought disconcerted Leoni.

Xavier strolled in. 'Hey.' He kissed her cheeks fondly. 'I've missed you, cousin. Where have you been?'

'Oh, just with friends. And I saw Ashton, too.' Leoni flung her arms round Xavier's neck and clung to him briefly. He smelt reassuringly familiar and the tang of cigarette smoke and cologne made Leoni feel grounded after such an unsettling morning. She adored Xavier. Apart from Ashton, who was a different kettle of fish altogether, Xavier was the closest thing she had to a brother now that Olivier had gone. And he was a damned sight more reliable. Well, unless it came to women, of course, but that didn't concern Leoni.

Xavier looked as glamorous as ever in a pair of jeans and a black polo shirt with the collar all twisted up – accident rather than design, Leoni presumed, but he got away with it.

'Bad morning?' Xavier asked.

Leoni shuddered. 'You could say that.' She filled him in about her confrontation with Cat.

'I was pretty vile to her.' Leoni chewed her lip. 'She might be genuine, but I'm not sure. Would you really marry someone without knowing who they were or what their background was?'

Xavier rolled his eyes. 'Exactly. She's not normal – she can't be. If she really did love him and she's not after his money – and we don't know that for sure yet – then at the very least she's certifiable. Hey, are you attending this meeting with her later?'

Leoni's brow furrowed. 'No. I wasn't asked.' She slammed her hand down on the counter, making her coffee cup shake. 'Don't tell me, you were? Damn it! How typical is that? I am so involved in this business, far more than you, Xav, and yet your father and our grandmother *never* take me seriously—'

'Leoni, calm down!' Xavier held up his hand. 'The only reason my father asked me to attend the meeting is because he was making yet another unsubtle attempt to draw me back into the business. Don't take it personally, he's just using any old excuse to try and get me involved.'

Leoni couldn't help thinking Guy had a point; after all, now that Aunt Elizabeth had died, Xavier's exceptional talent as a *senteur* was their only way of advancing the business. Otherwise, it would slide into obscurity. Leoni was itching to say as much but she kept her mouth shut because she didn't want to be on the receiving end of Xavier's hot temper. Guy was putting enough pressure on Xavier, he wouldn't welcome more from her.

Toying with his lighter, Xavier changed the subject, clearly bored. 'How was Ash?'

Leoni leant against the kitchen counter, her hand wrapped round her coffee cup. 'Fine. He was working on a gorgeous property in Mougins and then I think he went back to Paris. He's missing Olivier but aren't we all?' She sighed and rubbed her temples. 'I just wish it would all get sorted and then I can concentrate on work again. I have so many big plans but I can't seem to concentrate. The sooner Olivier's widow is out of here, the better, as far as I'm concerned.'

Xavier nodded but said nothing, watching Leoni over the top of his coffee cup. He admired her dedication to work but he couldn't help wondering if she was ever lonely. She rarely had boyfriends and he couldn't remember the last time she'd had a serious relationship. All she seemed to care about was the business. Spreadsheets and perfumes got Leoni going, not men. He looked up as Therese came into the kitchen, her red hair all over the place.

Leoni's eyes widened. Xavier's girlfriend was wearing a silky lavender robe that didn't do much to disguise her jiggling, bra-less breasts.

'This is Therese,' Xavier explained, looking slightly exasperated at Therese's appearance. He didn't care personally but he thought she could have made an effort in front of his family.

Therese nodded at Leoni briefly and looked around for something to eat. Picking up a fresh brioche she found in a basket, she bit into it as though it was an apple. Leoni watched her, thinking how child-like she was for a grown woman. Catching Xavier's eye, she could see he was thinking exactly the same thing and she almost giggled.

'Anyway, I can't wait to hear what happens at this meeting,' Leoni said distractedly, watching Therese helping herself to Xavier's coffee without asking. 'Grandmother can be so intimidating.'

About to comment, Xavier was cut short by Therese, who seemed to have some thoughts on the matter.

'*I* wouldn't be intimidated,' she informed them confidently. 'But then I'm not after something the way she is.'

Leoni said nothing. Personally, she thought Therese was no better than Cat; she was out for what she could get from Xavier and although he was undeniably gorgeous, his wealth had to add another string to an already appealing bow.

'Therese!' Xavier reprimanded her, trying to recall exactly why he had thought she was girlfriend material in the first place. Apart from a penchant for skinny-dipping, the attraction was beginning to wane. Idly, Xavier wondered if Monique was still in Provence or if she'd gone off on another modelling assignment.

'I'm going to have a shower.' Therese sniffed, tossed the remains of her brioche on the table and flounced out of the room.

Leoni picked the brioche up and put it in the bin. 'She's nice,' she mocked Xavier. 'So grown up . . . so intelligent.'

'Oh, shut up,' Xavier snapped, dropping his cigarette into his coffee cup with a hiss.

Cat took a deep breath as she made her way to the top floor of La Fleurie for her meeting with Guy and Delphine. She had changed into the only vaguely formal dress she had thrown into her luggage, which was a belted grey number she used for work, and some high heels.

She hesitated at the open door to the boardroom and Guy beckoned her in. Beside him at the head of a glossy oval table sat a stern-looking woman in a strawberry-pink Chanel suit.

'This is my mother, Delphine,' Guy informed Cat politely.

Delphine's austere brown eyes assessed Cat coolly.

'How nice to meet you at last,' she said in fluent English, her voice friendlier than her eyes. 'We have been so looking forward to meeting Olivier's widow.'

'Er . . . thank you.' Cat was uncomfortable with the word 'widow'. At twenty-six, she felt far too young for the title. 'I understand French so please don't feel obliged to speak English on my account.'

'Good. Listen, this is all rather delicate,' Guy started, uncapping a gold fountain pen, 'but I'm afraid it has to be done. When it comes to finances, I always find it best to be as open as possible.'

'Finances?' Cat stared at him and he found her direct gaze unsettling. He felt rather like the spider chatting casually to the fly before devouring it and it wasn't a role he was comfortable with.

Delphine's eyes narrowed. 'Surely you knew Olivier was a very wealthy young man when you married him?'

'No, I did not,' Cat said firmly. 'He never mentioned it and I had no idea he lived in such a beautiful château.' She could have added that he'd denied his family's very existence but the last thing she wanted to do was destroy their positive view of Olivier.

'Really?' Delphine responded, her eyes disbelieving. 'I find that astonishing.'

'It doesn't really matter either way,' Guy cut in. 'What is important now is to protect our family.' He pushed the papers towards Cat. 'Hopefully you can understand our position. All you need to do is sign where the crosses are marked and then our business is concluded.'

Cat scanned the papers quickly. Most of the legal French was too complex to understand fully but she grasped enough of it to comprehend that the Ducasse family were trying to ring-fence Olivier's inheritance. The final paragraph stated that she would be paid a lump sum in euros – a huge one – if she agreed not to contest Olivier's will and if she relinquished all claims to his shares in the Ducasse-Fleurie perfume empire.

'Ducasse-Fleurie,' she said slowly, her mouth suddenly

feeling rather dry as the penny finally dropped. The perfume empire.

Guy nodded, his eyes watching her astutely.

Cat was pale with shock. 'Dear God. You . . . you own Ducasse-Fleurie Perfumes.' The Ducasse family, the château called La Fleurie – she simply hadn't made the connection. The family crest was stamped on the legal papers, and it was one she'd seen on boxes and bottles in duty free in department stores all over the world. This family were surely millionaires . . . several times over.

'We *are* Ducasse-Fleurie Perfumes,' Delphine snapped. 'But you already knew that, of course.'

Cat put down the paperwork with shaking hands. Far from being a penniless waiter, Olivier had been an heir to what had to be a multimillion euro fortune. Why hadn't he told her? Cat's eyes filled with tears. Hadn't he trusted her? Had he assumed that like many women before her, she would only have been interested in him for his money? But if so, why hadn't he told her after their marriage? Why hadn't he thought enough of her to tell her the truth then? She had been so sure he loved her, but now . . .

Guy fixed his eyes firmly on Cat, thinking how ghostly pale she looked. 'We dropped the Fleurie part of our name some years ago but kept it for the brand. I assume you've heard of us.'

Cat nodded. 'Who *hasn't* heard of you?' Ducasse-Fleurie Perfumes were as famous as Lancôme or Dior. No wonder the Ducasse family had been treating her with such suspicion and hostility! They hadn't wanted to get to know her at all. They just wanted her signature on some papers that would get her out of their lives for ever. She was nothing more than a problem Olivier had created, a bit of mess his untimely death had unearthed.

Cat felt both fury and sadness. She had never felt more unwelcome or unwanted in her life. Without thinking, she

72

glanced at her watch, wondering how quickly she could book a flight back to England.

'You want to pay me off,' she said in a flat voice. 'You want me to take this . . . this money and leave. And there was me thinking you'd invited me here because you wanted to get to know me . . . to get to know Olivier's widow. Christ! How stupid of me.'

Guy, to his credit, had the grace to show some embarrassment but Cat couldn't even look at him. His part in this hurt her the most because he was the one person in the family who had been decent to her from the start. But it was obviously all a front.

Delphine simply stared at Cat. 'Will you sign the papers?' she asked without emotion. 'We would really like to get this issue tied up as soon as possible.'

Cat got to her feet, colour flooding her cheeks. 'No, I will not sign the papers!' She tore them in half for good measure. 'I didn't want you to know this but Olivier never said a word about you, he never spoke about any of you. He told me he was a penniless waiter when I met him. He told me he had no money and no family. And I married him anyway.' She swallowed. 'Which probably makes me stupid in your eyes, but I loved him.' Hot tears threatened but Cat held them back with a monumental effort. She would not break down in front of these scheming, heartless people.

Guy felt thoroughly ashamed. He believed Cat. Her shock and dismay were obviously sincere.

Delphine, however, remained unconvinced. 'Please do not humiliate yourself any further, Miss Hayes,' she said in clipped tones. She refused to call Olivier's widow Madame Ducasse – that would be nauseating and utterly unacceptable. 'This is difficult enough as it is. We have lost a dear relative and we need to ensure that our family is protected. Nothing is more important.'

Cat nodded. 'I quite agree. Family *is* everything. And as I am not family, I will leave and get on with my life. I have no desire to be part of your business or to take anything from you, not even this pay-off.' She squashed the thought that the enormous sum of money would be extremely useful since she was out of a job and had no home to go to.

'We need you to sign something,' Delphine insisted. 'If you don't, you could come back and claim Olivier's share of the business at any time. As his widow, you are his sole heir but I cannot allow you to just leave without legally stating your intention to step down.'

Cat prickled at the suggestion that she might come back at some later date and demand a share of the perfume business. Judging by the vast sum of money they were offering her to leave quietly, they weren't concerned about finances; they simply wanted legal confirmation that Cat wouldn't ever become part of Ducasse-Fleurie. What kind of person did they think she was? 'I don't want Olivier's money. Why can't you understand that?'

'This is a legal matter,' Delphine returned tersely. 'And you cannot leave until this matter is concluded.'

'What are you going to do, lock me in my room?' Cat demanded belligerently. 'I've said my goodbyes to Olivier and I have no wish to stay here. I'm going to pack and I'll be on the first flight home.' With that, she turned and left the room.

Guy gathered up the torn papers and slowly shuffled them together.

'What a performance!' Delphine sneered. 'She can't leave, Guy. We can't possibly allow her to go back to England without formally stating that she has no claim to our fortune.'

Guy frowned. 'What are you going to do? Lock her in her room as she suggested?'

'Don't be ridiculous,' Delphine snapped. 'We have to think of something. Actually, aren't the airports on strike again? Yes, I think I saw something about them being closed again this weekend. Which means we have a few days' grace . . .' Delphine looked thoughtful. 'The family meeting is arranged for Monday. We should invite Miss Hayes, make sure she understands how critical it is that she formally declines involvement on Olivier's behalf.'

Guy shrugged. 'As you wish.'

'I'll get Seraphina on the case. I saw her chatting to Miss Hayes. She can probably convince her the family meeting is a good idea. And maybe Xavier can assist us,' Delphine added, not at all sure what she had in mind for him. 'What do you think?' she asked Guy.

Guy's manner was offhand. 'Anything that will get Xavier interested in the business again is fine with me, you know that.'

Delphine narrowed her eyes. 'What's the matter, Guy? Surely you didn't believe what that girl said?'

Guy looked at his mother. 'Maybe. If it was an act, it was a very convincing one. And she has seemed overwhelmed by her surroundings since she arrived.'

'Ah, Guy, you always did have a soft spot for a pretty face.'

Guy's face darkened. His mother's disdain reminded him of when he'd first brought Elizabeth home to meet the family; they had disapproved of her and Delphine had always resented Elizabeth's blond beauty.

He got to his feet. 'Do whatever you want,' he snapped. 'Let's just get these papers drawn up again and signed. Then, perhaps, we can all move on.'

Frowning, Delphine watched him stride from the room. The Ducasse men were all so volatile and headstrong, she thought crisply. It was just as well she was on hand to sort out this preposterous mess Olivier had got them into.

Chapter Five

The following morning, Leoni stood outside the walled-off graveyard, trying to pluck up the courage to go in. She hadn't visited her brother's grave once since he'd been buried because she'd been too angry. She didn't feel any calmer now but after everything that had happened, Leoni knew she had to get a few things off her chest. Unaware Cat had done the same thing only a couple of days before, albeit in a more peaceful fashion, Leoni stalked towards Olivier's shiny headstone and allowed her emotions to come to the fore.

'How could you, you stupid idiot?' she cried. 'How could you leave me alone like this? And how dare you marry that girl without even telling me?' Her chest heaved. 'There's no one here on my side any more,' she wept. 'Selfish bastard!' She yelled.

Leoni cried and cried until finally she couldn't cry any more. She got slowly to her feet and dusted her dress down. She was glad she'd told Olivier how she felt – or his headstone, at least – because it was better than keeping it all bottled up inside, as her grandmother always insisted she should do. She glanced at her parents' crusty-looking gravestones. Why couldn't she lose herself in an addiction the way the rest of her family did? Or maybe she did, Leoni acknowledged with a jolt. Instead of drink, narcotics or flings with the opposite sex, business was her addiction – perfume sales and advertising. Business might be challenging but it wasn't messy and it wasn't unreliable and it didn't leave you vulnerable and exposed. Or with some bloody beautiful widow who suddenly had claim to your inheritance because you'd flown off a jet ski doing a backflip.

Leoni choked down a sob and then suddenly froze. She'd heard movement behind her. She spun round and caught sight of Ashton's blond hair through the mimosa trees in front of the graveyard. She flushed, hoping fervently that he hadn't heard her screaming like a banshee.

'Er, is it all right if I join you?' Ashton emerged cautiously from behind the trees.

'Of course,' Leoni said awkwardly. She must look a sight.

'Have you been giving him a piece of your mind?' Ashton asked with a smile, gesturing to Olivier's grave. He saw the panic in her tear-swollen eyes. 'Don't worry, I didn't hear you. I've only just arrived. And I don't blame you one little bit if you were letting rip at him.'

Leoni managed to smile back. He was always such a rock. 'Is our trip to England still on?' she asked, taking his arm.

Ashton nodded. 'My parents are dying to see you again. I said we'd stay with them for a bit, is that all right? Then we can go to London and do some research on those brands you mentioned.'

Leoni nodded, feeling almost content for the first time in ages. The trip to England to research her home fragrance line would be the perfect antidote to everything going on here. Cat Hayes would probably be gone soon and everything would settle down and feel normal again.

Sitting beneath a beautiful old sycamore tree, Cat gazed out across a sea of white, frothy almond trees. To the left, she could see what looked like olive trees, apricot trees and jasmine that would no doubt give off the most delicious aromas later in the year.

Cat let out a heavy sigh as she munched on a slice of French bread smothered with apricot jam. La Fleurie really was stunning but beautiful surroundings didn't mean anything when you weren't wanted. Cat didn't feel alone, exactly; the army of staff who tended to the needs of the Ducasse family were highly visible, albeit discreetly. Guy and Delphine always dined together, joined by Seraphina and Max much of the time. Loathe to face the family, Cat had taken to eating alone, usually after the others had left. She had barely seen Xavier, although he apparently resided at the château and Leoni, thankfully, had her own apartment near the perfume warehouse and she drifted in and out – presumably based on her business commitments. Cat wished she could book a flight home but the French were on strike again. How she wished she hadn't bothered to come! Every time she thought about the legal papers she'd been presented with, she was stung all over again by the insult.

'Hey,' Seraphina said, squatting down next to Cat, clutching some brochures and a bag of chinking bottles. She was wearing a grubby pair of black jodhpurs and a tight black T-shirt with a picture some French songstress on the front.

'Hey,' Cat said, giving Seraphina a mistrustful glance, as she finished her lunch.

Seraphina put the brochures down. 'Don't be like that! I'm not the one who tried to get you to sign things and buy you off.'

'You knew about it and that's just as bad,' Cat retorted. Instantly, she felt bad. 'Sorry. I feel like such an idiot.'

'You shouldn't. It's what our family are like. When you have this much money and a château, you end up being very protective of it. The family worked very hard to create the business. It's natural they want to look after it, isn't it?' She pushed a brochure towards Cat. 'Have a look, read up about it. You should know what you married into.'

Cat glanced at the brochure but didn't take it. 'What for? As soon as I can book a flight, I'm out of here.'

'If you think Grandmother will allow you to leave before

you've signed something, you've very much mistaken. And creating new documents could take ages.' Her mouth twitched. 'You know, since you tore the other ones up and threw them at my relatives.'

'I didn't "throw" the papers at your relatives. I tore them up and sort of . . . scattered them.'

'So I heard.' Seraphina grinned.

Cat clutched her hair. 'Jesus! I just want to go home. I mean, I don't have a job or anything but I need to sort one out and I can't do that here. This is like being in prison, a gorgeous one admittedly, but it's still a prison because I don't want to be here.'

'Thanks.' Seraphina pouted. 'I'll try not to be offended.'

'Actually, it's your father I'm most upset about. I thought he liked me but I was obviously wrong.'

Seraphina shrugged. 'I'm sure he does like you, but Grandmother's the boss around here.'

Cat flipped through the perfume brochure listlessly.

'Why don't you attend the family meeting on Monday?' Seraphina suggested brightly. 'Then you can see exactly why everyone is freaking out and going on about you signing papers.'

Cat looked up, her eyes fixed shrewdly on Seraphina. 'Did your grandmother put you up to that?'

Seraphina held up her hands. 'Guilty, I'm afraid. But honestly, I think it's a good idea. It's serious stuff, the family business. Once you see it with your own eyes, you'll understand why Grandmother is doing what she's doing. She's not all bad, I promise.'

Cat grudgingly agreed to attend the meeting. Glancing at the brochure again, she couldn't help reading about Maxim Ducasse–Fleurie, the first family 'senteur' – or 'nose'. 'So your great-grandfather created Rose-Nymphea?'

Seraphina nodded. 'It was the first Ducasse-Fleurie perfume, launched in nineteen fifty-one, thirty years after the legendary

Chanel No. 5 came on the scene.' She stopped and grinned. She was quoting from the brochure.

'Hush, let me read,' Cat said with a smile.

Inspired by his love of both roses and his beloved Monet paintings, she read, Maxim had given Rose-Nymphea, the rose and waterlily-scented perfume, a floral revamp in the early seventies before his death. But apart from a few minor fragrances, he hadn't been able to match the success of Rose-Nymphea which became the signature scent for Ducasse-Fleurie.

Seraphina drew a bottle out of the bag. 'Our great-grandfather was the first official "nose" in the family. My twin brother is named after him but, sadly, he's missed out on the talent. That all went to Xavier.'

Cat turned the bottle over in her hands, realising she remembered it from her mother's dressing table. It was a slightly old-fashioned bottle with a large stopper and swirly writing but it had a sophisticated air about it. She lifted the stopper and sniffed; the fragrance was familiar – sweet, floral and enduring.

'And Xavier and your mother created L'Air Sensuel together,' she said, referring to the brochure again.

Seraphina produced the relevant bottle from her bag with a flourish.

' "A rich, sweet fragrance featuring green fig with honey notes," ' Cat read aloud. She took the bottle and sniffed. The perfume had become a celebrity favourite; it had been followed by a lighter, summer version, as well as a moodier alternative with a musky base note. Xavier, clearly the most innovative of the family, had also, according to the brochure, developed a series of seasonal eau-de-toilettes that hit the top ten lists every summer and every Christmas because of their universal appeal and youthful accents.

'I've worn these,' Cat realised, recognising the packaging. 'I bought them in duty free. They're gorgeous.'

'They're sold as a pack of three,' Seraphina said, handing them over. 'The first is sharp and zesty, the second a romantic, floral concoction, and the final one is a rich "gourmand". See, I know my perfumes – well, the family ones, anyway. Especially these ones. They're Xavier's best creations, I think.'

Cat wasn't entirely sure what a 'gourmand' was but she knew she liked it; that particular fragrance had been one of her favourites. She felt her keen advertising mind spark up with interest as she skim-read the rest of the brochure. Elizabeth had obviously married into the family rather than being an original Ducasse, so her talent for perfume blending had been purely coincidental. But it had been much needed.

'Here comes Max,' Seraphina commented, spotting her twin's dark head in the distance. 'I'm surprised he's managed to prise himself out of Vero's clutches. Vero's this nasty girl Max has been hanging out with, you see. She goes to our college but she's older than us and she's bad news.' Seraphina fiddled with her ponytail. 'Max is . . . he's a bit mixed up at the moment. Problems with our father but he never talks about it. I don't even know if Max himself knows why he's so angry, to be honest.'

Cat raised her eyebrows but said nothing. She wasn't about to update Seraphina on Max's smoking but she hoped his drug habit didn't spiral out of control. Glancing at him, she noticed that his longish dark hair flopped over his face, obscuring his eyes, but his cheekbones were to die for. Now they were together, Cat could see the resemblance between Max and Seraphina, even though she was as fair as he was dark.

'I thought you might be out with Vero,' Seraphina said slyly.

Max scowled. 'We're not joined at the hip, you know.'

Cat squinted up at him. 'I'm Cat. I'm not sure we've been properly introduced.'

Max shook her hand politely, his ever-present scowl lessening slightly. 'I saw you at the party,' he said, his liquid brown eyes meeting hers as if he was daring her to say she'd seen him doing drugs.

Seraphina frowned. Max hadn't mentioned seeing Cat at the party.

'Did you?' Cat shrugged and met Max's gaze. 'I can't say I remember. It's nice to meet you finally, anyhow.'

Relieved, he squatted down next to them. 'You actually look as though you're reading that,' he said, swatting the brochure.

Cat closed it. 'Seraphina made me, but to be honest, it's fascinating. I had no idea the process of scent creation was so personal. I love it that the idea behind L'Air Sensuel was "sticky, hot Provençal summers, fig and honey compote and romance". Your mother sounds so creative.' She glanced sideways at them. 'Sorry, does it upset you if I talk about her?'

They both shook their heads. 'Not at all,' Max mumbled, looking emotional. 'It's just . . . no one talks about her around here.'

'Really? How strange.' Cat wondered why that was. 'All right, so I'm attending this family meeting but I don't have a clue who does what.'

Max sat up. 'Well, we're just shareholders so no one lets us make any decisions yet. Our father is managing director of the whole company and Leoni is creative director. She also looks after the team of staff who package up all the perfumes for us.'

'Grandmother looks after press and advertising,' chimed in Seraphina, 'which she usually does from her office in Toulouse. She's only here now because . . .' She stopped, looking embarrassed.

'She wants to make sure I'm dealt with,' Cat finished for her sourly. 'It's fine; I know the score now. And what about Olivier, what did he do?'

Max grinned. 'Well, loosely speaking, Olivier was in charge

of sales but he didn't do much selling. He was really just Leoni's sidekick when it came to supporting her in meetings. She comes up with all these outlandish ideas and everyone thinks she's nuts but Olivier always used to stick up for her.'

'Leoni's really sweet when you get to know her,' Seraphina offered earnestly. 'I know she seems really aloof and scary but that's only because no one takes her seriously in the business.'

Having only seen Leoni venting her spleen like a fishwife, Cat remained unconvinced. 'What about your father?'

Max's expression became bitter. 'Oh, he's like Leoni, he's all about the business.'

Seraphina nodded sadly. 'It's true. It's pretty much all he cares about.'

Cat watched them, wondering why they seemed so hurt. Guy, despite the way he had deceived her, seemed like a genuinely caring man so what was stopping him from connecting with his children?

'And Xavier?' Cat glanced at the glamorous photo on the back of the brochure, wishing her only other view of Xavier hadn't been him skinny-dipping in the family pool.

'He's like Olivier,' Max said with a laugh. 'He loves women, has several on the go at the same time. Lucky bastard,' he added enviously.

Seraphina shot him a glance. Xavier was nothing like Olivier! Trust Max to say something immature like that.

Cat didn't really like hearing about Olivier and all his women but he had told her he'd been a bit of a playboy in his time. As for Xavier, sleeping around was just the sort of shallow behaviour she'd expect from him. From what she'd seen, anyway. 'I meant, what's Xavier like when it comes to the perfume business?'

Seraphina looked glum. 'He's not involved any more. He used to be the family nose, he's so talented and intelligent but he's just not interested, not at the moment, anyway. He stepped out around two years ago.'

When Elizabeth died, Cat realised. 'Your mother's death has affected you all greatly,' she commented gently.

Max looked away. 'The riding accident . . . it was devastating for all of us.'

Cat frowned. A riding accident? That was the reason Olivier had given for his own parents' deaths. Did they all go around falling to their death from horses? It was unlikely but Cat couldn't bring herself to question it, not right now.

'But it wasn't just our mother's death that made Xavier step out of the business,' Seraphina commented. 'There was also this woman— ow!' Jumping, she glared at Max who had just elbowed her, hard.

'Shut up!' he hissed. 'You know Xavier hates being talked about.' He spoke rapidly in French. 'He'd go mad if he knew you were saying things about him . . . he thinks she's insane, remember?'

They didn't realise how good her French was; Cat understood every word. She smarted, wondering why Xavier had been bad-mouthing her.

'That's so rude! He doesn't even know her,' Seraphina defended Cat hotly.

Max stood up. 'He said she must be mad to have got married so quickly, that only crazy people do things like that.' He rolled his shoulders. 'I reckon he's got a point.'

Cat went scarlet. She hadn't even spoken to Xavier! Yet apparently he had formed a very clear opinion of her.

'I think she's been very unlucky,' Seraphina hurled back. 'All those women Olivier was stringing along just before he went to St Tropez . . .' Suddenly noticing Cat's expression, Seraphina clapped a hand over her mouth. 'You understand what we're saying,' she gasped, mortified.

Cat just nodded.

Max shoved his hands in his pockets and walked off.

'I'm so sorry,' said Seraphina. 'Please don't start thinking badly of Olivier.'

'Really?' Cat met her eyes. 'I think we both know I probably should.'

Seraphina got to her feet. 'I'm really sorry.' Slowly, she walked away, wishing she'd kept her mouth shut.

Left alone, Cat felt angry tears pricking her eyelids again. She gritted her teeth and pushed them back. Who were you, Olivier? She asked silently. Why did you marry me if you had a stable of other women? And why didn't you tell me about Ducasse-Fleurie?

If Olivier really hadn't been the genuine, loyal man she thought she'd married, Cat thought, feeling her heart constrict painfully, that turned everything upside down.

Xavier glanced upwards to search for the next handhold. He was halfway up Ceuse, the northernmost cliff in the Alps, which some said was the best and most beautiful cliff in the world. Certainly the orange and blue-streaked crest of limestone perched at the top of the Ceuse massif was exceptional.

Tethered to the cliff face by cables from the heavy-duty belt around his waist, he was totally focused on pulling on those handholds and balancing on footholds. He found climbing Ceuse hard, it pushed his body to the limits, but that was why he enjoyed it so much. It released his mind and enabled him to think clearly.

Xavier paused to take in the breathtaking view, dazzled by the blue and gold streaked limestone. His mind drifting, he wondered what had happened at the meeting with Cat Hayes. He couldn't imagine it being much fun and he wouldn't be surprised if she had gone by the time he got back if his grandmother had anything to do with it. He would find his grandmother simply terrifying if he didn't know her; as it was, he found her austere and frosty – and he was allegedly her favourite.

Xavier slotted the toe of his boot into a small pocket, wondering how the hell he was going to secure his next draw.

He wished Therese hadn't come with him, even if she was sat in the car. She always found his rock-climbing tedious, yet she insisted on accompanying him all over Provence. Sometimes he just needed a break from her.

'What are you doing?' asked Matthieu. Matthieu was a friend of Olivier's whom Xavier occasionally went climbing with. 'Are you contemplating the view, Ducasse? Come on, I bet I can beat you to the top.'

Xavier never could resist a dare. Shrugging off his thoughts about Therese and Cat Hayes, he matched his friend's handholds and bounces with increasing vigour. This was what it was all about! Xavier reached the top seconds before Matthieu and as soon as he'd unclipped himself, he rolled over and stared up at the sky.

'Can't believe you managed to beat me,' Matthieu moaned, lying down next to him, exhausted. 'I shouldn't have said anything; I should have just charged past you.' He glanced at Xavier. 'What were you so lost in thought about, anyway? That red-headed girlfriend of yours?'

'Therese?' Xavier shook his head. 'Not really. She's pretty but she's not the most intelligent person I've ever met.'

Matthieu shrugged. 'Does she need to be brainy? With tits like that, I could forgive her lack of intellect. Hey, shame about Olivier.' He took a swig of water and offered the bottle to Xavier. 'I read in the paper about his widow turning up. Was that the one he used to take to Morocco all the time?'

Xavier shook his head and frowned. 'Morocco? No, he met her in St Tropez, of all places.'

'Really?' Matthieu looked puzzled. 'Olivier always said he hated St Tropez. Still, he went wherever there were girls so he wasn't exactly choosy.' He paused and sat up. 'I could have sworn the girl he was nuts about a while ago used to meet him in Morocco a lot.' He took back his water bottle and shrugged.

Xavier thought Matthieu must be mistaken – but then Olivier had no doubt enjoyed liaisons with girls all over the place.

Sometime later, Xavier joined Therese in the car. She was slumped over her book in the front seat, clearly bored senseless.

'You took your time,' she grumbled. 'I've practically read this entire novel.'

Xavier doubted it. He doubted Therese had finished a novel in her life, not even one by Jackie Collins. 'You could always join me next time,' he suggested mildly, wondering what on earth they actually had in common.

Therese shuddered. 'What, crawl all over a massive mountain with just a rope and a bit of metal holding me up? No thank you.' She looked affronted. 'Why do you like doing such dangerous things, anyway? You've got all the money in the world, can't you just play polo or relax on a speedboat like ordinary rich people do?'

Xavier sighed. Her asinine comment proved that Therese didn't know the first thing about him. Sometimes the Ducasse millions were a curse, he thought, tight lipped, as he started the car. If only he could be more like Olivier used to be and not care about anything or anyone, Xavier was sure he'd find his life less irksome.

The day before the family gathering, Delphine was still seething about the meeting with Cat Hayes. It had been an unmitigated disaster; Guy had been totally hoodwinked and somehow the girl had turned the tables on them.

Her fingers tightened around the head of her cane. The girl was not as easy to intimidate as she'd hoped. And if the very generous offer they'd made wouldn't buy her off, something else was needed. Which was why she had invited Yves Giraud to La Fleurie this morning.

Hearing a knock on the door, Delphine looked up. He was

punctual; a good sign. 'Come in,' she called, taking a seat at a table by the window. A tallish man with brown hair and a swarthy tan came in. Delphine assessed him critically. He was younger than she'd expected – thirty, thirty-five perhaps – and he was wearing a flashy brown suit with a colourful lining and no tie.

Delphine's mouth tightened in disapproval. But did it really matter what he looked like? She wasn't hiring him for his wardrobe. She held her hand out.

'Yves Giraud, at your service, madame,' Yves murmured, bending over her hand deferentially.

Unmoved, she motioned him to a chair. Sycophantic gestures bored her.

'What a wonderful château.' Yves took a seat and gazed out at the magnificent view. It was a clear day and acres of gorgeous Provençal countryside could be seen from the window, along with an impressive collection of stables. 'What beautiful views . . .'

Delphine inclined her head. 'Indeed. But we are not here to discuss the delights of my family home.' She linked her pale fingers together. 'Before we begin, I assume I can rely on your absolute discretion?'

'Of course.' Yves drew a small, moleskin notebook out of his suit jacket and a slim gold pen. 'I have worked for extremely well-known celebrities, as well as some of the best families in France.' He touched his rather large nose with the pen. 'You would be surprised what I know but I never reveal my findings. Not unless I am asked to, naturally.'

'Good.' She outlined what had happened since Olivier's death, sparing no detail and filling Yves in on everything she knew about Cat Hayes.

'So you see, Monsieur Giraud, I have a dilemma on my hands.'

Yves nodded. 'Call me Yves, please. Yes, I do see your problem. The Ducasse-Fleurie empire must be protected.'

Delphine stood up restlessly, staring out of the window. 'Nothing is more important to me, Monsieur Giraud.'

He hid a smile, noting her refusal to call him by his first name. And why would she? Delphine Ducasse was a traditionalist, one of only a few left of her kind, but she was paying him handsomely so he would keep his mouth shut and his eyes peeled. His role as a private detective to the rich and famous had left him relatively well off but opulence and breeding never failed to impress him.

Yves glanced out of the window again. He caught sight of a tall, handsome man by the stables, wearing what could only be an extremely expensive designer suit. Xavier Ducasse, Yves realised. Ever since Delphine's phone call, he had been researching the family, making sure he was prepared. Xavier was the eldest of Delphine's grandchildren, the famous 'nose', who no longer took part in the creation of scents for Ducasse-Fleurie. Yves was also aware of two other children, a boy and a girl, but no one had seen much of them over the past two years, not since Delphine's son Guy had packed them off to a private boarding school whose annual fees could finance a couple of racehorses.

'So you want me to find out everything I can about this Miss Hayes,' Yves summed up. 'Everything about her background, her upbringing, her old boyfriends – anything that could potentially discredit her in some way.'

Delphine winced. Put that way, it sounded so crude. But she nodded. It was exactly what she was hoping for – some detail, some fact about Olivier's widow that could send her packing for good if she didn't go of her own accord. 'Check their marriage,' she instructed. 'Find out if it's legitimate. If not . . .' She let the sentence hang.

'Leave it with me, madame,' Yves said smoothly. 'I will return when I have more information.' About to kiss her hand again, he caught her expression and thought better of it. He gave her a polite bow instead and left the room. He planned to have a good look around the château before he went home, despite his proclamations about discretion.

In her room, Delphine stood by the window, watching Xavier. His dark head was bent and he was stroking his beloved horse Cassis, the horse he hadn't ridden since his mother Elizabeth's death.

Xavier has far too much time on his hands, Delphine decided. He needed a project, something to occupy him, preferably something that would benefit the family business. Delphine's eyes gleamed as a germ of an idea occurred to her. As it took shape in her mind, her spirits lifted and she felt back in control again.

Chapter Six

Guy watched his mother impatiently checking the slim gold Patek Phillipe watch on her wrist for the umpteenth time. She had called the meeting for nine o'clock sharp and she was clearly livid that he was the only member of her family seated at the boardroom table so far.

'Do you think Miss Hayes will join us?' Delphine inquired, her hazel eyes quickly scanning the agenda Guy had prepared.

'I have no idea. She probably can't stand the sight of us right now so I wouldn't blame her if she didn't bother.'

Guy felt awful about Cat; he had honestly liked her as soon as he met her and his warmth towards her had been real. He had known they would be presenting her with the legal papers, of course, but he hadn't anticipated the meeting turning so sour, nor had he expected Cat to feel so let down by all of them.

Guy glanced at Delphine. He had an idea his mother hid a soft-centre beneath the neat suits and the harsh tone she always used but the last glimpse he'd had of it was so long ago, he'd begun to wonder if it was wishful thinking rather than a distant memory.

'I hope she makes the right decision,' Delphine said imperiously. 'That girl needs to understand why it's imperative that she signs those papers.'

'Any idea how long it will take to draw up new ones?'

'I've instructed Pascal to get on to it immediately,' Delphine told him, sounding more hopeful than she felt.

Guy let out a short laugh. 'Good luck with that! It's bound to take ages. And what's to stop Cat leaving before she's signed anything?'

Delphine averted her eyes. 'Nothing, I suppose. As you keep reminding me, we can hardly keep her under lock and key, can we? If she decides to leave, we have no choice but to let her go.'

Guy narrowed his eyes at his mother. Her casual air was at odds with her usual insistent tones but she looked back at him haughtily, her hazel eyes clear and direct. Guy straightened his blue tie and shrugged his arms into the sleeves of his well-cut suit jacket. He always wore suits to family meetings like these because formal attire sharpened his mind. Still, today, all he could think about was how Olivier's poor widow was going to cope with a full-scale family onslaught.

In her room, Cat had more important things to deal with. She had spent the past three hours turning the guest room upside down searching for the one thing she couldn't get home without, but it was nowhere to be found.

Practically tearing her hair out in sheer frustration, Cat finally admitted defeat and tried to come to terms with the fact that she had lost her passport. She had never lost it in her life – nor when she'd backpacked through Thailand with friends, not even when she had undertaken a spontaneous but gruelling solo trip through the rainforests of Venezuela when her parents had died. Yet somehow, in a luxurious, sophisticated guest room in a château in Provence, she had managed to do just that.

Aware that she was late for the family meeting she'd promised Seraphina she would attend, Cat let out a howl. It was so infuriating! Her bags were packed and she was all set to make a quick getaway after the meeting. She had intended to tell the Ducasse family that any legal documents they wanted her to sign could be sent to her in England. But she wasn't going anywhere now that her passport had disappeared.

Had she left it in the limo Guy had sent? No, surely someone would have phoned and told the family about it. Had it fallen out of her bag when she'd dumped it in the garden? Cat felt a flash of hope. That seemed likely. It was very possibly sitting in a flower bed somewhere.

Feeling more optimistic, Cat caught sight of the photo album Seraphina had given her. Unable to resist having another look at Olivier's handsome, smiling face, she opened it, then shut it abruptly and threw it in the drawer of her bedside table. Cat had finally started to face facts: she'd married a man who was not only adept at lying, he also didn't rate faithfulness very highly. She did not know how many women Olivier had been juggling at once or how many lies he had told her, but she knew he was far from the perfect man she'd believed he was before he died.

Cat put her shoulders back and headed to the board-room. She was certain she must be the last to arrive but she found she didn't care too much about how rude she might appear. Tardiness hardly seemed significant up against accusations of being either insane or a gold digger.

To her surprise, when she entered the boardroom, only Guy and Delphine were there. Feeling slightly reckless in view of her recent aggravation, she deliberately took a seat in the middle of the table, knowing that Delphine would expect her, as a non-family member, to sit discreetly at the end.

Guy hid a smile as his mother bristled at the sight of Cat taking what was usually Xavier's seat. She was looking particularly attractive in a pair of black trousers and a water-lily green top that made the most of her butterscotch hair and aquamarine eyes. He poured Delphine a cup of black coffee and raised the pot in Cat's direction.

She shook her head, not meeting his gaze.

'So are you leaving us after this meeting?' Delphine asked.

'I can't.' Cat drummed her fingers on the table. 'I've lost my passport,' she confessed, feeling idiotic.

Guy looked up. 'Really? Surely it must be in your room.'

'You'd think,' Cat muttered. 'But it's not, I've looked everywhere.'

'Oh well, I guess you'll be staying with us for a little longer then,' Delphine said, averting her eyes.

Cat shot a glance at her. Why didn't she seem surprised by the news? Suspicion crawled up her spine. Could Delphine be behind the disappearance of her passport? Surely not! It was unthinkable . . . wasn't it?

Max appeared in the doorway.

'Sorry we're late,' he muttered, swaggering in wearing black jeans and a T-shirt with some French slogan emblazoned across it. He reeked of cigarette smoke and looked every inch the bratty teenager as he threw himself into one of the chairs at the far end of the table. 'Breakfast can be *so* time-consuming.'

Delphine looked furious but she bit her tongue. Guy shot him a disapproving look and didn't hold back.

'Max! Don't be so disrespectful. You know what time this meeting is. And since when do you eat breakfast?'

Max glowered, spoiling his good looks.

Seraphina, more sedately dressed in a pair of tailored trousers with a pink silk shirt, took a seat next to her brother, hiding a rolled-up magazine behind her back. Leoni arrived next, carrying a thick folder bursting with paperwork. Ignoring Cat, who she had hoped would be gone by now, Leoni smoothed down the skirt of yet another black tailored dress and sat down opposite Guy.

'Xavier is on his way,' she informed them, flipping open her folder.

Cat was astonished to see what looked like pages and pages of research, with neat, handwritten notes backed up by articles clipped from magazines and colourful sketches. Leoni certainly took her role in the business seriously, Cat thought, impressed but not really surprised. It was what she used to do at the advertising firm to ensure she was fully prepared and able to answer any unexpected questions in meetings. Watching Leoni push her glasses firmly up on to the bridge of her nose, Cat could tell she had something to discuss. Swallowing, she hoped Leoni's already spiky claws weren't being sharpened in her direction.

As Xavier, clutching his cigarettes and his mobile phone, slid into the seat next to Cat with a polite but distant nod, Delphine took charge of the meeting.

'Thank you all for coming,' she started, giving everyone a cool stare.

As managing director, Guy should surely be running the meeting, thought Cat. She wondered if he minded that his mother assumed control like this. Noting the way he was smoothing his silver hair down with an irritable flick of his hand, she decided that perhaps he did.

Next to her, Xavier shifted in his chair. Wearing a crisp white shirt with well-fitting grey trousers, he looked more professional than his younger brother but his laconic expression indicated he was there out of duty rather than desire. Glancing down, Cat saw that her assessment was accurate; beneath the table, Xavier was surreptitiously reading a text, no doubt from his girlfriend . . . or *one* of his girlfriends, she thought tartly, remembering what Max had said about Xavier sleeping with most of France.

'We have many things to discuss,' Delphine was saying, 'such as sales, promotions and general targets.' She threw figures at them blithely, comparing them to the previous quarter and painting an upbeat picture of Ducasse-Fleurie's finances, despite the fact that they sounded slightly lacklustre, even to Cat's untrained ear.

Moving on swiftly, as if she was aware she was effectively attempting to throw glitter over what was clearly a dull ornament, metaphorically speaking, Delphine handed round a copy of a recent review of Rose-Nymphea. It had been placed in the top ten in one of France's best-selling but rather turgid magazines and Delphine waxed lyrical about it, seemingly impressed by the rather uninspiring review.

'Oh, who cares about that?' Leoni interjected rudely. 'That magazine is only read by geriatric women who wouldn't know if they were dabbing on wee or Chanel No. 5.'

Max grinned and Xavier burst out laughing.

Leoni met her grandmother's eyes. 'Seriously, what does it matter if that magazine rates Rose-Nymphea? It's hardly a five-star review in French *Vogue*, is it?'

'It is still a glowing review of our most beloved perfume and I think we should all be grateful for that,' Delphine hissed, her eyes blazing in Leoni's direction, even though the boys had been far more disrespectful. Cat was beginning to understand why Leoni acted like such a martyr all the time; Delphine didn't even bother to hide the fact that she favoured the men in the family, despite their lack of interest in the perfume business and regardless of Leoni's obvious dedication and commitment.

After a brief pause, Delphine handed out a sales report and systematically went through it.

Without realising it, Cat's advertising antennae automatically pricked to attention. She had been determined not to allow herself to become even vaguely interested in Ducasse-Fleurie because there was no point. She didn't want Olivier's share in the business so she had no reason to even listen to the sales data, let alone make any kind of assessment of it. But she couldn't help mentally collating the figures and drawing the conclusion that not everything in the Ducasse-Fleurie empire was rosy.

By most people's standards, the company was generating a healthy profit, but considering profits amassed during previous years, as detailed in the report Delphine had provided, the brand was flagging, mainly due to the fact that no new fragrances or other products had been created for a number of years now.

'So, nothing has changed since the last meeting then.' Max yawned, clearly bored. Seraphina, surreptitiously devouring French *Vogue* under the table, noticed a gaping silence had occurred and looked up guiltily, stuffing the magazine out of sight.

Delphine laced her fingers together so tightly, her knuckles turned white. 'I really wish you'd show more interest, Maxim,' she snapped. 'My father . . . your grandfather invested years of his life in this company. Perfume might not be your thing but without it, you wouldn't have all of *this*.' Delphine swept an elegant hand in the air to encompass the house and everything in it.

'Oh, I know, we're all *so* lucky,' Max responded derisively. He grabbed Seraphina's magazine and pointedly began reading it.

Guy, barely containing his rage at his younger son's behaviour, gritted his teeth. 'Any other business?' he growled, keen to wrap the meeting up and get back to work.

Leoni cleared her throat loudly. 'I have some other business,' she said, rustling her paperwork importantly.

Halfway out of his seat already, Xavier sat down with a sigh. 'Forgive me, Leoni,' he said. 'I thought the meeting was over. Do continue.'

Cat noted that Leoni betrayed her nerves as she flicked her hair out of her eyes. Not that Cat blamed her; whatever Leoni had to say, Cat had a feeling it was going to be met by disdain.

Leoni deftly handed out some pamphlets she had put together, reluctantly sliding one across the table towards Cat. 'As you see, I have prepared some information for you all,' she started, her delivery speeding up as excitement took over. 'These are my ideas for the future of Ducasse-Fleurie. A new fragrance would be marvellous, of course.' At this, she shot

Xavier a pointed glance and grimaced as his expression remained impassive. 'But in any event, I feel Ducasse-Fleurie needs to branch out and join its modern competitors. As such, I am proposing a home fragrance line. This would incorporate exquisite candles using our signature scents and also some upmarket sprays for the home and for linen. This way, our brand would become synonymous not just with luxury and wealth but with stylish, everyday living.' Leoni paused, her brown eyes sweeping the room. She wasn't about to mention her idea for a store in Paris just yet. Knowing her family, it would be rejected out of hand. Bracing herself for what she felt sure would be an unenthusiastic reaction, she surveyed the room.

'What do you all think?'

There was silence. Delphine perused Leoni's handout as though she was sucking lemons and Guy's brow furrowed in displeasure. Xavier flicked through it with vague interest but he made no comment.

Cat felt irrationally irritated by Xavier's apathy but reminded herself it was only because she knew he had a low opinion of her.

'It would be very expensive,' Guy said finally. He gestured to Leoni's pamphlet. 'It's all very nice but I can't see the idea working for us.'

Delphine tossed Leoni's carefully constructed pamphlet to one side.

'We have always been a fragrance-only company,' she said dismissively. 'What value would it add to have customers spritzing our perfumes around their homes?' She touched the soft sleeve of her suit. 'Coco Chanel didn't feel the need for candles and linen sprays so I don't see why we should.'

Guy agreed. Xavier shrugged. Max and Seraphina weren't even pretending to listen.

In spite of herself, Cat felt impatient with their dog-in-the-manger attitude. She couldn't care less about Ducasse-Fleurie but surely anyone with any business sense could see that Leoni's idea was a good one?

Without thinking, she found herself speaking up in Leoni's defence. 'Coco Chanel had many other strings to her bow and the brand now offers jewellery, watches and any number of other products. A home fragrance line is simply another take on skincare or make-up, when you think about it.' She felt Delphine's chilly stare fall on her like a bucket of cold water and faltered. She glanced at Leoni who was gaping at her as if she couldn't quite believe that Cat, the person she had been so hostile towards since her arrival, was her one lone supporter.

Remembering this, Cat had half a mind to back off and keep her thoughts to herself. But she had never been a petty person and she wasn't about to become one now, regardless of the way Leoni had cold-shouldered her. 'I think a home fragrance line would be the perfect way to bring Ducasse-Fleurie into a more commercial arena,' she said, her voice gathering momentum as she mentally slid on her advertising hat. 'It will also re-establish your company as a key player in the fragrance industry because it will instantly update the brand. And as long as the line retains the luxurious, extravagant feel of your fragrances and the promotion of the products is executed to a high level, it could revive Ducasse-Fleurie in much the same way a new fragrance would.'

Leoni was unbelievably impressed. Cat had detailed the concept of her home fragrance line far more eloquently than she had and even though Cat knew nothing about the perfume industry, she had somehow managed to capture the whole sense of her idea in a nutshell. Leoni eyed Cat suspiciously, wondering if she might be trying to sabotage her in some way; surely the last thing Cat would want to do is help her after the way she'd treated her.

'And what, pray tell, makes you an authority on perfume sales?' Delphine queried, unable to conceal her hostility. 'And on branding?' Somehow, she made it sound like a swear word.

'My background is in advertising,' Cat replied. 'In branding specifically. I've worked on fashion campaigns as well as make-up and fragrance.' Cat decided against mentioning that she'd lost her job. It wouldn't help Leoni's cause and it was none of anyone's business. Besides, she would sort another job out as soon as she got back to England – whenever that might be. Cat bit her lip but she met Delphine's eyes as directly as she could.

'I see. Do tell us about branding, then,' Delphine said, her voice dripping with sarcasm. 'As we, the owners of a highly successful perfume conglomerate, so clearly have no idea.'

Cat hesitated, but with a flash of defiance she decided to call Delphine's bluff. 'When you have a product you believe in, how you brand it is critical. You need to deliver a clear message and you want your target market to connect with your product emotionally.' Cat paused for a moment, marshalling the details of the last fragrance campaign she'd worked on. 'The thing about fragrance is that it triggers emotion, it stimulates the senses like . . . the smell of suntan lotion, for example. It transports you back to that tropical location in seconds. In exactly the same way, perfume taps into the memory banks in our brain that bring us pleasure. It's a bit like sex.'

Xavier turned round in his seat to look at her and Cat blushed, embarrassed by her analogy. He seemed amused by her discomfort but she resolutely ignored him.

Guy leant forward, intrigued. 'So, do you think there is something wrong with the way we're currently promoting ourselves as a brand?' The last person he had heard talking about perfume in such a way was his wife Elizabeth. Or maybe Xavier. 'Do you really think this home fragrance idea will make a difference?'

Cat nodded. 'The way you're perceived as a brand is that it

is luxurious and opulent. Your fragrances are an indulgence, one that is just about affordable but worth every penny. The problem is that because nothing new has been created for some time, the only way you're reaching any kind of market is with your old established fragrances. Classics, undoubtedly, but they're becoming viewed as being slightly dated, simply because Ducasse-Fleurie have nothing new on offer, nothing to entice the younger, sexier market.'

'Exactly!' Leoni slammed her hand on the table, making Max and Seraphina drop their magazine. 'This is what I've been trying to tell you all. Ducasse-Fleurie will continue to make money with our existing fragrances but don't we want more than that?' Her eyes became earnest. 'Don't we want to be seen as glamorous and sexy and vibrant, as well as reliable and classic?'

'Your two main fragrances sell well but they suit an older audience', Cat said. 'The trio of fragrances hit the mark perfectly,' she added reluctantly, detesting paying Xavier any kind of compliment but knowing it was the truth. 'They covered all mood bases as well as having that luxurious feel about them.'

'Thank you,' Xavier responded. 'You certainly seem to understand what I was trying to do when I created the fragrances.'

Cat shrugged, avoiding his intense gaze. 'What you all decide to do is up to you obviously. As we all know, it's none of my business.' She stood up, keen to search for her passport again. 'I saw in your brochure that this year is the fiftieth anniversary of Rose-Nymphea. I haven't a clue what you usually do to mark these sorts of events but, maybe you could relaunch the signature scent. Or tie it in with the home fragrance idea. Anyway, I'll leave you all to it. I must find my passport so I can go home.'

Cat left the room.

The Ducasse family stared at one another.

'Well,' Guy said at last. 'That was unexpected.'

Leoni grabbed one of the Ducasse-Fleurie brochures from a pile on the side and hurriedly leafed through it. 'How did none of us notice that it's the fiftieth anniversary of Rose-Nymphea?'

Delphine leant on her cane and stood up. 'Because we're all too busy running the business,' she retorted.

'Really?' Leoni wished she'd picked up on the anniversary date herself rather than Cat; tying it in with the launch of her home fragrance line was a wonderful idea.

'Leoni,' Guy said, 'I think you should put a formal proposal together for your idea. I'd like to see some samples and how you intend to market the line. In principle, I can see the benefits of the idea, certainly now that Cat has outlined them so expertly, but I'll make a final decision when you do your presentation. Is that acceptable?'

'Yes, thank you, Uncle,' Leoni said demurely, seething on the inside. Even if Cat had been succinct on the whole issue, couldn't her family take her at her word, just for once?

Guy rubbed his chin, wondering why it had taken an outsider to bring their branding issues so sharply into focus and to notice such a key date in their calendar. He realised they'd all underestimated Cat. 'That girl isn't what any of us expected,' he asserted. 'I think we've been too quick to judge her.'

Xavier frowned. He didn't think he'd been too quick to judge her at all but he was irked by her cool manner towards him. 'What the hell have I done to upset the girl? I haven't even spoken to her.'

Seraphina looked sheepish. 'We didn't realise Cat could speak such good French and she overheard us saying you thought she must be a bit mentally challenged . . . you know, for marrying Olivier when she didn't really know him.'

Xavier looked exasperated. 'Oh, great! No wonder she was throwing me evil looks.' He raked his fingers through his hair irritably. Did it really matter? Cat was leaving as soon as she found her passport and he couldn't imagine she was too deeply hurt about his opinion. Anyway, it *was* what he thought so what could he say to make things any better?

'And she now knows about all those girlfriends Olivier strung along,' Max threw in for good measure. 'She seemed pretty cut up about it, actually.'

Guy let out a sigh. They had all behaved deplorably towards the poor girl; no wonder she wanted to cut her losses and leave. 'We owe Cat an apology,' he said tightly, standing up. 'All of us. Before she goes back to England, we need to make amends.'

Delphine rolled her eyes. 'Oh, Guy, I'm sure Miss Hayes isn't crying into her pillow. And she's not going anywhere just yet, not until those papers are signed. How fortuitous that her passport has gone missing, it buys us some time.'

Xavier frowned. Did his grandmother know something about the missing passport? He dismissed the idea. No, it was not her style to stoop to such behaviour.

'This meeting is over.' Delphine wrapped things up. 'Maxim, next time, set your alarm, dress more formally and absolutely no yawning. Seraphina, ditto, and for your information, *Vogue* magazine is not a replacement for company data. Read it in your own time.' Drawing herself up to her full height, Delphine turned to her granddaughter. 'Leoni, don't you have better things to do than come up with silly ideas for the company when it is functioning very well as it is?'

Leoni flushed. 'There's a difference between functioning and flourishing, Grandmother,' she argued. 'Ducasse-Fleurie needs new lines. We can't keep coasting like this.'

Delphine pursed her lips. 'It's doing just fine, Leoni. If you'd listened to my report, you would know that. Wouldn't you be better off finding yourself a boyfriend?' she suggested nastily. 'Or a girlfriend, if that's your preference?'

'How dare you!' Pink in the face, Leoni leapt to her feet. 'Just because I don't parade men in and out of La Fleurie . . . How *bigoted* you are, Grandmother! How ridiculous!'

Delphine recoiled in shock. Leoni was outspoken but she was rarely abusive. She stared at Leoni icily. How like her brother Leoni was, so unpredictable, so out of control. Like Olivier, Leoni seemed to have no sense of practicality – every decision she made seemed to be based on a whim or a mad impulse.

'I am *not* Olivier,' Leoni snarled, reading her grandmother's mind like a book. 'Just because I have big ideas for Ducasse-Fleurie doesn't mean I'm unstable or out of control, like Olivier was. This is business. My brother didn't know the first thing about it and we all knew that years ago.'

In an attempt to lighten the atmosphere, Xavier grinned. 'I rather like the idea of you having a girlfriend, Leoni.'

'Oh, shut up!' Leoni screamed at him, paperwork cascading to the floor. 'And what about you? Don't you think you should stop screwing everything in sight and start pulling your weight around here?'

Xavier leapt to his feet. 'Back off, Leoni,' he snapped, his eyes darkening until they were almost black. 'You don't know the first thing about it.'

'Why don't you fill us all in, then?' Guy demanded. 'We'd all love to know why you can't bring yourself to get involved in Ducasse-Fleurie any more.'

His face stony, Xavier glared at his father before turning on his heel and stalking out.

Seraphina burst into tears. 'Leave Xav alone!' she yelled emotionally, her beautiful face distorted with pain. 'Stop trying to make him do something he doesn't want to do. If you knew more, you wouldn't harass him . . .' Grabbing Max's arm, she ran out with him, swiftly followed by an ashen Leoni.

Looking apoplectic with rage, Guy strode out of the board-room like a man possessed, leaving Delphine open-mouthed at her family's behaviour. What on earth had happened to them all?

Three days later, Cat was in the garden, nearly tearing her hair out. Her passport still hadn't turned up, despite in-depth investigations into every flower bed and shrub in the vicinity. Cat felt fit to burst.

Realising she hadn't spoken to her best friend in nearly two weeks, Cat decided to phone Bella. She was having lunch with Ben in some funky new bar that blasted out rock music as it served up gourmet sandwiches. Bella didn't hear her phone for a good five minutes before realising Cat was calling her from France.

'Cat!' Bella screeched, her delighted squawk almost drowned out by 'Love In An Elevator'. 'What's happening? Have the Ducasse family fallen head over heels in love with you? Do they want you to stay with them forever? Have you found closure?'

'Er, no, to all the above,' Cat replied drily, wincing as something by Bon Jovi kicked in. Giving Bella a quick rundown of the situation and ignoring the cries of 'Shut *up*!', 'No way!' and 'You've got to be fricking *kidding* me!' that punctuated the conversation, Cat finally managed to inform Bella about her missing passport.

Bella was taken aback. 'But you've never lost your passport before, not even in the rainforest in—'

'Venezuela, I know.' Cat sighed. 'It's so frustrating. I just want to come home and I can't leave until I sort out this passport issue. I feel like a bloody prisoner.' She glanced over her shoulder ruefully, taking in the breathtaking sight of the sweeping valley and the stretch of dormant lavender fields that the Ducasse estate encompassed. 'If you could see the view I'm looking at now, you'd think I was mad for moaning but it's no fun here, not when the family think I'm the devil incarnate.'

'It must be because they thought the world of Olivier,' Bella assured her soothingly. 'It's probably nothing to do with you personally.'

'Oh, no, it really is,' Cat insisted. 'And the worst thing about it all is that I'm now beginning to realise Olivier wasn't exactly the lovely, genuine guy we thought he was.' Haltingly, she filled Bella in about the other girls and confided her suspicions about Olivier having lied about his parents' death, just to get her sympathy. 'I don't know for sure because I can't face asking anyone at the moment, but they can't all have died in riding accidents, can they?'

'Probably not,' Bella said slowly. So she'd been right to have concerns about Olivier; it seemed he was a cheat and a liar, after all. Bella felt immeasurably sorry for her friend and pulled a face at Ben who was holding up his phone. 'Oooh, yes, Ben has some news. He got in touch with his old company and they're very interested in hiring you. *Very* interested. I'm quoting here: "Cat Hayes would be an asset to our company and, frankly, we'd rip our right arms off to get her in." What do you think of that, my friend?'

Cat's mood improved. 'That's amazing! Wow, Brian would be spitting feathers if I went to work for the company's direct competitor.'

'Perfect revenge, right?' Bella said gleefully. 'I don't think they're hiring for a few weeks but the girl Ben knows in HR says she'll call him as soon as they start recruiting. Hey, do you want me to start the ball rolling on a new passport, just in case your one doesn't turn up?'

'Would you?' Cat said gratefully. 'That would be great. Anything to speed things up here.' She looked at the ground glumly. 'I'm surrounded by bloody pictures of Olivier and by people who think I'm either a gold digger or a complete numpty for marrying him when I hardly knew him. I've felt more welcome, let's put it that way.'

'Leave it with Auntie Bella,' Bella said brightly. 'We'll get everything sorted, don't you worry. Nothing is insurmountable.

A wise old woman called Cat once told me that. Chin up, love.'

'Thanks, Bel. Love to Ben. Well, you know . . . a friendly wave, or whatever.' Cat finished her call, feeling buoyant for the first time in days. It was true; nothing *was* insurmountable. Even lost passports.

The following weekend, Seraphina wrapped her arms around her knees and wished it was the summer. The beach wasn't as much fun without sunshine.

'It's been so long since we did this!' she exclaimed to her friend Adele as she stretched out luxuriously and wiggled her toes. They were wearing jeans and T-shirts rather than bikinis because of the chilly breeze that kept whipping up the towels on their loungers. The Ducasse family had their own private beach but Seraphina preferred to go to the public ones, like everyone else.

Adele shivered. 'It's hardly beach weather,' she moaned. 'But I guess we're not here for the weather.' Grinning at a boy in tight jeans, she flipped her hair so hard, she nearly fell off her lounger.

'Stop trying so hard,' Seraphina chided her with a giggle.

'Easy to say when you look the way you do,' Adele retorted, turning beetroot.

Seraphina snorted. People always told her she was pretty but all she could see when she looked in the mirror was skin that never tanned and a lanky body that always seemed to tower over the men she fancied. Still, it didn't stop her wanting to be a model . . . but models weren't conventionally pretty, they were a blank canvas.

'When are you coming back to school?' Adele asked, scooping up some sand and letting it run through her fingers. 'And is Max coming back? He seems hell-bent on getting expelled!'

Seraphina shifted uncomfortably. She wasn't proud of the

way she and Max behaved at their expensive boarding school but the rules were so strict, it was impossible not to rebel against them. God only knew why Max rebelled because he didn't exactly want to be at home either, Seraphina thought glumly. 'We'll be back soon,' she assured her friend. 'That girl Madeleine Lombard was asking me about Max the other day too. I think she has the hots for him. Waste of time. Max only has eyes for Vero and her motorbike.'

Adele pulled a face. 'Vero's a junkie. Max should be careful.'

Seraphina looked up as a man in a suit crouched by her lounger.

'Have you ever considered being a model?' he asked.

Seraphina gasped and Adele sat up excitedly. The man continued, his eyes serious, 'I own a large, successful modelling agency and I would be very interested in representing you.' He handed her a silver card with numbers across the bottom. 'Call me.' He strode away, leaving the girls clutching each other breathlessly.

'Oh my God . . . this is unbelievable!' Adele said, with glazed eyes. 'It's like Kate Moss being discovered at JFK airport . . .'

Seraphina leapt off her sun lounger. 'I have to go and tell my father!' She gathered her bag up and pulled a jumper over her head. 'Come on,' she called to Adele, who shook her head and waved her away. Jumping into the car that was waiting for her and for the first time grateful for the privileges being a Ducasse afforded her, Seraphina dashed through the doors when she arrived home and took the stairs to her father's office two at a time.

'I got a modelling contract!' she cried, bursting into this office.

'What?' Flipping through some of Elizabeth's old notes and wondering if he could possibly put a perfume together from them, Guy nearly jumped out of his skin. With barely concealed impatience, he listened as Seraphina eagerly recounted her story from the beach. Taking the card from her hand, he glanced at it.

'I've never heard of this man or this modelling agency.' Dismissively, he tossed her treasured card across his desk. 'Honestly, Seraphina, you should know better! He's probably just some old pervert who picks up girls using that tired old chat-up line.' Guy stared at his daughter. 'It's the oldest trick in the book. I bet if we look him up, all he has is a shop full of grubby underwear and hidden cameras. And why on earth would you want to model anyway? The idea is ridiculous.'

Seraphina was shaking all over. Biting down hard on her lip, she welcomed the rush of blood as it flooded into her mouth because it drowned out the acrid taste of disappointment. Out of the blue, she felt like a child again; a naughty little girl who couldn't do anything right. Fighting a sob, she gazed at her father beseechingly.

Guy returned to Elizabeth's folder. 'Get back to your studying and stop being so immature, Seraphina. I have work to do here.'

Gasping, Seraphina ran out of the room and slammed the door as hard as she could behind her. Inside, Guy looked up, startled as several perfume bottles clinked and nearly fell off the shelf. What on earth was the matter with his daughter? Had she taken leave of her senses? He rubbed his head and got back to work.

Outside the door, Seraphina's pride was stinging. How *could* he? How could he have so little faith in her? It wasn't just his casual disregard about the modelling opportunity, it was the crushing realisation that her father didn't believe she was capable of actually achieving her dream.

Perhaps she simply wasn't special enough, Seraphina thought bitterly. She knew she wasn't conventionally pretty but maybe she didn't have unusual enough looks to be a model either. Her father didn't seem to think so, anyway. Not looking where she was going, Seraphina crashed straight into someone. Her nose connected sharply with a brown suit that smelt of cigars and a strong, woody aftershave she recognised.

Dior's Fahrenheit For Men, she thought to herself almost mechanically, catching wafts of cedar and bergamot. Unashamedly masculine and brash, it took a certain type of man to wear it.

Seraphina looked up, realising she was clinging to the man like a limpet. She let go of him abruptly, all the while thinking he was rather attractive. He looked a bit old and his suit had a loud purple lining but at least he was tall, she thought, gazing up at him. Men weren't usually taller than her – or maybe that was because they were boys, not men, Seraphina thought.

'Well, hello,' he said, giving her an oily grin. His eyes ran over her body fleetingly before he held a friendly hand out. 'I am Yves. You must be Seraphina. I am a friend of your grandmother's,' he explained when he saw her eyeing him suspiciously. 'I was here for a meeting. You look upset,' he added with a sympathetic smile. 'Are you all right?'

Seraphina looked at the ground. Not sure why, she found herself telling this stranger she had just met everything that had happened. 'I know I shouldn't be vain and think I could be a model but is it really such a crime?'

'Of course not.' Yves dark eyes were fixed on hers intently. 'How sad. It's so distressing when a parent doesn't believe in you.' With obvious regret, he checked his watch. 'Apologies, I'm late for another appointment.' He bent and kissed her hand briefly, hiding a smile as she shivered slightly at his intimate touch. 'But if I may say . . . and what do I know, so feel free to ignore me, but really, you are an exceptionally pretty girl. If you want to be a model, you should follow your heart.' Tucking a strand of platinum-blond hair behind her ear, Yves gave her a winsome smile. He stared at Seraphina for a moment. She could only be in her teens but she had a luminous quality about her that made it difficult to guess her age. She was beautiful, though, astonishingly so. Far too young for him, however, and she no doubt had boys queuing at her door.

Turning on his heel, Yves made his exit.

Flattered but still crestfallen, Seraphina headed outside and found Max and Cat chatting over coffees in the pool house.

'I think we should go back to college early, Max,' Seraphina announced, scuffing her feet on a wicker chair.

Max narrowed his eyes at her. He could tell his twin was suffering but he knew better to ask her when she looked as destroyed as she did right now. Besides, he'd probably say the wrong thing and put his foot in it.

'I'm game if you are,' he responded, meaning it. He'd had enough of playing happy families. Besides, Vero had promised him all sorts of fun if he made it back to school soon. Max settled back in his chair, his eyes sparking up decisively. 'Let's do it,' he told Seraphina. 'It's no fun here anyway.'

Cat's mood darkened. The twins were the only friendly faces around La Fleurie. She wasn't sure if she felt drawn to them because they knew about loss at such an early age or if she just felt sorry for them for being so misunderstood, but Cat knew she would miss them if they went back to their college. The rest of the family seemed to have written them off as naughty and rebellious, but she couldn't help thinking the twins were incredibly vulnerable. How could Guy treat his children this way? she thought. He had no idea how much he was hurting them with his cruel dismissals and his preference for spending his time focused on the business rather than them. Cat knew it wasn't her place to say anything but she sincerely hoped Guy came to his senses before it was too late.

'Might you still be here when we come back for half-term?' Seraphina suddenly felt a bit tearful about the possibility of never seeing Cat again.

'Oh . . . er . . . I doubt it.' Cat shook her head. 'Although I haven't a clue what's going on yet, to be honest. Bloody passport,' she added to herself in English.

She almost told Seraphina her suspicions about Delphine being responsible for its disappearance, but she reminded herself that the old lady was Seraphina's grandmother. It wouldn't go down well, however austere Delphine was.

Seraphina hugged her tightly. 'I really hope you stay,' she whispered in Cat's ear. 'I know you want to go but I wish you could stay for a bit longer.' She didn't know why she felt so attached to Cat. It was madness, really.

Max nodded. 'It'd be good to see you when we get back,' he said in a gruff voice, kissing her cheeks politely.

Feeling dismal, Cat watched them as they drifted off to pack.

Chapter Seven

Xavier was about to have a shower when he found a handwritten note from his grandmother slipped under his door. What on earth did she want? Handwritten requests from her never boded well; it either meant he was about to get his knuckles rapped or she wanted him to do something, neither of which was remotely appealing. Xavier couldn't help hoping she might go back to Toulouse in the near future. Sweet as she could be at times, his grandmother had the knack of making him feel like a schoolboy, which Xavier detested.

Since the disastrous family meeting Delphine had been conspicuous by her absence, shutting herself away in her quarters and emerging only for meals. Leoni, relieved not to have to discuss the heated row that had taken place in the boardroom, saw it as a positive sign and even thought it might mean their grandmother felt remorseful about her meanness. Xavier, knowing his grandmother better, thought otherwise. Far from hiding away because she was licking her wounds or feeling repentant, Xavier was convinced his grandmother simply needed solitude and privacy in order to plot and scheme and do whatever was necessary to bring the family back into line.

'Come back to bed, darling,' Therese cajoled, flipping the sheet back to expose a rather slutty red thong and not much else.

'I have a meeting,' Xavier replied.

He had a quick, hot shower. Therese was becoming

increasingly demanding, he thought impatiently. And she bored him. It was time for a change. He and Therese were just too different, he thought as he quickly shaved. She was laid-back and lazy and he liked to be active. Aside from his daily swims, he had his climbing, he loved beach sports and he always enjoyed casinos and eating out. A few years back, he would have ridden every day but that was out of the question now. Another great love ruined by circumstances, one he sorely missed if he was being honest with himself.

He emerged from his ensuite bathroom to find Therese snoring like a French horn, with her legs wide open and her pale breasts lolling. Xavier flipped the sheet over her before dressing in a freshly ironed shirt and a pair of smart trousers and then made his way to his grandmother's rooms. She was seated on the rose-pink silk chaise longue in the corner. In front of her on the table was a silver tray bearing an exquisite Limoges porcelain coffee pot with a floral design on it and some matching cups that looked as though they wouldn't bear the weight of the coffee inside them.

Delphine poured him a strong, black coffee, just the way he liked it and, smiling, she patted the place next to her on the chaise longue. She admired his ability to look so stylish considering he had probably only just got up. She wondered if his unsavoury girlfriend was waiting for him in bed. The girl was reasonably pretty but she was hardly good enough for someone as handsome and gifted as Xavier.

Xavier sat down and picked up the delicate cup warily. The informal setting, the antique china – he was right, something was definitely up.

'Thank you for joining me at such short notice,' she said, her hazel eyes warm. 'I felt we should talk after that terrible meeting the other day.'

'Oh?' Xavier regarded her coolly.

Delphine nodded. 'Yes, I was so upset after . . . after everything that happened and I wanted to ask your opinion on it.'

Xavier drank his coffee. 'I see. And which particular aspect would you like me to comment upon?' He sat back, his manner casual but his eyes alert. 'Are you after my opinion on Leoni's extravagant but quite possibly sound ideas for the business? No? Perhaps you'd like me to assess the sales figures for the last quarter.' Xavier met her eyes. 'Or would you like to discuss what to do about Cat Hayes, especially since she had the audacity to speak up and make her presence felt in a family meeting.'

Delphine smiled approvingly. Xavier might have spent the last two years doing nothing apart from sunbathing and sleeping around, but he was as sharp as a tack. And contrary to what her son Guy thought, Delphine was certain Elizabeth's death wasn't the only reason for Xavier's indifference towards the perfume business. That was another matter, however, and one Delphine planned to deal with once this particular problem had been resolved.

'I'll get straight to the point,' she said. 'You're right, Cat Hayes is posing a problem. As you know, she turned down the money Guy offered her and she is keen to leave as soon as possible. Her passport is missing but I'm sure it will turn up shortly. In any case, she has probably been on to the British authorities to organise another one.' Delphine glanced out of the window thoughtfully. 'In the meantime, Miss Hayes is at a loose end. Or rather, she *is* a loose end.'

Xavier didn't smile at the weak joke. 'What does this have to do with me?'

'What it has to do with you is that bearing in mind Miss Hayes', shall we say, insight into the perfume business the other day, it made me wonder if she might be useful to us while she's still here.'

'Useful? In what way?'

Delphine refilled his cup and offered him a plate of exquisite, handmade macaroons which he refused. 'No? They are your favourites. Anyway, as I was saying, I am loathe to admit it but the girl did come up with some interesting thoughts about the business. Even Leoni's idea seemed to make more sense once it was explained properly.' Delphine pursed her lips. 'I can't say I fully approve but I can see the sense in maximising the business and I suppose we should be grateful that Miss Hayes pointed out the anniversary of Rose-Nymphea. What about a little trip to Grasse? You could take her to the perfume factories. You could tell her all about the art and science of creating scents.'

'And why would I want to do that?'

'Because you don't have anything better to do,' Delphine fired back crisply, the warmth evaporating from her voice. 'Guy and Leoni are far too busy to undertake such a trip.' She sipped her coffee, regarding him over the paper-thin rim.

Xavier stared at her. He knew exactly what she was up to. His grandmother thought that if he went on some trip to the place he had learnt his craft, he would fall back in love with the perfume-making process. She hoped he would get so carried away telling Cat Hayes all about his apprenticeship and about his passion for scents that he would come back renewed, refreshed and raring to get back into his lab again. Filled with contempt at the obviousness of her plan, his lip curled.

Delphine guessed what he was thinking and stared him down. 'Cat Hayes might be able to assist with the business and if anyone can get her to do it, you can.' Delphine raised her eyebrows delicately when she saw Xavier's expression. 'No one is asking you to sleep with the girl, Xavier! That would be highly inappropriate. She was married to your cousin, however briefly. No, I am simply asking you to be persuasive, to see if she can tell us anything useful. Blind her with science, give her the whole, heady perfume experience.' Delphine flapped her hand in the air. 'If nothing else, I want her to understand why this is all so important to us, and why we need her to sign

116

those papers as soon as Pascal can arrange them. It is in the family's best interests.'

Xavier stiffened. He wasn't ten years old any more. The emotional blackmail she always fell back on had worked then because he had been too young and immature to spot it. These days, he recognised that the family's 'best interests' simply meant his meddling grandmother had no other argument to get her own way.

Xavier stood up. He could say no but the fact was he didn't have anything better to do and he probably was the best man for the job. His expertise in the perfume business was second to none and a part of him resented Cat Hayes' obvious low opinion of him as an empty-headed philanderer. He just wished his grandmother wasn't so manipulative.

'Fine. I'll do it,' he said with bad grace. It would get him away from Therese, at least, and as soon as his duty was done and he was back at La Fleurie, he could give Monique a call and go out on the town.

Delphine nodded. 'Thank you, Xavier. I knew I could rely on you.'

Xavier paused by the door, feeling the need to score a point of his own. 'Are you organising anything, as Cat suggested, to celebrate Rose-Nymphea's half-century?'

Delphine bristled. 'Yes,' she admitted. 'A party. Guy thinks it's a splendid idea and I suppose I can see the appeal. I intend to create a spectacular event, one befitting our signature perfume.'

As Xavier left the room, Delphine decided to put to one side the fact that Cat had been the only person to notice the anniversary. It was too vexing for words.

'So why were your family initially so against your home fragrance idea?' Ashton asked Leoni as they stood outside Jo Malone in Sloane Street. As usual, Leoni was wearing a stark but tight-fitting dress, in slate-grey this time, with a black wool coat over the top and a Hermès scarf knotted at her throat. He caught a waft of her perfume, L'Air Sensuel, which she sometimes wore.

Leoni's lips tightened. 'They were against the idea because they don't like change. Anything new and daring has them retreating into safety, especially when it comes to the visions I have for the perfume business; you know that.'

'They clearly don't know they have a genius idea in their midst.' Ashton threw her a smile. 'It's a shame Xavier has ducked out of the business because otherwise I'm sure he'd stick up for you.'

Grateful for Ashton's support, Leoni wrapped her coat more tightly round herself. February in London was predictable for its unpredictability and although she had anticipated a chill in the air, she was astonished to find herself in sub-zero temperatures with the threat of sleet overhead. She glanced at Ashton. He was wearing a dark overcoat with a cornflower-blue shirt from Pinks that matched his eyes. A group of girls teetered past in high heels, giving him quick, appreciative glances. His preppy blondness and lovely eyes probably made Ashton quite a catch when he was on home turf, Leoni realised.

'So the family meeting was stressful?' Ashton asked as he rubbed his hands and blew on them for warmth.

'Terrible!' Leoni replied with feeling. 'That girl, Cat Hayes, came up with all sorts of suggestions and really made her presence felt. Very inappropriate.'

'I thought you said she supported your ideas?'

Leoni relented. 'Well, yes, she did actually and it was very generous of her in the circumstances. I suppose I just thought she'd sit back and say nothing. Grandmother was in charge as usual and you know how scary she can be.'

Ashton did a mock shudder. 'God, yes. She's absolutely terrifying.'

'It's just . . . Cat Hayes made it obvious she didn't want to be at the meeting and that she just wants to come back to England but I have to admit she made some very good points,' Leoni said grudgingly.

Ashton smiled at her unwillingness to admit that Cat Hayes had impressed her. He opened the door to the Jo Malone store and they went in.

Leoni admired the light, airy space and the calming cream and mirrored decor. If only she could have the chance to create a shop like this! One step at a time, she reminded herself. She needed her family to agree to the idea before she started planning her own shops in Paris and London.

'Wow, this place is amazing,' Ashton exclaimed.

Leoni nodded. A woman was receiving a luxurious-looking hand and arm massage in one corner and another – a bride, if the bulging folder of coloured swatches and sample invitations was anything to go by – was sitting at a counter having a skin consultation. Fragrances mingled in the air and their combined scent was enticing rather than overpowering. A table in the centre of the shop had a neat crescent of fragrance bottles displayed on it. They were identical in appearance but Leoni knew that each one contained its own identity, totally different from the scent in the bottle next to it.

She moved over to the home fragrance area and paused by the section devoted to candles. She loved candles; they created such a warm, inviting atmosphere and having a subtle fragrance drifting in a room somehow transformed it from drab to cosy.

'I like the way they're divided up into home, luxury and travel,' she commented to Ashton as she picked one up. 'By doing that, you're covering all angles, from an affordable, everyday luxury to a more extravagant treat at home or abroad. Fruity, citrus and floral – something for everyone.'

Ashton sniffed one. 'Have you arranged a meeting with that candle-maker chap yet?'

Leoni shook her head. 'No, I must do that. Guy wants to see samples and Jerard is supposed to be one of the best so I'm sure he can create something beautiful to show off my ideas.'

They wandered around the shop together, inhaling the scent of zesty linen sprays and 'Living Colognes' in sensual Amber and Sweet Orange and heady Blue Agave.

'The perfume you have on today would be good in one of these,' Ashton said, gesturing to a candle. Looking up, he caught the surprise on Leoni's face and flushed slightly. 'You . . . often wear it,' he explained, wondering if he'd made a mistake. 'Don't you?'

She nodded thoughtfully. 'You're right, it would make a lovely romantic candle, wouldn't it? We could promote it that way, maybe with a book of matches with the Ducasse-Fleurie monogram on it . . . or maybe a silk flower.'

'Sounds good. Maybe instead of marketing the candles in terms of where they'll be used, you could focus on the mood,' Ashton suggested. 'You know, romance, relaxing, that sort of thing.'

'Genius,' she exclaimed. 'As you would say. Hey, I thought you were just coming along for the ride. I didn't realise architects knew about marketing.'

Ashton laughed. 'We don't. I just had a moment of brilliance, that's all. Make the most of it.'

They mooched around the shop and then Ashton hurried Leoni outside. 'We need to jump on the train,' he said, checking his watch and turning up his collar.

The journey slipped by in companionable silence, with Ashton responding to messages on his phone and Leoni leafing through the brochure she'd picked up in Jo Malone. In Surrey they caught a cab. Leoni enjoyed the scenery as it zipped past the windows, even though it was almost dark. With its wide expanses and interesting green and brown tones, it was very different to Provence but she liked it. Ashton's parents' house, which she hadn't visited before, was neat and understated. It was also tiny compared to La Fleurie, but then, most places were, Leoni acknowledged wryly. The Lyfield residence was cosy and welcoming and that was the main thing.

'Leoni, how wonderful to see you again!' Joyce Lyfield, Ashton's mother, bustled forward, wiping her hands on an already floury apron. 'Gosh, it's been so long, darling, five years maybe, since we visited you and the family in Provence?'

Leoni kissed her cheeks politely, letting out a squeak as Joyce hugged her enthusiastically. This wasn't what she was used to; at La Fleurie, everyone was so self-conscious and painfully formal. Leoni wasn't sure if it had always been that way but she certainly couldn't remember the last time anyone had given her a rib-crushing bear hug.

'I've been baking all afternoon,' Joyce was saying as she took Leoni's coat and led her to a comfy armchair by a lovely period fireplace. 'I've made some cheese scones, some cupcakes and, if I say so myself, a very tasty banana loaf.'

Ashton's father, Arthur, a nice-looking man in his fifties, rolled his eyes. 'The kitchen looks like a bloody bombsite,' he chided, giving his wife a wink. He shook Ashton's hand heartily, delighted to see him after such a long time. '*Really* good to see you, son. Still loving Paris?'

Ashton nodded. 'God, yes. You must come and visit again soon, the spare room's all done now. Oh, and I've seen this incredible building . . .' As he still hadn't mentioned it to Leoni, Ashton took his father into another room to show him some of the photographs he'd taken on his phone.

Joyce brought a tray to the table by the fire. 'I hope you're hungry, darling,' she said, slathering some butter on to a thick slice of banana bread. She gave Leoni a critical once-over, observing her thin calves. 'If you don't mind me saying so, you could do with putting on a few pounds, Leoni. I know you French women don't eat much because you want to wear those lovely dresses – and you look gorgeous, don't get me wrong – but I just worry about you not getting all your vitamins . . .'

Warmed by the flow of friendly chatter, Leoni took a small bite of the banana bread. It really was delicious and even though she didn't usually eat cake, she found herself demolishing an entire slice.

'It really is good to see you again, darling,' Joyce said, perching her bottom on the edge of a red sofa. She placed her hand on Leoni's. 'We were so sorry to hear about Olivier. You must miss him very much.'

Leoni gulped, almost choking on the last of her banana bread. She nodded.

Joyce squeezed her hand. 'Brave girl. It's tough when you lose someone. I lost my brother when I was young. Tommy, his name was.' She looked upset for a moment then pressed on. 'Ash told us about Olivier's new wife – what a shock for all of you! I do hope she's a genuine girl and that she cared about him.' Joyce got up and bustled around, pouring tea and fussing over Leoni. 'I'm so excited about this home fragrance line you're researching . . . oh, I know all about it because Ash told me. I hope that's all right.' She looked at her guest. Leoni smiled and, satisfied she hadn't put her foot in it, Joyce handed her a large mug of tea.

After tea, Ashton invited Leoni out for a walk in the garden while Joyce prepared dinner. Arthur was a keen gardener; the earth in the flower beds was moist and full of freshly planted bulbs, and roses in every colour sat in large, glazed pots.

Leoni looked pensive. 'That relaunch Olivier's widow suggested, the one for Rose-Nymphea . . .'

Ashton stuffed his hands into his pockets. 'I'm guessing you hate the idea.'

Leoni laughed. 'Actually, no. I only wish I'd thought of it myself! Grandmother's furious that Cat dared to make a suggestion about the business but Uncle Guy put his foot down so now she is arranging the biggest party France has ever seen.' She pushed a log with the toe of her shoe. 'Cat is still at La Fleurie. She's lost her passport. I'd think she was making it up except for the fact that she's been in a monumental strop ever since.'

Ashton watched as the wind lifted Leoni's hair from her face. He realised she was still talking and forced himself to listen.

'I feel so resentful towards her, Ashton, but I don't know why.'

Ashton thought for a second. 'Maybe you feel jealous of her.' The words came tripping out before he could stop them. Seeing the colour rise in her cheeks, he backed away, laughing. 'Bloody hell, L, calm down! I just meant that perhaps the thought that someone . . . someone who wasn't you, I mean, spent so much time with Olivier before he died is eating away at you.' He watched her polish her glasses on the sleeve of her dress, something he knew she did when she felt emotional. 'You were very close, the two of you,' he added gently. 'It's natural to feel anger towards Cat when she got to see him at the end and you didn't.'

Leoni tugged at the collar of her coat with shaky fingers. 'It's not just that, it's the fact that he didn't even tell me about his marriage. I mean, we all know he was a liar but he never lied to me.' She sniffed. 'At least, I thought that was the case but it obviously wasn't. I was just the same as everyone else in his eyes . . . I must have been.' She let out a bitter laugh. 'And there was me thinking I was special to my brother.'

Ashton didn't know how to respond to that. What could he say? Olivier had been his best friend and he hadn't known about his marriage to Cat Hayes either. Ashton was aware that Olivier had lied to him on several occasions but he'd put it down to Olivier's devil-may-care attitude and had never taken it to heart. But for Leoni, he knew, it was different.

Knowing that words couldn't make things any better, Ashton pulled Leoni into an awkward hug. As expected, she stiffened, but as he held her, she relaxed and leant against him, crying quietly into his shoulder. Ashton said nothing; he simply held her because he knew that was all Leoni needed at times like these.

'Dinner's ready!' Joyce called out through the kitchen window, starting as she noticed them embracing in the garden.

Ashton drew back and, using his thumbs, wiped the tears from Leoni's cheeks. 'Now, do you think you can hold it together enough to eat a massive plate of my mother's shepherd's pie? No one likes a sissy.'

Leoni laughed, punching him on the shoulder. 'Of course I can. Honestly, you're so rude sometimes, I don't know why I put up with you.'

Following her back down the garden towards the house, Ashton stared after her thoughtfully. Giving his mother a bright, warning smile, he headed indoors.

Slightly chilly in a pair of white trousers and a baggy beige jumper, Cat was immersed in a book called *The Emperor of Scent* by Chandler Burr. Sitting by the pool on one of the luxurious loungers, she was surrounded by books about perfume. She'd been at La Fleurie for nearly a month now and she felt the need to do something with her time until her new passport arrived. And at this time of year, Cat couldn't imagine it would take too long now that she'd sent all the forms back to Bella.

Still feeling trapped and claustrophobic at La Fleurie, Cat couldn't help enjoying the book she was reading. Perhaps it was because the ball was now rolling again in terms of her departure or maybe it was because Leoni was in England and the atmosphere in the house suddenly seemed less intense. Leoni was so uptight, she had a way of making everyone around her feel like a coiled-up spring as well. Delphine was also still giving her a hard time, throwing frosty looks in her direction at every opportunity and Cat was beginning to wish she could escape from the château, even for just a few days to release the tension.

She glanced down at her book again. The perfume business was fascinating and under different circumstances she knew she would really enjoy immersing herself in it. She had only happened upon the books when, furiously visiting Olivier's headstone again, she had discovered the nearby library that overlooked the private Ducasse graveyard. On a whim, Cat had picked out three books on perfume to take her mind off her dead husband's betrayal. As a result, she now knew about top notes, middle or 'heart' notes, and base notes.

She had learnt that the top notes of a scent – the *tête* or *départ*, as they were known in French – were the most volatile odours and the first to make themselves known. They then faded into the background to allow the heart notes – the heart and soul of the perfume – to take centre stage, before the base notes, the most persistent, revealed themselves. They lingered and 'fixed' the scent. This was also apparently known as the 'dry down'.

Cat flipped through another one of the books she had borrowed. An 'accord', she saw, was a composition of harmonious notes which blended to form a perfume, and an 'absolute' was a term used to describe a pure substance which, once obtained and refined by rinsing in alcohol, smelt exactly like the plant from which it had been extracted. Florals, citrus, chypres, orientals – there were so many different fragrance families, all with their own unique identity. Cat couldn't help feeling swept up by the romance of scent and its creative process.

She heard her phone beep over the sound of rustling almond trees beyond the swimming pool and was pleased when she saw a text from Bella saying she'd sent the passport forms off. Apparently, Prism, the rival advertising agency Ben had been liaising with, were putting a job proposal together for her to review as soon as she was back in England. Bella also gleefully reported that the word on the street was that Cat was sorely missed at her old job and that the ad agency had gone spectacularly downhill since she left. Who knew if that part was true, but Cat appreciated Bella's efforts to cheer her up.

A shadow darkened the page of her book and Cat looked up to find Xavier towering over her, darkly handsome in a black shirt and jeans.

'What are you reading?' he asked. Picking up one of her books curiously, he raised an eyebrow. 'You look as though you're studying for an exam.'

She really was beautiful, Xavier thought taken aback, and mainly because of her eyes, which sparkled and changed colour like the sea. Xavier dismissed the poetic notion. He had a job to do.

'I'm reading up about perfume and how it's created,' Cat explained, realising it must seem strange that she was suddenly so interested in the family business. 'Not so I can take Olivier's share away from the family or anything,' she added defensively.

'Of course not,' Xavier said politely. 'Not all of us think that.'

'No,' Cat replied. 'Some of you just think I'm completely mental for marrying someone I barely knew.'

'Ah, yes . . . that.' Xavier met Cat's eyes, inwardly cursing the twins for letting his thoughts about her slip. He wasn't sure how to smooth the waters. He still thought Cat was foolhardy for marrying Olivier but if he didn't make some sort of effort to justify himself, he had no chance of getting her to come to Grasse. Swallowing a sigh, he did his best, hoping his grandmother appreciated his efforts.

'Look, all I meant was that marrying someone so quickly comes with . . . consequences. I don't mean because Olivier died; I mean because you can't have known him that well. Even when you know someone intimately, they can still do something unexpected and surprise you.' He linked his fingers together tightly. His words had conjured up memories he'd rather forget. 'And when you don't know someone, the only result you can count on is getting hurt.'

Cat looked away. 'Yes, well . . . you're right there,' she admitted, still smarting. 'I had no idea Olivier had so many women on the go at the same time. Runs in the family, I see,' she added without a smile.

Xavier's eyes became hard. 'Well, we all have our cross to bear.' He felt his temper rising but reined himself in, remembering the task in hand.

'Look, I wondered if you might be interested in taking a short trip. I . . . suppose I know a fair amount about the perfume business.'

'Seraphina says you're one of the best "noses" in the world.' Cat said the words with slight scorn.

Xavier bristled. 'My sister is biased, but I do have some sort of talent. My mother, now she was impressive. She knew exactly what ingredients blended together, how one odour can intensify a scent, how the velvety tone of a fragrance can be changed to a sensual one by just a fractional addition.' He paused. 'My mother was a true *senteur* because she was both a chemist and an artist. Everything I know, I learnt from her.' Xavier stopped talking abruptly. What on earth was he doing, talking about his mother and what she could do?

'Is that your lab?' Cat pointed at a nearby barn that had remained under lock and key since her arrival.

Xavier glanced at it and nodded, wondering where this was leading.

'It looks deserted. As if no one cares about it any more.'

He narrowed his eyes. She was trying to wind him up; he could tell. 'Would you like to see it?'

Cat seemed bemused that he had called her bluff. She shrugged non-committally, but followed him to the lab which was at the edge of the pool area.

Outside the door, Xavier hesitated. He hadn't been inside for two years now. Did he really want to go back in there and

127

rake up all those old feelings? He drew out the key he always carried around in his pocket and slotted it into the lock. The door opened easily and he stepped inside. Cat followed him in, glancing around as she did so. Inside, it was deadly quiet, almost as if it was sound-proofed. As Cat strolled past him, Xavier caught a waft of the Jo Malone perfume she wore.

'Wow,' Cat said, impressed in spite of herself. She sniffed. The air inside the lab smelt strange – clean but imbued with something else. She supposed it was probably many other aromas mingled together. She walked over to a counter, intrigued. Its rows of gleaming equipment would have looked more at home in a school science class. There were several computers lined up on the counter and hundreds of boxes of white blotting paper, cut into thin strips like wands. There were bottles labelled 'Essences' and 'Absolutes', some from obscure places in the world. She read some of the labels. Beeswax . . . leather . . . champagne . . . blood orange . . . marigold . . . galbanum . . . The essences and aromas were grouped together under headings like 'Citrus', 'Animal Sources' and 'Resins and Balsams'.

'You can really use all these sorts of things to create a fragrance?' she asked, trying to sound casual.

Xavier nodded. 'Of course. Sage, wheat, sesame, cardamom – you name it, you can blend it. You'd probably be surprised if you knew what was in some fragrances, not just the ingredients themselves but how many of them are used in any one perfume.'

Cat frowned as she discovered a large section labelled 'Chemicals'. The bottles were called things like 'Aldehydes', 'Cashmeran' and 'Ambretone'. 'I had no idea it was all so technical, so scientific,' she commented, bewildered by what she was seeing. 'It feels almost clinical. But making fragrances is surely a creative process?'

Xavier picked up the bottle marked 'Galbanum'. Removing the lid, he inhaled the distinctive bitter scent. 'Scent creators are essentially skilled chemists,' he explained, 'but they are also creative. You need an in-depth knowledge of a vast number of materials and you need to be able to recognise and compare, as well as measure out the correct quantities of your ingredients to create your fragrance. I usually map out my vision of a scent on paper first before moving into the lab to try out different combinations.' A shadow passed across his face. 'Or rather, I used to.'

Cat wanted to ask him about that but she didn't dare.

'For example,' he said, his voice animated as he found himself back on familiar and much-loved territory, 'what does a woodland smell like? Woody, of course, but it's more than that. Mossy, perhaps? Fresh because of the air, but also sensual, due to the earthy aromas of the bark and the muddy ground underfoot.' Xavier felt his senses stirring as he spoke. 'This has to be captured but other elements must be added to layer the fragrance and give it character and body. Floral tones, as an example, or maybe something musky to give it a really erotic hit.'

He picked up an empty perfume bottle and held it up. 'Once the bottle is opened and applied to the skin, the scent will change, depending on the skin's acidity. Which is why the most exquisite of perfumes can smell divine on one woman and like cat piss on another.' Abruptly, Xavier laughed.

Cat was startled to hear his laughter. He hadn't so much as smiled in her direction before. 'I know what you mean. I really want to love Chanel No. 5 because it has this glamorous image – Marilyn Monroe famously only wore it in bed, et cetera – but it smells terrible on me. *Disgusting*.'

'Chanel No. 5 can be difficult to wear.' Xavier ran his hand along the clean, empty counter rather as if he was caressing the slender waist of a lover. 'It's a floral,' he informed her, 'but a powdery one containing rose and jasmine. And, so legend has it, an accidentally generous slug of aldehydes.'

'Right.' Cat felt rather dizzy from all the information. 'I

can't imagine you in a chemistry class as a kid,' she teased. 'Can't really see you in goggles and a lab coat.'

Xavier held up a pristine white coat. 'Really? I think I used to carry it off well.' He hung it up, the ghost of a smile lifting the corners of his mouth. He paused, looking uncomfortable as he remembered his task. 'Would you like to join me in a visit to Grasse? It's the perfume capital of France. I think you'd find it very interesting.'

Cat eyed him suspiciously. What was he up to? Why was he suddenly being nice?

Xavier avoided her eyes. 'We could visit some factories. I could tell you a bit more about the history of fragrance, that sort of thing. I just thought until things were sorted with your passport … who knows, you might be able to come up with some other brilliant ideas.'

Cat was puzzled. She couldn't help thinking there was something else behind Xavier's offer but she didn't have a clue what it could be. She didn't trust him – that was for sure.

'Maybe,' she said, off-handedly. It would be a good excuse to get away from La Fleurie for a while. The tension in the air was unbearable and she had never felt more unwelcome in her life. Could she tolerate Xavier for a few days? Cat reckoned, at a push, she could manage it. 'I suppose I haven't anything else to do,' she added.

Xavier nodded curtly. 'Good,' he said. 'I'll arrange everything.' He turned to leave.

'Why don't you make perfumes any more?' Cat blurted.

'What?' Xavier returned her stare coldly.

She gestured at the rows of bottles. 'It seems a bit silly if you're so good at it. Any particular reason?'

'Not one I wish to discuss with you,' Xavier snapped, his blood racing.

Cat couldn't believe his rudeness. 'Not very nice when someone thinks decisions you make are total nonsense, is it?' she retorted.

Xavier's dark eyes flashed at her dangerously. 'It's not the same thing at all,' he shot back. 'You have no idea what you're talking about. You have no fucking right to question me like this.'

Cat swallowed, realising she had obviously hit a very raw nerve.

Before she could apologise, he stalked out of the lab, slamming the door behind him.

Boy, did he have a temper! Cat thought. Could she really see herself going to Grasse with this man?

Cat headed out of the lab and sighed gloomily as she contemplated her options. She could stay at the château and be frozen out by Delphine and Leoni when she returned from England or go to Grasse with Xavier who exploded if anyone dared to challenge him. Not for the first time, Cat cursed Olivier for putting her in this situation in the first place.

Chapter Eight

Back at boarding school, Seraphina emerged from a classroom clutching some books. Checking her phone, she found she didn't have any messages. Disappointed, she tossed her phone back into her school bag.

'God, that was boring!' Max moaned, sloping out behind her. He chucked his bag over his shoulder, almost smacking Madeleine in the face. 'Who gives a fuck about history, anyway?'

Seraphina wasn't listening and she fiddled with her hair distractedly. She found most of her lessons dull but she had learnt to switch off and think about other things when time was dragging. Thoughts of modelling and fashion kept her going if she needed to daydream, but today, Seraphina's mind was occupied with something quite different.

'See you later,' Adele called as she and Felicity shot past in their gym clothes.

Seraphina raised a hand and, seconds later, her mobile rang and she scrabbled around in her bag to locate it.

'Hello?' she said breathlessly, turning away from Max.

He frowned, not used to his twin being secretive. Since when had she needed to hide the identity of a caller from him? he thought moodily. Barely noticing Madeleine hovering nearby, Max watched Seraphina turning pink with pleasure as she chatted to whoever was on the other end of the phone. Hearing her cagey, monosyllabic answers to whatever she was being asked, Max wondered uneasily if it was the guy from the modelling agency who'd approached her on the beach. He wouldn't dream of admitting it but on this particular issue, Max agreed with his father for once; the guy sounded like an opportunistic pervert. Seraphina was only sixteen, for fuck's sake! Dirty bastard, he thought angrily.

'Who's on the phone?' he demanded, grabbing his sister's arm. Whoever she was speaking to was turning her into a simpering flirt and he didn't like it one bit.

Seraphina finished her call and spun back round to face Max. She was positively glowing and her brown eyes were sparkling.

'Who was it?' he repeated doggedly. His sister might be more mature and sensible than him but she was also incredibly fragile. He didn't want some dirty old man taking advantage of her. 'Was it that dickhead from the beach?'

Seraphina frowned. 'What? Oh, no, it wasn't him.' Her mouth curved up into a mysterious smile.

Max scowled. 'It had better not be. If he lays one finger on you, I'll kill him.'

'It wasn't him,' Seraphina insisted. 'It's nothing. Don't worry about it, Max.'

Max stared at her. Not once, in all their sixteen years together, had Seraphina ever kept a secret from him.

'You're not still thinking of doing modelling, are you?' he demanded. 'It's not safe, anything could happen to you.'

Seraphina frowned. 'Not you too, Max! I thought you were on my side.' She couldn't believe it, not her twin as well! The one person she could usually rely on to take her side, and now even he seemed to feel the need to warn her against the career she had set her heart on. Seraphina felt let down and all at once she realised why Leoni was always so resentful. It was crushing not to be taken seriously by one's own family, especially when it concerned an important issue like a career.

'I *am* on your side,' he told her intently. 'I just don't want you to come to any harm.'

Seraphina shook her head in exasperation at Max's assumption that she was too immature and gauche to handle a career in modelling and turned away to read a text message. Disturbed, Max was about to dig deeper when he felt a hand slide into the back pocket of his jeans. It was Vero, her black hair tied up in a sleek ponytail.

'Fancy going somewhere?' she murmured in his ear as Pierre and Thierry sidled up behind her with another girl Max didn't know.

Madeleine stepped forward. 'We have English next. You should stay for that.'

Max glared at her. Slinging his arm casually round Vero's neck, he nodded, even though Vero's unsubtle perfume was almost making him gag. 'Let's go.'

'Please don't,' Madeleine said, putting her hand on his arm. Seeing his withering look, she removed it. 'I-I just don't want you to get into trouble,' she stammered.

'Such a *good* girl,' Vero smirked as she and Max swaggered off in the other direction. 'Go to your class, little girl. We're off to have fun.'

Max laughed and they disappeared round the corner. Seraphina watched him with some resignation.

'You're wasting your time, I'm afraid,' she told a deflated Madeleine kindly. 'Max is . . . he has issues. You probably know our mother died a few years back . . . Max is still really screwed up about it.' And about our father ignoring us, Seraphina reminded herself silently but she wasn't about to spill the beans to Madeleine, whom she barely knew.

Madeleine nodded. 'I . . . just don't want him to feel as though anyone is giving up on him,' she said, biting her lip.

'None of us are,' Seraphina said drily. 'But Max does whatever he wants, he won't listen to anyone.' Remembering her phone call, she felt euphoric again and hugging herself as she headed to her next class, she forgot all about Madeleine.

*

Standing outside the gorgeous, rococo-style building again, Ashton felt a flash of excitement. He'd been away in England and hadn't seen the place for a while; he'd almost convinced himself it wasn't as special as he'd first thought.

But it was. It was perfect. The location was ideal; it was close enough to busy Boulevard Haussmann to bring a stream of customers past it but it was also discreetly positioned in a pretty side road. This gave the building a 'boutique' feel, accessible but high end, which was exactly what a perfume shop should be, Ashton thought, gazing up at it. And he loved the shell motifs that sat above the window. They added a touch of playful humour which stopped the building from being too intimidating or formal.

Having asked for the keys, Ashton opened the door and walked inside, feeling as though he was entering Aladdin's cave. Placing the keys and his phone on a nearby counter, he sucked his breath in. The building might be empty but in his mind's eye he could see it taking shape and assuming an identity. He paused then refocused his attention on the building. Taking out a notepad, he started sketching his ideas in pencil, using rapid strokes and approximate measurements.

The fluid lines of the shopfront lent themselves to similar curves inside – elegant, undulating counters and softly rounded shelves that flowed around the side of the shop in one continuous curve. Ashton quickly pencilled in the small chandeliers he had originally envisaged, with muted, hidden bulbs around the wide window to highlight each beautiful Ducasse-Fleurie product. He didn't want to get carried away with the interior so he focused on the structure. He checked the floor area of the flat above and then went back downstairs. He jumped when he realised someone was standing just inside the street door.

'*Bonjour*,' said a husky, teasing voice.

Turning round, Ashton came face to face with a glamorous woman in her forties. Instantly, he recognised her as the woman he'd seen eyeing up the building when he'd viewed it before. Today, her russet-coloured hair sat around her shoulders like a glorious, autumnal shower. She wore the same black trench coat, this time with ruby court shoes that had dagger-thin heels.

Ashton blinked at her, wondering what she was doing there. Women like her made him feel uneasy. 'Hello. Can I help you?'

'Mmmm, how *delicious*, you're English,' she murmured. She undid the belt of her trench coat and took it off in one smooth movement, placing it carefully on the cleanest surface she could find. Underneath she revealed a scarlet dress with an asymmetric neckline and a tight skirt that emphasised every curve. With her flowing hair, immaculate red lips and statuesque figure, she was like a Hollywood siren from a bygone era.

'Let me introduce myself. My name is Marianne Peroux.'

Ever the gentleman, Ashton shook her hand, aware that she held his far longer than was necessary. 'It's very nice to meet you, madame. I'm Ashton Lyfield.'

'Ashton. It is *so* nice to make your acquaintance.' Letting go of his hand, she instead held his gaze with bewitching green eyes that seemed to mock and beguile him simultaneously.

What an attractive man, she thought to herself. He was like a shy but very fanciable prefect at one of those posh English boarding schools, someone most girls would want to ravish and lead astray.

Marianne smiled inwardly. She was going to enjoy this game. 'What a wonderful building,' she commented, her airy tone at odds with the determination etched on her face. 'A truly magnificent specimen of its period, don't you think? And so . . . utterly . . . perfect.' She said the words in a deliberately sensual manner and strolled purposefully around the space, her sharp heels making snapping sounds on the dusty floor.

'Perfect for what?' Ashton felt compelled to ask.

'Why, a perfume store, of course!' Marianne let out a throaty laugh and put her hands on her hips. She gave him a keen glance. 'I head up one of the biggest perfume houses in Paris,' she informed him. 'Armand.' She threw the name out with the casual confidence of someone who knew they held all the aces.

Ashton felt his spirits plummet. Armand were one of the most commercial, well-known brands in France. Originally a luxurious, upmarket make-up line that catered to the exceptionally rich, Armand had branched out into fragrance ten years ago and their top-selling perfume, L'Ecarlate, meaning Scarlet, had been an instant bestseller. Bold, brash and unforgettable, the fragrance had benefited from a very provocative ad campaign featuring a famous French actress, her semi-naked pose now synonymous with the perfume. L'Escarate had made record sales for the first five years and thereafter Armand, as a brand, were unstoppable.

If Marianne – and Armand – were interested in this building, which they clearly were, Ashton knew he was going to have his work cut out securing the property for Leoni.

Marianne paused at Ashton's elbow. 'I love your ideas for the space,' she said, running a finger topped by a flame-red nail through his notebook of sketches. 'You are an architect? I love these sexy, flowing lines and the way you plan to capture the light. It's perfect.' She puckered her mouth until it resembled a ripe cherry and regarded him. 'Would you consider renovating the building for me? I would hire you in an instant and I will pay double your normal rates.'

Taken aback, Ashton smiled politely. He didn't want to alienate her, not when she was clearly a rival buyer. 'I'm flattered but I'm afraid that's not possible. I plan to renovate this building for someone else once they've purchased it. It's . . . it's personal.'

'Really?' Marianne looked put out. She narrowed her green

eyes at him, moving closer. 'Who is it, this person you are so keen to do such a thing for?'

Ashton shook his head, giving her a genial smile. 'I'm so sorry but it really wouldn't be appropriate for me to tell you.' His phone rang and he groped for it in his pocket, before remembering he'd left it on the cracked counter by the door.

Marianne scooped it up helpfully and glanced at the screen. Catching her breath, her mouth fell open in surprise. 'Leoni Ducasse?' she said incredulously. 'It can't be . . . You want this building for Ducasse-Fleurie, don't you?'

Taking his phone from her, Ashton looked pained. He couldn't very well deny it now. He wondered why Marianne had been so astonished to see Leoni's name.

Marianne was pacing the store. 'I cannot believe it . . . this is incredible! After all these years . . .'

'What do you mean?' Ashton asked finally, totally nonplussed.

Marianne let out a short laugh. 'Well, let's just say that I knew Guy Ducasse a long time ago.' She nodded, her russet hair falling over one eye. 'Oh yes, me and Guy, we knew each other before he met Elizabeth. How is she, by the way?'

'She's dead,' Ashton said bluntly. He suspected Marianne didn't really care much for Elizabeth's welfare. 'She died two years ago.'

'Riding accident?' Marianne guessed correctly. 'I knew she'd come off that silly horse one day. Such a dangerous sport but some people have to get their thrills. So Guy is alone now. How very interesting.' She turned her attention back to Ashton, gazing into his eyes. 'You have the most arresting eyes, you know. We should go out to dinner and discuss this wonderful building.'

Ashton felt slightly panicked. Marianne would eat him for breakfast. 'Oh, I really don't think that's—'

'Let me make myself clear,' Marianne interrupted, her voice taking on a sharp edge. She shrugged her arms into the sleeves of her black trench coat and did the belt up smartly. 'I have no intention of letting this building go to someone else, least of all Guy Ducasse. So you can either join me or fight me. It's your choice, Mr Lyfield.'

Ashton believed her. With all the confidence of an older woman in her prime, she leant against him deliberately, pressing her full breasts against his arm as a pungent waft of L'Ecarlate threatened to overwhelm him. He wanted to push her away but good manners prevented him.

'Are you sure you won't join me for dinner?' she asked, running a hand boldly down his thigh. 'I plan to go somewhere romantic that serves lobster and vintage champagne. Such things always put me in the mood.'

Ashton gulped. 'You're too kind,' he said, knowing he sounded ridiculously British, 'but I'm afraid I must decline. Loyalty to the Ducasse family and all that.'

Marianne was unabashed. 'No matter,' she said, fluttering a hand carelessly. 'We will have countless opportunities in the future, I am sure of it.' Turning on her heel, she left the building, leaving it feeling drab but, from Ashton's perspective, safe again. He knew he needed to get the Ducasse family on board as soon as possible. Otherwise Armand, with forceful, terrifying Marianne at the helm, would steal this magnificent building out from under them.

'Let's go for coffee,' Delphine announced, surprising Cat in the breakfast salon the following morning. 'We should get to know one another.'

Feeling her heart sinking to join the croissant she'd just demolished, Cat put her cup of coffee down. She guessed Delphine meant they should go somewhere else for coffee rather than have one at the château, but she had no idea why. She also felt rather unnerved by Delphine's suggestion. What did the old lady really want? Cat wasn't naive enough to think the invitation was an innocent one and she wondered how she could wriggle out of it. After the heated altercation with Xavier, the last thing she wanted was another run-in with a member of the Ducasse family.

'There's a pretty café in town,' Delphine added, in case Cat didn't understand what she meant. 'We can talk there without being interrupted.'

Feeling a sense of impending doom settle on her shoulders, Cat got to her feet. 'That sounds . . . lovely.' She glanced at Delphine's cane. 'Er . . . shall I drive?'

Delphine gave her a sneering look. 'No, thank you. I'm more than capable. Besides, we have drivers for such things.' As she turned and headed for the door, Cat cursed herself for being so crass. A woman as independent as Delphine would obviously hate to be viewed as a cripple in any way, and of course the family had drivers! Why drive when you could pay someone to do it for you?

Cat followed Delphine out, forgetting to grab her handbag on the way. She felt at a slight disadvantage as she slid into the limo next to Delphine who placed her smart black crocodile bag between them like a fence. The short journey was completed in silence, apart from Delphine pointing out the occasional sight – an unlikely tourist guide, Cat mused – and they were soon settled in the window of a pretty café with coffees in front of them.

'Tell me about your home life,' Delphine asked pleasantly.

Warily, Cat eyed her, hoping she appeared open and friendly, even if she felt cagey on the inside. She wasn't sure how far back Delphine wanted her to go so she presented her with a potted history. 'I grew up in a lovely village near Cambridge,' she provided. 'I enjoyed school and I had a very happy childhood. My parents were wonderful and they enjoyed lots of different sports like sailing, cycling and skiing.' As ever, mentioning skiing made her wince slightly. Cat pushed ahead. 'They both worked in advertising. They were very creative, which I suppose, is where I get it from.'

'Did they own their own company?' Delphine asked. She wasn't sure what she had hoped would come out of this chat but Cybille had suggested it and Delphine thought she should do it, just to see if anything new came to light. If it did, she could get Yves on the case to see what he could discover.

Cat nodded, wishing she'd tied her wayward hair back. Delphine's look was so neat and precise, it made her feel positively dishevelled. 'Hayes Advertising. Not very original, I know, but I always liked it because it was such a joint venture.' Sitting back, she toyed with her cup, her expression unconsciously wistful. 'My parents would often come home fired up after receiving a new brief and they would tell me about it, debating their ideas, arguing sometimes. They spent a good deal of time working in Paris together and we spent lots of summers over here when I was a child, which is why I can speak French. Not brilliantly, as you can tell, but I get by.'

'Your French is very competent,' Delphine allowed with some reluctance. 'Your accent needs work but overall you have a good grasp of the grammar and construction.'

Coming from Delphine, Cat guessed that probably came under the banner of a compliment. 'Anyway, my parents were great fun—'

'Were?' Delphine asked delicately. 'They are no longer with us?'

Cat met her eyes. 'That's right. They both died in a skiing accident.'

Delphine nodded slowly. She could tell Cat was telling the truth and that, unlike Olivier, this wasn't something invented for sympathy. Delphine berated herself for being so soft. Plenty of people had lost someone – look at what the Ducasse family had been through!

'It changed my perspective on life,' Cat went on. 'Instead of feeling scared about doing things, I went down the "life is too short" route. I ski, I climb, I do reckless sports because I enjoy them. Sometimes I do stupid things and fall in love with people more quickly than I should.' Delphine bristled across the table and Cat glanced away. 'Not always the best thing to do. But I don't want people to feel sorry for me; I'm not a victim.'

Straightening her back, Delphine realised Cat and Xavier had much in common. Whether or not Xavier knew it, he lived life with the same attitude as Cat. It was only when it came to love that he held back. Dismissing the thought, Delphine went through her list of questions, carefully watching Cat's reactions. Cat answered each one immediately, not batting an eyelid at anything that was thrown at her, not even the more intimate questions about her past boyfriends (surprisingly few serious ones, if she was telling the truth) and openly discussing her life in London.

'I've had a good life so far,' Cat stated with a friendly smile. 'I mean, obviously losing one's parents isn't ideal, especially when you're a teenager, but that's about it in terms of tragedies. Well, apart from Olivier,' she added, realising too late how insensitive that sounded. 'I'm so sorry, I didn't mean to sound so . . . It was a huge shock to me but Olivier's death must have hit you all very hard.'

'Oh, it did,' Delphine returned sharply. 'But we are used to loss.'

'Are you?' Cat leant forward. 'Does anyone ever get used to loss? I was talking to Seraphina about this and I think that all that happens is that maybe you get stronger with each blow.'

'Seraphina? Why?' There was a brittle edge to Delphine's tone.

Deciding she had nothing to lose as she was leaving soon, Cat carried on. 'She . . . and Max too . . . they both seem a bit . . . depressed. Seraphina told me about Elizabeth's death. Have they had any proper counselling?'

'Counselling?' Delphine snorted. 'They don't need counsel-ling! They need discipline. Rules, regulations and boundaries to keep them under control. That's all there is to it.'

Discipline? Cat gave Delphine an earnest look. 'It's just that . . . I had counselling when my parents died and it really helped me. I know it sounds like a load of rubbish but talking about things can make such a difference. Max and Seraphina just seem as though . . . as though they're really hurting,' she ended lamely.

'Well, thank you for your opinion,' Delphine said tightly. 'I'm beginning to see that it's part of your charm, offering your thoughts on anything and everything.'

Recoiling, Cat went bright red. Delphine stood up, leaning on her cane.

'Thank you for the chat,' she said primly. 'I have some errands to run but please use my car to go back to the château. I can easily call another.' She left with her back erect and her snow-white chignon rigidly in place.

Cat stared after her, feeling as though she'd been dismissed.

Later that afternoon, Guy hurled the phone down with a howl of frustration. He had been trying to get hold of the family accountant for the past three hours and being told he would need to be put on hold again was just too much.

Leaning back in his chair tiredly, Guy rubbed his eyes. He was normally so in control. What the hell was the matter with him? He pushed all the paperwork on his desk to one side and left the room. His mother called him bossily from her quarters (how did she even know he was out of his office?) but Guy ignored her and headed downstairs. Gathering up his car keys, he went outside, his shoes crunching on the gravel driveway. He needed to get away. From La Fleurie, from the business, but most of all from his family.

Jumping into the silver and grey Bugatti Veyron Elizabeth had treated him to for his fiftieth birthday, Guy shot down the driveway at high speed. His head was pounding as though it was going to explode, but Guy knew it was just stress. His children were driving him nuts, for one thing. They all seemed to be going off the rails at the moment and he was at a loss to know how to deal with them.

Seraphina, admittedly not the most academic of children, was so focused on becoming a model she was neglecting her studies, according to the report Guy had just received from the college the twins attended. She would need to repeat a year if she wasn't careful, Guy thought, gripping the steering wheel tightly as he shot round a sharp bend. All these silly notions of becoming a model – Guy shook his head disapprovingly. Seraphina was beautiful, no one thought that more than he did. She was the very image of her mother, something Guy found both endearing and heart-wrenching. Elizabeth would want Seraphina to get an education, he told himself fiercely, completely forgetting that all Elizabeth had ever wanted was for her children to be happy.

As for Max, Guy thought, swerving to avoid a car that was on his side of the road, he had such an attitude – all that scowling and backchat. If he behaved like that at school, he'd get thrown out if he wasn't careful.

Xavier worried him too. He had gone badly downhill since Elizabeth's death. Who would have thought he would stop working in the business the way he had? Was it really just Elizabeth's death that had affected Xavier? Guy wondered. He vaguely remembered a woman Xavier had been seeing at the time, a stunning, sexy girl who did something arty for a living. She had disappeared around the same time they had buried Elizabeth but if it had damaged Xavier in some way, he wasn't talking about it.

Taking a hairpin bend at speed, Guy smashed his hand on the steering wheel. What had gone wrong with his family? They were out of control – all somehow lost and screwed up. Guy felt tears pricking his eyes and he wiped a hand across his face, hearing a loud horn as though it was in the distance. Quickly, he grabbed the steering wheel again and his eyes widened in horror as he realised he was millimetres from smashing into a sleek red Ferrari. Veering wildly to avoid a collision, Guy briefly saw the bald, ageing man who was driving the Ferrari mouthing off to his bimbo girlfriend. Shuddering to a halt, Guy felt his heart racing. That had been a close call. He had taken his eye off the road for a mere second but he had been driving so fast, he had nearly caused a major accident.

He got out of the car shakily. He leant on the bonnet, yelping as he burnt his hand. Fuck! The Bugatti's engine was hot enough to sear a steak on. He stared out across the Provençal countryside desperately. Why was he alone? Why wasn't Elizabeth here to help him, to guide him towards making the right decisions for their children? Not even realising his cheeks were wet with tears, Guy stood by his car helplessly. Elizabeth was gone and he was going to have to face up to it. And somehow, he needed to figure out what it was his children needed.

More discipline, he thought grimly as he flung himself back in the car. That was what Max and Seraphina needed, at any rate. As for Xavier . . .

Feeling heavy hearted, Guy realised he had absolutely no idea how he could reconnect with his elder son.

Leoni was on her way to a candle shop to meet the owner, Jerard Monville. In her sports car with the top down and an Hermès scarf fluttering behind her, Leoni looked glamorous and in control. She still felt Olivier's loss acutely but she was determined to get on with her life and prove to her family that she was capable of masterminding her home fragrance idea.

Leoni thought about the trip to England. It had been wonderful, and just what she had needed. Her research had gone well; visits to Jo Malone, Miller Harris and a few other stores had been both productive and inspiring. Ashton had been a good friend, listening patiently to her rants about

Olivier, and Joyce and Arthur had been the perfect hosts, attentive, friendly but not too intrusive, and Leoni had eaten heartily, better than she had in a long time.

She let out a sigh of satisfaction. She was glad Ashton had suggested the trip. It had been good to get away from home and everything associated with Olivier, Cat Hayes included. And more importantly, creative thoughts about possibilities for the Ducasse-Fleurie line had been flowing ever since the trip. Leoni's notebook was positively bulging with ideas and sketches. She wanted to make sure her home fragrance concept had something different, something which made it stand out from other products on the market. What exactly she needed was eluding her for the time being, but Leoni was confident she would come up with a winning formula by the time she presented the campaign to Guy.

She glanced down at her mocha-brown dress with matching heels in soft brown suede and checked that her trademark slick of red lipstick was intact before getting out of her car. Standing outside the shop, Leoni thought it looked rather unimpressive; it was small and the sign above the main window badly needed painting. But as she stepped inside the cool, darkly lit building, Leoni caught her breath.

Candles in all shapes and sizes sat on every available surface in the slightly rounded room, and with its low, star-studded ceiling, Leoni felt as though she had stumbled into a magical cave. Behind the counter, black and white boxes were stacked up on top of one another and there were piles of glossy tissue paper in all the colours of the rainbow for wrapping.

'Hello,' said a pleasant-looking man of around thirty with light brown hair. He was wearing scruffy jeans and a black T-shirt with multi-coloured splashes of candle wax splattered from neck to hem. 'Leoni Ducasse, I assume.' His eyes twinkled at her in the dim light, their colour unidentifiable. 'I'm Jerard Monville. Welcome to my shop.'

'Nice to meet you,' she responded formally. 'Sorry I'm a few minutes late.'

Jerard smiled, giving her a discreet once-over. 'No problem at all. Would you like to see the team at work?' He gestured behind him. 'This place is bigger than it looks.'

Leading the way, he showed Leoni round a small workshop which was neatly kitted out with rows of counters and shelves containing moulds of different shapes and sizes. Staff members were lined up behind counters peeling moulds away from candles and efficiently wrapping them in crisp white tissue paper. Another set of people were responsible for packing them up into boxes, which they were doing carefully but with some speed.

'We're a happy team here,' Jerard said as he held a door open for her.

She accidentlly brushed against him as she went into his office and, flustered, she apologised. She noticed that he had quite a Gallic nose, but it suited him.

'No need,' Jerard said with an easy grin, making it clear he'd be happy if it happened again.

'Right. Good.'

Edgily, Leoni pulled out the fat notebook she used for all her ideas and took a seat by Jerard's desk. Her business meetings were usually conducted quickly with suited types who watched the clock even more than she did. 'I sent you some information but, basically, candles are a love of mine. I'd like us to produce a good range of luxury items using some signature Ducasse fragrances.'

Instead of taking a seat behind his desk, Jerard leant against it and pushed his hands into his pockets casually. 'Sounds like a great idea. You sent me some fragrance phials a while back and I'd be interested to get your feedback on the sample I've knocked up. While I dig it out, have a look at this. I did some estimates based on the quantities you told me about.'

147

Leoni was taken aback at how organised Jerard was. Considering how laid-back he appeared, he certainly knew what he was doing. She skimmed through the numbers and couldn't help being impressed. To have such detailed figures, Jerard must have done a great deal of research into Ducasse-Fleurie.

'And what sort of deal could you offer for orders of a much larger size?' she asked aggressively when Jerard returned bearing a box. She felt the need to assert her authority.

Before he could answer, a pretty brunette entered the room carrying a cup of coffee. 'Here you are, Jerard,' she said, handing him the cup. She was dressed in a simple yellow T-shirt and jeans that somehow looked provocative on her curves. She gave Jerard a wide smile before turning to Leoni. 'Er, sorry. Would you like something to drink?'

Leoni shook her head.

'My assistant,' Jerard explained as the girl disappeared. 'Now, where were we? Ah, yes, a deal. Well, we can discuss that as and when it happens.' Jerard pushed the box towards her. 'Go ahead, open it.'

Leoni lifted the lid and pulled out a bundle wrapped in snowy white tissue paper. She gasped as the tissue came away to reveal a beautiful white candle, encased in glass, with a small white and lilac label on the front. There were three wicks poking out of the top of the candle and it felt heavy and luxurious.

'Wow.' Leoni caught a waft of something familiar and moved her nose closer. The candle was imbued with the aroma of L'Air Sensuel and it smelt divine. Delighted, she looked up at Jerard with shining eyes. 'It's lovely . . . really. Perfect, in fact.'

Jerard grinned. 'Glad you like it. The design can be changed – the candles can be any colour you like and any shape. Here's a brochure. We can do it in glass, silver, trio box sets, single items in packaging of your choice . . . so many decisions.' His eyes twinkled at her again. 'Perhaps we should go out to dinner so we can talk about it properly.'

Leoni almost dropped the candle. Was he asking her out? No one ever asked her out! Men tended to find her intimidating, especially when they met her to discuss business, but Jerard seemed completely at ease with her. She blushed as Jerard's blue eyes flirted with hers. Was he genuinely attracted to her or was this just a ploy to get a better business deal? She was hardly dressed to seduce; her brown dress suited her figure but it wasn't exactly sexy. It was professional and formal, just the way she liked to appear.

Jerard leant forward, his expression now sober. 'I am passionate about business . . . I've built my company up from nothing and it's my life. Nothing is more important. I'd still like to take you out to dinner, if you'd like to come?'

Leoni nodded and busied herself putting the candle and her notes into her bag. She was attracted to him; she couldn't deny it. His passion for business, the way he talked about his company, it was exactly how she felt about Ducasse-Fleurie. Leoni faltered. She had never met anyone whose business focus matched hers . . . well, Ashton, perhaps, but he was an architect; it wasn't the same thing. Something about Jerard's intense gaze was making Leoni feel wobbly around the knees. Going against her staunch belief that she should never mix business and pleasure, she found herself agreeing to dinner at the weekend.

Absurdly flattered, she left the factory on a high. Men so rarely asked her out.

She felt buoyed up and sparkling with enthusiasm, something she hadn't felt since Olivier died.

Delphine put the phone down and surveyed her pristine office with satisfaction. Decorated in cool blues and greys with white furniture and its own *balcon* overlooking the fields to the side of the stables, it was a serene and restful space.

149

Organising the event to celebrate Rose-Nymphea was turning out to be easier than she had thought and it was all coming together nicely. They had the perfect venue in La Fleurie so she didn't need to worry about hiring somewhere at short notice and the colour scheme was easy because she could simply use the signature Ducasse-Fleurie colours, lilac and white. Several guests had already verbally accepted, even though the invites hadn't gone out yet, and she had been able to line up a dazzling group of celebrities who happened to be in the area.

Delphine preened, pleased with herself. In fact, if the suggestion had been made by Xavier, for example, instead of Cat, she would have been over the moon about the party. She loved creating events like this, and celebrating Rose-Nymphea was such a wonderful idea because it was an excuse to dress up and invite the rich and famous to their home. Scribbling down some notes, Delphine decided silver fairy lights would be stunning along the outside of La Fleurie and perhaps fresh sprigs of lavender could be tied together with fragrant bunches of the beautiful Romantica roses that grew in abundance in Provence in pinks and whites . . .

Looking up, Delphine was surprised to find Yves, the private detective, loitering at her door. 'Come in.' She flapped her hands so he didn't dawdle in the doorway. She didn't want anyone spotting him and asking questions. Delphine wasn't afraid to take control of a situation to protect her family but she had a feeling they might all think she'd gone mad if she admitted she'd hired a private detective.

'You have news for me?' she asked, gesturing to a seat and trying not to take offence at the sight of another of Yves' shiny suits. This one had a scarlet satin lining that resembled the inside of a tart's boudoir. Or what Delphine imagined a tart's boudoir would look like.

Smoothing his hair back with a smarmy smile, Yves took a

seat. 'Yes and no,' he said mysteriously, clearly enjoying having knowledge to impart.

Delphine, irritated by such behaviour, gritted her teeth and waited.

'Forgive me,' Yves said, flashing her a very charming smile as he took out his notebook. 'It's just that I did find out something very interesting about Cat Hayes.'

'Yes?'

Yves referred to his notes. 'So far, I haven't been able to find out anything to discredit her, as such. She was very well respected in her advertising job and she also worked at a design company for a number of years, learning about branding. Both companies had nothing but good things to say about her, even her most recent place of work, who fired her.'

Delphine sat up, her brown eyes gleaming. 'They fired her? Why?'

'For taking too long on her honeymoon with your grandson, Olivier,' Yves explained with raised eyebrows. 'Hardly a major crime, especially when Miss Hayes hadn't been on holiday for three years. By all accounts, the advertising firm has lost four major contracts since she left because the clients only wanted to work with her.'

Delphine stiffened. This wasn't what she wanted to hear! She had hired Yves on the understanding that he would dig up some dirt on the girl, not arrive with glowing references about her professional capabilities.

'What else?' she barked. 'Miss Hayes must have some skeletons lurking in the cupboard.'

Yves eyed her keenly. 'She does, but not what you might be expecting.' He handed Delphine a photocopy of a newspaper. 'Her parents died when she was a teenager. Quite a horrific accident, by the looks of things. It was in Austria. They were both on a black run and there was an avalanche. Not having any other family, Cat was orphaned.' Yves shrugged. 'Sad, isn't it?'

Delphine nodded. 'I know about this. She told me herself.' It did at least prove that Cat was telling the truth, and that Yves was doing his job. Delphine's mind wandered to Olivier and Leoni. They had been devastated by the death of their parents when they were in their teens and they had been fortunate enough to have a family to support them and pick up the pieces. Whereas Cat had been left all alone to fend for herself with no one else to lean on. It must have been hard for her, not having parental guidance at such a tender age, especially when . . .

Briskly, Delphine pulled herself together. This was no time for sentimentality or unnecessary sympathy. What Cat Hayes had suffered as a teen was neither here nor there; all that mattered was finding some way to show her character to be immoral or untrustworthy, or that her marriage to Olivier was false in some way.

'Did you find out anything more about their marriage?' Delphine asked, handing the photocopy about the skiing accident back impassively. 'That's what I'm really interested in. There has to be some way we can prove it is not legitimate and then the problem of Olivier's inheritance will disappear, regardless of whether Miss Hayes agrees to sign legal papers or not.'

Yves shook his head apologetically. 'I will look into it further but so far I cannot find anything that indicates the marriage isn't legal.'

Delphine frowned at something she'd seen through the window. Yves stood up. 'Right, I'll come back when I have more information, then.'

Delphine waved a hand distractedly. Staring out of the window, she watched Cat strolling to the pool wearing a pair of very unsuitable denim cut-off shorts that were hardly appropriate attire in a chilly February. As she sat at the edge of the heated pool and trailed her fingers in the water, Xavier, on his way into the main house, paused and watched her. It was a brief, fleeting moment and a dark shadow crossed his face before he marched into the house.

Delphine smiled smugly. Good. No chance of Xavier ending up the same way as Olivier. The trip to Grasse was all arranged and Xavier could pick the girl's brains while she herself worked to ensure that Cat was out of the family for good. She felt badly for Xavier, though; he never seemed to be happy these days.

Thinking about Xavier's love life, an idea occurred to Delphine and she reached for the phone. It is *not* meddling, she told herself, knowing it was. Still, it was the best thing for the family in the long run. And as her father Maxim had taught her from a very young age, family was all that mattered.

Chapter Nine

Excitedly clutching the details for the property in Paris in a rolled-up sheet under his arm, Ashton arrived at La Fleurie in search of Leoni. She wasn't at her apartment or at the perfume warehouse, so he guessed she'd retreated to the safety of her office at the château. Ashton had an idea Leoni felt closer to Olivier there. Sure enough, he found her poring over some quotes for the linen spray she was designing, her hair falling forward as she frowned at the page. Behind her glasses, her nut-brown eyes looked bloodshot and tired, as if she had been toiling away at her desk all night.

'Hey,' he called softly.

Leoni's head snapped up. 'Ashton! What are you doing here?' Remembering her manners, she jumped up and kissed his cheeks, inhaling his aftershave before pulling back. She glanced at her watch. 'Look at the time. I've been here since the early hours. I had this idea and I had to get it down.' Ruefully, she smiled, realising she must look a mess. Thank God it was her good friend Ashton standing in front of her and not Jerard Monville, otherwise she'd be dying of embarrassment. There was a time when she would have felt that way about Ashton but those days were long gone.

Ashton grinned at her. 'Listen, I have some plans to show you. I've found this incredible property in Paris.' He pulled the roll of paper from under his arm and unravelled it across her desk. 'I think you're going to absolutely love it.'

'Wow,' Leoni breathed as she walked round her desk, taking

in every angle. There were photographs and sketches and she could immediately see how perfect it could be with the right changes and the appropriate fittings. 'It's stunning, Ashton! Where is it?'

Filling her in quickly on the location and surrounding area, Ashton ran through the ideas he had for the structure and design of the interior. 'Small shelves here, do you agree? And then a wonderful long counter that curves around this side.' Moving round the desk to join her as he enthusiastically outlined his thoughts, he pointed to the ceiling. 'And stunning lights here . . . something like this, I thought.' He showed her a photograph of some magnificent chandeliers with elegant teardrop crystals.

'I love it!' Leoni declared, her tired eyes lighting up with sheer delight. 'The location is ideal for a perfume shop and the building is superb. I can just see our beautiful perfumes lined up in that window, lit from above . . . and the shelves, they would be so perfect for the home fragrance line!'

'That's what I thought.' Ashton nodded. 'You could use your new candles to fill the store with fragrance and maybe some boards advertising the perfume could go here?' He pointed to a section at the back.

Longingly, Leoni ran a finger over one of the photographs. She wanted the building. She didn't know how they were going to get it but it was everything she had hoped for when she had envisaged a store in Paris. Everything and more. Ashton must know her so well to have found this building and she felt deeply grateful to him.

'Is it up for sale yet?' she asked, feeling panicky.

Ashton shook his head. 'Yes, but it's going to auction. I was lucky enough to get the keys recently, so I was able to go in and measure up and get a head start on the plans.' His cornflower-blue eyes met hers keenly. 'I'm guessing all we need to do now is convince Guy.'

Leoni sank down into her chair dispiritedly. 'That's the

problem, Ash. Guy is . . . well, you know, I love my uncle, but he's in the Dark Ages when it comes to such things.'

'What things?' Unexpectedly, Guy poked his head around the door.

Leoni felt guilty. His eyes seemed dull and his shoulders were drooping. Guy seemed rather depressed and she hoped it wasn't her fault.

Guy's dark eyes lit up, however, when he caught sight of Ashton. 'Hey, great to see you, Ash! Always a pleasure.' He came in and shook Ashton's hand energetically, seemingly upbeat again. 'What have you got there?' he said, gesturing to the plans.

Leoni felt defensive. This wasn't how she wanted to approach the subject. She had hoped she could catch Guy in a good mood, when he was relaxing, because that was when he was at his most amenable. It was too late now, however.

'We were just talking about a property in Paris,' she confessed, watching his face carefully. 'Ashton found it and he's drawn some plans up for us.' She took a deep breath, knowing how much was riding on this. 'It could be the first Ducasse-Fleurie perfume shop in Paris. It's small and not remotely flashy but it's in a great location and with Ashton's suggestions I think it could be beautiful and classy, just right for our brand.'

Guy was silent as Ashton quickly talked him through the plans. When he had finished, Guy seemed unimpressed. 'I just can't help thinking it would be difficult to control the business in Paris without one of us visiting it constantly,' he said eventually. 'It's so much easier with everything based in the south of France. The store is local and we have total control over the sales, the staff and the output.'

Leoni slumped over her dcsk, disappointed. She knew Guy would never agree to the idea but just for a moment she had allowed herself to hope. And the trouble was, when Guy made his mind up, he rarely changed it. As stubborn as the proverbial mule, he seemed to think it was a weakness to ever go back on a decision, even if he was patently in the wrong.

Guy stepped away from the desk, the very action underlining his decisiveness on the issue. 'I really don't think it's viable right now. We have so much going on and opening a store in Paris would take up too much time.' He shook his head again. 'Leoni, I'm sorry but it's too much to take on. And I thought you were focusing on your home fragrance line?'

'I am!' Leoni flung her arm out to encompass her piles of notes. 'I've been up most of the night working on it. But opportunities like this building don't come along all the time. It would be awful to lose such a perfect property.' She could cry she felt so disappointed.

'What a shame,' Ashton interjected, feeling as frustrated as Leoni. 'It's such an incredible space, Guy, really. If you could see it, I honestly think you'd be totally won over.' He rolled the plans up with obvious regret. 'I'm not the only one who thought it was perfect for a perfume shop either so I guess it will come down to who makes the best offer at auction.'

'Really?' Leoni sat up. She hadn't even seen the building but already the thought of someone else buying it, let alone using it to create a perfume store, was unbearable. 'It wasn't anyone we knew, was it?'

Guy headed to the door. 'Whoever it was is irrelevant. The timing is all wrong, Leoni.' His mouth in a tight line, he made his final point firmly.

Ashton stared at him, thinking how much Guy reminded him of Olivier right now. His friend had been equally obstinate. 'Her name was Marianne Peroux.' Ashton turned to Leoni. 'She's the owner of Armand.'

Leoni put her head in her hands. 'Brilliant. One of our main competitors.'

By the door, Guy spun round. 'Marianne Peroux?' He went pale beneath his tan. 'Are you sure?'

Ashton nodded. 'She said she knew you. Unfortunately she

found out I was looking at the building for Ducasse-Fleurie and now she's absolutely hell-bent on acquiring it.'

'Is she now?' Rubbing his chin, Guy's brown eyes were gleaming. He began to pace the office. Leoni watched him in astonishment. What on earth was going on? And who was Marianne Peroux?

Realising Ashton and Leoni were eyeing him expectantly, Guy sighed heavily and sat on the edge of the desk. 'Marianne is an old flame,' he explained, looking rather uncomfortable. 'Before I met Elizabeth, I was working in Paris in a flagging perfume company in the sales department and Marianne and I fell in love.' His eyes stared past them as he became lost in memories. 'We were due to be married but she was so competitive! She had ambitions to take over the company and between us we came up with a plan. I thought she was taking too many risks . . . I discovered she was intending to sack thousands of people. I did my best to talk her out of it but . . .'

'I'm guessing she went ahead and did it anyway,' Ashton provided, thinking about the way Marianne's mischievous green eyes had taunted him as she had made her salacious dinner invitation. 'Having met her, I can only imagine how ambitious she was back then. She is certainly not a woman who is easily ignored.'

Leoni glanced at Ashton briefly, wondering if he fancied this Marianne woman but dismissed the thought immediately. Having met a couple of his previous girlfriends many years ago – timid, unassuming girls – she didn't think Marianne Peroux sounded like his type at all.

Guy started pacing the office again. 'Oh, you have no idea, Ash! She got rid of the department, including me, and she stole a number of my ideas along the way. It didn't take her long to topple the CEO and take his place.' He shoved his hands into his pockets, old feelings of anger resurfacing. 'I couldn't forgive her for what she'd done and we broke up. I moved back to Provence and I met Elizabeth the same year. She was working as an au pair – absurd really, when she had such a natural talent as a "nose".'

Guy reminisced for a moment. They had both been unaware of her talent for the first three years of their marriage and it was only when Elizabeth began showing an interest in the business that she discovered her natural ability to blend fragrance.

'Marianne is nothing like Elizabeth,' Ashton commented. 'Elizabeth was sort of innocently beautiful, wasn't she? And really caring, whereas Marianne is—'

'Well, quite.' Guy shot Ashton a meaningful look. Man to man, they both knew what they were talking about. Marianne was a *femme fatale* – alluring, seductive and ultimately dangerous.

'Wow,' Leoni said. 'I had no idea you'd had some big romance before you met Aunt Elizabeth.' She glanced at Guy but he was looking out of the window, apparently lost in thoughts of Marianne. Abruptly, he spun round, a look of utter determination in his eyes.

'Get that building,' he instructed Ashton.

'Really? I can definitely try—'

Guy cut him off sharply. 'Don't try, just get it. Do whatever it takes and pay whatever you need to. I'll sanction any budget to ensure we get it and then I'll pay you handsomely to renovate it for us.'

Leoni put her hands to her mouth. Guy was giving the go-ahead for the store! Her delight was tinged with a flash of annoyance that Guy had argued that her home fragrance idea might be too expensive when he had literally just offered a blank cheque to Ashton for the Paris property. Leoni had always known the company – and the family, for that matter – had more than enough money at their disposal but it irritated her that Guy's willingness to loosen the financial reins seemed to depend on a personal whim rather than sound business reasons.

'Marianne must not get her hands on that building, do you understand?' Guy told Ashton.

Stunned, Ashton nodded. 'Whatever you say, Guy.'

'Leoni, I want you to oversee this and keep me up to date.' Guy turned back to Ashton. 'Don't underestimate Marianne for a *second* and believe me when I say she will stop at nothing to get her own way. Do not trust her, all right?'

Wordlessly, Ashton nodded and Guy strode out of the room.

Over the moon, Leoni did something rash and threw her arms round Ashton's neck. She smiled from ear to ear as he swung her up in the air.

'What a week!' she exclaimed breathlessly. 'First I'm asked out on a date and now this!'

Ashton's smile faded. 'A date?'

Leoni nodded, smoothing her hair down. 'You know the candle man, Jerard Monville? He asked me out on a date after our business meeting.'

'And . . . you accepted?' Ashton couldn't quite understand why he felt so jolted by the news. There was something in Leoni's eyes, a glimmering excitement, that he hadn't seen before. This Jerard man must be quite something because she was never this animated over anything other than spreadsheets. Moreover, Leoni never accepted dates, she was all about the business.

'I know, isn't it unlike me?' Leoni beamed, looking happier than she had in months. 'But Jerard is, well, let's just say we have a similar work ethic.'

Ashton felt an irrational rush of relief. 'Oh, so you don't fancy him as such, then?'

Leoni blushed. 'Well, he's very attractive, actually. Nice looking, I suppose you might say . . . handsome even. We're going out to dinner at the weekend and I'm looking forward to it.' She paused. 'Very much so, in fact.'

Ashton's mood plummeted further.

'Aren't you pleased for me?' Leoni looked up, puzzled by Ashton's silence.

'Er . . . yes, of course.' With a monumental effort, Ashton pulled himself together. 'Of course I'm pleased for you. I hope you have fun.' Brandishing the plans for the shop, he gave her a hearty smile which was totally at odds with his feelings. 'I must get back to Paris and get the ball rolling,' he added, trying to sound jovial.

'I'll call and let you know how my date goes,' Leoni said happily as Ashton headed for the door.

'Can't wait,' Ashton said cheerfully. Shutting the door, he leant against it, feeling utterly sick. All the old, intense feelings he had for Leoni – ones he'd tried to bury years ago – came rushing to the surface. Leoni had never had a clue that when they were younger, Ashton had started to see her as more than his pen pal's older sister. She wasn't his usual type at all, but he had fallen head over heels with her quirky looks, intriguing personality and her endearing earnestness. He knew that no matter how prickly she was on the outside, to those who knew her well, she was soft and sensitive on the inside. And he loved her for it.

Still, it had all come to nothing because one day back then, Ashton had confided in Olivier about his feelings. Olivier had flung his head back and guffawed before telling him Leoni only dated rich Frenchmen and that he was wasting his time. Humiliated, Ashton had shrugged the comment off, telling Olivier he hadn't been serious about Leoni anyway.

Olivier had been right, though, Ashton thought bitterly. Leoni, when she decided to date anyone, went for rich Frenchmen. The trouble was, no other woman seemed to have measured up to Leoni since. He had tried bloody hard to stop thinking of her in that way but no one had quite got under his skin the way she had.

*

Keeping watch by the college library window, Max was on tenterhooks. Seraphina had sneaked out hours ago to meet someone and she still wasn't back. He checked his watch again. It was midnight. Where the hell was she? She'd promised him she would be back by eleven, before the main gates closed.

Max cursed. If she was caught by the teacher in charge of their year, Seraphina risked being kicked out. Monsieur Gaultier – no relation to Jean-Paul, sadly – was strict, sadistic and looking for an excuse to get rid of them, especially since Seraphina had been caught reading a copy of English *Vogue* in his English lesson twice in the past week.

It was so stupid, going out like this on a week night! All Seraphina would say was that she wasn't meeting the sleazy guy from the beach and Max believed her, but judging by the amount of make-up she'd plastered on before she left, she was meeting some other man. And Max had a bad feeling about it. Maybe it was because Seraphina was taking risks and being furtive, something she never normally did, or maybe he was just wary about whoever this man was she might be dating. Either way, he couldn't help worrying. He had thrown a jumper on over the black shorts he slept in, just in case he had to go looking for her.

Squinting through the window into the inky darkness, he saw a flash of white-blond hair in the distance. It had to be Seraphina but she still had a football pitch to negotiate, as well as getting through the locked doors at the side of the building. Max dashed down towards the doors so he could let her in, his bare feet squeaking on the scrubbed floors. Arriving at the door, he was bemused not to find Seraphina there waiting to be let in. Turning round, he saw her emerge from a window that was slightly ajar further down the corridor, wearing her dressing gown over the silver dress she'd gone out in. She had obviously prepared for her late return by leaving her robe outside and the window ajar.

Max's jaw tightened. Couldn't she have told him that,

instead of pretending she wouldn't be late? She landed awkwardly and crashed into the wall, hard. In shock, she clapped a hand over her mouth and pointed frantically at the wall. Baffled, Max stared back at her. There was a moment's silence and then a shrieking siren started, filling the corridor with a deafening wail. It was the fire alarm. Max and Seraphina put their hands over their ears, exchanging horrified glances. They heard shouts and yells from people overhead.

Without warning, the sprinklers went off and showered them both with water and soon the corridor was awash.

'I'm so sorry!' Seraphina cried. Her mascara was sliding down her cheeks in gothic streaks. 'I didn't see the alarm . . .' She glanced over her shoulder, her eyes panic-stricken. 'What are we going to do?'

As people in dressing gowns and pyjamas started to appear, Max didn't waste time thinking. Catching sight of Madeleine frenziedly beckoning them at the end of the corridor, he grabbed Seraphina's hand. They started to run and headed in Madeleine's direction but as they shot through the doors, they crashed into someone. Stopping dead and looking up, their hearts sank as they realised it was Monsieur Gaultier. In spite of it being midnight, he was pristine in a striped dressing gown, his blond hair neatly brushed.

Madeleine, having intended to send them out through a side entrance before Monsieur Gaultier arrived, was gutted. She threw Max an apologetic look but Max was too busy trying to think how on earth they could emerge from this unscathed to notice. Crowds had gathered either side of them and eyes were goggling as everyone strained to hear what was being said over the noise of the alarm.

'Well, well, well,' Monsieur Gaultier said with obvious satisfaction. 'What do we have here then?' He scrutinised Seraphina's face but most of her make-up had been washed away by the sprinklers. Petrified, she tightened her belt in case her silver dress was showing.

Max stepped forward. 'It was my fault,' he said in a clear voice. 'I . . . er . . . got up to get a drink and I accidentally set the fire alarm off.'

'You got up to get a drink,' Monsieur Gaultier echoed sarcastically, his eyes resting on Max's jumper. 'But the bathrooms are *that* way.' He pointed in the other direction. 'You, Maxim Ducasse, have pushed me too far this time. Give me one good reason why I shouldn't send you straight home.'

Elbowing Seraphina back, Madeleine bravely stepped forward. 'It's true, Max was going to the bathroom but I made him accompany me to the medical room because I felt unwell.' With a flash of inspiration, she rubbed her tummy discreetly. 'Women's problems, Monsieur Gaultier,' she murmured, casting her eyes to the ground. 'Please don't tell anyone . . . it's so embarrassing.'

Eyeing her doubtfully, Monsieur Gaultier grunted. He didn't believe the Ducasse boy for one minute but Madeleine Lombard was one of his best students and this was the first incident she had ever been involved in. Regretfully and only because he felt sure he could get Madeleine into one of the best universities in France, Monsieur Gaultier decided to give the Ducasse twins the benefit of the doubt. He would, however, let their father know what had been going on.

'That had better be the truth, Madeleine. You,' he stabbed a finger at Max, 'are lucky you're not on the first train home.' Turning, he roared at the goggling crowds. 'To bed, all of you!' and he herded them back to their rooms.

'Thanks,' Max said to Madeleine, regarding her curiously for a moment. He had no idea why she would choose to save him like that but he was grateful for her intervention. Madeleine smiled shyly and left them to it.

Turning to Seraphina, Max grabbed her by the shoulder. 'What were you thinking? You almost got us both expelled!' The expression in her eyes was dreamy and he was infuriated. 'Were you meeting your boyfriend?' he demanded.

Seraphina nodded. 'Oh yes. And it's serious, Max. I think I'm in love.'

Max gazed at her worriedly. Who the hell *was* this guy? He hadn't even met him and now Seraphina was saying she loved him. 'Is he older than you?' he asked suddenly, wondering if that was why Seraphina was being so guarded.

She went red and defensively she pulled away from him. 'Maybe. But Vero is older than you so you have no right to judge me.' She flounced away from him and Max bit his lip. Something didn't feel right about any of this. Shivering in his wet clothes, he headed back to his bed and peeled off his wet jumper. Whatever Seraphina thought, he intended to get to the bottom of her mystery man, however old he was.

Having risen early in her apartment to head over to La Fleurie the following morning, Leoni was fired up with enthusiasm but she needed a strong coffee to wake her up a bit. Her good mood plummeted when she found Cat trying to work Xavier's high-tech coffee machine.

Wearing no shoes, a pair of denim shorts and a bluebell-coloured T-shirt that kept slipping off her shoulder, Cat was cursing as she waggled the handles and pressed the buttons. Her bra-less breasts were almost visible through the thin material of the T-shirt. The washing machine was full and it was rattling around alarmingly, almost as if it was about to explode, and Cat kept shooting it nervous glances as if she expected foam to start seeping out of it at any minute.

Leoni rolled her eyes. Cat might be dressed like something from the eighties and she clearly couldn't work a coffee machine but with her hair tumbling down her back and her naturally golden-brown skin, she looked like something out of a Pirelli ad. All she needed was some oil and a spare tyre, Leoni thought spitefully.

'Oh, let me,' she said impatiently pushing Cat out of the

way. Within seconds, the coffee machine was purring away with steam chugging out of it, filling the air with the aroma of roasted coffee beans.

'You've obviously got the knack,' Cat commented nervously, wrapping her bare arms round her body.

'And you obviously haven't.' Leoni glared back.

Cat bit her lip. Forcing a bright smile on to her face, she gestured at what she was wearing, shivering slightly. 'I didn't bring much with me and I'm doing some washing.'

'We have staff for that,' Leoni snapped.

Cat flushed. 'Yes, well. I'm used to doing my own washing … and I didn't want anyone to think I'd made myself too much at home.'

About to agree that Cat should certainly do no such thing, Leoni stopped herself. She knew Cat was desperate to get home and that if she hadn't lost her passport, she'd be back in England now.

'Any joy with your passport?' she asked, trying not to sound as though she couldn't wait for Cat to leave.

Hearing the hope in Leoni's voice, Cat almost laughed out loud. 'Unfortunately not. There's a postal strike on at the moment and my friend Bella doesn't even know if my forms have arrived at the passport office yet.' She pulled a face, clearly vexed. 'Everyone says the French like a good strike but, trust me, the English aren't far behind.'

Leoni nodded. Ashton had always said the same. She remembered what he had said about her being jealous of Cat. Was it true? Reminding herself that Cat was probably just as hurt by Olivier's lies and that she must feel more betrayed than anyone else, Leoni made an effort to be civil.

'I met up with someone who could produce the candles for us the other day,' she said. She took out some fragile-looking coffee cups with slender handles and placed them on the counter. 'Jerard, the owner of the store, seemed confident he can handle our orders, even if they end up being large.' Going slightly pink, she pushed the box she'd brought with her towards Cat, who was wondering why Leoni looked so keyed up. She took the candle from the box, turning it round in her hands. 'This is exquisite.' Cat inhaled the aroma and held it up to the light. 'It's luxurious and it feels expensive.' She placed it on the counter and stood back to view it. 'I'd love one of these. I wonder if pearlescent glass would look good . . . or maybe this is just perfect as it is.' She gave Leoni a sideways glance. 'If you need any help presenting this to Guy, I'd be happy to provide back-up. I mean, if I'm still here, that is.' She looked gloomy. 'At this rate, I'll still be here at Christmas.' Seeing Leoni's startled expression, she couldn't help laughing. 'Oh Leoni, I was only joking! Even the English post isn't that bad.' She picked up the candle again. 'Anyway, this is absolutely beautiful. Your Jerard certainly knows his stuff.'

'He's not *my* Jerard,' Leoni said defensively. She hesitated then realised she couldn't wait to tell someone about her date. She'd told Ashton but that didn't count; he was one of her best friends but he wasn't female. 'At least . . . not yet. We're going on a date at the weekend.'

'Really?' Cat was surprised. From everything Seraphina had told her, she had Leoni pegged as some sort of workaholic nun.

'Just for dinner.' Leoni shrugged casually, the sparkle in her eyes giving away how excited she was. 'And mainly to discuss work. It's nothing serious.'

Cat blew on her coffee. 'Sounds nice.'

Leoni picked up her coffee cup, looking almost disheartened that Cat had agreed with her.

Cat hid a smile. God, Leoni was complicated! Cat wondered at how different Leoni and Olivier were. Olivier had certainly got more than his fair share of the confident genes, Cat thought wryly. Leoni seemed far less self-assured, at least when it came to matters of the heart. And she obviously had no idea that

that lovely English guy – Ashton, was it? Cat couldn't remember – had feelings for her. Or maybe she did and she wasn't interested.

Leoni made a mental note to ask Jerard about pearlescent glass. 'So, what are your plans over the next few days?' she asked.

Cat sipped the coffee Leoni had made and did her best not to wince. It was so strong it nearly took the enamel off her teeth. 'Well, Xavier offered to take me to Grasse but I don't think we'll end up going.'

Leoni's head snapped up. 'Grasse? Why did Xavier ask you to do that?'

Cat's aquamarine eyes met Leoni's. 'I have absolutely no idea. I was hoping you could shed some light on it.'

'Me? Oh, don't ask me what makes Xavier tick. I haven't the first idea.' Leoni looked irritated.

Cat frowned. 'Well, it's not because he wants to spend time with me. He can't stand me. I think he might be following orders from above.'

'Grandmother?' Leoni felt both relieved and appalled at the same time. 'That wouldn't surprise me. Although why she'd make him do such a thing is beyond me.'

'Yes, well.' Cat put her coffee down, unable to stomach it. 'We had a fight the other day and he looked as if he wanted to throttle me so I can't imagine us going now.'

'What did you have a fight about?' Leoni was curious. Xavier had a terrible temper but he had to be pushed pretty far before he lost it.

Cat's mouth twitched. 'I . . . er . . . I asked him why he didn't make perfumes any more.'

'Ouch!' Leoni looked taken aback. 'You're brave. We all get our heads bitten off if we dare to bring that subject up.'

Cat shrugged. She wasn't scared of Xavier. 'I think I probably did it because I was so frustrated about all the secrecy and lies Olivier fed me, to be honest. I wasn't expecting Xavier

168

to yell at me, though.' Seething at the memory, Cat didn't notice that Leoni had fallen silent.

Leoni was feeling rather guilty, mainly because she understood exactly what Cat was talking about. How often had she wanted to take out her anger over Olivier on someone else? In fact, she had done the exact same thing. She had directed her fury at Cat, venting her spleen at every possible opportunity. Knowing she should apologise, Leoni also knew she wasn't big enough for that . . . at least, not yet.

'Do what I did,' she offered instead. 'Shout at Olivier's grave. Very therapeutic.'

'I already have.' Cat got up and eyed the shuddering washing machine. 'Let me know if you need a hand with that proposal. If I'm still here, I'd be happy to help.'

Leoni nodded. She knew she wouldn't be as gracious in Cat's shoes, not after everyone had been so hostile. 'If you do end up going to Grasse, keep your hands to yourself,' she joked without thinking. 'One Ducasse is quite enough, isn't it?'

'You have nothing to worry about on that front,' Cat told her stiffly. 'I don't trust your cousin one little bit.'

Leoni felt defensive on Xavier's behalf. 'Look, I know you don't care either way, but seriously, Xavier is nothing like Olivier. He's a good man, one of the best. Don't be fooled by all the women. It doesn't mean he's a cheat or a liar.'

Cat looked away. 'As you say, I don't care either way.' She left the room, her shoulders taut.

Leoni sighed. Why had she said that about Cat keeping her hands to herself? It had been totally inappropriate and she had really pissed Cat off in the process.

A few days later, Cat was staring out at the valley rather glumly. Bella had been in touch to say that the passport office had received all the paperwork but that they had a three-week backlog to clear, so she was going to have to stay put for a bit longer.

Cat was consumed with frustration. She wanted to get back home and start working again. She had hardly any money left and she was dying of boredom. She was also worried the job at the rival firm might disappear if she didn't get home soon, although Bella had assured her that the company said they would wait for her. Cat sighed. God, she needed to get away from this place.

'There you are.' Xavier appeared, his hair still wet from the shower. Wearing a simple white shirt – albeit a hand-made one with the Ducasse-Fleurie monogram discreetly stitched on to the pocket – and dark, belted jeans, he looked the epitome of European casual but his expression was inscrutable.

'About the other day . . .' Cat began. She wasn't sure what to say about it but it would be weird not to refer to it at all.

Xavier shook his head. 'Forget it. I have.'

Cat stiffened. She was glad she hadn't wasted time beating herself up about it. He clearly hadn't lost any sleep over it, despite his livid outburst.

'That trip to Grasse, how about going today?' Xavier said, shoving his hands into his pockets.

Cat gaped. Was he being serious? 'Er . . . do you think that's a good idea?'

Xavier shrugged. 'I'm sure we can manage to be civil to one another for a few days. We're both mature adults.'

That's bloody debatable, Cat thought, almost laughing as she realised how immature she sounded in her own head. 'Yes, of course we are. What time would you like to go?'

'Now sounds good to me,' Xavier replied, already striding away. 'I'll get my car and meet you out the front.'

Cat scratched her head. And people said she was impulsive. Did she really want to go anywhere with this man? He had the most awful temper and he was so touchy, he put a hormonal woman with a chocolate craving to shame. But the alternative was mooching around the château in total boredom, avoiding Delphine and Leoni. Unappealing to say the least.

Cat hastily packed a bag. She had no idea what she might need and conscious that she didn't want to look like a silly female who brought fifteen pieces of luggage for a few days, she kept it simple and packed the bare minimum.

She found Xavier leaning against an immaculate silver Aston Martin. She knew a little about cars. It was a DB9, a stunning, sporty number with a long, smooth bonnet and a sleek, curvy frame. To complete the image, Xavier, looking nonchalant and suave, was leaning against the car wearing Ray-Bans to combat the weak February sun.

Handsome twat, Cat thought irritably. She watched him put her luggage in the boot and frowned when he held the door open for her politely.

'Nice car,' she commented. 'Flashy.'

Xavier didn't rise to the bait. 'I agree. But it's lovely to drive so it's worth it.'

He drove down the driveway at speed. His phone beeped and he glanced at it before switching it off and slipping it into the pocket of his shirt.

'Your girlfriend?' Cat asked sweetly.

'Ex,' Xavier replied shortly.

Cat studied the road ahead. 'It must be difficult keeping track of them all.'

'Not really.' Xavier's expression darkened. 'My organisational skills are excellent.'

They travelled in silence until they were past Mougins. Heading in the opposite direction to the sea into some lovely countryside, Xavier surprised Cat by telling her a bit about Grasse.

'It produces something like two thirds of France's perfume aromas and food flavourings,' he informed her, lighting a cigarette after courteously checking she didn't mind him smoking. 'It's far enough away from the sea air to encourage flower farming and with its sunny climate, it's perfect,' he continued. 'It has a high altitude and there are plenty of hills and forests around it to be useful for farming.'

'I had no idea it was so close.' Cat leant out to get a better view of the pretty, medieval town in the distance. She suddenly wondered where they'd be staying and guessed Xavier must have booked a hotel.

'It's only fifteen kilometres from Cannes, actually. Molinard, Fragonard, Galimard, they all have factories here.' He pointed to a vast field that hadn't yet come into bloom. 'That's jasmine. Nearly thirty tonnes of it are harvested in Grasse every year; they even have a festival in August to celebrate it. There are floats decorated with flowers and they drive through the town soaking onlookers in scent.' He tossed his dying cigarette out into the road. 'In the old days, people used to have little jasmine fields next to their houses but most of them have been sold off over the years. In the eighties, Chanel bought their own jasmine farm which is looked after by the Mul family.'

'Chanel have their very own jasmine farm?' Cat raised her eyebrows. 'That was smart of them.'

'Wasn't it? I detest the smell of jasmine but that's just me. Most people love it.' Xavier's jaw became set for a brief moment and Cat wondered what his problem was. 'They now grow rose de Mai as well, because it's such an important component in fragrance.'

Cat inhaled gulps of fresh, Provençal air punctuated with wafts of earthy mimosa. She knew from the information she'd read that Grasse produced quantities of the bright yellow mimosa that grew at La Fleurie, as well as rose and lavender. She couldn't help expecting to see houses covered with floral, scented blooms, as if everyone in the town mixed their own special fragrances, although Cat knew that couldn't be the case.

Xavier took the turning to Grasse. 'Don't get too carried away with romantic notions about the process,' he told her wryly, reading her mind. 'The industry now relies on synthetic chemicals as well as on flowers and natural produce. Some substances, ambergris, for example, are far too expensive and rare to use naturally.'

'What's ambergris?'

'It's a strange substance found in the bellies of sperm whales.' Xavier caught sight of Cat's appalled expression. 'It sounds disgusting, I know, but it has a uniquely pungent and powerful aroma that blends well with other scents, as well as making them last longer.' He turned into a street alongside a large square signposted Place Aux Aires, with a three-tiered fountain in the centre and a busy food market. 'It's illegal to trade in ambergris now, except any that might be washed up on a beach. Amber resin is often used instead.'

They passed under an arched tunnel and, at the roundabout, Xavier took an exit marked Saint Antoine. Cat had no idea where they were going but she noticed they were driving into the heart of some olive groves.

'Do most noses come to Grasse to learn their craft?'

Xavier pointed out an impressive view of the surrounding plains and the Bay of Cannes. 'Definitely. Many noses train here because of the abundance of natural ingredients and because of the history of the place.' He pulled up outside a stunning hotel set amongst exactly the kind of beautiful flowers and shrubs she had been envisaging.

Xavier climbed out of the car. 'An English aristocrat took this place on in eighteen sixty-four and he added a new wing and landscaped the gardens.' He gestured to some lawns. 'A Frenchman took it over some years later and he hosted fashion shows and showbiz parties here. I have it on good authority that the Rolling Stones lived here for a year in the seventies. I thought you might enjoy the thought of that.'

Cat got out of the car before he could help her and gazed at the hotel with its pale blue shutters and elegant statues on the neatly clipped lawn. It was called La Basticle Saint Antoine and it was breathtaking. They checked in and Xavier disappeared to his room, saying he'd meet her downstairs for a drink. Cat made her way to a wonderful, Provençal-style room with painted wood furniture and a quilted bedspread. She freshened up and added a slick of nude lip gloss. Staring at herself in the mirror, she rubbed the lip gloss off in case Xavier thought she'd done it for him and headed downstairs. She found him on the terrace and as she drew closer, she caught a waft of another one of his aftershaves. This time, it was something warm and woody that reminded her of visits to the Far East.

'I ordered us some pastis,' Xavier said, pushing a glass of dark, transparent yellow liquid towards her. 'If you don't like it, I'll order something else, of course.' As he topped it up with water, Cat watched the liquid change colour to a soft, milky yellow. She took a large sip, choking slightly.

'Oh my God! That's so strong.'

Xavier couldn't help laughing. She looked quite funny with tears streaming down her cheeks, her nose bright red.

'Don't order anything else,' she said tartly, unamused. 'I can cope.'

'I'm sure you can,' Xavier replied.

Cat heroically swallowed the pastis, even though the aniseed taste reminded her of horrible cough medicine she'd had as a child. She admired the view of Grasse stretching out below, wondering if they could get through the trip without rowing. And maybe, she thought hopefully, by the time she got back her passport might have arrived and she could go home.

'So what do you think?' Guy asked, passing Delphine a photograph of the property in Paris as they relaxed over a glass of wine. 'Leoni thinks it will be perfect for a Paris shop and I agree. I told Ashton to go ahead and buy it.' He didn't add that he had sanctioned an unlimited budget because he knew his mother would be outraged. She would also demand to know why and Guy wasn't about to discuss Marianne with his mother. She wouldn't understand.

'Pah!' Delphine tossed the photo back without even looking at it and held her glass out for a top-up. 'I thought you didn't approve of a store in Paris, Guy?'

Looking uncomfortable, he avoided her gaze. He filled her glass with more of her favourite wine, a nutty, straw-coloured blanc de blanc from Cassis. He couldn't deny he had been opposed to the idea. But now that Marianne was back on the scene, he couldn't help feeling compelled to get involved. Guy rationalised the situation in his mind by telling himself Leoni had a point about him being stuck in the Dark Ages when it came to business.

'Don't you think we should move with the times?' he said lamely, knowing his mother had no intention of doing any such thing.

Delphine snorted. 'Absolutely not! Why have you started taking risks at a time when we really need to be stable and secure?' She hit the floor with her cane for emphasis. 'Have you thought what might happen to our cash flow if . . .'

Guy barely listened as his mother outlined every potential flaw in the plan. Having worked with Marianne all those years ago, he wasn't inclined to take risks. He had seen the effect it could have on a business and on the people working within it and he valued loyalty too much to challenge it. The competitive edge he had been known for back in Paris had been buried in favour of family loyalty and fairness.

Thank God he had met Elizabeth, Guy thought, feeling a stab in his heart. Elizabeth had restored his faith in women and she had shown him that it was possible to be successful without screwing people over. Marianne might be one of France's most accomplished businesswomen but she had no scruples whatsoever. Guy gripped the stem of his wine glass. He had charted her rise in the newspapers over the years and he had hardened his heart as they became rivals. But he had forgotten the way she had made him feel – reckless and with a strong need to compete.

Delphine stared at Guy, aware he had tuned out. 'What is the point of it?' she griped, raising her voice. 'We are a Provençal business and we have always operated locally without needing to display our wares in vulgar stores.'

'That's not true,' Guy protested. 'Without our fragrances being stocked in all the major stores in London, Paris and the rest, we wouldn't be making any profit at all!'

Delphine gave him a sour glance. 'Don't be obtuse. Frankly, I think Leoni is being allowed far too much freedom in the business. A shop in Paris and a new line in home fragrance!' She sipped her wine. 'Leoni would do far better finding herself a husband and settling down with a couple of children.'

Guy sighed.

Delphine scrutinised him. He seemed different. Making bold decisions wasn't his thing. He was reading a text he had just received and suddenly looked as if he was about to explode.

'It's the twins,' Guy growled. 'They're in trouble again.' Christ, since Elizabeth's death, his two youngest children seemed incapable of behaving.

Delphine rolled her eyes. 'What now?'

Guy stared past her. He couldn't deal with her constant disapproval right now. His mind returned to the property in Paris, and to Marianne. Feeling deeply disloyal to long-departed Elizabeth, Guy wondered if Marianne still wore clothes that made her gorgeous body look as though she had been poured into them . . .

Chapter Ten

'So this is the Fragonard factory,' Cat said, gazing up at the building. Painted a rich terracotta with the palest blue shutters, it looked more like a very grand house than a perfume factory. Located in the heart of the old town in Grasse, the historic factory was one of the oldest around and it was still a family-run enterprise.

Xavier finished his cigarette. 'It took the name of Fragonard in nineteen twenty-six as a tribute to the great painter Jean-Honoré Fragonard.'

Cat raised her eyebrows. 'I've heard of him. Gorgeous paintings.' She noticed Xavier's surprise. 'My father absolutely loved art,' she explained, 'mostly paintings by the Impressionists, but Fragonard was supposed to have had quite an influence on them. Renoir in particular.'

She took a good look around the grounds. 'What a lovely place. This would be good for an ad campaign – for a young, wild fragrance, anyway.' Cat turned to Xavier. 'You have such beautiful views at La Fleurie, you could always shoot something there, couldn't you? It's ravishing.'

'I've never really thought about it,' Xavier admitted, realising she was probably right about La Fleurie. 'Our ad campaigns have never really been that brilliant, we've always just featured the bottle of perfume and some sort of tag line. I never got involved with that side of things, to be honest.'

Cat nodded. 'Such a waste, really. You've got some great products and they could really benefit from good promotion.

Still, it's none of my business.' She looked away. She didn't want Xavier to think she was interested in Olivier's money or his share in the business.

Xavier gestured to the building. 'Shall we go in? The museum inside covers three thousand years of perfume-making.'

Cat nodded and Xavier followed her in. Her knowledge of art intrigued him. She'd obviously spent her childhood surrounded by paintings. He wanted to ask her more about her upbringing but he felt sure she wouldn't tell him. She was obviously wary of him but then, he thought, the feeling was mutual.

They walked around the first floor of the perfume factory in silence. Cat gazed at the collection of antique scent bottles in awe. They ranged from Egyptian to the nineteenth century and came in every shape and size – slender, graceful vessels, silver flacons, ones made from shells, tortoiseshell and even sharkskin.

'Lucrezia Borgia used tiny skull-shaped pomanders which she filled with pungent musk,' Xavier informed Cat. 'Some pomanders, engraved with silver and worn round the neck, came apart like orange segments. They were used to ward off evil, by all accounts.' He couldn't resist telling her more. 'Perfume bottles have historically been objects of great beauty. They were supposed to signify the allure of the perfume contained within. Art Nouveau Lalique bottles emerged in the nineteenth century but you can't get them any more. François Coty asked Lalique to design a selection of bottles for him, you know.'

Cat was fascinated. 'They're like ornaments. They're so lovely, it's hard to believe they have a practical purpose.'

Xavier agreed, casually giving her a potted history of glass-making by the Romans and perfume decanters inspired by Renaissance art. He pointed out elaborate, moulded stoppers shaped like flowers and birds before moving on to the collection of perfume equipment and apparatus.

'Wow, if only I'd seen all of this when I did that perfume campaign a few years back,' Cat said. 'I would have had so many ideas for perfume bottles and God knows what else if I'd seen all this first.'

Xavier frowned. 'Such as?'

Cat allowed herself to indulge. 'If I was designing a perfume bottle, for example, I'd probably come up with something heart-shaped . . . no, maybe not.' She grabbed a brochure and started sketching on the back of it. 'Something like this . . . more teardrop-shaped. If it was made in the right way, it would be really lovely to hold in your hand. See?' She held the sketch up.

Xavier was impressed with both her drawing skills and her creativity but he said nothing.

Cat added some detail to the bottle and sketched out the stopper. 'Shimmery glass, something that would really catch the light. A modern bottle but with a vintage feel, something that would look incredible on a dressing table.'

Xavier's eyes met hers briefly. 'I see. And would you change the Ducasse colour scheme?' Discreetly, he pocketed the sketch. He had no idea what his grandmother would think of Cat's ideas but he was doing as he had promised.

Surprised he had even asked her such a question, Cat contemplated the lilac and white packaging the Ducasse perfumes were famous for. 'I like the lilac but it feels a little old fashioned, if you really want to know. I'd have to think about it but I reckon you could update it without completely changing the brand. Are you thinking of rebranding?'

'Not really.' Xavier was offhand.

'Because I was going to say that it's sometimes better to introduce what's called a sub-brand rather than a whole new one, something that is still synonymous with the original but targets a younger market.' Xavier was staring at her intently and Cat fell silent. His eyes gave nothing away.

'Shall we move on?' he said.

He started to talk about the perfume-making process. His voice became animated as he described the early technique of distillation, which used steam to capture essential oils, and absorption. 'This involves animal fat naturally absorbing odours,' he added. Without going into too much detail, he touched on the cost-effective use of carbon dioxide extraction then moved on to the origin of materials used in perfume making.

'As I mentioned on the way here, most ingredients originating from an animal have now been replaced by synthetic materials, to protect the animals. Ambergris, musk, that sort of thing.' Xavier noticed distractedly how bright Cat's aquamarine eyes became when she was stimulated. 'Anyway, synthetic products are totally acceptable now in the process of scent creation. Lilac, lily of the valley – these are not natural aromas. Veltol is a newly discovered molecule which smells just like caramel. The point is, when synthetics are blended with natural flowers and plants, the results can be magnificent. Rose, jasmine, tuberose, orange blossom, lavender, mimosa, aromatic herbs such as rosemary, thyme, mint and basil.'

'What about citrusy aromas?' Cat couldn't help asking.

Xavier shrugged. 'Of course. Lemon, orange, mandarin, even grapefruit are popular ingredients. So are spices and seeds like nutmeg and pepper, as well as leaves and roots, woods and resins. Personally, I love sandalwood and cinnamon, especially for aftershave.'

'Like yours?' Cat blurted out before she could stop herself. She felt her cheeks go pink. Christ, the last thing she wanted him to think was that she'd noticed his aftershave. 'It's . . . quite strong,' she added lamely, adding a slight criticism so he didn't think she was being flirtatious in any way. 'You know, pungent.'

Xavier almost smiled. 'Pungent? Oh dear, I'll have to address that. I mix my own aftershave, we don't sell it commercially.' She had a fairly good nose, he noted in surprise. She had

180

recognised two of the ingredients in his aftershave, which was unusual for someone not used to picking out single aromas from a blend. But Xavier was certain his aftershave wasn't remotely strong or pungent so he felt irked that she had criticised it.

'So, the creation of a scent, is it a science or is it creativity?' Cat asked as they headed outside into the pale sunshine.

'It's both. Imagination and memories also play a part.'

'Memories?'

'You mentioned it yourself at the family meeting,' Xavier reminded her as they took a seat together awkwardly. 'Suntan lotion or coconut aromas transport us back to that beautiful beach and memories of the fun we had . . . the sex . . .' His eyes slid to meet hers but slid away just as quickly. 'So, in my opinion, fragrance creation is about both the science of mixing aromas and the imagination needed to re-create those memories and stir the senses.'

Cat wondered if he was laughing at her. 'You must have been quite an asset to your family,' she commented coolly. 'They must be devastated that you're no longer part of the process.'

His jaw tight, Xavier gazed at her. 'I suppose they must be. Shall we head into the old town?'

He was politeness itself, pointing out various pretty shops and stalls; if she had annoyed him, he didn't show it.

'Oh, look at that lovely lavender,' she said, admiring a faded bunch on a stall. Tied with a Provençal-style blue and white ribbon, it was really sweet. She took out her purse to buy it. She was surprised when Xavier got there first. He handed some euros over and presented it to her with a careless wave of his hand.

'Please . . . take it.'

Cat accepted the lavender with slightly bad grace. She sniffed it, thinking the aroma would always remind her of the south of France. And probably of Olivier, she thought, putting it into her bag with a pang. She nodded when Xavier suggested coffee and they took seats outside in the pretty square.

'So what's the best perfume ever created?' Cat asked, reverting to safe territory to keep the peace. 'Seriously, what's the most gorgeous scent in the world?'

Xavier grinned. 'Well, there's a question!' He considered. 'There are so many, it's impossible to choose. Chanel No. 5, of course. Shalimar has its place too. Did you know it was supposed to have been created when Jaques Guerlain accidentally tipped vanilla essence into Jicky?'

'That's a great story but those fragrances are so old fashioned,' Cat said, rather unnerved by Xavier's sudden grin. He looked totally different when he smiled, handsome and rather charming. She steeled herself.

'Old fashioned?' Xavier looked outraged. 'How can you say that? They're classics, the star players of their time. They're the fragrances that set the bar for the newer ones out there. Did you know that many are just replicas of a bygone era?'

'Well, no, I didn't but—'

'Of course there are some wonderful new fragrances – Thierry Mugler's Angel, Jo Malone's Lime, Basil and Mandarin . . .'

Cat's head snapped up. 'I wear that!'

'I know.' Xavier looked sheepish for a second, obviously loath to admit he admired the fragrance she wore, let alone that he had noticed it. 'It's a good choice.' He relaxed slightly. 'Do you think we sound slightly ridiculous, debating such an issue?'

Cat's mouth twitched. 'I guess so.' She laughed. 'My mother always said I was argumentative. Did yours say the same about you?'

Xavier's expression became sober. 'She did. But we had a lot in common too. After a moment's silence he continued. "Noses" are essentially artistic and nostalgic by nature. They enjoy music or art or literature. They tend to study chemistry as it's a good basis for the technical side to perfume creation but deep down they lean towards the arts. I did and so did my mother – we both loved paintings.'

'Do certain smells remind you of her?' Cat sipped her coffee. The tension felt as if it might have been broken between them but she was aware she was on delicate ground discussing Elizabeth. As the twins had mentioned, no one ever seemed to talk about her.

Xavier toyed with his coffee cup. 'Ocean smells, pine forests . . . iris really reminds me of her. Orris root is used in make-up and many perfumes, you see. It is reminiscent of violets but when distilled into an essential oil, its fragrance is heavy and woody.' He stared past Cat, preoccupied. 'It makes me think of chatting to my mother while she put her make-up on. It's . . . both evocative and painful for me.'

'You miss her a great deal,' Cat stated.

Xavier rubbed his thumb along his coffee cup, his dark eyes downcast. 'More than I can say. She was a beautiful woman but she was a real mother to me too. She taught me so many things.' Stopping abruptly, he wondered what the hell he was doing telling Olivier's widow something so meaningful.

Not noticing the shutters going down behind Xavier's eyes, Cat nodded numbly. She knew exactly what he meant. Sometimes she missed her own mother so much, it hurt. It was about always having someone there when you needed them, that unconditional love that only a mother could provide.

'Wouldn't your mother want you to carry on her legacy?' Cat asked out of the blue. She knew she was on dangerous territory but she really wanted to know the answer.

Xavier's eyes flashed. 'It's not as simple as that,' he returned angrily, throwing some cash on the table. 'It wasn't just my mother's death that destroyed my love of perfume.' He stood up. 'There was something else, *someone* else who changed everything but I hate talking about it. Shall we go?'

Smarting at his anger, Cat followed Xavier back to the car, struggling to keep up with his strong strides. 'I'm sorry if I said the wrong thing. I just think it would be amazing if you created another perfume. Don't bite my head off; I'm just saying.'

Xavier's phone rang. He took it out and frowned. 'No, it's not one of my many girlfriends,' he informed Cat drily. 'It's my grandmother.' Leaning against his Aston Martin, he took the call.

Seraphina returned to school through a side entrance and headed to the unisex bathrooms nearby. Catching sight of her reflection in one of the mirrors hanging over a neat row of white sinks, she gasped. Her hair, originally in a sleek ponytail, was loose and dishevelled and her mouth resembled a crushed strawberry because her lipstick had been kissed off so messily. Her cream silk shirt was buttoned up the wrong way and her jeans were so low-slung, her lace thong was showing.

Seraphina urgently raked her fingers through her hair in an attempt to tame it. Rubbing her mouth with the back of her hand and desperately re-buttoning her shirt before anyone saw her, she jumped as Max strolled in. Dressed in black jeans and a black T-shirt with a marijuana leaf on the front, his own hair was all over the place.

He scowled. 'Been out with the boyfriend again?'

Seraphina tried to look nonchalant, despite her churning stomach. 'Maybe.'

'Well, you missed English, Maths and Art, so you must have been somewhere good.' Max bit his fingernails. 'Whoever he is, he doesn't give a shit about your education, does he?'

She pulled her jeans up discreetly, not really able to disagree with her twin. She'd been thinking the same thing herself recently. But then, her boyfriend worked strange hours so she really didn't have too much choice when it came to arranging their dates.

'Did you have fun?' Max asked belligerently.

Seraphina chewed her lip. Fun? She wasn't sure if she would describe her dates as 'fun'. Going out with someone so much older had seemed exciting at first; she had imagined being taken out to classy places, eating out in elegant restaurants, dancing, perhaps . . . Eliza Doolittle to her very own Professor Higgins, Seraphina thought with a smile as she remembered her mother's favourite novel.

But the reality was very different. There was the odd elegant restaurant and classy bar but there was also a lot of making out . . . and a fair amount of pressure to go all the way. Seraphina stared back at her reflection, feeling gauche and unsophisticated. Still a virgin, the thought of sleeping with someone was both thrilling and terrifying and she was only just managing to hold her boyfriend at arm's length. She felt totally out of control and she didn't have a clue what to do about it.

But I can't hold him off forever, Seraphina fretted, coaxing her hair back into a ponytail. A sob caught in her throat. She wished her mother was still here so she could talk to her about it. She couldn't exactly discuss such things with her father. Imagine the look on his face if she asked him about sex!

Turning to Max, Seraphina wondered if she should confide in him. They rarely had secrets from one another, so he was the natural person for her to turn to.

'I've got this . . .' Noticing his distant expression, Seraphina faltered. Staring past her, Max was lost in thought. She had no idea what was on his mind but she sensed that now wasn't the time to dump her problems on him. She didn't want to worry him when he seemed to have the weight of the world on his shoulders.

'Sorry, what?' Snapping to attention, Max straightened and frowned at her.

'Nothing.' Seraphina shook her head and picked up her bag. 'Haven't we got another lesson?'

As Max sloped off, Seraphina pushed down her worries and followed him.

Hosting a cocktail party at La Fleurie the following day for some of her more influential friends, Delphine was in her element. Yves was due to visit again soon with an update. She contentedly sipped her Black Rose cocktail, a revival of an old-time Parisian classic made with French vermouth and blackberry cordial. She had no idea what she was expecting Yves to find but she felt certain there had to be a loophole somewhere that would remove Cat Hayes from their lives completely. The thought filled her with happiness and she smiled benevolently at her affluent friends. An eclectic group of rich wives sporting handmade shoes and husbands and ex-husbands of varying importance, they were rather like a well-shod mafia; they shot victims down without preamble and thought nothing of turning on their own if need be.

'What a wonderful idea to celebrate the launch of Rose-Nymphea,' announced Delphine's good friend Cybille, the one who had recommended Yves. 'Ducasse-Fleurie's signature scent, an absolute classic, in my view,' she added in a way that suggested she was bestowing some sort of honour. She lit a cigarette airily, forgetting to ask if she was allowed to smoke inside the château.

'Isn't it?' Delphine replied, pleased, and prepared to let Cybille off for smoking indoors. 'My little notion for a celebration is just what the family needs after everything we've been through.'

Her friends murmured their sympathies.

Guy, unaware there was a cocktail party in progress, strolled in to help himself to a glass of wine and found himself surrounded by fluttering old ladies. He wished he'd stayed in his office and cringed as all the perfumed geriatrics flocked round him in delight.

'Oh, Guy, how lovely to see you again!'

'It's been so long!'

'How are you managing after Olivier's death?'

Guy smiled with an effort. 'I'm very well, thank you, ladies. I had no idea you were all here, actually. Do forgive me for intruding.' He attempted to leave and found he couldn't without being rude.

'Don't be silly,' said Cybille. 'Delphine was just telling us all about her idea to celebrate Rose-Nymphea.'

Guy shot his mother a look. So she was taking credit for that now, was she? He shook his head at her in mock disapproval.

'I do so love Rose-Nymphea,' commented Cosette, the wife of the owner of one of France's largest chain of department stores. 'It's always been my scent of choice.'

Delphine frowned, well aware that Cosette had worn Miss Dior for years. A singularly inappropriate fragrance for her aged friend, Delphine felt; it was a timeless but rather powdery chypre, not something Cosette could pull off at all. Delphine also thought her friend was letting the side down by being so overweight. She watched Cosette tucking in to the miniature but highly fattening pastries that were doing the rounds and frowned. All the other women knew they were just for show.

Cybille cocked her head one side astutely, considering Delphine. 'Are there any new scents planned?' she asked in a sweet voice, knowing it was a thorn in Delphine's side that no new fragrances had been created since Elizabeth's death. 'It would be so lovely to report back to society that Ducasse-Fleurie has created something original.'

Guy raised his glass cheerily at Delphine. How was she going to get out of that one?

'Actually, I think there might be a few little surprises on the horizon,' Delphine hinted coyly.

'Really? How thrilling!' Cybille declared, already taking her small, expensive-looking phone out of her pocket.

Guy was alarmed. 'Mother, what are you doing?' he asked,

taking her to one side. If she wasn't careful, she would sabotage herself – and the family business.

Delphine threw him a triumphant glance. 'I spoke to Xavier yesterday and I heard the passion in his voice. He's all set to create a new fragrance, I just know it!'

Guy scoffed. The only thing that got his elder son's juices flowing these days were gorgeous women. Guy thought it was far more likely Xavier's new-found passion was for the pretty English girl he was spending time with, not a renewed vigour for blending aromas.

'Mark my words, Guy,' Delphine told him, supremely confident. 'We will have a new scent to promote before the year is out.'

Guy shook his head. 'It can take two years to create a new fragrance, five years, in some cases.'

Delphine dismissed his comment with a wave of her hand. 'Xavier has many half-started formulas, probably even some scents that are near completion. He just needs something to kick-start him and get him back in the lab.'

Guy stared at her. How did she know such things about his son when he didn't have the first idea? And why was she so sure Xavier was about to get working again?

Guy's scepticism turned to concern. What games was his mother playing with Xavier?

'So what has been your favourite moment so far?' the interviewer asked, practically falling into Angelique's gravity-defying cleavage.

Angelique considered, leaning forward and affording him an even better view. In his sixties, Robert Duland was one of the biggest talk show hosts in France and she was overjoyed to be on his show because of the profile it would afford her.

'Well, Robert,' she said with a smile, 'I think the film I've just finished is one of my favourites. It's so raw . . . so sexual.'

'Is that so?' Robert could barely keep his groin under control. If she leant any further forward, he was certain he was going to get a first-hand glimpse of her raspberry-pink nipples. Under her cream silk dress, it was obvious she wasn't wearing a bra and Robert could barely concentrate on his notes.

He cleared his throat and made an effort to get the interview moving. It was live and being watched by millions and if his boss didn't stop screeching in his ear . . . 'Do you feel you can relate to the character you play in this movie?'

Angelique let out a throaty laugh and covered his hand with hers. 'Oh, Robert, not really. No man has ever left me for another man! But you never know.' Batting her eyelashes coquettishly, she gave him a ripe smile. Inside, she was aching with boredom. She was so fed up with portraying and talking about sordid sexual issues. It was about time people respected her.

'I can't imagine that ever happening,' he told her gallantly, flattered she hadn't let go of his hand. 'And what's on the horizon for you now?'

'Who knows?' Angelique finally let go of his hand but she did so with mock reluctance. She crossed her legs slowly, watching as he salivated. 'Offers are coming in all the time, of course, but I'm feeling the need to branch out a little . . . to show my audience something different.'

Robert wondered if she was wearing any knickers and his penis jerked at the thought. 'I'm sure we'll all look forward to whatever you decide to do next,' he said, hoping she would come for a drink with him after the show.

'Thank you so much, Robert,' she simpered. 'You're very kind.' Angelique tossed her blond hair over her shoulder and sparkled at the audience as the cameras continued to roll. As soon as they shut down, her expression changed and she stood up.

'Do you fancy a drink?' Robert said, his balls aching with lust. 'Or . . . something else?'

'No thank you,' she snapped dismissively. 'I do not fancy a drink or "something else".'

Stalking off, Angelique left Robert scarlet in the face and with an erection he didn't quite know what to do with.

'What a pervert!' Angelique sniped, taking refuge in her dressing room.

'You've had a few calls from your agent about some Hollywood films,' her assistant Celine said. 'Isn't that exciting?' She handed Angelique a note with some carefully written messages attached and consulted her BlackBerry again. 'And Delphine Ducasse called. Several times in fact.'

'Delphine Ducasse? Really? How very interesting.'

'I have no idea who she is,' Celine was saying. 'Some deranged fan probably but I told her you wouldn't be calling her back anytime soon.'

'You did what!' Angelique leapt out of her chair and snatched Celine's BlackBerry from her, her dress slipping off her shoulder. 'You don't make decisions like that for me, do you understand? Do that again and you're fired.'

Celine nearly burst into tears. At that moment Angelique's agent arrived. Mason Tyrone was an American, a big man with a hooked nose. He favoured sharply tailored, pinstripe suits and his neck was thickset, like a rugby-player's. Mason lived in Paris because he liked it and in Los Angeles for business – he travelled between the two constantly. Angelique had chosen him partly for his reputation for ferocious negotiating and also because of her aspirations to break America one day.

'What's going on?' he asked Angelique as Celine made herself scarce. His voice was loud and rasping.

Angelique gave him a withering glance, never sure whether she found him repulsive or disturbingly sexual. She had often wondered if he was gay as he seemed so unmoved by her but he was so manly and butch, she couldn't imagine he was anything but heterosexual.

'My assistant is making decisions for me and as I don't even let you do that, you can understand why I'm annoyed.'

Mason's eyes darkened and he bristled at her rudeness. Angelique might be sexy but she was a bitch. He'd love to tell his most lucrative client where to go, but he knew which side his bread was buttered on. 'Of course. I'm sure she won't do it again. What decision did she make for you, out of interest?'

'She told a very good friend of mine not to call me,' Angelique replied tersely. Delphine Ducasse wasn't a good friend but she couldn't really explain the nature of her relationship with her to someone like Mason, who was nothing more than a brute in a suit.

Angelique couldn't help wondering why someone with Delphine's influence liked her. Women usually despised her, especially ones of Delphine's age. Although perhaps older women admired her for her success. Delphine obviously didn't know the full story from her time in Provence, that much was obvious, but then only one person did. And Angelique was pretty sure he wasn't about to tell. Nor was she going to bring it up and ruin everything.

Angelique started to undress. 'I'm changing my clothes,' she pointed out deliberately to Mason. God, the man was a Neanderthal!

Mason folded his arms. 'So what? I have business to discuss and no time to waste. Other men might find you irresistible but I think I'll cope.'

Angelique pulled her dress from her shoulders and let it fall to the floor. Standing in nothing but her heels and a pair of virginal-looking, cream silk French knickers, she regarded Mason coolly, her nipples tightening as she felt his eyes on her.

Mason's expression remained blank, however. 'As I said, I have some business to discuss. I've heard rumours of a big Hollywood film and some of the bosses at Paramount want to talk to you.'

'Really? What do they need? The token French actress who'll get her clothes off?' Furious that Mason found her so unappealing, Angelique hooked her thumbs into the edge of her French knickers and insolently shimmied out of them.

Mason's expression was impassive. 'So what if they do? It'd be madness to turn it down.'

Kicking her knickers away, Angelique gave Mason an unadulterated view of her enviably flat stomach and the thin strip of hair she tolerated because her films tended to demand some show of adulthood. Turning away from him and exposing her smooth buttocks, Angelique wriggled into a bottle-green jersey dress.

'And since when have you cared about showing your tits?' Mason demanded in a raspy voice. 'You're hardly the shy and retiring type.'

Angelique dismissed him with a flap of her hand. 'Oh, what would you know about it, Mason? You have no idea what I want out of my career. I should fire you, really.'

Mason rolled his eyes. 'No one else would put up with your shit. And I know exactly what you want from your career – you want to be taken seriously. But stripping off is what you do.' He shrugged. 'You have a good body and you use it. End of. So what's the problem with getting your tits out in Hollywood? No one said you had to show your fucking bush which is an improvement on what you get up to here.'

Angelique flushed. God, the man riled her! 'I'm just saying that it doesn't have to be written into every contract I get given. Maybe I'm fed up with it. Maybe I want to take a different direction.' She gazed at her reflection, touching a hand to her perfectly coiffed hair. 'How about Angelique, the brand? How does that sound to you?'

'Arrogant,' Mason barked in response. 'Do you really think people want that? What did you have in mind? Clothes by Angelique? Sex toys, perhaps?'

Angelique almost hurled a bottle of champagne at him. Who did Mason think he was? He was supposed to have her best interests at heart. Instead he was like a one-man assassination crew, determined to bring her down.

Mason's expression softened slightly. 'It's Hollywood, Angelique. The big time. Maybe you'd have to do some nudity once or twice but so what? It didn't kill Halle Berry's career, and it won't kill yours.'

It was certainly tempting, and she had wanted to break America for so long. But the timing was all wrong. She couldn't risk screwing up her opportunity with the Ducasse family, not when it might result in her being set for life.

'I need to make a call in private,' Angelique snapped. 'Please can you fuck off, as you vulgar Americans say?'

'You've got a cheek calling *me* vulgar,' Mason growled. But he left her to it.

Angelique dialled quickly. 'Delphine! How lovely to hear from you,' she purred. 'Yes, I have five minutes. Please go ahead.' Listening intently, her mouth curved into a smile as Delphine outlined her proposal.

She had been desperately trying to think of a way to get back into the Ducasse family fold and now Delphine Ducasse, the woman who had, mysteriously, always approved of her, had solved the problem for her.

'I'd love to,' she told Delphine, agreeing instantly. 'Yes, really. I can't wait.' She finished the call and handed the BlackBerry back to a trembling Celine who had reappeared. Angelique could tell her assistant was worrying about losing her job.

'You are forgiven,' Angelique told her curtly, 'but don't ever do that again.'

So grateful she was moved to tears again, Celine shook her head. 'I won't.' She wouldn't; all her friends envied her for her spectacular job. 'Um . . . did you tell Mason you'd start the Hollywood talks?'

Angelique shook her head. 'No. I'll be in the south of France for the foreseeable future.'

'The south of France?' Celine looked bemused.

'That's right. Now get me a glass of Veuve Clicquot.' Angelique crossed her legs and stared into the distance. It had been a long time since she'd been at La Fleurie and she could barely wait to get back. It didn't matter what offers she'd had from across the pond; there were more important things at stake. How lucky that Delphine had phoned when she did.

Chapter Eleven

Leoni headed into the restaurant to meet Jerard. She liked his choice; it was cosy but smart. She was due to fly to Paris the following morning, the flight booked purposefully so she had a good excuse to get home at the end of the night. It was important not to let Jerard think she was a pushover.

Wearing a classic black Dior dress with a scooped neck and a low back, Leoni felt sexy for the first time in ages. She wore high heels and sheer black stockings but she kept her jewellery chunky so she looked on-trend and chic. Leoni had debated wearing contacts but decided not to bother; she didn't want to look as though she'd tried too hard. She'd also decided against taking a car so she could drive herself – another way to ensure she didn't get too drunk and make a fool of herself.

Jerard was sitting at the bar inside.

'Leoni!' He greeted her with a warm kiss on each cheek. 'I'm starving. Shall we order straightaway?'

She nodded. If only her heart would stop beating at a hundred miles an hour. Leoni eyed Jerard as he took his seat opposite her at the table. He was dressed relatively casually in a white shirt with no tie and a pair of jeans but he looked well turned out.

And quite handsome, Leoni thought. 'I half expected your assistant to be tending to your needs,' she said, feeling a bit light headed. 'You seem so close.' Leoni kicked herself. How obvious.

Jerard shook his head. 'Suzanne is very pretty but she's not my type. I like a woman who's intelligent, businesslike *and* sexy.' He gave her a pointed glance.

Leoni went slightly pink and lowered her head to study the menu.

'The châteaubriand is fantastic and so are the mussels,' Jerard told her, giving her a wide smile.

'I'll have the sea bass,' Leoni told the waiter, noticing that Jerard had very nice blue eyes. Not the piercing blue of Ashton's but they were lovely. She frowned. Why had she suddenly thought of Ashton?

Jerard ordered a good bottle of red and when they both had full glasses, he raised his across the table. 'To . . . business,' he said, his eyes twinkling at her.

'To business,' she agreed, chinking her glass. 'What's that?' she asked curiously, indicating a file Jerard had brought to the table.

'Just some ideas for the designs.' He smiled, tugging some paperwork out. 'That's what we're here to discuss, isn't it?'

'Er . . . yes.' Leoni felt a thud of disappointment. Of course Jerard had said that it was essentially a business meeting but she had spent all week telling herself it was a date. Now she felt foolish.

Jerard's mouth twitched. 'It's just some design ideas, Leoni,' he said softly. 'And then I thought we could get down to the more serious business I had in mind for tonight.'

Leoni raised her eyes to his. 'What's that?'

'Getting to know one another,' he said.

The following morning, Leoni awoke early, hugging herself. The evening with Jerard had been lovely. He had made her laugh, he had complimented her and over a mouth-watering pot-au-chocolat for two, they had also discussed the candle deal in more detail. He had walked her to her car where he had put his arms round her waist and pulled her in for a slow kiss, one that had left her slightly breathless and eager for more. With obvious regret, he had told her he had an important meeting in the morning and wishing her a good trip to Paris, he had waved her off. It had been perfect . . . romantic, sexy without being over the top and deliciously flattering. Leoni really felt as though she was being swept off her feet. Finally, after all her pointless longing for Ashton, it was her turn to be happy.

She had a hurried but steaming hot shower to revive herself after the late night and she put on the rather masculine-looking camel Celine trouser suit she'd bought recently, teamed with a black silk blouse with a pussycat bow. Not sure what Ashton had in mind for their Paris trip, Leoni added just one dress to her suitcase and one pair of high heels. She headed downstairs to collect her briefcase. Her car was already waiting outside on the gravel driveway and, about to leave, she was surprised to see Delphine emerging from the salon.

'Grandmother! You're up early.'

'I'm always up early,' Delphine returned snippily, gripping her cane with tense knuckles. She eyed Leoni's suitcase. 'So, you're off to Paris, I see. To view this shop, no doubt.'

Leoni nodded, checking she had her wallet and mobile. 'Have you seen the plans? Ashton has some wonderful ideas to turn it into a boutique-style store with elegant fittings and lots of personal touches.'

'Yes, I've seen the plans.' Delphine shifted her weight to the other hip, wincing slightly. 'I must say, I'm surprised Guy has given you the go-ahead.'

Leoni glanced at her. So her uncle hadn't mentioned Marianne – not surprisingly.

'You were late last night,' Delphine commented as Leoni headed towards the door. 'You weren't actually out on a date, were you?'

Leoni turned scarlet. What on earth did it have to do with her grandmother?! 'That's . . . that's none of your business,' she stuttered, furious at being questioned like a teenager.

Delphine smiled smugly. 'Ah, I thought so. Good. It's about time you settled down and made someone a good wife.'

Leoni seethed. 'Really? Like you, you mean?' Her grandmother's eyes narrowed irritably. 'I seem to remember that you married Grandfather but somehow still found time to be involved in Ducasse-Fleurie.'

Delphine's cheeks coloured delicately. 'I admit I have dabbled with the business now and again over the years, but my marriage always came first.'

Leoni spluttered. 'Did it? Throughout my childhood, Grandmother, all I remember is you talking about perfume – the new fragrances that were being created and the buzz it gave you when the business was doing well.' She felt her own cheeks reddening and she looked away. 'It was *your* passion that got me so fired up in the first place!'

Delphine was taken aback. She hadn't known she had been any kind of inspiration to her granddaughter. 'That's flattering, Leoni, but I maintain that my marriage was always the most important thing in life. My father taught me that family was everything. Business is obviously vital but family, relationships, love, these things matter more than anything.'

Meeting Delphine's clear, hazel eyes, Leoni saw the truth behind them. It astonished her; her grandmother had always been a successful businesswoman and Leoni had never really considered where Delphine had placed Ducasse-Fleurie in relation to the other aspects of her life.

'You think I'm saying all this just to give you a hard time?' Delphine said gently, reaching out to take Leoni's arm.

Leoni looked down at her grandmother's softly wrinkled hand on her arm and felt thoroughly unnerved by this exchange.

Delphine shook her head. 'Trust me, Leoni. Business . . . success . . . they will get the blood pumping round your body like nothing else. Well, almost nothing else.' Her eyes glinted humorously. 'But when all is said and done, spreadsheets won't keep you warm at night. And they certainly won't be there for you in times of trouble. The exact opposite, if anything. Life is about balance and love has a far more enduring presence than business ever will.' Nodding sagely, she let go of Leoni's arm.

Leoni stared at her. Since when had her grandmother ever been this frank with her? 'I . . . I have a flight to catch,' she muttered.

'Indeed.' Delphine squared her shoulders. 'Do give my love to Ashton, won't you? Dear boy . . . I have such a lot of time for him. Don't you?'

'Er, yes, of course.' Bemused, Leoni headed outside to her waiting car.

Watching Seraphina skiving off yet another lesson, Max couldn't help feeling concerned about his sister. Seraphina hadn't missed a single lesson before she met this boyfriend of hers and her grades were dropping alarmingly. Still, he was hardly a paragon of virtue himself. A recent incident had involved him almost burning down the library whilst smoking a sneaky joint. Feeling an uncharacteristic flash of guilt, Max had left an anonymous donation of two thousand euros in a copy of Albert Camus' *L'Étranger* on the library desk to pay for it. But, Seraphina was pushing her luck, in his opinion.

'What are you looking at?'

Max turned to find Madeleine Lombard behind him. She was wearing a pretty floral top with jeans, her black velvet jacket over the top and a cute pair of ballet pumps. He stared at her impatiently. Why did she keep hanging around him? She was like his shadow at the moment.

'Nothing,' he snapped curtly. Madeleine was rather pretty, he realised. She had long brown hair, nothing special but it was clean-looking and shiny, and she had green eyes that seemed somehow kind. She looked through the window.

'Oh, I see. Seraphina's sneaking out again.'

'You can't say anything,' Max told her fiercely, walking away.

'I wouldn't dream of it.' Madeleine looked shocked as she hurried to catch up with him. 'Why would I do something like that?'

Max shrugged. Suddenly irritated by her presence, he turned to face her. 'I don't know if I've given you the wrong impression but I'm not interested in a relationship, all right? We're just friends.' He started walking again but turned slightly, almost as if inviting her to accompany him.

Madeleine looked pained but she continued to walk alongside him. She was happy to spend time with him in whatever capacity he allowed her to. She followed him to the college stables and watched him saddling up one of the chestnut mares.

'Want to come?' he offered on the spur of the moment.

She didn't need asking twice. Borrowing a pair of riding boots from one of the grooms, she was soon sitting astride a beautiful ebony stallion, looking very much at home. They cantered across the college grounds, ducking beneath trees and darting between them. As he always did when he rode, Max felt his anxieties melting away. He glanced at Madeleine, impressed by her skills as a rider. Vero could barely identify one end of a horse from another and he found it irksome.

'Thanks for saving my skin when the fire alarm went off,' he said gruffly as they pulled up by some trees. He slid off his horse and helped Madeleine down. Her eyes were bright from the ride and she shrugged.

'Any time. I was worried you'd get kicked out.'

Max pulled up some grass. 'Me too. My father would go ballistic. He's such a stickler for rules.' He said the words bitterly and kicked the grass with his boot. Madeleine put a calming hand on his arm. Impulsively, Max pulled her down on to him. He lost himself in the softness of her lips on his and his heart pounded in his chest. Abruptly, he pulled away. He didn't want to care for her – he didn't want to care for anyone. Pushing her away roughly, he leapt on to his horse. Glancing down at Madeleine, he saw how upset she was.

'It's all right,' she told him as she got to her feet and dusted herself down. 'You don't need to say it. We're just friends, nothing more.'

Sincerely regretting what had happened but having no idea how to fix it, Max kicked the flanks of his horse and cantered away, leaving a crestfallen and very confused Madeleine behind.

A week later, a restless Delphine summoned Yves to her office once more. She hadn't heard from him for days and he had proved hard to get hold of, so she had left a brusque message on his answerphone, demanding a breakfast meeting at 7 a.m., making it clear that she would terminate his contract with immediate effect if he didn't show up.

'Ah, there you are, Monsieur Giraud,' she said briskly as he appeared in the doorway of the breakfast salon. The shiny suit he was wearing today made him look like a cheap gangster. Delphine swept an arm grandly towards a chair.

Yves, looking slightly sweaty around the collar, took the proffered chair gratefully. He smoothed his already seal-like hair back with the palm of his hand. 'I must apologise for not responding to your messages. I have been incredibly busy.'

'Working on my case, I hope,' Delphine interjected sharply.

'Oh, yes.' Yves nodded as he accepted the cup of coffee she had poured him. He glanced outside, enjoying the view of the splendid swimming pool with its rippling turquoise water and sloping, mosaic-covered steps. 'What a marvellous pool . . . so inviting. Even in this weather, it's just asking for someone to take a quick dip, isn't it?'

Delphine scrutinised him. In her opinion, Yves was far too

interested in La Fleurie; every time he visited, his admiring eyes would wander around the property as if he were sizing it up and giving it a mental valuation.

'So, what has been distracting you to such an extent that you were unable to return my calls, Monsieur Giraud?'

Yves cleared his throat uncomfortably, wondering how he could wriggle out of the situation.

Delphine watched him, growing more impatient by the minute. He looked as though he was playing for time and that could only mean one thing – he had nothing to tell her. In which case, what the hell had he been up to all this time? Delphine was beginning to regret hiring him. She couldn't understand it; her good friend, Cybille Thibault, had spoken so highly of him, describing him as 'a veritable shark' when it came to detecting, yet apart from their initial meeting some weeks back, Yves had appeared to be little more than a bumbling, incompetent fool. Unless he had a very good reason for his apparent ineptitude, Delphine planned to sack him on the spot.

Yves laced his fingers together. 'The marriage between your grandson and Miss Hayes is definitely legal, and I can find nothing to discredit her. But maybe there is something else we can do to ensure she does not remain here at La Fleurie?'

Delphine's eyes lit up. 'Such as?'

Yves shrugged. 'Perhaps I can do some digging here for a while. See if there is anything I can find out about Olivier and his life which would explain why he married her so suddenly. Did she know something about him, I wonder?'

'Blackmail?' Delphine uttered the word distastefully. 'Surely not. Miss Hayes is an annoying inconvenience but I'm not sure blackmail is her style.'

'Ah, but can you be certain?'

Delphine hesitated. She couldn't help thinking Yves was clutching at straws. Cat Hayes, as much as she hated to admit it, seemed like a pleasant enough girl and Delphine really couldn't imagine her in the role of blackmailer. Still, Olivier was worth an awful lot of money . . .

'Very well,' she said decisively, giving Yves a cold stare. 'No one, and I mean *no one*, must know what you are doing here. You must be discretion itself while you go about your business.'

Yves nodded, getting to his feet. 'No one will even know I'm here,' he assured her.

Delphine felt a moment of disquiet. The look in Yves' eyes had seemed almost triumphant. She didn't like the man. Delphine wished for the hundredth time that Olivier hadn't died. Or if he was going to, she thought resentfully, he might at least have done it as a single man.

Feeling nervous, Seraphina lay coiled round her boyfriend in the back of his flashy but rather dilapidated red Alfa Romeo. They were fully clothed but she knew he was itching to get her clothes off. Why wouldn't he be? He was in his thirties and he'd been with tons of women – he'd told her as much.

Seraphina sighed, wishing she could pluck up the courage to go all the way. She stiffened slightly as she felt his hand stroking her denim-clad thigh. She liked it but she could never let her guard down – the thought made her panic.

Her phone buzzed in her handbag. Seraphina guiltily ignored it. She was sure it was her twin, demanding to know where the hell she'd got to and when she'd be back.

'So, what happened with that model scout?' her boyfriend asked, lazily trailing his fingers down her side.

Seraphina wriggled as he reached a ticklish bit and flipped her blond hair over her shoulder rather sulkily. 'He turned out to be a creepy guy on the make,' she admitted, feeling irrationally annoyed with her father for being right about him. 'Bastard. Can you believe he tries it on with young girls like that?'

Seraphina had asked someone she knew from home to

check out the address on the card the 'model scout' had given her. It didn't exist and, after doing some digging, she'd discovered a dodgy website with dozens of sordid photographs on it, no doubt provided by innocent girls like herself who desperately wanted to be a model. It was disgusting and Seraphina couldn't help feeling stupid that she had been so naive.

Her boyfriend shrugged. 'It just shows you can't trust anyone these days,' he said smoothly, slipping her top off her shoulder. 'So, am I invited to this perfume celebration party thing at your family's house or not?' he asked, languidly dropping kisses on to Seraphina's shoulder.

Seraphina frowned. Had she mentioned the party at La Fleurie? She supposed she must have done. How else would he know about it? 'Yes, of course you're invited.' She shivered, enjoying the feel of his mouth on her bare skin.

'You might feel more . . . relaxed there,' he suggested, his voice loaded.

Anxiously, Seraphina swallowed. 'I-I definitely think I'll be more relaxed at La Fleurie,' she stammered, confused by the way she was feeling. Her body was reacting strongly to his touch but inside, she still felt like a child. A part of her wished he would give her more time.

'Great,' he murmured, removing his mouth from her shoulder and slipping her T-shirt back into place. 'I can't wait.'

'Me neither,' she said, feeling terrified but thrilled at the same time. She'd agreed to it now and she couldn't back out.

Knowing Leoni was on her way, Ashton hurried from a meeting towards the coffee shop round the corner from the rococo-style building. He paused by Galeries Lafayette, which was lit up like a beautiful Christmas tree, despite the early hour. Catching sight of his reflection in the window, Ashton raked a hand through his hair impatiently. It was all over the place and his chin was stubbly because he hadn't had time to shave that morning due to his early breakfast meeting.

Having registered Ducasse-Fleurie's interest in buying the property, Ashton felt all the more determined to secure the building. The way Leoni's lovely brown eyes had lit up when she'd seen the plans – she'd clearly fallen in love with it the same way he had. He couldn't wait to show her round it.

Ashton went into the coffee shop, relieved to find that Leoni hadn't yet arrived. He ordered a coffee and took a seat. He wondered what had happened with the date she had told him about last time and his stomach tightened. He had spoken to her once or twice since he had last seen her and she hadn't mentioned it again.

'Penny for them?' asked a throaty voice.

Ashton looked up to find Marianne Peroux standing over him. Wearing a bright red coat with glossy black boots and leather gloves, she looked sleek, beautiful and dangerous.

'Isn't that what you English say?' Marianne slid into the seat opposite Ashton.

'Er, yes. Yes, it is.' Ashton's gaze darted to the door but Leoni was nowhere to be seen.

Marianne allowed her eyes to run over his delectably English blond hair and his stubbly chin, which gave him a far sexier edge than when he was clean-cut. And those cornflower-blue eyes . . .

'So. What is occupying your thoughts? Or should it be who?' She gave him a knowing smile.

Ashton hoped he wasn't going red. He caught a waft of Marianne's perfume, a new one this time but just as pungent as the last one.

Disconcertingly, she held her wrist out and turned back the cuff of her leather glove. 'It's our new fragrance.'

'It's . . . very strong,' Ashton responded with a slight cough.

Marianne let out a peal of laughter. 'I know. It's called La Vengeance.'

Ashton raised his eyebrows. 'Revenge. Why choose that name?'

'It is a joke, nothing more.' Marianne waved an airy hand then leant over and tucked a scented card into the top pocket of his suit. 'I see the Ducasse family have registered their interest in the sale of the building.' Her green eyes met his unflinchingly. 'I hope you know I won't give up without a fight.'

Ashton inclined his head. 'Of course. You seem like a woman who … who's used to getting her own way.'

Marianne pursed her lips. 'Most of the time.' She got to her feet. 'Keep the stubble,' she instructed him, cupping his chin with her gloved hand. 'It's very sexy.' Planting a kiss on his mouth before he could pull away, Marianne laughed and left the coffee shop.

Outside, her mouth falling open in surprise, Leoni watched the exchange. Ashton was certainly a dark horse; he hadn't mentioned anything to her about dating anyone. His usual type, she noticed ruefully; as Olivier had said all those years ago, Ashton obviously still liked curvy redheads. It bothered her slightly that Ashton was keeping secrets from her. She went inside and slid into the seat Marianne had just vacated.

Ashton's startled expression sat oddly with the smear of lipstick on his mouth.

'Well, well,' Leoni said, eyeing his lips. 'Who was that?'

Blushing slightly, Ashton rubbed his mouth with a handkerchief. Leoni was wearing a businesslike suit and she looked as professional as usual but there was a glow about her. Ashton felt a stab of unease.

'It was just Marianne making a point,' he said.

Leoni sat back. 'That was Marianne Peroux? Ashton, far be it for me to tell you what to do with your love life, but is it advisable to date Marianne while the building sale is going through?'

Ashton looked horrified. 'Me? Dating Marianne?' How Leoni could possibly think such a thing? 'You couldn't be more wrong, Leoni.' Ashton shuddered. 'She frightens the bloody life out of me.' He pulled the scented card out of his pocket. 'And as for her latest perfume . . .'

Leoni sniffed the card he was holding out. 'Eeeguh! That's awful. How have Armand done so well over the years?'

'God knows. I suppose certain women must like fragrances like that.' Ashton glanced at his watch. 'Would you like a coffee or shall we go straight to the shop?'

'Straight to the shop, please,' Leoni said, giving him an excited smile. 'I can't wait to see it!' She tucked her arm through his as they walked to the door. 'And then I can tell you all about the perfect date I went on with Jerard last night . . .'

Feeling his heart constrict painfully, Ashton plastered a smile onto his face.

Chapter Twelve

Xavier glanced at Cat across the table as she gazed at the view. They were dining on halibut with crab Hollandaise at a lovely restaurant high up in the hills. The vista was gorgeous and even as the sky darkened Cat couldn't help wishing she was here in different circumstances. They probably looked like a reasonably happy couple enjoying a spot of lunch but in reality the air was still rather tense between them.

Xavier was actually quite likeable – when he wasn't being disagreeable. Over the past few days, they had crossed swords on more than one occasion but when they chatted about perfume, he was intelligent, relaxed and quite funny. He was just incapable of talking about anything remotely personal. The shutters would come down, his sensual mouth would curl contemptuously, and he would become distant and overly polite. Cat had learnt that as long as she stuck to the safe topic of fragrance, she and Xavier could get on reasonably well; in fact, she actually rather enjoyed his company. She was doing her very best not to compare Xavier to Olivier but it was difficult when his phone kept alerting him to texts from various girlfriends. It was also impossible to tell what he thought of her.

'So tell me who's who in the perfume world,' she said as she sipped her Sancerre.

Xavier sat back. They had visited most of the *parfumeries* in the area – Fragonard, Galimard and Molinard – and Cat's luggage was now weighed down with beautiful perfume bottles and a collection of scents she hadn't been able to resist, despite the depleted money supply she had mentioned in passing. In Galimard, several of the male assistants had fawned all over Cat as if she were a celebrity, leaving her laughing in bewilderment and reluctantly accepting all the free samples they had insisted she take. To her credit, she had been admirably modest about it, claiming it was simply down to her 'kooky' French accent but Xavier wasn't so sure.

'Well, there's Sylvaine Delacourte, Azzi Glasser, Camille Goutal, and Roja Dove, of course,' he said. He noticed that the pale, hazy sunshine had given her skin a rose-gold hue and that her shoulder, exposed by the mint-green top she was wearing, had caught the sun too. Xavier had half a mind to tell her she might need some after-sun but he refrained, thinking it would sound too intimate.

'Roja Dove is like a walking encyclopaedia on all things perfume-related,' he continued. 'I was obsessed with him when I was younger, he's a bit of a hero of mine. He used to collect perfumes and perfume bottles when he was a kid and he got a bit of a name for himself pestering experts. He was offered a job by Robert Guerlain in a factory near London and even though he has never trained as a nose, he worked with the perfumers and eventually opened his own boutique in Harrods.'

Cat smiled at a waiter as he removed her plate. 'I didn't even know there was a perfume boutique in Harrods. Did Roja create his own perfumes in the end?'

Xavier nodded, raising his eyebrows to ask if she wanted to see the dessert menu. When she shook her head, he ordered them coffees. 'Oh yes. His boutique had a crystal Caron fragrance fountain and Clive Christian hand-engraved bottles which were diamond-encrusted. They sold for more than a hundred thousand pounds.' He pointed at her with his wine glass. 'For a certain sum of money, Roja will make a bespoke scent, just for you.' Xavier mentioned a figure.

Cat gulped. 'That's a bit pricey for me.'

'But worth it,' Xavier asserted. 'Trust me.'

'Couldn't you make me one for less than that?' She grinned to show she was just teasing him.

'I could,' he said cautiously, feeling his jaw clench. Letting it go, Xavier reminded himself that he shouldn't always feel as if he was being attacked. Feeling relaxed after several glasses of wine, he decided to indulge her. 'What would you like it to smell like?'

Happily surprised that he was playing the game, Cat thought for a moment. 'Well, I'd call it Reckless, or something, I know that much. Leoni would probably want it called Scarlet Woman or the Black Widow Spider, I'm sure.' She pulled a face.

'Are you reckless?'

Cat let out a laugh. 'What do you think? But seriously, I like dangerous sports, I suppose, parachute jumps, climbing, that sort of thing, and I used to ride a lot . . . I love horses, actually.'

Xavier was impressed. 'You like climbing? I didn't know that.' He told her about his recent climb and Cat was envious – that stretch of mountains was famous for its views and its complexity. She was equally amazed to find that Xavier enjoyed something as physical and as dangerous as climbing; it was at odds with the rather lazy persona he projected. Maybe he was only cautious when it came to love, she mused.

'I distracted you,' Xavier said. 'You were about to describe what you'd like in this new fragrance I'm allegedly creating.'

'Right, yes.' Cat tried to remember what she'd learnt in the perfume factories. 'It should have an outrageous brief, like the ones you told me about. Something like the scent of an ocean wave as it crashes down on a sandy beach while a coconut falls on a man's head.'

Xavier laughed.

'I suppose I would need to choose a type, wouldn't I?' Cat

went on. 'What about a gourmand? I liked the one you made in that trio of scents.'

Xavier shrugged. 'Gourmand scents are a more recent addition to the fragrance family. DKNY's Be Delicious, for example, has a coffee accord, and Angel, by Thierry Mugler, features candyfloss and toffee apples. They're usually child-hood scents, to create nostalgia.' He paused. 'How about a blast of sweet rose, orchid and white lily, to start with?' he suggested.

Cat blinked at him. 'Wow, that was quick. Sounds gorgeous. What next?'

Xavier's eyes met hers. 'Some creamy amber and a touch of freesia to stabilise the top note.'

'Perfect, I love all those.' Xavier made it sound so easy to come up with a new fragrance on the spot. 'What about the heart notes – the middle bits?'

Xavier nodded. 'Something fruity but also deep and full bodied. Plum, red berry and orris root for a raw hit. I think also some mandarin . . . a tropical accord is unusual but if it's done properly, it can really work.'

Cat felt sure he couldn't have worked out the perfume he had just described in the past few minutes. 'All right, time to confess. You didn't just come up with that, did you? This is something you've already given a lot of thought to.'

Xavier pulled a rueful face. 'Sort of. It's something I was working on before and after my mother died.' He stopped, as though he felt he'd said too much. The unfinished fragrance had had all the makings of a modern classic, the kind of fragrance that would be aimed at the younger consumer but could still bridge the generation gap. Something that could offer that much sought-after sense of decadence, sophistication and glamour.

Cat wanted to know more but she was aware she had to be careful. 'Did you . . . identify the base notes?'

'Almost. Honeyed cedarwood, ambergris – synthetic, of

course – and sandalwood. And something else . . . but I hadn't identified that part.'

Cat fiddled with her hair. 'So it's unfinished?'

He nodded, his eyes downcast. 'It's . . . something happened and I stopped working on it.' Xavier couldn't bear to say it out loud but the perfume had been based around his idea of the 'perfect woman'. If it ever saw the light of day it would probably surprise most women to know – one, in particular, Xavier thought with a grimace – that it hadn't been based on anyone he knew. It was simply a concept created with certain characteristics and attributes in mind.

Cat itched to question Xavier about why he had abandoned what sounded like a beautiful fragrance, but she knew better. It would put an end to their pleasant lunch and Xavier was likely to erupt. Cat glanced up at the sky, aware of a chill in the air. Dark clouds were gathering and the wind was picking up, tossing the surrounding almond blossoms.

She looked at Xavier's closed expression and changed the subject to something she'd been meaning to get to the bottom of. 'Olivier's parents, how did they die?'

Xavier drained his coffee, disconcerted by the abrupt change of subject. He glanced up at the darkening sky and realised they should make a move. 'Uncle Henri and Aunt Paulette died taking drug overdoses at the party of all parties. Did Olivier tell you something different?'

Cat nodded. Of course he had. 'He told me they died in a riding accident,' she said flatly.

'No, that's how my mother died.'

'Why would Olivier lie about such a thing?' Cat blurted out. 'I didn't need him to make things up . . . I thought we had so much in common. Leoni was right; I didn't know Olivier at all. I'm just an idiot for falling for his stupid lies . . .' She stopped and looked away. 'God, sorry. I thought I was over him.'

'Olivier was a pathological liar,' Xavier asserted. 'Even as a

212

child he used to make stuff up. He used to run rings around my grandmother, if it makes you feel any better.'

Cat pleated her napkin. 'Christ. Love . . . isn't it shocking what it can do to you?'

'Tell me about it.'

Cat wished he *would* tell her about it. She wanted to know what had made him the way he was, what had caused him to ditch the one thing he loved doing most in the world.

Xavier hesitated. He was tempted to confide in Cat. She was so open and honest. But it was ridiculous, he had only spent a few days in her company and he couldn't even bring himself to talk to his own father about what had happened back then. What was he thinking?

Cat lifted her head and leant forward. 'The thing is, the death of our parents was what we really bonded over. Mine died in a skiing accident,' she explained. 'They lived life to the full and they died doing just that. They were caught in an avalanche in Austria when I was fifteen.'

Xavier stared at her, suddenly seeing her in a completely different light. He'd had no idea she'd suffered such a tragedy at a young age. 'That must have crucified you,' he commented.

She nodded. 'It did . . . it really did. They were everything to me . . . I was an only child so I guess I was probably a bit spoilt.'

'You don't seem spoilt,' he replied. 'Not like me,' he added lightly. 'Pampered playboy and all that. Tell me about your parents.'

About to retort that she didn't want to talk about them, Cat faltered, knowing she was being petty. She loved talking about her parents; she couldn't help smiling, just at the memory of them. 'They were amazing. I spent my life around so many incredible things like music and art and they travelled all the time and I went with them. We spent a lot of time in France. They had this zest for life, this astonishing way

213

of grabbing it with both hands and living it to the full. I admire them so much for it . . . and since they died, I've tried to live my life that way too, you know, as a sort of tribute to them.'

Xavier nodded. He had always lived his life impetuously, not so much because of any wounding loss – those had come much later – but perhaps because he had always battled with his privileged upbringing. Sure, he enjoyed the good things in life but, unlike Olivier, who had positively embraced the easy wealth he had grown up with, Xavier had gone out of his way to take risks and prove that he didn't rely on the Ducasse name to get by.

He was about to tell Cat when spots of heavy rain began to patter around them. The sky was very dark and most of their fellow diners had ducked inside. Xavier knew there was about to be a torrential downpour, punctuated by jagged, bright-white lightning. But he didn't want to break the moment. He was jolted when Cat looked up with tears in her eyes.

'There are some days when I just miss them so, so much. They taught me everything . . . they shaped who I am and how I live my life.' Her mouth crumpled. 'Of course I make mistakes – look what happened with Olivier! Maybe if they were still here, I'd have been able to ask them what to do, instead of throwing myself headlong into a marriage that should never have happened.' Her voice cracked and, at the same time, the heavens opened.

Cat leapt to her feet. Tearing off his jacket, Xavier threw it round her shoulders and grabbed her by the hand. The wind whipped up around them and they were soaked in seconds. Xavier pulled Cat out of the rain, underneath a canopy, holding her tightly.

Xavier stared down at her, his eyes focused on her mouth. God, she was irresistible. Feisty, opionionated, vulnerable, trusting and open . . . The tangible hurt and loss in her aquamarine eyes, her trembling shoulders . . . the way she had opened up so readily . . . all of it was making him want to gather her up in his arms and kiss the life out of her.

Cat swallowed. The look in his eyes could strip paint. There were gold flecks in their depths, she noticed.

Xavier cupped her face with his hands, pulled her closer and kissed her mouth. He felt her stiffen against him, but he held her more tightly, sinking his hands into her sopping wet hair. Cat threw caution to the wind and kissed him back. Her head was telling her it was wrong but her heart – or more accurately another part of her body altogether – was telling her it was very, very right. Pushing his thigh between Cat's buckling legs, Xavier took her weight, kissing her on and on as the rain thundered down around them.

A huge bolt of thunder exploded overhead, and they both jumped, their mouths separating. Cat's face was lit up by a spectacular fork of lightning.

Xavier stared at her. What had he just done? He was supposed to be picking her brains not kissing her senseless. But the kiss . . . it had been . . . Xavier didn't even have the words. Desire shot through him, followed by guilt. What would Olivier think if he could see him now? Xavier took a deliberate step backwards.

'That . . . shouldn't have happened,' he said. The shutters came down; Cat saw it happen in front of her eyes.

'It really shouldn't,' she said, feeling suddenly chilled to the bone, and not just because she was soaking wet.

As Cat stumbled away from him, Xavier bit his lip. No doubt he had just succeeded in convincing Cat he was the serial lothorio she thought he was.

Angelique couldn't believe it was finally happening. After being left out in the cold for the past two years, she was actually sharing tea and sandwiches with Delphine Ducasse. Ensconced at a private table in an alcove hidden from view, Angelique had readily agreed to meet Delphine in the upmarket tea rooms in Toulouse, Delphine's home town.

'How have you been?' she asked Delphine warmly, pouring them both cups of fragrant mint tea. 'I must say, I've missed chatting to you.'

Delphine regarded her coolly. She had arranged the meeting with Angelique because she wanted to sound her out; she needed to be clear about her strategy when Xavier returned home from Grasse.

Angelique was aware that this was a test. She didn't know why Delphine had broken her silence but she intended to play the situation to her advantage.

'I see you've made a few more films since our last meeting,' Delphine said, her disapproval clear.

Angelique refused to blush. Her films made her an awful lot of money and provided her with the sort of celebrity lifestyle she craved. She did, however, want a different sort of life now, one a relationship with Xavier could provide.

'Yes, needs must, I'm afraid. But I would love to move in another direction if at all possible.'

'Really?'

'I would love to do more adverts,' Angelique explained. 'Classy ones, of course. Something that might raise my profile . . . that might allow me to make more serious films. If I wasn't lucky enough to become a wife and mother, of course,' she added demurely, looking down at her mint tea, in case shrewd Delphine spotted the insincerity in them. Angelique wouldn't dream of giving up her career to become a stay-at-home housewife, not in a million years. What had happened with Xavier proved that, not that Delphine knew about that issue, naturally.

Before meeting Delphine, she had received a message from Mason saying she'd been offered the cover of *Playboy*. That was her point, in a nutshell. Years ago, she would have jumped at the chance, but now, she had different ambitions. Her own line of products – Angelique, the brand. That was her ultimate aim. She made an effort to focus on what Delphine was saying, knowing this was her big moment.

'I'm so glad to hear that,' Delphine commented, with slightly more warmth in her tone. 'I think moving your career in a different direction would be the right thing to do. Especially if you were to move in our circles again . . . and perhaps settle down.' She let the words hover, certain it was what Angelique wanted to hear.

Angelique could barely contain her excitement. She could deal with the issue of 'settling down' later but if Delphine was offering her a free pass back into the Ducasse family fold, she was going to grab it with both hands. The tea and chatter continued in a friendly fashion for the next hour or so, with Angelique employing all of her acting skills. As Delphine left, promising to get in touch soon, Angelique let out a sigh of relief and paid the bill. It had been hard work but well worth it. All she had to do now was wait for Delphine to call.

In Paris, Ashton was showing Leoni the changes he'd made to his apartment. 'As you can see, I've added those shelves and now the balcony really stands out with the addition of the period lighting.'

'I love it, Ashton.' Leoni looked round in wonder. 'You have captured the essence of the building to a T.' She smiled at him. 'I know how much this place means to you.'

Ashton nodded. 'I wouldn't give it up for anything.'

'I don't blame you,' Leoni said. Through the window the Arc de Triomphe was outlined dramatically against the darkening night sky. She smoothed a hand down the skirt of her dress. It was a frothy number in a deep red, almost black crepe, with a square neckline and a full skirt. In truth, it was rather out of character for her, but it was beautiful and it was fun. Leoni couldn't help thinking Jerard might not like it as he had mentioned how much he admired her sleek, businesslike style, but she quite liked wearing something that felt quirky and different.

'Where are we off to again?' she asked Ashton, thinking he looked rather dashing in his dark suit and snowy-white shirt. He had shaved, which she found slightly disappointing, and his hair was neatly combed.

'A bar I discovered recently. You'll love it. It has a dance floor too. It's quite . . . romantic, actually.' He faltered, wondering if he'd made the right decision to promise Leoni a night out there – it was all soft lighting and music to sway to. He had arranged it before he realised how besotted Leoni was with Jerard. But it was too late now.

Ashton put on a tie, his fingers hovering in mid-air as Leoni leant over and straightened the knot. 'What do you call this knot again?'

Ashton smiled. 'It's a Windsor,' he told her for what must be the tenth time.

'Charming,' she said with a smile. 'So English . . . so very you, Ash.'

'That's me . . . so very, very English,' Ashton said wryly, wondering why he felt irked by this description all of a sudden. Ever since Leoni had got together with Jerard, he had felt like a clunky spare part; Leoni's boring, English sidekick who was good as a friend but nothing more. It had been that way between them for years but he supposed he had always felt heartened by the fact that he had never seen Leoni crazy about another man . . . therefore providing him with a shred of hope.

'You look really pretty in that dress,' Ashton blurted out, to cover his silence. 'It's not your usual style but it really suits you. It's very . . . feminine.'

'Thank you.' Leoni blushed. She couldn't remember when she'd last been described as feminine. 'You are a true gentleman, always. Let's go.' She took his arm and they headed out of his apartment. Twenty minutes later, they were sitting at the bar of the new club Ashton had discovered.

'It's gorgeous,' Leoni enthused, her cheeks flushed. She glanced over her shoulder at the band who were setting up at the edge of a stunning dance floor with glossy black and white checked tiles and moody lighting. It was full of couples, both old and young, and Leoni was particularly taken with an old couple who were already swaying on the dance floor, even though the band hadn't properly started. With neat, grey hair and smart clothes, the couple moved in unison as though they could predict each other's movements – no doubt from many years spent together. Leoni felt quite sentimental at the sight of them.

Feeling desolate, Ashton could only think Leoni's happiness was due to the text message she had just received. It had to be from Jerard; no one else's texts made her smile from ear to ear. He ordered some of Leoni's favourite champagne and watched her eyes spark with happiness. Did Jerard see Leoni's beauty? he wondered. Did he see beyond the mannish glasses and the stiff, designer clothes to the incredible woman within?

'You are lovely,' Leoni said, her eyes shining behind her glasses as she waited for the champagne to be poured. 'This trip has been great, you know. The building is exquisite and we've had so much time to talk. It's been like old times … minus Olivier, of course.'

'Let's drink to him,' Ashton said, raising his glass with a smile. 'To Olivier. May he be drinking Dom Perignon in the sky – or in the ground – wherever he might have ended up.'

Leoni sipped her champagne ruefully. She was fairly sure Olivier wasn't wearing a halo and floating around with fluffy angels now that he'd passed on.

The band struck up and Leoni recognised one of her favourite tunes. She threw Ashton a coy glance.

'Nothing to do with me,' he said, shaking his head. 'Damn, I could have lied and said I'd arranged it and you'd have thought I was brilliant and the most thoughtful guy around.'

'Shall we dance?' She smiled, slipping off her seat. 'Or do you have two left feet? I can't remember.'

Ashton straightened his tie. 'Me? I can dance like a pro. My parents sent me to lessons when I was a child so I didn't end up standing in the corner like a loser.'

Twirling her around in the centre of the dance floor, he pulled her in close. With one hand on her waist and the other cupping her hand, Ashton swayed to the music, occasionally spinning Leoni out and pulling her back in again. She laughed breathlessly, taken aback that he was such a good dancer.

'We've never danced before,' she realised, surprised. 'In all this time, we haven't ever done this before. Isn't that strange?'

Ashton nodded, feeling her soft cheek against his, breathing in her perfume.

Leoni smiled. She hadn't enjoyed herself this much in ages – aside from the date with Jerard, of course. But that had been different, it had been more serious. Leoni decided she would bring Jerard here one day. It was so romantic with all the candles and the band playing live. If he wasn't too busy with work, she would love to bring him to Paris – although she reminded herself that it was Jerard's dedication to his company that made him so attractive. Leoni frowned; she couldn't quite summon up his face but she supposed that happened when you didn't see someone every day.

'Isn't it nice to do something like this?' Ashton said out of the blue, pulling away to glance down at her. 'I mean, business is important and we're both very committed to what we do, but there's something to be said for having fun, isn't there? You know, love, family, relationships, all that kind of thing.' He put his cheek against hers again.

Ashton's words mirrored what her grandmother had said before she left for Paris, Leoni thought with a jolt. She didn't answer. In truth, she didn't know if she should be prioritising business or pleasure right now.

When the dance ended, Leoni pulled away and mumbled something about needing to go to the restroom. She found the old lady she'd noticed on the dance floor there, and was startled when she patted her cheek.

'Such a lovely couple, you two,' she said with a dimple. 'Aaah, young love . . . it reminds me of when I met my husband.'

'Oh, but we're not a couple,' Leoni corrected her, smiling.

The old lady frowned. 'No? You looked so right together.' She shrugged. 'Perhaps you *should* be a couple.' She winked. 'That much chemistry shouldn't be ignored!'

The old lady left the restroom, leaving Leoni pensive. She supposed a man and woman dancing together so closely would look like a couple to anyone who didn't know them. But she felt unsettled.

Leoni took out her mobile phone and dialled Jerard. She just wanted to hear his voice.

'Jerard? It's Leoni. I . . . just thought I'd call from Paris and see how you are.' She stared at herself in the mirror and waited for his response. 'You're on a break from a meeting? Lucky I caught you for five minutes then.' Forgetting all about Ashton waiting for her outside, Leoni willed Jerard to – verbally, at least – sweep her off her feet again.

The day after the kiss at the restaurant, Cat found herself packing her bags with a heavy heart. The past twenty-four hours had been fraught with tension. She and Xavier had barely exchanged more than a few words afterwards. As ever, the only safe topic of conversation thereafter had been perfume but even that had become strained. Cat sat down abruptly on the bed.

The heady kiss at the restaurant, with the rain pelting down around them, had been incredible. Knee-trembling, mind-blowing and utterly unforgettable. Her body let her down constantly by filling with desire at the memory at the most inappropriate moments.

She stood up and threw the last of her clothes into her bag. But the look on his face afterwards . . . Xavier's eyes had been full of guilt, regret and intense disappointment in himself. It had been like a slap in the face. Cat guessed Xavier felt guilty about Olivier, and she knew she should be feeling that way too but she didn't. His lies had seen to that. She didn't feel remotely bad about kissing his cousin.

Cat paused. Olivier had married her, so she supposed she had meant something to him. What had his long-term plans been? Had he even thought that far ahead – or had Olivier intended to pass himself off as a penniless waiter indefinitely?

Cat sighed. She guessed she'd never know for sure now and unfortunately, the fact that Olivier had taken the step of marrying her didn't provide much comfort any more.

She put on a cream jumper over her jeans and hurried downstairs. She was due to meet Xavier outside and she didn't want to keep him waiting. She found him leaning against his Aston Martin looking like a bloody film star and Cat wished he was less charismatic. Thoroughly fed up with the tension between them, she decided to bite the bullet.

'Listen, about that kiss . . .'

'What about it?' Xavier threw her bag into the back of the car, his expression unreadable.

Cat sighed. 'Don't you think you're being a bit childish about it?'

He let out a short laugh. 'Childish? No, why on earth would you think that? It was a mistake, that's all.'

Offended, Cat leant on the car. 'Yes, Xavier, we both know it was a mistake. You don't have to rub it in.'

He shrugged, as if he found the conversation tiresome. 'We should just forget it.'

Frustrated, Cat smacked her hands down on the Aston

Martin. 'What the hell is wrong with you?' she yelled. 'You can't even talk about a stupid kiss! Are you emotionally retarded or something?'

Xavier recoiled as if Cat had slapped him. *Emotionally retarded?* How dare she! If anything, he was far too passionate about the things that mattered to him. He didn't want to tell her about his past because he knew he'd be in danger of breaking down, and then what might she think of him? Would she think him pathetic for falling in love so deeply before falling apart when it all went wrong?

'You don't know me at all,' he said coldly. 'So don't make assumptions about me.'

Cat hardly heard him, she was so angry. 'If you weren't so screwed up, you'd understand that sometimes people do crazy things. People fall in love when they haven't known each other for very long, they even occasionally kiss in the heat of the moment. These things happen!'

Xavier opened his mouth to respond but Cat was on a roll.

'And you're a fine one to talk about making assumptions, Xavier! When did you make your mind up about me? When you heard Olivier had married me? Or was it when you saw me for the first time, while you were frolicking naked with one of your many girlfriends?'

Xavier flushed. 'I admit I had preconceptions about you but why wouldn't I? Do you know how many people target our family because they know we're wealthy?'

'That doesn't justify tarring everyone with the same brush. Oh, and by the way, thanks so much for letting me cry into my napkin and tell you intimate details about my family and my life, whilst you sit there on your high horse and decide that I'm too naive and silly to warrant any kind of openness back.'

'That's a ridiculous thing to say,' Xavier told her in clipped tones. 'That's not what it is at all.'

'Then what is it?' Cat demanded, her hands on her hips. 'Are you scared? Worried about what I might think of you? Or do you just hate feeling vulnerable?'

All of the above, Xavier thought to himself tersely as he threw himself into the driving seat of his car. 'We need to leave now,' he said, putting his Ray-Bans on and staring straight ahead.

'Too bloody right, we need to leave,' Cat muttered under her breath and got into the car like a petulant child. She gritted her teeth and looked resolutely out of the window.

Chapter Thirteen

Hard at work at La Fleurie, Leoni had barely thought of anything else but her home fragrance campaign, apart from the odd intrusion when Jerard flashed into her head. The campaign was taking shape nicely and it kept her focused whilst Jerard was busy with a large new contract he'd taken on; he was working on it pretty much night and day.

Leoni had experienced the odd pang of anxiety over Jerard's preoccupation with his new contract. She knew all about putting business first, especially when it was important, but she couldn't help panicking that he was using it as an excuse to avoid her. Still, he'd sent her so many texts, as well as a bouquet of lilies, she had no real reason to doubt that he was simply caught up in business and too busy to visit.

She eyed the large bunch of flowers which she'd displayed in a Lalique vase. Unfortunately lilies always reminded her of funerals. It wasn't Jerard's fault; he didn't know her well enough to have any idea about her favourite flowers, or to know how many times she had seen lilies on fresh gravestones. Ashton, having known her for so many years, would of course know to send her lush, velvety pink roses should he ever feel the inclination to do so. It was going to take time for Jerard to get to know her, that was all.

And vice versa, Leoni thought, realising she didn't even know what Jerard did in his spare time, let alone what his favourite things were. She sincerely hoped he liked Paris because if they secured the shop, the first thing she wanted to do was take him there. Leoni had loved every minute of her recent trip there but it had been missing one thing – romance. Idly, she wondered if Ashton had taken anyone else to the lovely bar yet. He didn't seem to be short of admirers; his answerphone had been full of messages from both English and French girls.

And there had been a fair few messages from Marianne Peroux too, Leoni thought with pursed lips. She was fairly sure the woman applied the same rules to men as she clearly did to business: she wouldn't stop until she got what she wanted. Leoni only hoped Marianne was after the building and not Ashton – for his sake.

Something suddenly occurred to Leoni. Not once had Jerard made a move on her – not a serious one. She had planned to keep him at arm's length – for a while, at least – but she hadn't really needed to. Leoni felt a moment of panic. Perhaps he didn't see her that way, perhaps he thought she was interesting but not sexually attractive. Although he had called her sexy at their first dinner date, hadn't he? In a roundabout way, at least.

Leoni tried to reassure herself. Why would Jerard be dating her if he didn't find her physically attractive? Surely there wouldn't be much point in that. Deciding to do something she hadn't ever done before where a man was concerned, she did an internet search on Jerard. Taken aback, she discovered that the small store Jerard ran nearby was actually the tip of the iceberg – or rather, the cornerstone of his empire, as it were. He had stores selling all sorts of different items all over Europe and he had a huge business arm in Japan, of all places.

Leoni looked up his website. Jerard wasn't just quite success-ful, he was a self-made millionaire, she thought with a gulp. He might have come from relatively humble beginnings and he might dress casually in the office but he was very rich. Leoni frowned, not sure how she felt about Jerard not telling her the extent of his business. But perhaps he was just modest. After all, how was he supposed to drop being a millionaire into the conversation? And she didn't make a habit of talking about her own substantial wealth, so why should Jerard?

Hearing a sound outside, she looked up. It was quiet at the château; the twins were at college and Xavier was still in Grasse with Cat Hayes, by all accounts. A head poked round the door and Leoni immediately recognised Jerard's tufty brown hair.

'What a lovely surprise! Come in, come in.' Quickly closing the internet page down, Leoni smoothed her hair and hoped her red lipstick was still in place.

Jerard grinned. 'Ah, hard at work, I see. A woman after my own heart.' He leant in and kissed her, his hands moving round her waist. Leoni kissed him back, pleased that he was being so tactile.

Pulling away reluctantly, Jerard tucked her hair behind her ears, the gesture oddly distracted when it should have been intimate.

Leoni discreetly let her hair fall back around her chin. She hated showing her ears; she always thought they stuck out.

'Sorry I've been so busy,' Jerard was saying. 'This deal is taking up all of my time at the moment. I can't believe it, just as I meet you, my company takes on the biggest contract it's ever seen.'

'But great for your company,' Leoni told him, delighted that he felt the need to explain himself. It was almost as if he had known she was anxious about his feelings for her.

Jerard kissed her again. 'You're very understanding, Leoni. I can't believe we're so compatible.' He glanced at her teetering pile of paperwork and pulled a face. 'Don't you just hate paperwork? My assistant files everything for me, thank God, otherwise I think I'd drown under it all.'

Leoni frowned at the thought of Jerard's very pretty assistant Suzanne.

'Hey, I was just about to invite you to a party,' Leoni said, changing the subject. She handed him an invitation, hot off the press. 'My grandmother is organising it to celebrate the fiftieth anniversary of Rose-Nymphea. It was an idea Olivier's widow had, believe it or not, but I have to admit it's a good one. It's creating such a positive buzz about Ducasse-Fleurie, and all the attention will be fantastic for my campaign.' She hoped her grandmother had remembered to send Ashton an invite and made a mental note to check with her. Maybe he would bring a girlfriend . . . maybe he would even bring Marianne, Leoni thought with some distaste.

Jerard read the invitation, looking impressed. Taking out his phone, he checked something and Leoni realised he was scrutinising his calendar.

'Oh no, can't you make it?'

'It's fine. I have a big dinner the night before but it seems I'm free on this date, so I'll book myself in right now.' Leaning over, he gave her another kiss, noticing the lilies in the vase behind her. 'You got my flowers, I see. Do you like them?'

Leoni hesitated, about to say she hated lilies but she nodded instead. 'Yes, I do. Thank you so much.'

'Great.' Jerard's phone went off and, glancing at it, he let her know he needed to take it. 'Sorry,' he added. 'I was on my way to a meeting, but I really wanted to see you.'

Leoni smiled as he left. Things were on track between them; she was sure of it.

When Cat arrived back at La Fleurie, she just wanted to disappear to her room to get her head together. She was dying to call Bella to tell her what had happened but, more to the point, she needed to get away from Xavier and the crackling tension that sat between them. The silent drive back had been almost unbearable. But they were greeted in the hall by Guy who looked suave in grey trousers and a pale pink shirt. His silver-grey hair was neat and his brown eyes lit up at the sight of them.

'You're back! Did you have a good trip?'

Xavier nodded, not looking at Cat as he put their bags down. 'Yes, thank you.' He sighed to himself as Delphine appeared, resplendent in an apricot woollen suit and court shoes. The last thing he needed was his grandmother stirring things up.

'How lovely to see you . . . both,' Delphine said. 'I do hope your trip was successful. While I remember, Xavier, a girl came looking for you while you were in Grasse. Monique, I think her name was. Pretty, but rather cheap looking.'

Xavier looked pained. He didn't dare look at Cat.

'Therese also called many times – didn't you have your phone with you?' Delphine seemed determined to make him look like the gigolo Cat obviously thought he was.

Xavier stiffly thanked her. 'I'll deal with my calls later, Grandmother. For now, I'd like to get unpacked and grab a bite to eat.'

'I assume my passport hasn't arrived? I need to get on to my friend about it,' Cat muttered, about to head towards the stairs.

Delphine reached out and grabbed her arm. 'Actually, I wanted to have a chat with you about something, if you could wait a moment.'

Cat noticed Xavier hesitate, as if he felt he should stay. Then he clearly thought better of it and disappeared upstairs. Guy also made his exit, leaving Cat alone with Delphine.

Cat bit her lip. A cosy chat with Delphine was the last thing she wanted right now.

'So, how do you think your trip went?' Delphine asked.

Cat shot her a suspicious glance.

'It was . . . fine,' she provided with a frown. 'Very . . . informative.'

Delphine nodded slowly. 'And how did Xavier seem?'

Cat was beginning to feel exasperated. What was Delphine driving at? 'I don't know. He was happy when he was talking about perfumes, I guess.'

'I see.' Delphine's eyes seemed to brighten and, for whatever reason, she looked satisfied. 'Preparations for the Rose-Nymphea party are fully underway,' she added. 'I insist you stay for it.'

'Er . . . well, if my passport arrives . . .' Cat felt panicked. As soon as she had her passport, she intended to leave.

Delphine waved away her hesitation. 'Please, you must. It was your idea to mark the anniversary. Let's call it a farewell to your time here.'

'I'll see,' Cat muttered non-committally. Why on earth did the old lady want her to stay for the party all of a sudden?

Up in her room, Cat began to put her clothes away in the drawers of the dresser by the door. The belt on her jeans caught on something in one of the drawers and she bent over to look inside. There, at the back, caught between the bottom and the end part of the drawer, was something small, flat and burgundy coloured. Tugging it out, Cat stared at her passport in utter amazement. Had it been there all along? Surely not. She had checked the drawers in the dresser, even right at the back . . . hadn't she?

Sitting back on her heels, Cat couldn't be sure. For a moment, she wondered if someone had planted her passport in the drawer to make it look as though it had been there all the time.

Was she being totally paranoid? Cat quickly dialled Bella for a second opinion. She was in the toilets at her work reading *Heat* magazine. Cat filled her in on recent events, turning beetroot as she recounted the kiss, and waited to hear Bella's response.

'Well, firstly, are you insane? What the hell did you kiss that Xavier bloke for? I know you said he was handsome but he sounds like a total dickhead . . .' Bella sighed. 'Or he is actually drop-dead gorgeous and you fancy the pants off him?'

'No way, he's totally infuriating. Look, I know it's not my finest hour – can you imagine what the family would think if they found out?' Cat shook her head gloomily. 'Anyway, enough of that. What about this passport business? Do you think Delphine is behind it?'

Bella made doubtful noises. 'I don't know, Cat. Aren't you being a bit dramatic?'

Cat realised she probably was. 'I'm just feeling really paranoid right now, Bel. I can't work out who I trust here and who even likes me. It's tough.'

'The sooner you get home, the better, right?' When Cat didn't respond, Bella pressed her. 'Trouble is, now that we've applied for a new passport, the one you've just found will have been cancelled.'

'Damn,' Cat said, vexed. 'I forgot about that. Any news on the job?'

'Ah, about that.' Bella swiftly explained that the head of the company had put a freeze on all recruitment until the team had completed a campaign they were lagging behind on. 'It's a really stroppy client, apparently, but they still really want you to join them. Ben checked they weren't mucking you around and they're not at all. It just might be another month or two before they can offer you something.' There was a rustle as Bella rolled up *Heat* magazine and tucked it in the back of her skirt. 'I've got to get back to work. Cat?'

'What?'

'Do me a favour? Please try your hardest not to snog any other members of the family before we talk again?'

A few days later, feeling slightly hesitant, Xavier turned the key to his lab and went in. He hadn't said a word to anyone about returning to the lab, not Cat, not his father and most certainly not his grandmother, but it felt like the right thing to do. The visit to Grasse had unlocked a door in his mind and he was totally consumed by thoughts of perfume-making, particularly the half-finished fragrance he'd abandoned when everything went wrong.

Well, that wasn't strictly true, Xavier admitted to himself. He had also thought quite a lot about that kiss with Cat, that reckless, erotic, wonderful kiss they'd shared. But what was the point? Cat thought he was 'emotionally retarded'. Xavier winced. He had no idea how to change her opinion of him without revealing everything about his love life and he really wasn't sure he wanted to do that. Who was Cat Hayes to him, anyway? She was Olivier's widow and he'd do well to remember that.

He put on his white coat, a shiver of anticipation filtering through him. The coat felt like a familiar friend; comfortable, safe and like coming home. He dug out some of the formulas he had developed a few years ago before his mother's death and went through them, discarding some and selecting the ones he kept going back to. The air became thick with aromas and he was soon totally immersed in the perfume-making process all over again. Scents of vanilla and caramel emerged, immediately summoning up childhood days spent in the family kitchen; bitter-sweet, orangey petit grain and almond blossom, reminiscent of La Fleurie in full bloom; and the distinctly oriental aroma of rich, musky jasmine.

Angelique. Xavier grimaced, holding the phial at arm's length before daring to inhale again. The scent of jasmine was synonymous with her and a mere waft of it brought memories thundering back into his mind. When they were together, she had drenched herself in jasmine oil and every inch of her skin had been imbued with the heavy, exotic aroma. Angelique had adored perfume with a passion; it had been one of her favourite indulgences. She had even talked about creating her own fragrance one day.

At the time, Xavier had found her obsession with perfume

exhilarating; it had almost felt as though they were meant to be together. His work became an extension of their relationship, a heady compulsion that, like Angelique, Xavier had been almost powerless to resist. It was only later that he realised her interest was merely self-serving. What she wanted was the place in society that the perfume business brought with it. For her, bringing out her own perfume was a means of introducing herself to the world in a way that might give her the accolades she felt she deserved.

Sitting in his lab, assailed by memories, the strong, unforgettable aroma of jasmine wound around Xavier's throat and almost choked him. This was the woman who had crucified him emotionally. If he was 'emotionally retarded', Angelique was the reason. She had destroyed him just after his mother had died, hurting him more than any other woman in his life had before. Xavier couldn't bear being reminded of her. Revolted, he tossed the phial of jasmine oil into the bin.

He let out a breath. Could he do this again? Was he capable of making a new fragrance, one that would make the world sit up and take notice? It was time to turn his back on the past and embrace something new, he decided, trying to find the courage from somewhere. Finally, it felt right to let go, and this fragrance, one with not a drop of jasmine to its formula, would mark the start of a new beginning.

Xavier pulled out the notes relating to the fragrance he'd talked about in Grasse. Yes, it was just as he'd remembered it, heady, memorable and intoxicating. The perfect scent . . . conjuring the perfect woman. Xavier knew he was an ingredient or two away from absolute perfection.

The new fragrance needed to be special, it had to be dynamic enough to pull Ducasse-Fleurie into the modern age.

Xavier started to jot down words as they came to him. Classy. Romantic. Sexy. Unforgettable. Timeless. Sensual. Ideas were bubbling up and he struggled to capture them all as his mind raced ahead. Beach, rain, earthy, fresh, clean.

Did he need peony, gardenia or geranium? All three? Pink honeysuckle, marigold . . . moss, musk, cedar. No, none of them was right.

Xavier suddenly believed in himself again. He felt as though a weight had been lifted off his shoulders and he felt hopeful. He pulled a box of phials towards him, thinking about the scent. What was missing? What were those elusive final ingredients that would make this scent extraordinary? He would work day and night if he had to until he found them.

A few days later, Guy received a phone call from Max and Seraphina's college.

'He's done what?' he shouted, almost dropping his phone. 'Right. I'll be there as soon as possible.'

'What's going on?' Leoni was at his side. She had been trying to summon up the courage to approach Guy about her home fragrance line which was more or less ready to present, but Ashton hadn't been in touch much since Paris and she felt oddly put out and unsure.

'It's Max,' Guy snapped, barely keeping himself under control. 'He's been expelled.'

'Oh no! What for?'

Guy's hands were shaking. 'Doing drugs on college premises.' He clutched his hair, making it stand on end. 'What the hell was he thinking, Leoni! Doing drugs . . . I had no idea. Who would have got him into drugs, for God's sake? Someone must have made him do it – surely Max wouldn't be stupid enough to try cocaine without being encouraged?'

Leoni bit her lip. She remembered Olivier passing a spliff to Max once at a party and she sincerely hoped it wasn't because of her brother's cavalier attitude towards drugs that Max now found himself on the same slippery slope. She knew Xavier had swept many of the details of Olivier's life under the carpet to protect their feelings – hers, in particular. He needn't have bothered. She had done her fair share of secretly bailing Olivier

234

out of many a dodgy situation; she was all too aware of her younger brother's more dubious habits.

'Shall I come with you?' Leoni asked.

Guy shook his head. 'I'd rather go alone, thanks.'

The drive to the school did nothing to calm Guy and he stormed to the head's office where he found. Max lounging in a chair like the obstreperous teenager he was. His dark hair was a mess and there were shadows under his eyes. He looked as though he hadn't slept in a week and for a moment Guy faltered, alarm replacing his anger.

What could be so wrong in Max's life that he had ended up like this? Guy wondered anxiously.

'It wasn't my fault,' Max stated morosely, folding his arms in the universal gesture of defensiveness.

Guy's rage returned. 'Of course it wasn't,' he fired back with steely sarcasm. 'It never is, is it?'

'Monsieur Ducasse,' said Madame Muret smoothly. 'I think it's important for you to know that Max has apologised for his mistake.'

Max glanced at her in surprise. He had done no such thing! He half wished he had apologised but he couldn't exactly do anything about it now.

Madame Muret pushed a seething Guy into a chair opposite her desk. 'I think we all need to take stock of the situation,' she began, feeling the need to give Max a fair hearing. What he had done was unforgivable but the family had been through an awful lot recently. She wondered why Guy's face was slowly turning pale.

'Perhaps I have been a little hasty, talking about expulsion,' Madame Muret added, frowning at him over her glasses. Honestly! Here she was, doing her best to put things right and all Guy Ducasse could do was stare over her shoulder like a man possessed. What was so interesting beyond her window?

Max, too, had seen something He stood up abruptly and his mouth fell open. 'No way,' he gasped. 'Seraphina . . .'

'She's not . . . tell me she's not doing that,' Guy gibbered, rising out of his chair slowly.

Madame Muret whipped her head round. Her mouth formed a perfect 'o' as she saw what they were looking at. Cantering round the front lawn on one of the college's best chestnut mares was Seraphina. But that wasn't what had Guy ashen and Max open mouthed.

Seraphina was completely naked, her pale skin stark against the dark flanks of the horse. Only her platinum-blond hair stopped the scene from being a centrefold shot. Her small breasts were bouncing, popping in and out of sight as she turned the horse sharply as though she was on a polo pitch.

Some senior officials were just finishing a tour of the college and were being shown back down the driveway. They stopped as one and gaped. They were soon joined by a crowd of teenagers who shouted and pointed. Madeleine was there, as well as Vero and Max's friends. Teenagers started flooding out of the building, followed by disgruntled lecturers.

The window to Madame Muret's room was open and Seraphina came trotting towards it.

'If Max is being expelled then so am I!' she yelled spiritedly.

Guy groaned and put his head in his hands.

'Good for you!' Max yelled back, whooping and punching the air in delight. 'That's family loyalty for you,' he told his father smugly, no longer caring what happened. Max felt terribly proud of Seraphina. If their roles had been reversed, he would have done the some; neither of them could stay at the college alone.

Guy looked at Madame Muret. 'I'm guessing you don't think you've been too hasty talking about expulsion now,' he stated flatly. He did not wait for an answer. 'If you could please have someone pack their things and send them on, it would be appreciated. Max, follow me.'

Guy strode outside. He tore his jumper off and threw it at Seraphina.

'Put it on,' he hissed, 'and get off that fucking horse right now.'

Exchanging a glance with Max, Seraphina did as she was told, wriggling into the jumper and sliding quickly off the horse. She tied it safely to a tree and they all walked past the crowd of spectators. Guy held his head high and glared at some of the officials.

'She's a child!' he hurled at them hoarsely. 'Perverts!'

'Sorry, Dad,' Seraphina mumbled into the collar of his jumper, inhaling the tobacco and iris smell of the Dior Homme he always wore. For a second, she was transported to her childhood.

'What were you thinking?' Guy stormed, not quite believing what he had just seen.

'I couldn't stay here without Max.'

Max flung his arm round her protectively. 'Thank you,' he mouthed at her.

'Madame Muret was this close to changing her mind about the expulsion before you did that,' Guy shouted, maddened. A tiny part of him was impressed by Seraphina's shocking stand. It was just the sort of thing Elizabeth would have done years ago. But she wasn't here any more and there was only him to pick up the pieces. Hardening his heart, he stalked to his car, got in and waited for them to do the same. They climbed in, silently.

'Look, Dad,' Max said, leaning forward.

'Don't speak,' Guy cut him off curtly. 'Don't either of you speak. I can't even look at you right now.'

Driving far faster than he should have done, Guy shot back to La Fleurie with red mist dancing before his eyes.

Later that day, having heard about their shocking expulsion, Cat went in search of the twins. Worriedly, she looked all over the house, then headed for the games room by the pool but it was empty. She went towards the graveyard, not quite sure why she was going there.

She stopped immediately when she discovered Guy slumped over Elizabeth's grave. She read over his shoulder: '*Ici repose ma chère épouse, Elizabeth. Une femme et une mère dévouée. Aimee de tous, elle sera toujours parmi nous.*' Here lies my dearest wife, Elizabeth. Devoted wife and mother. Cherished by all . . .

Cat's heart went out to Guy. He was sobbing as if his heart was broken.

'Help me,' he pleaded with her silent headstone. 'Tell me what to do. I'm a fucking terrible father without you . . . I can't do this on my own . . . you have to tell me what to do . . .'

Cat backed out of the graveyard. Guy needed help.

Chapter Fourteen

Bored out of his brain at a cocktail party in the sixth arrondissement, the Luxembourg, Ashton tried Leoni's mobile again. It went straight to voicemail and just like all the other times he had tried her, he didn't bother to leave a message. Ashton's heart sank. Ever since Leoni had started seeing Jerard, she had been as difficult to track down as Lord Lucan.

Gloomily, he glanced down at the pamphlet in his hand. 'Celebrating Five Decades of Parisian Architecture', it said. Normally, he loved this kind of event but since Leoni had left Paris to no doubt dive back into Jerard's warm arms and bed, he had no enthusiasm for anything.

He stared out across the Seine sightlessly, not noticing how beautiful it looked with moonlight dappled across it. He wished for the millionth time that he didn't feel the way he did about Leoni. What was the point?

Behind him, on a stage, someone made a speech about celebrating some of Paris's most famous architecture but Ashton couldn't be bothered to listen.

'Having fun, Monsieur Lyfield?'

Marianne's potent perfume caught in the back of his throat. Turning, he found her beside him, wearing a glamorous cream coat with a red and grey scarf coiled round her neck and red suede gloves. She pulled them off and slipped the coat from her shoulders to reveal a red wrap-around dress. Her red hair was piled up on top of her head in graceful, sweeping waves and her neck looked pale in the dim light.

Ashton wasn't sure he was up to the high-octane verbal banter Marianne demanded. He politely kissed her scented cheeks but made no effort at small talk.

Marianne regarded him quizzically. Noting that his blue eyes were dull and that his chin was covered in pale-gold stubble again, she guessed his love life wasn't going too well. Dips and troughs at work made a man look tense and stressed, they didn't cause his shoulders to droop like Ashton's were doing.

Marianne turned away thoughtfully. Ashton seemed to have no idea how attractive he was. His reserve and immaculate manners might give him a serious air but Marianne had a feeling that beneath that buttoned-down exterior there was a passionate heart. And there was nothing she liked more than a man who was sex on legs but oblivious to the fact.

'She's a fool,' Marianne stated, slipping her arm through Ashton's.

'Who?' He drained his champagne listlessly and handed his glass to a passing waiter. He felt Marianne's fingers digging into his arm.

Marianne smiled. 'Leoni Ducasse, of course. Who else?' She glanced at the Seine impassively. 'Take it from me, the Ducasse family aren't easily won over.'

Ashton wondered how it was that he kept bumping into Marianne Peroux. The city of Paris was huge. Marianne was in the perfume business, not architecture, yet everywhere he went, there she was. Like Delphine Ducasse, she scared the hell out of him, albeit in a very different way. Ashton had a feeling that if he didn't keep his wits about him, he would find himself pinned to the wall with his trousers round his ankles.

'What are you doing here?' he asked her.

Marianne shrugged. 'A friend of mine is an architect. I enjoy the thrill of finding the perfect building but discussing trends and changes over the past five decades isn't exactly my idea of fun. But I felt I owed my friend a favour. He's the one who found the lovely building we both like so much in the ninth arrondissement, actually.' Marianne waved to a handsome, tanned man who grinned back at her.

'Your boyfriend?' Ashton asked. The man rather resembled his mental image of Jerard – good looking and sexy, with lots of confidence, the kind developed through years of always getting the girl. Ashton told himself to stop being such a twat; he had no idea what Jerard looked like or what his track record was with women.

Marianne let out a raucous laugh. 'I don't have boyfriends, Ashton. My life is far too busy and complicated for that. I have lovers instead.' She didn't elaborate on whether or not the handsome man was her lover but her eyes ran over him hungrily.

Ashton was too tired to deal with her. 'I'm afraid I must be going, Madame Peroux. I'm really not in the mood for this event.' He went to kiss her cheeks but she held her cream coat out to him.

'I'll join you,' she said, allowing him to help her into it. 'Paris can be a little unpredictable at night, as you know. Perhaps I could call a cab from your apartment?'

About to point out that Marianne could just as easily call a cab from here, Ashton hesitated. He didn't want to antagonise her, not when the building sale was still undecided.

Marianne pulled her red gloves on and slipped her arm though his as they strolled towards his apartment. They said nothing, they simply walked.

'You live . . . *here*?' Marianne said when they reached his apartment. She was clearly astonished and Ashton smiled proudly, in spite of himself.

'Stunning, isn't it? And yes, rather more opulent than you might imagine for an architect. At my age, anyway.'

'Can we go in? I'd love to look around. This is one of the most desirable buildings in Paris!'

Flattered, Ashton showed her to the elevator. When they

reached his doorway, he let her in and switched some lights on. He gave her a quick tour, noting the excitement her eyes.

'It's magnificent,' Marianne breathed, walking around and trailing her fingers across sculpted mantelpieces and perfect archways.

'Isn't it? I oversaw the renovation myself, just to make sure every detail was spot on.'

Marianne raised an eyebrow. 'You did an amazing job. It's superb. Not one thing jars . . . everything has been restored beautifully.' She nodded approvingly at the richly coloured curtains and the exquisite furniture. 'I see you have a wonderful eye for interiors too.'

Ashton shook his head. 'No, a friend helped me with all of that. I'm afraid my creativity runs out when it comes to colours and textures.' He wondered what he could offer as a drink and settled on Scotch, because it was all he had.

'Thank you.' Marianne seemed unable to tear her eyes away from each detail of the apartment, but finally she refocused her green eyes on Ashton. 'You must be lonely, living here all by yourself,' she said, moving closer.

Ashton sidled towards the window. 'Not really. I enjoy my own company.' He wished Marianne would sit down; she was making him nervous.

'Ah, but everyone needs someone, don't they? Now and again.' Marianne had somehow managed to shimmy forward and pin Ashton to the window. She ran a finger down the lapel of his dinner suit.

Ashton gulped. He felt like Benjamin Braddock in *The Graduate*. And Marianne made the perfect Mrs Robinson.

'I'm in love with Leoni,' he asserted, hoping Marianne would take the hint.

She didn't. Slotting her leg between his, she looked up at him, her full mouth curving into a smile. 'I know that. But it's not your heart I'm interested in.'

Ashton quailed. This was going to be tougher than he'd

thought. 'I don't sleep around. I mean, I probably should and, believe me, I've tried, but it doesn't make any difference.'

Marianne gave him a withering look, sensing he meant what he said. 'You love her that much?'

Ashton nodded. 'I'm afraid so.' He pushed his hair out of his eyes, looking rueful.

Marianne let out an impatient sound and removed her knee from his thighs with obvious regret. 'What a shame,' she said lightly. 'I think we could have had fun.'

Ashton wasn't so sure; being eaten alive wasn't his idea of a good time. He hoped he hadn't offended Marianne. The sale of the building was so important but when it came down to it, Ashton wasn't ready to take one for the team.

'You're beautiful,' he told her, meaning it. To most men, she probably was. Only Ashton preferred women with earnest brown eyes and severe bobs that revealed a slender, vulnerable neck . . . 'I'm just a lovesick fool. What can I say? Leoni . . . she means everything to me and while she's still in my life, I can't be with anyone else.'

Marianne felt irrationally envious of Guy's silly niece. What was wrong with the girl? The Ducasse family wreaked havoc wherever they went, Marianne thought, even more determined to get the building now.

'I'll see you at the auction,' she told Ashton and drained her Scotch. 'Prepare yourself for a battle.'

Ashton felt a shiver of apprehension. 'Shall I call you a cab?' he asked politely.

She let out a tinkling laugh. 'No, thank you, that won't be necessary. I can take care of myself . . . I always have done.' With one last, lingering look around the apartment, she sashayed to the door and left.

Ashton ran a hand through his hair with a shudder. He couldn't help thinking he had made an enemy of Marianne by rejecting her but there was nothing else he could have done.

He picked through his post lethargically and discovered a

card bearing Delphine's distinctive spidery handwriting on the front. Opening it up, Ashton saw he'd been invited to the celebratory Rose-Nymphea party at La Fleurie. Would Leoni attend with her new boyfriend, Jerard? Probably.

Ashton picked up the open bottle of Scotch and decided to get absolutely plastered.

Having spent the morning sorting paperwork on her desk, Delphine was restlessly sifting through the pile of party RSVPs that had been delivered to her by the housekeeper. She was looking forward to the party; it would be glamorous and extravagant with plenty of celebrity attendance.

Delphine put the RSVPs down and stood by the window. Crossly, she saw that Cat was sitting by the pool with Seraphina, no doubt lending a sympathetic ear when in actual fact Seraphina was in disgrace and should be ostracised. Fancy riding a horse naked round a school field! Delphine was shocked to the core and her lips tightened at the mere thought of the incident. She couldn't imagine what had possessed her granddaughter to behave so outrageously. And what about Max? Doing drugs on school grounds like that . . . something had to be done about the pair of them but Delphine had other things to attend to at the moment.

'Plan Angelique', as she liked to call it, was shaping up nicely; she simply needed to utilise Cat to her advantage to get everything up and running. Delphine tapped an RSVP idly and wondered what Xavier would say when he clapped eyes on Angelique again. She felt sure she had made the right decision and that Xavier would be delighted. Angelique was the one woman he had been serious about, the love of his life; whatever had come between them could surely be resolved after all this time.

Opening a box, Delphine took out the celebratory bottles of Rose-Nymphea she'd had especially created for the party. Nestling in small white boxes lined with satin, they were 30ml versions in frosted glass the colour of blush-pink tea roses, with silver ribbons spiralling from the neck. They were perfection.

Delphine realised she was late for a meeting. Hurrying to the library, she waited for Pascal, shivering slightly as she realised it was the first time she'd been in the library since Olivier's funeral. Out of the corner of her eye, she could see the edge of Olivier's headstone but she refused to look at it. It didn't do to be sentimental, she reminded herself, her chin in the air. Life was tough; people died and it was sad but life went on. Firmly telling her hands to stop shaking, she turned as she heard the door open.

'Good morning, Pascal,' she said, her voice devoid of warmth. Pascal had been very disappointing of late; she couldn't understand what was taking so long with the legal documents she had asked him to draw up to cut Cat Hayes out of Olivier's will. Delphine was all for loyalty but if Pascal didn't get his finger out, he could find employment elsewhere. He had been baffled by her urgent phone call the night before but Delphine had cut him off before he could make excuses. She didn't want to make it easy for him by allowing him to pass off his failings on the telephone; she wanted him quailing and apologising in front of her.

Pascal shuffled in, his spectacles threatening to fall off his nose. As ever, he was clutching a bundle of paperwork tied up with ribbons and no doubt full of legal jargon no one understood.

Delphine sighed and rubbed her temples. Pascal, Yves – why were these men so incompetent? She wished she could do her own investigating and her own legal work and then she wouldn't have to waste her time chasing people all over France.

'What do you have for me?' she demanded, not wasting time with small talk.

Pascal looked confused. 'I don't understand, Madame Ducasse. What is it you are expecting me to produce?'

'The legal documents, of course, Pascal! Why else would I have called you here?'

'That's what I was trying to tell you last night on the phone,' Pascal explained earnestly.

'What, exactly?'

Pascal cleared his throat. Delphine always made him feel nervous, even when he hadn't done anything wrong. 'The documents were completed last week and I sent them over to you this week. I have a photocopy but if you need another formal set with the original stamps, et cetera. I would need to have them drawn up again.'

Delphine looked astonished. That was the first she'd heard about the documents arriving. 'They must have gone missing,' she snapped, feeling foolish. 'How irresponsible to send them in the post when you know how unreliable it is.'

'I didn't send them in the post,' he protested hotly. 'I had them couriered over and your housekeeper signed for them.'

Delphine frowned. This was highly embarrassing, as well as irregular.

'Well, I apologise, Pascal,' she said stiffly, detesting the fact that she was having to say sorry to a man she felt was barely able to do his job properly. 'I didn't realise. I'll make sure my housekeeper is punished for not letting me know the documents had arrived.' She waved him to the door. 'That will be all, thank you.'

Pascal scuttled away in relief, hearing her call for the housekeeper before he'd even closed the door. Pascal pitied the woman; whatever she had done with the documents, Delphine was unlikely to let her off the hook.

The housekeeper was unrepentant. She had signed for the documents at the beginning of the week and she had immediately taken them to Delphine's private quarters, where she had locked them safely in her desk.

Rather overcome, Delphine sat down on one of the

uncomfortable library sofas. She didn't need to go upstairs and check if the documents were there; she had cleared her desk out that very morning. So where had the documents gone and, more to the point, who had them? Delphine pondered their disappearance. Could Cat Hayes have gone into her desk to retrieve them herself? Would she know the documents had arrived? Surely not. She had been in Grasse until the other day. What about the twins? They had been back for a few days and they were known for being mischievous. Were they so desperate to keep Cat here that they had taken the documents?

Delphine didn't have a clue. She stood up, tight lipped. Once the Rose-Nymphea party was out of the way, she would find out exactly who had dared to thwart her plans and they would sorely regret their interference.

She headed outside to get some air. Starting, she realised someone was inside Xavier's lab. Catching her breath, Delphine realised it was Xavier. A slow smile spread across her face. So her plan had worked; going to Grasse and immersing himself in perfume again had reignited Xavier's love of fragrance, just as she'd hoped it would.

Feeling uplifted, Delphine left him to it.

Holed up in her flat near Mougins awaiting further instructions from Delphine, Angelique was being massaged by her petite Japanese masseuse, Mai Ling, whom she had finally managed to track down. Mai Ling was masseuse to the stars and she would fly anywhere in the world to pummel the stress out of the rich and famous with her magic, probing fingers – for a price. Known for her rudeness as well as her expertise, she was much sought after and fought over among celebrities. Angelique squirmed on the couch; Mai Ling's touch was both painful and exquisite.

'You so tense,' Mai Ling tutted, kneading Angelique's shoulders with expert hands. She moved the mane of blond hair out of the way, drizzled some more jasmine oil through her fingers and resumed her rhythmic pummelling. She spoke perfect English but she knew her clients preferred her to play dumb and act out the stereotype. And for the money she charged, Mai Ling was happy to go along with it, dressing and acting like a subservient geisha girl. Hell, for her rates, she'd put on a funny wig and dance a jig, if asked to. As it was, her dumb-dumb, I-no-speaky-English persona allowed her to be privy to all sorts of gossip and drama, something Mai Ling enjoyed immensely. She was discretion itself but she loved knowing intimate details about her famous clients.

'I have a big event to attend,' Angelique announced.

'Really?' Mai Ling sounded bored.

Angelique's mind flipped through her plan. As far as she could see, it was foolproof but, as always, she was on her guard. Men were tediously predictable but she had a few aces up her sleeve just in case; even the most typical of men could occasionally be resistant. And Xavier could hardly be described as a typical man. Deep in thought, Angelique rested her head on her hands. Her entrance had been planned meticulously and she wanted everything to go like clockwork. There was so much at stake, so much to play for. Angelique forced herself to relax. Why couldn't she just trust that everything would work out the way she wanted it to? And worst case, if it didn't, she was still holding all the cards.

'What's that?' Mai Ling asked, pointing a child-sized finger at a red, slinky dress that was hanging over the back of the door.

'A dress for a party I've been invited to,' Angelique said, without lifting her head. 'It's Dior.'

'Fancy,' Mai Ling commented, moving her hands down Angelique's spine slowly. Her entire back and shoulders had been taut and knotted and it had taken some serious finger work to remove the stress. Mai Ling moved the towel, exposing

Angelique's slender legs. She started massaging her smooth calves, her mind and ears alert.

'This could be the start of something very important,' Angelique mused, her mind still torn between giving in to Mai Ling's practised strokes and mulling over her situation.

Mai Ling said nothing, sliding her oily hands up and down Angelique's toned thighs. Then she concentrated on Angelique's feet, cradling them in her tiny hands before flexing them up and down and circling them in her palms.

Angelique felt Ma Ling's hands cupping her thighs as she lifted and stroked her skin. She spread her legs slightly, letting out a groan and relaxing into the couch. Mai Ling didn't break a stroke, easing her hands up and down with fluid strokes, her thumbs darting in and out of Angelique's inner thighs. Angelique sucked in her breath as Mai Ling's hands moved higher, the edge of her fingers just touching between her legs before teasingly moving away again.

Angelique gripped the edge of the couch. She shouldn't . . . she really shouldn't . . .

'Miss want usual?' Mai Ling murmured, her eyes narrowed.

Angelique hesitated. In view of her plan, she really should try to be good. She felt Mai Ling's tiny fingers flicking at the edge of her buttocks and gave up trying to be good. Where had that ever got her?

'I think that's exactly what I need, Mai Ling,' she murmured, wriggling expectantly on the couch.

Mai Ling rolled her eyes. With a body as beautiful as Angelique's, it wasn't exactly a hardship. Flicking the towel away, she climbed up on to the couch and parted Angelique's legs with her knees. Using her skilful fingers for an entirely different kind of massage, Mai Ling did what she did best and proved once more why she was in constant demand all over the world.

As Angelique squirmed and gasped, Mai Ling held her

down and firmly applied her tongue. As her client came and let out a shuddering howl of release, Mai Ling smiled smugly and climbed off.

'Miss better now?' she said, placing a fresh towel over Angelique's body.

'So much better,' Angelique responded in a husky voice, luxuriating in the afterglow of her orgasm.

'Good. Mai Ling charge extra for that.'

'Mai Ling can charge whatever she pleases.' Angelique grinned, resting her head on her hands as her masseuse bustled around tidying up and packing her oils away. Finally, her head was clear. That . . . release was just what the doctor ordered.

'Dad's never going to speak to me again,' Seraphina groaned, hugging her knees. Wearing a white sundress with her platinum-blond hair loose around her shoulders, she resembled an angel.

Or, rather, a fallen one, Cat thought, trying to read Seraphina's masked expression. Her eyes, with purple shadows beneath them from lack of sleep, looked bruised and her skin was sallow because she had spent the past few days shut in her bedroom. Cat still couldn't believe Seraphina had cantered round her school front garden naked and even though she could see the funny side of it, she was more concerned about what was really going on inside Seraphina's mind. Something had tipped her over the edge and Cat couldn't believe it was all down to Max being expelled.

'He'll come round,' she assured the girl. 'Your father is just angry right now.'

Seraphina jumped up, her mouth twisting defiantly. 'Well, so am I! I'm angry too but no one cares about that, do they?'

'Sit down,' Cat told her calmly. 'I mean it, Seraphina. What's the point of us trying to talk about this if you're just going to lose your temper every five minutes?' She waited until

Seraphina gave in and sank down on to the sun lounger again. 'Now, talk to me. Why are you so furious with your father?'

'Isn't it obvious?' Seraphina's brown eyes, when she lifted them to meet Cat's, were full of hurt. 'He doesn't want us here, Cat! That's why he sent us away to that stupid college in the first place. When Mum died, he shut us out, he sent us away because he couldn't bear to have us around.'

'Is that what you really think about your father?' she asked her gently. 'That he sent you away because he didn't want you here?'

'Why else would he do it?' Seraphina's shoulders were tense and hunched as she clutched her legs. 'Seriously, Cat, however hard you try, you won't be able to come up with another alternative. He rejected us just when we needed him the most and that's all there is to it. I know it, Max knows it and unless he's an idiot, our father knows it too.'

Cat sighed. She didn't want to betray Guy's confidence by telling Seraphina about him sobbing over Elizabeth's gravestone but she felt duty-bound to at least try to defend him.

'Maybe he can't cope with his own grief,' Cat offered, treading carefully. 'That doesn't mean it's right or that I'm on his side, all right? I'm just saying it's possible, isn't it?'

Because she liked Cat so much, Seraphina gave the suggestion a chance. She mulled it over, her small nose wrinkled with concentration, but finally she shook her head. 'No, sorry. I just can't see it. I don't think Father is suffering at all. I think he's just obsessed with business and he can't find time for us in his busy schedule.'

Cat gave up. Perhaps she could speak to Guy about it, but then it wasn't exactly any of her business. She chewed her fingernails. The longer she stayed at La Fleurie, the more deeply she was being drawn into all the issues the Ducasse family were facing. In reality, they were nothing to do with her.

'My passport turned up,' Cat told Seraphina, wondering if

251

she could voice her suspicions aloud without sounding crazy. 'In a drawer I'd already checked more than once.'

Seraphina missed the inference, her face falling. 'Oh no, does that mean you're going home?'

With a frown, Cat explained about her old passport being cancelled. 'So I have no choice but to wait for the new one. I still have the legal papers to sign and your grandmother has asked me to stay for the party, but either way, I'm trapped here until my new passport arrives.'

'Well, I'm glad you're here for a bit longer,' Seraphina confided, her eyes meeting Cat's. 'I . . . could do with a friend right now.' She changed the subject, hating sounding needy. 'So how was Grasse?'

'Incredible,' Cat murmured without thinking, her mind returning to the delicious kiss.

Seraphina raised her eyebrows. Cat was doing her best to look nonchalant and Seraphina wondered if something had happened between her and Xavier. Looking ridiculously pretty with her butterscotch-blond hair tied up in a ponytail and her aquamarine eyes all wide and innocent, Seraphina couldn't help thinking Cat was hiding something.

'Incredible. I see. In what way?'

Fully composed now after her slip-up, Cat waved an airy hand. 'Oh, it was just interesting, you know. All those perfume factories and the scenery was to die for.'

Seraphina flipped over on to her front but she didn't take her eyes off Cat. 'And what about my brother, Xavier. Was he incredible too?'

Cat looked away quickly. She wondered where Xavier was. She had barely seen him since they had returned from Grasse. She glanced at his lab. As she did so, she thought she saw the shadow of movement inside but she knew she must be mistaken. Xavier was more likely to be on the beach somewhere, half naked with a new girlfriend.

Seraphina rested her head on her hands. 'I expect you think

Xavier is just like Olivier, don't you?' Seeing Cat's startled expression, she nodded. 'Thought so. And I can see why. I mean, on the surface of it, they must seem very similar. The privileged background, the good looks . . . the women.' Seeing Cat flinch, she apologised. 'Sorry, I know that must sting. But what I'm trying to say is that I would hate you to not trust men any more just because of Olivier.' Seraphina sat up. 'He was such a selfish bastard. He was spoilt and lazy and all of us thought he needed a kick up the backside. But not all men are liars and cheats, you know. Xavier isn't and . . . and there are other men out there who aren't like that too.'

Cat's lip curled. 'What's so different about Xavier? He might be more talented than Olivier when it comes to the perfume business but I honestly can't see too much of a difference when it comes to shagging around. Sorry,' she added, realising she was slating Seraphina's beloved brother.

Seraphina hesitated. 'Look, there's more to Xavier than meets the eye. He's only with all those women because . . . there was this woman, you see, and she really hurt him . . .'

Cat made an impatient sound. She didn't buy it; Xavier wasn't some tortured soul, damaged by the love of his life.

Seraphina could tell that Cat didn't believe her. 'I know he looks like he doesn't care about anything but you couldn't be more wrong.' She pulled a face. 'I wish I could tell about this woman but Xavier hasn't even told the family about it, only me and Max, and I swore I wouldn't say anything.'

'You don't need to explain,' Cat told her firmly. 'His life is none of my business. He made that very clear when we were in Grasse.'

To her surprise, Seraphina laughed. 'Typical. He's ridiculously private and so hot headed. Look, I can't say too much but I will say that he hasn't always been like this. Olivier . . . I'm afraid he was born that way but Xavier, well, something changed him, all right?'

Cat shrugged. Seraphina seemed earnest in her attempts to

get her to think differently about Xavier but she wasn't sure if she believed her. Maybe she had Xavier all wrong, maybe she didn't. The fact remained that he still thought badly of her for marrying Olivier. She said as much to Seraphina. 'It's just that he clearly thinks I'm an idiot . . . but love makes you do reckless things, doesn't it?' Cat paused. 'What am I saying? You shouldn't know about such things.' When Seraphina was silent, Cat touched her arm. 'You don't, do you?'

Seraphina went pink. 'Not yet. But I want to.' Her brow furrowed. 'At least, I think I want to. I have this boyfriend, you see, and he's much older than me.' Realising she'd said too much, she hurriedly corrected herself. 'Well, not *much* older than me, just a bit older.'

Concerned, Cat leant forward. 'Seraphina, don't ever do anything you don't want to, all right? Men say all sorts of things to make you think you should have sex and God knows what else but at your age, no one should be pressurising you.'

'I'm not a child, Cat!' Seraphina was clearly offended.

'I know that. I wasn't suggesting you were. All I was saying is that you sound unsure and if you are, you need to know something.' Cat brushed a lock of hair out of Seraphina's bruised-looking eyes. 'Any man, any decent man, will wait for you.'

'Will he?' Seraphina looked sceptical.

Cat nodded firmly. 'Yes, he will.' She paused. 'Seraphina, are you all right? If you need to talk to someone, I'm here. I know I'm absolutely no substitute for your mother but I can still listen and support you.' Seeing Seraphina's eyes fill with tears, Cat put her arm round the young girl's shoulders. 'It's just . . . no one should make you do anything you don't want to do. Ever. And if they do, they're not worth it, do you understand?'

Seraphina nodded and did her best to stop her lip trembling. Cat wondered who this older boyfriend of hers was. If she

254

wasn't much mistaken, he was putting serious pressure on Seraphina to sleep with him.

And that, Cat decided, made him a major league creep.

A few days later, Xavier emerged from his lab and squinted at the brightness outside. Lighting a cigarette and inhaling deeply, he realised he'd been working almost non-stop for the past week or more. He was desperate for a break.

Tearing off his white coat and tossing it back inside the lab, he undid his shirt collar and immediately felt more relaxed. He strolled to the pool and felt a mild stab of disappointment that Cat had gone. He'd seen her out of the lab window but, checking his watch, he realised that must have been hours ago. Xavier wasn't sure what he would have said to her if he'd managed to bump into her but he was conscious that the air needing clearing. Also, ridiculously, he felt the urge to talk to her again, not about what had happened but about what he was doing.

Glancing at the pool, Xavier decided to take a dip. Not a proper one, he was fully dressed. His cigarette hanging out of his mouth, he rolled his trouser legs up and dangled his feet in the pool. The water was cool and refreshing and just what he needed. Sitting back, he flicked his dark hair out of his eyes and saw that Max was skulking around the pool house.

'Hey!' Xavier called him over. What was he doing back from college?

Max, wearing a black T-shirt, black jeans and an equally murky expression, came over. His dark-brown curls were dishevelled and his eyes were wary. 'Where did you just come from?'

Xavier looked sheepish. 'The lab. I've been . . . trying some things out.'

'What, creating a new fragrance?'

Xavier blew smoke in the air. 'More like resurrecting a new

one . . . I don't know. I'm just experimenting at the moment. Anyway, what are you doing back from school?'

Max looked incredulous. 'Don't you know? Hasn't Dad told you?'

Baffled, Xavier shook his head. 'I've been shut in the lab for days. What's going on?'

Knowing he was probably in for another ear-bashing, Max sat down next to him, and undid his baseball boots. Dropping his feet into the pool, he filled Xavier in about his drugs bust and about Seraphina's naked canter round the college grounds.

'Fuck.' Xavier didn't know whether to laugh or whack Max round the head.

Max braced himself. 'Go on then, let me have it. Everyone else has.'

Xavier sucked on his cigarette. He felt immensely sorry for the twins. After their mother's death, they had pretty much been left out in the cold and he couldn't help thinking the current situation was simply the result of that. At the time, Xavier had been far too caught up in his own fucked-up situation to be as supportive as he would have liked, and their father, well, he had literally fallen apart.

Bearing all this in mind, Xavier decided to go easy on Max. It was fair to assume the rest of the family wouldn't have held back. Someone had to be on the twins' side at a time like this.

'I think Seraphina's got guts,' he said. 'I can't believe she rode round the college naked!' Xavier could just imagine how his father would have reacted to that. He was glad he'd been locked away in his lab whilst it was all kicking off. 'As for you, Max . . .'

Max hung his head. 'I know. I'm an idiot. You don't need to tell me.'

'I didn't say that. But while we're talking, what's it all about?' Xavier asked, blowing smoke into the air. 'The drugs,

I mean. Do you really enjoy it or are you just trying to get Dad's attention?'

Max shrugged. 'A bit of both, I suppose. It made me feel as if I was letting off a bit of steam, you know?' He waggled his feet and Xavier couldn't help thinking how young he looked with his jeans up round his knees and his head hanging sorrowfully. 'Getting Dad's attention didn't work – not in a good way, at any rate.'

'Well, it wouldn't really, would it?' Xavier pointed out reasonably. He put an arm round Max's shoulder and gave him a brotherly hug. 'You know you can always talk to me, don't you?'

Max nodded, turning away. 'Yeah.' His voice sounded gruff.

'Sometimes you just need a father, I know, and we haven't really had one of those for the past couple of years.'

Max scowled. 'He's just useless.'

About to defend his father, Xavier realised he had thought very much the same thing about him over the past two years. Practically all of their conversations revolved around him returning to work, not about anything meaningful and certainly never about their mother.

Max jerked his feet in the water angrily. 'He doesn't even know about Seraphina and this boyfriend of hers.'

'What boyfriend?'

'He's older than her and that's about all I know about him.' Max shrugged helplessly, wishing he could do something about it. 'I have a bad feeling about it, Xav. Don't ask me why because I don't know but she's changed since she's been with him.'

Xavier's brown eyes were full of concern. 'Should I speak to her?'

'No, she'd only be furious with me for talking about it. I just hope she doesn't do anything stupid, that's all.'

Xavier sighed. 'All right. Now, do we need to talk about this drugs thing?'

Max shook his head. 'I've learnt my lesson, Xav. I didn't even really enjoy it that much,' he confessed. 'Vero and the boys . . . it was more about hanging out with them. They're older than me. They're cool, with their motorbikes and all that stuff.'

'Have you heard from them since you've been expelled?'

Max frowned. 'No, but I'm sure they'll be in touch soon.'

Xavier wasn't convinced. Kids like Vero and those boys who followed her around only hung around with rich, screwed-up kids like Max because they thought it added something to their group. Max, with all his hang-ups and his rebellious attitude, had probably attracted a great deal of attention due to his daring antics and complete disregard for rules but now that his wildness had tipped over the edge into expulsion, Xavier suspected Vero and the rest of them wouldn't have much time for his younger brother.

Max changed the subject. 'Seraphina told me you and Cat had a good time in Grasse.'

Xavier shot a glance at him but said nothing. He'd hardly describe it as a 'good time' and he was certain Cat wouldn't have said that either.

'What has Dad said about you being back in the lab?' A bitter expression flitted across Max's face but it was fleeting. He couldn't resent Xavier for doing what he loved most in the world. It was his father he was furious with.

'He doesn't know. At least, if he does, he hasn't said a word to me about it.'

Max raised his eyebrows. 'So what's this new fragrance then?'

Xavier played with his cigarette packet. 'I suppose, loosely speaking, it's a floral with a blast of sweet rose and orchid as a top note with some creamy amber and white lilies, and the base notes are a honeyed cedarwood, musk and a really dry, lemony frankincense.' He stared past Max, his mind darting. 'It's the heart notes I'm struggling with. I want a fruit accord but something isn't quite right. I think mandarin but it needs something else too, as does the base note.' He needed to talk to someone about it but the only person who seemed able to listen to him properly and spark off his creativity, unbelievably, was Cat.

Max was impressed. He didn't understand everything Xavier was talking about but he knew enough to see that his brother was on to something big.

'If I get it right, it's going to be the best thing I've ever done,' Xavier admitted, the thought filling him with momentary anxiety. 'Is Cat still here?' he asked, as casually as possible.

'For now.'

Xavier felt a moment of irrational panic but he squashed it down. 'What does that mean?'

'Rumour has it Pascal's completed all that paperwork,' Max shrugged. 'Once she's signed it, she'll have no reason to stay. Although, I did overhear the housekeeper gossiping and she reckons someone stole the first set of papers.' He looked gloomy. 'I thought I might get the blame. Everyone around here seems to think I'm capable of most things. No one's said anything to me about it, though – not yet, anyway.'

Xavier's brow wrinkled in confusion. 'How strange,' he said. 'Still, Cat's old passport will have been cancelled if she's applied for a new one, I should think, so it doesn't really matter about the legal papers.'

'Oh well.' Max didn't really care what Cat did or why she was here. He liked her, she was extremely pretty and she had always been nice to him, but he had far too much going on in his head to worry about his cousin's widow. Grabbing his baseball boots, he shot Xavier a curious look. His brother was staring into space. Max shrugged. Most likely Xavier was pondering the elusive missing ingredient in the fragrance he was working on because he always got like this when he was developing something new. Leaving Xavier chain-smoking and

259

thoughtfully swishing his feet in the water, Max headed to the stables to saddle up Le Fantome.

There was nothing for it, thought Xavier, he was going to have to speak to Cat. He couldn't get her out of his head and the only thing he could do was talk to her again to check how he felt. For all he knew, he was imagining things and he had to know for sure.

Chapter Fifteen

Nursing a sore throat and taking a break from her home fragrance campaign, Leoni was sitting in the main salon drinking a cup of honey-infused tea with a slice of lemon in it.

She leant over the edge of a sofa and stared out of the window in bemusement watching the preparations for the Rose-Nymphea party getting underway, suppressing a laugh as she noticed her grandmother bossily clutching a clipboard and presiding over events as though she was the conductor in charge of a wayward orchestra. Case after case of wine was being delivered, as well as some crates of vintage champagne which Leoni happened to know came with a heart-stopping price tag.

It was like watching a gigantic wedding being organised, Leoni thought with a frown, wondering if Delphine would go to half as much trouble if her granddaughter was about to get married. Although, on reflection, she probably would, Leoni decided. If only to celebrate the fact that her granddaughter had finally managed to find a man to settle down with, just as all Ducasse women should. Leoni wished her grandmother wasn't so bigoted.

Still, perhaps Jerard was the man who could change all that. Nice looking, hard working, caring – what more could she ask for? All right, so she hadn't experienced any particular knee-trembling when they'd kissed and Jerard hadn't exactly thrown her into bed and torn her clothes off, but so what? Lust was overrated. Leoni had allowed herself to be caught up in such silliness when she was younger – look at the way she had lusted after Ashton! And it had been such a waste of time too.

Leoni swallowed. No, at her age, she should be thinking about a stable, lasting relationship with plenty of shared interests; passion and desire were for childish crushes, not a mature, serious relationship. Feeling her mood plummet slightly at this sensible but rather uninspiring thought, Leoni ignored her feelings and checked her phone to see if Jerard had sent her any texts. He had. Short but sweet as always and mostly about the meeting he was attending or what time he would be back but it still made her smile that Jerard took the time to let her know his whereabouts.

She realised she hadn't heard from Ashton for a while and sent him a quick text to check he'd been invited to the party. He sent her one back telling her he'd received his invite and that he'd probably be there. Unreasonably, Leoni felt disappointed that he didn't seem to want to indulge in any general chat the way he usually did – she and Ashton always chatted about nonsense, he was the one man she could say anything to, however absurd it might sound.

Perhaps Ashton was busy too, Leoni thought, wondering why she seemed to be surrounded by men who thought more about business than relationships. Well, friendships, in Ashton's case, but still. Wondering if he might bring a date to the party, Leoni couldn't resist sending him a quick text about it. When he didn't immediately come back, she sighed and headed outside for some air.

Discovering a group of men stringing up fairy lights and fixing unlit torches into the lawns nearby, she wondered why it was taking so many of them to sort out what seemed to be a relatively simple job. Then Leoni realised Cat was taking a swim in the pool. No wonder the men were so distracted, she thought tartly. Cat was all butterscotch hair and golden-hued skin and as she swam to the edge of the pool and smiled, Leoni realised with annoyance that the dark, sooty lashes framing the outrageously pretty aquamarine eyes were clearly natural.

Shivering, Cat gestured to the water. 'Fancy a dip? The air is chilly, but the pool is so well-heated, it's not that bad once you get in.'

'I have far too much work to do,' Leoni snapped in English, shoving her hands into the pockets of her sleek, black dress and omitting to mention that she had been doing nothing more useful than drinking tea for the last hour or so. Randomly wondering why she found it endearing that Ashton spoke French like a bumbling fool, Leoni reverted to her mother tongue grudgingly, knowing Cat preferred it. 'Some of us have jobs, you know.'

Cat flushed. 'Indeed.' She leant on the edge of the pool, her expression glum. 'I thought I had a new job sorted back home but it's all on the back burner again. Christ, I hate not working. It's not natural, is it?'

Leoni contemplated her. She'd forgotten Cat had a life back in England and she supposed that being stuck out here in France wasn't exactly conducive to getting another job sorted out.

'Why did you get fired from your old job?' she asked out of interest.

'Er . . . for taking an extended honeymoon,' Cat replied abruptly, not wanting to set off Leoni's temper by talking about Olivier. Seeing Leoni staring back at her expectantly, she continued grudgingly. 'I hadn't had a holiday for years but for some reason, my boss took exception to me getting married and staying in France for a few more weeks.' She lifted herself out of the water, revealing a toned body in a sky-blue bikini she had borrowed from Seraphina. It was slightly too small but it highlighted her curves perfectly.

Leoni suddenly envied Cat – not for being a widow at such a young age, naturally – but really, when was the last time she, Leoni, had gone for a swim or done something relaxing? Her work schedule was so tight, it simply didn't allow for down time in the form of a calming swim or even a rejuvenating massage. Although, if Leoni was honest with herself, it was a self-imposed pressure but she didn't know how else to live. Her life had always been about work; after a series of terrible dates in her youth and the realisation that nothing would ever happen between herself and Ashton, Leoni had devoted herself wholeheartedly to the family business. Until now, Leoni reminded herself. Now, she had Jerard.

What must it be like to look like Cat, she wondered. Even wrapped in an emerald-green towel with messed-up, wet hair, Cat looked sensational and Leoni couldn't help envying her, despite her losses.

'Did you hear about the legal papers going missing?' she asked.

Cat nodded, looking exasperated. 'Can you believe it? My passport mysteriously turns up and then those papers disappear into thin air.'

Leoni perched on the edge of a sun lounger, giving a nearby workman a pointed glance when she noticed he was fiddling with an already secured string of lights. He moved away, throwing a final look of longing in Cat's direction.

'What do you mean, "mysteriously"?' Leoni asked, referring to Cat's passport.

About to offer her thoughts about it, Cat closed her mouth. She hadn't a clue which members of the family she could trust around here. And even though she knew Leoni was frequently irked by Delphine's interfering ways, Leoni's loyalties would reside with her family when it came down to it.

'Oh, nothing,' she answered finally, her eyes downcast. 'I'm getting carried away with conspiracy theories at the moment. Ignore me.' Cat buried her head in the towel, rubbing her hair briskly. 'It doesn't matter, anyway; I still need to wait for my new passport.'

Leoni held her face up to the emerging sun, allowing herself to relax for a moment. She realised she must look incongruous reclining on a sun lounger in a tight dress and high heels but right now she suddenly couldn't care less. Why did she push herself so hard? she wondered. Why did she put herself under so much pressure there was no time for fun?

Leoni suddenly felt unsure of herself and she found herself questioning why she didn't have more free time to enjoy herself. Her girlfriends were in Rome on a hen break, no doubt eating deliciously fattening gelati and chatting up handsome Italian men. She had declined to join them, citing heavy work commitments. Yet in reality she could have done with a break and she would still have had plenty of time to get back for the Rose-Nymphea party at the weekend. Leoni sighed. She really did seem to have her life–work balance all wrong.

'How's your pitch going for the home fragrance line?' Cat asked, emerging from under the towel. 'I meant what I said about helping if you'd like me to.' She sat down on the lounger nearest Leoni. 'Actually, I'm dying to do something – anything, really. It's beautiful here and I hate to admit that I'm bored, but I'm used to working, you know?'

Leoni nodded, hesitating. Why wasn't she taking Cat up on her offer of help? She had far too much on her plate to manage it all single-handedly and Cat, out of everyone in the vicinity, was the best placed person to assist her with the pitch. She had probably delivered this kind of thing hundreds of times before and judging by the way she had handled herself in the family meeting, Cat would know just the right thing to say to win Guy over.

About to take her up on the offer, Leoni noticed Seraphina approaching them wearing a robe over a bright pink bikini with a straw hat, her platinum-blond hair tied in a side ponytail. She looked as though she belonged on the pages of the glossy fashion magazines she was so attached to. Feeling frumpy and invisible in her smart dress and heels, an aggravated Leoni got to her feet. Why were Cat and Seraphina swanning around in

265

bikinis, anyway? It was only just spring! Leoni had never felt more undesirable or drab in her life and her mood turned frosty.

'Thanks, but I don't need your help,' she said to Cat tersely, changing her mind in a heartbeat. 'I just can't concentrate because of this stupid party. Not with all the crashing and banging going on around me.' She shot the lighting men a hostile glance but they were too busy checking out the doubly rewarding sight of Cat and Seraphina to notice. Leoni came to an important decision. After the party, she and Jerard were going to sleep together. It was about time they cemented their relationship and, for once, she was going to urge Jerard to put pleasure before business. As a bare minimum, Leoni decided, she wanted some sort of confirmation of his commitment to her. All of a sudden, it seemed important to know Jerard had real feelings for her. Not just romantic ones but sexual ones, too.

Seraphina sighed at Leoni's curtness and turned to Cat. 'Do you have something to wear for the party?'

Cat sat up. 'God, no, I haven't. My friend Bella said she was going to send me some of my party dresses from storage but nothing's turned up yet.' Her eyes clouded over. 'I totally forgot about it, to be honest.'

Leoni narrowed her eyes. 'So you're staying for the party, are you?'

Cat looked pained. 'I have no choice. Well, I could sit in my room during the party, I suppose,' she added, sure Leoni would think that the best idea. 'And without anything suitable to wear, I might do just that.'

'I can lend you something,' Seraphina offered. 'I have tons of gorgeous clothes.'

'Not that you wear them much these days,' Leoni interjected sarcastically, feeling left out of the girly chatter. Missing Jerard and narked that Ashton hadn't come back to her about his date for the party, she lashed out. 'Did you really think that riding bareback around your college was the best way to get your father's attention?'

Seraphina went pink. 'I wasn't trying to get his attention,' she fired back, hurt. 'I was trying to make a stand about Max being expelled, that's all.'

'What, by getting yourself expelled at the same time? Very clever, Seraphina, very commendable.'

Cat frowned. 'That's a bit unfair,' she said heatedly, then held her hands up apologetically. 'Sorry; obviously this is none of my business but I think we all know that Seraphina's naked horse-riding was a protest. Besides, Guy does need to pay the twins some attention . . .'

Leoni's lip curled. 'Oh, I see, now you know more about my family than I do. Don't start getting ideas above your station. You're Olivier's widow and nothing more, do you understand?' Spinning round, she hurried off, her high heels savagely stabbing holes in the perfectly clipped lawn.

'I'm not likely to forget that fact, am I?' Cat muttered dejectedly as Leoni disappeared from sight.

'Oh, ignore her!' Seraphina flapped a hand. 'She's just ridiculously uptight. Nothing a good bout of sex wouldn't cure.'

'Seraphina!'

'Well, it's true.' Seraphina smiled. 'Leoni's got this new boyfriend, Jerard, but they haven't done the deed yet.'

Cat was shocked at Seraphina's directness. 'How do you know that?'

'Because she's like a cat on a hot tin roof and there's no way she'd be like that if she was getting some.' Seraphina flipped over on to her front, her expression rueful. 'Trust me, I know. And no, I don't mean me.'

Cat glanced at her worriedly. She was becoming increasingly concerned about Seraphina's older boyfriend but she had no idea what to do about it. She had thought she might be able to approach Leoni and get her take on it but judging by Leoni's aggressive reaction just now, she was the last person Cat should think of confiding in.

'I wonder if Ashton's coming to the party?' Seraphina said casually.

Cat turned to look at her. 'Why does it matter?'

Seraphina shrugged, her brown eyes full of mischief. 'I'm just thinking, he's single, you're single, he's English and so are you . . .'

'Oh my God, you're matchmatching,' Cat said in disbelief. 'Is that appropriate? I'm your cousin's widow, for heaven's sake!'

'Yes, but that's all in the past.' Seraphina slid her sunglasses on. 'Isn't it about time you met someone else? Of course, I've always thought Ashton was madly in love with Leoni but now that she's hooked up with Jerard, it might be time for a change ...'

Cat put her head on the lounger guiltily, wondering what Seraphina would think if she knew about the kiss she and Xavier had shared. Would she be as friendly then? Cat had no idea and she supposed that it was irrelevant, in any case. The kiss was a regrettable moment of madness, never to be repeated, so it wasn't worth mentioning and it was best forgotten.

So, forget it, Cat told herself brutally. Forget the kiss and forget about Xavier. He wasn't worth her time and he was, most assuredly, not someone she should get close to in the future. Listening with only half an ear to Seraphina's bright chatter, Cat wished she didn't find it so hard to put Xavier and the passionate, rain-soaked kiss out of her mind.

Deeply engrossed in his formula, Xavier glanced up to see his father standing in the doorway. Looking utterly incredulous, he clearly hadn't been expecting to find his son ensconced in his lab again.

Xavier felt mildly exasperated. His grandmother had visited him in the lab the day before, pretending to ask casual questions but really, she had been intent on finding out what he was up to. Informing her that he was creating a new fragrance using a formula he had almost perfected some years ago, she had gone into raptures of delight. When she learnt that the fragrance could possibly be launched in the summer if he could finalise the missing ingredient he was searching for, Xavier had been concerned his grandmother might keel over and have a heart attack in front of him, she was so ecstatic. Giving her carte blanche to look into a suitable ad campaign if she so desired, Xavier had finally managed to get rid of her so he could concentrate. And now his father was here, clearly wanting to know more.

Xavier sighed. Being back in his lab was big news as far as the family were concerned but he couldn't help wishing everyone would leave him alone to get on with it.

'What . . . what are you doing in here?' Guy stammered, staring at Xavier.

'I'm . . . creating a new fragrance,' Xavier admitted.

Guy looked as pleased as punch. 'A new fragrance? How wonderful.' For a while, he wandered around the lab while Xavier worked, finding pleasure in the sight of Xavier's chemistry and perfume books piled high and open at various pages. There were Post-it notes dotted along the surface of the counter and rows of labelled phials in storage boxes sat with their lids open expectantly. Xavier's laptop was on with several internet pages on the go and his notepad was filled with distinctive scribbles.

Guy couldn't believe it. This was a scene he hadn't witnessed for more than two years now and he didn't dare hope his elder son was finally back doing what he did best. He glanced at him. Xavier was sitting on a stool, his lab coat hanging open to reveal his shirt and jeans, his dark hair falling across his face in concentration. He looked up and Guy could see that his chocolate-brown eyes were alight with passion.

Xavier held up an empty perfume bottle. 'Do you think this

needs updating? The bottle, I mean.'

Guy shrugged. 'It's classic, I suppose. Why, what did you have in mind?'

'Something younger, perhaps? Nothing too funky that will alienate our older customers . . . in fact, I'm thinking of something with a vintage vibe. A very curvy bottle made of beautiful glass that will make customers want to pick it up as soon as they see it.' He pulled a sketch out of his pocket – the one Cat had knocked up in Grasse. 'Something like this.'

Guy looked at it. 'You didn't draw this. Who did?'

'Cat,' Xavier admitted, not meeting his father's eyes. 'What do you think?'

'It's good. Very good. But I'd rather you focused on the fragrance itself, if I'm honest.'

Xavier smiled. 'I will. But I have a friend in Limoges who owns a glass factory. I thought he might be able to make us a prototype if I fax him the drawing.'

Guy looked thoughtful. 'I wonder if Cat would have any ideas about a proper ad campaign? Leoni's always going on about us being more commercial and I'm finally coming round to the idea.'

'She knows her stuff.' Xavier shrugged, not wanting to seem too keen on Cat. 'I guess you could always ask her.'

'Well, if Cat's inspired you to be back in here in any way, then I'm grateful,' Guy said, wondering why Xavier looked so uncomfortable.

Xavier started. Cat hadn't inspired him – had she? He'd like to say not but he couldn't help thinking she had lit a flame under him somehow. Not once in the past two years had he felt galvanished into action the way he was now. Not once had any of the women he'd spent time with, girlfriends or one-night stands, shown a remote interest in fragrance or the business or why he no longer took any part in it.

Xavier put down his notepad. He was sick and tired of

skirting round what had happened in Grasse. He needed to speak to Cat and he needed to do it soon.

Pacing restlessly around the stable area for something to do a few weeks later, Cat wasn't best pleased to find Delphine limping towards her. Boredom was bad enough but she really wasn't sure she could face the Spanish inquisition right now.

Or the French inquisition, Cat told herself glumly. She couldn't believe another few weeks had passed with no sign of a new passport or the legal papers.

'There you are,' Delphine said with a bright smile. She was carrying a magazine in her free hand but she held it down by her side. 'I've been looking for you.'

'Really?' Cat felt unnerved by the sight of Delphine's teeth; most of the old lady's smiles, the rare few that were directed at her, tended to be tight-lipped ones. 'Listen, I know you must be keen for me to get home now. As soon as I sign those papers and my new passport makes an appearance, I'll be on my way.' She bit her lip, wondering why it seemed so hard to imagine being back in England. 'I must get on with my life. Jobs, flats, you know . . .' Cat's voice petered out. She couldn't exactly tell Delphine her desire to leave was mostly because of Xavier so she preferred to make it sound as though she had pressing issues to deal with in England. Although, obviously, a job and somewhere to live *were* critical issues in reality.

'I'm sure you must have things to attend to.' Delphine frowned. 'In the meantime, I was wondering if you could help me with something.' Gesturing to a nearby bench, she sat down and waited for Cat to join her. 'Obviously I'm now aware that Xavier is creating a new fragrance.'

'He is?' Cat was jolted. She'd worked out that Xavier was back in his lab again but not that he was getting down to the serious business of making perfumes.

'Yes. I spoke to him about it briefly yesterday and he hinted that we might be able to release something new in the summer.'

Cat was taken aback. 'Wow. You must be delighted about that,' she said, unable to keep the sarcasm out of her voice.

Delphine ignored it with an effort. 'Of course, it's the most wonderful news. The trip to Grasse clearly unlocked something for Xavier.' Her hazel eyes met Cat's briefly.

Cat stared at her, irritation creeping up inside her. Was that what the trip had been about?

'But that's not what I wanted to discuss with you,' Delphine said, 'although it is related in a roundabout way.' She flipped the magazine open. 'When Xavier releases his new fragrance, I was wondering if we might need to be a bit more creative this time. Leoni has always wanted us to use someone more famous in our ads and I thought you might have an opinion on that.'

Cat was surprised. Why was Delphine asking for her opinion all of a sudden? She'd made it clear she found her suggestions irksome. 'I think it always helps to use a well-known face for a campaign. Someone recognisable catches the eye, and if the person is aspirational – you know, someone others look up to and aspire to emulate – it can really give a fragrance the right vibe.'

'Excellent.' Delphine looked pleased. 'This is the person I have in mind.' She showed the magazine to Cat and waited.

Cat glanced at the photograph. The woman, whoever she was, was stunningly beautiful. With full, pouty lips and acres of blond hair, she was sexy with an incredible figure. She read the name – Angelique Bodart. It was only vaguely familiar to her but presumably the actress was very well known in France.

'She has an agent,' Delphine said. 'But I wouldn't have the first idea how to go about contacting him.'

Cat looked up. 'Are you saying you'd like me to do it?'

'Could you?' Delphine's eyes lit up. 'That would be perfect, and at least it would give you something to do until everything else is sorted out.'

'I guess . . .' Cat wasn't sure if she wanted to do anything for Delphine. At the same time, she was bored out of her brain. Leoni refused to accept her help on the home fragrance campaign and there was nothing else going on. 'All right, I'll do it.'

Delphine looked thrilled. 'Thank you! I'd really appreciate that. I wonder, could you possibly keep this whole thing a secret? I wouldn't want anyone to think I was interfering. Xavier, for one, is very anti such things.'

Xavier was anti most things, Cat thought acerbically. 'Of course. Leave it with me and I won't breathe a word to anyone.'

Delphine patted her hand in a disturbingly friendly way and got up. 'I can't thank you enough, really. I'll leave the magazine in your room so you have the agent's details and I'll make sure Xavier provides you with a brief so you can sell the idea to Miss Bodart.' She glanced over her shoulder and saw Xavier approaching. Putting a finger to her lips in a rather girlish fashion, Delphine gave Cat a wink. 'Not a word, remember?'

Cat nodded distractedly as Delphine headed off. What did Xavier want? He had been avoiding her since their return from Grasse and she had decided it was probably for the best to keep out of his way so he couldn't mess with her head again.

He gestured to the bench. 'May I?'

'Help yourself.'

'Sorry we haven't spoken since Grasse,' Xavier started, staring at her intently.

Mesmerised by his chocolate-brown eyes, Cat shrugged, but she couldn't break his gaze.

'I promise I wasn't avoiding you . . . at least, maybe I was.' Xavier rubbed his chin. 'I'm back in my lab, I needed to concentrate.'

'So I hear.' Cat told him what Delphine had said, carefully avoiding saying anything about the potential ad campaign.

'I thought perhaps we should clear the air,' Xavier said, sounding absurdly rational. 'You know, after what happened.'

Cat gave him a half-smile. 'What, that terrible kiss that we both regret so much?'

Xavier shot her a glance. Did she regret it? Did he? He pulled himself together. Of course he regretted it. However ravishing Cat was, she was Olivier's widow. Inappropriateness aside, they were totally incompatible – apart from an apparent ability to irritate the hell out of each other, Xavier thought crossly.

'Yes, that. I can only apologise. I'm not sure what came over me,' he said, wondering why his words sounded so empty.

Cat allowed her gaze to linger on Xavier's mouth. He really was attractive but, that aside, they had nothing in common.

Xavier frowned, leaning back on the bench. 'It was . . . there was something you said over dinner.'

'What did I say?'

'The thing about your parents, about how you live your life to the full, out of tribute to them. It struck a chord with me. It's how I see life, I guess. Not because anyone had died at that point, but because this,' he gestured to his surroundings, 'all of this makes me seem so unfairly privileged. I suppose I wanted to show the world that I didn't live in a secure little bubble.'

Cat was stunned that he was opening up to her, even if it wasn't deeply personal information he was offering. 'That does make sense,' she said slowly. So they did have something in common, after all. His honestly suddenly made him even more attractive and Cat struggled to focus on what he was saying.

'I just thought we should clear the air,' Xavier said again, looking straight into her eyes. How had they ended up sitting so close? he wondered. There was barely a breath between them, which meant that her full mouth was mere inches from his. Shocked at himself, Xavier realised he was longing to kiss her again. It was madness, but he knew he'd be lying if he said he didn't want to feel her soft lips against his again, that he didn't want to sink his hands into her wonderful hair or that he didn't want to tear the clothes from her body and find out just how exquisite her skin was beneath them.

Cat, unable to tear her eyes from Xavier's, felt herself trembling all over. What the hell was wrong with her? Xavier was the last person she should be attracted to – she didn't even like him, for heaven's sake! But his tanned nose, the smattering of golden freckles, the vulnerable look in those devastating eyes . . .

'You're not like Olivier,' she murmured without thinking.

Xavier sat up sharply. Mentioning Olivier had been like hurling a bucket of cold water all over him. It was a stark reminder that he was having improper thoughts about his cousin's widow – who was, quite frankly, one of the most exasperating women he'd ever met. One of the most desirable too, Xavier thought, running his eyes over her gorgeous body, but that was irrelevant.

'Of course I'm not,' he snapped, getting to his feet. 'How many times do I have to tell you that?'

Affronted, Cat blinked. She hadn't meant to say the thing about Olivier out loud but, on reflection, wasn't it a compliment to Xavier? God, he was touchy!

'I have work to do,' Xavier told her curtly. 'I'm so glad we had this chat.'

'Oh, me too,' she replied in a saccharine tone. She had never felt more like slapping someone in her life. Watching him stride off like some bloody matinee idol, Cat wanted to let out a scream of frustration. Xavier had got under her skin and whatever she did, she couldn't seem to stop her feelings for him spiralling out of control. After the party, she was definitely going back to England to start again.

Otherwise, Cat thought, as she closed her eyes and willed

the image of Xavier's sexy, soulful eyes out of her mind, she was in danger of losing her heart completely.

Sitting outside La Fleurie on a crumbling wall waiting for Vero and the boys to turn up, Max was beginning to feel agitated. It was Friday night, where the hell were they? Without fail, they would drive into the local villages on their motorbikes and visit some bars, whether they were at college or not. And they had always picked him up on the way. But tonight there was no sign of them and it was an hour after their usual bar-visiting time.

Max lit a cigarette moodily. Bastards. How could they let him down like this? If they'd just been hanging around with him because he was the messed-up rich kid, he'd be gutted. It wasn't that he missed Vero or the boys particularly, it was just that he hated the thought of being used. Vero was off her head most of the time anyway, Max reflected, and the boys were like a couple of willing lapdogs doing her dirty work for her. Just as they had always been the ones to score the drugs for the gang, Max half expected the boys to turn up on their bikes to snidely let him know Vero wouldn't be putting in an appearance.

Feeling morose, he blew smoke into the air. The château was lit up like a Christmas tree as the party preparations reached fever pitch. Staff were running around like headless chickens and his grandmother was behaving like a mad dictator. She had made several of the girls cry and had even managed to reduce one of the men to tears with her demands.

Who cared about a stupid party? Max thought sulkily. Especially when it looked as if he wouldn't have any of his friends there. He had invited them a few weeks ago and they had promised to be there but now, Max thought it extremely unlikely. Hearing a noise, he looked up hopefully but he was flooded with disappointment when he realised it was only Madeleine.

'Hey,' she said shyly. She sat down on the edge of the wall. Her long dark hair hung over one shoulder and she was wearing jeans and a long-sleeved striped T-shirt. 'Are you waiting for Vero?'

Max shrugged. He noted that Madeleine was wearing Cool Water by Davidoff, a perfume he really approved of. It smelt of crab apple, woody citrus, amber and musk and it was one of his favourites. He wondered why he hadn't noticed before that she wore it. Having grown up around fragrance, identifying perfumes and aftershaves and whatever they contained was something all the family did without thinking. He supposed he had never thought of Madeleine in that way, despite the brief kiss they had shared.

'I don't think Vero's coming,' Madeleine said apologetically. 'I heard her and the boys saying something about going to Marseilles for the weekend.'

Max swore and threw his cigarette on the ground.

'Sorry.' Madeleine winced. 'I just thought you should know.'

'It's not your fault.' Max pushed his dark hair out of his eyes. 'I thought they might not want to know me now but I was hoping I was wrong.'

'Sorry. So, how are you? Is your dad furious?'

Max shoved his hands into his pockets, glad of someone to talk to. Apart from his brief chat with Xavier, he felt like a pariah. 'Like you wouldn't believe! He's barely speaking to me and Seraphina – I'm not sure if he's worked out who he's angrier with yet.'

Against her better judgement, Madeleine giggled. 'It was amazing when she cantered past on her horse. I wish I had the guts to do something like that.' She cast her eyes to the ground. 'I'm way too strait-laced. And my father really would disown me. He thinks I'm going to be the first female president.'

'Better not be seen talking to a delinquent like me, then,'

Max said abruptly, turning to head back inside. He didn't notice her face falling. He thought of something and glanced over his shoulder. 'Fancy coming to a party tomorrow night? It's formal and there will probably be loads of boring people there but . . .'

'I'd love to,' Madeleine replied, jumping up from the wall. 'You can count on me,' she added.

So maybe he had one person he could rely on, Max thought, sloping back up to the château. In spite of his mood over Vero and the boys, he couldn't help hoping Madeleine would turn up tomorrow.

Feeling utterly confused about Xavier, Cat was on her way to meet Angelique Bodart. Having borrowed a sporty little red Peugeot from Guy, Cat was heading towards a building near Mougins where, conveniently, Angelique was doing some shots for a French magazine.

Cat wondered what Xavier was thinking. Did he feel even the tiniest iota of what she was feeling right now? He was so hard to read but at one point sitting there on the bench, she had been certain he wanted to kiss her again. Hating herself for admitting it, Cat knew she had been dying for him to do it too.

She pulled to a halt at the address she'd been given, knowing she needed to stop thinking about Xavier. Inside the building, she was directed to the 'penthouse studio' and she found herself inside what looked like a very expensive boudoir. Decked out in pinks and reds, it featured a large bed with a scarlet throw across it and several plump fluffy cushions, mirrored walls and a dressing table with toiletries and make-up all over it. Loud music blared out of a stereo that was out of shot and a crowd of male and female staff were presiding over the photo shoot.

Wondering if all of them were legitimately part of the photographic team, Cat gasped as she caught sight of Angelique lying on the big squashy bed on her front, her blond hair reaching down her back almost to the cleft of her perfect, peachy backside. Completely naked save for a pair of black patent slingbacks and a velvet ribbon round her throat, Angelique looked like the archetypal sex kitten. Her eyes were made up with smoky greys and blues and her lips were red and glossy. It was an unsubtle image but it worked.

Angelique flipped on to her back and gave them all an eyeful of her luscious breasts. The photographs Cat had seen in magazines didn't do Angelique justice; in the flesh, she was jaw-droppingly gorgeous. As she coiled one leg across her body and flung her arms over her head, Cat heard an audible gasp from the crew.

'Are you Cat Hayes?' whispered Celine, Angelique's assistant, her hands full of paperwork, phones and a honey-coloured silk robe.

Cat nodded.

'Angelique said to let you sit here.' Celine gestured to a chair near the front and nearly let the silk robe slither out of her fingers. 'Oops. Thanks. This shoot, it's a "crazed lover" scenario, in case you're wondering about all the mess. All about some lover leaving her for another man.' Celine frowned. 'I'm not sure I could see that happening to Angelique but I suppose it's just acting.' She pointed at a man in a suit who was watching everything meticulously and prowling around the set restlessly. 'That's Mason, Angelique's agent.'

Cat took the seat, disturbed to find her eyes level with Angelique's groin. She glanced at Mason. He was a big man with a heavy jaw and a hooked nose and he was wearing a pinstriped suit that made him look more like a mafia boss than an agent.

'What sort of magazine is this shoot for?' she asked, doing her best to tear her eyes away as Angelique crawled up on to all fours and put her perfect butt in the air.

Celine's eyes darted to Angelique. She didn't want to get

caught gossiping but she loved talking about her famous boss. 'Just one of the usual men's magazines. She always has to strip off – it's what they want.'

'She seems very . . . confident,' Cat said, raising her eyebrows as Angelique contorted herself into a position a stripper would baulk at. She couldn't believe it was a shoot for a men's magazine; it looked more like a top-shelf effort.

'I know.' Celine nodded, looking slightly embarrassed. 'I thought I'd get used to all this but it's a bit overwhelming. She's so famous, you know. Me and Mason are worried she's having a mini breakdown at the moment,' she confided in a low voice.

'Really?' Cat thought Angelique looked totally in control. She moved easily, as if she knew exactly what she was doing and what was expected of her.

'She's usually so business minded,' Celine went on absent-mindedly. 'None of us can understand why she's turned this Hollywood film down. She actually had the role without auditioning for it – how often does that happen?' Celine tutted. 'I practically had my bag packed and my ticket to L.A. booked but then she did an about-turn and said she didn't want to do it.'

Cat frowned. Why on earth would Angelique turn down a chance at Hollywood? The place was hardly teeming with French actresses.

Suddenly remembering she was speaking to a perfect stranger, Celine went bright red. 'Oh my God, you can't tell anyone about that!' She jumped as Angelique stood up and snapped her fingers for her robe.

Cat shook her head as Celine dashed forward and helped Angelique into the honey-coloured silk.

'Cat Hayes? I speak a little English . . . oh, you speak French? Wonderful. I only know a few swear words in English anyway.' Angelique smiled charmingly and took a seat. 'My agent tells me you have some sort of offer for me.' Before she had finished the sentence, Mason was at her elbow.

He introduced himself to Cat briefly and took a seat without being offered one, his large frame filling it with ease.

Cat felt apprehensive. She'd offered actresses or models roles in ad campaigns a few times before but not often enough to feel particularly confident about it. It occurred to her that perhaps Delphine had set her up, hoping she would mess the whole deal up and the family would think she had done it on purpose, but Cat put the thought aside firmly. She had to stop being paranoid about Delphine.

Telling herself it was just like pitching a brand to a client in her advertising firm, Cat cleared her throat. 'I do. It's in the early stages but the Ducasse-Fleurie perfume brand is hoping to launch a new fragrance this summer. The family would very much like you to front the campaign.' She followed up with a few more details, handing some glossy brochures over and chatting about the company.

Close up, Angelique was even more breathaking. The honey-coloured robe complemented her colouring perfectly and even when she removed the red lip gloss and heavy foundation with a cloth Celine handed her, she was still stunning. It was difficult to pinpoint her age but Cat guessed Angelique might be only a few years older than she was – in her late twenties perhaps, early thirties at the most. As Cat watched her, she couldn't help putting the concept together in her mind – Angelique in exquisite, expensive underwear, being showered with purple, velvety petals. Her expression would be innocent yet knowing . . .

'I'm familiar with the brand,' Angelique informed her silkily, handing the dirty make-up cloth to Celine without even looking at her. Celine hovered for a moment before resigning herself to her redundant status and leaving. 'And I like it. I would certainly consider—'

281

'How much?' Mason demanded, butting in. He spoke in English.

Angelique shot him a furious look. 'Mason! Leave this to me, please.'

Mason looked fit to burst. 'I'm your agent, it's what I'm meant to do.' He fixed his beady eyes on Cat. 'And if you're going to do this campaign, it had better be worth it. It's only a fucking perfume, you know.'

Cat guessed he was struggling to understand why Angelique had turned down a role in Hollywood, especially before she knew what was involved in this offer. He would be thinking of the hefty percentage he had just lost and Cat couldn't blame him.

Why would she turn down such an amazing offer? Cat wondered again. Angelique would be perfect for a big budget film across the pond. She had no qualms about taking her clothes off, she was utterly self-composed and it didn't take an expert to spot that she had an ambitious streak.

Maybe Angelique saw it as selling herself out, Cat thought. Perhaps she preferred to be a very big fish in a small pond as opposed to the other way round. And she was French – perhaps the idea of living in La-la-land with all its craziness and image obsession wasn't for her.

'Ignore him,' Angelique said, crossing her legs. 'Tell me more about this new fragrance.'

Cat did so, using everything she could remember from her trip to Grasse with Xavier. She described the concept in great detail and glossed over the fact that she wasn't sure what the scent would smell like. She hyped up all the positive angles she could, highlighting Ducasse-Fleurie's achievements over the past few years and making the most of Xavier's world-renowned talent as a *senteur* to make the bait as tempting as possible.

'It sounds wonderful,' Angelique purred, while Mason looked ready to explode. 'We can work out the terms and conditions later on but for now, you can take my word for it that I would love to be involved. It sounds exactly like the sort of high-profile, well-respected project I'm going to become known for in the future.'

Cat stood up, pleased. She shook Angelique's hand. 'Just to warn you, you might need to come down to the family home at some point. There's talk of shooting the campaign there. It's really beautiful,' she added, in case Angelique needed convincing.'

'I'm sure you're right.' Angelique smiled, omitting to mention that she was more than familiar with La Fleurie. 'I have a flat in Provence so I will move back there for a while until I'm needed.' In her heels, she was slightly taller than Cat and her breasts were spilling out of the robe. She didn't bother to close it as she leant over and kissed both of Cat's cheeks.

Cat was enveloped in an overpowering waft of jasmine. She remembered Xavier saying he detested the smell and Cat found herself agreeing with him. It was such a strong, pungent aroma and it had a cloying aftertaste. Dry down, she corrected herself, remembering what Xavier had taught her. She frowned, wishing she could stop thinking about him at every turn.

'I'll be in touch,' she told Angelique. She gave Mason's big sweaty hand a quick shake and made her escape.

When Cat had gone, Mason turned on Angelique. 'What the hell are you playing at?' he demanded.

Angelique frowned. 'It's my decision, Mason,' she said. 'You get your cut but ultimately I decide what I want to do, just like I always have.'

'But there's a Hollywood film on the table . . .'

'I don't care!' Angelique's blue eyes flashed coldly at him. 'I am doing the Ducasse-Fleurie ad campaign and there is nothing you can do about it. Fuck the Hollywood film. They want me naked, just like everyone else. I told you, I want to be

283

a brand. I want the world to know who I am, not just Hollywood.'

Mason stomped out of the studio.

Celine was hovering nearby. Angelique pointed her finger at her. 'Are you going to tell me what to do as well?'

Celine shook her mousy head fervently. 'Of course not, Angelique! I wouldn't dream of it.'

'Good.' Angelique tightened her robe. 'Pack my bags, Celine, but don't bother about yours. I haven't decided if I need you in the south of France yet.'

In a few months, maybe even a few weeks, Angelique thought happily, she would be back at La Fleurie and, if she had her way, back in Xavier's bed.

Chapter Sixteen

On a balmy spring evening, Ashton arrived from Paris as the Rose-Nymphea party was in full swing. He stood outside La Fleurie, consumed with nerves. Leoni was somewhere inside and he had no idea whether she would have Jerard on her arm or not. Ashton knew he had no choice but to deal with it but now that he was here, it suddenly seemed like a much bigger thing than he'd imagined.

God, he had missed her. Since her last visit to Paris, Ashton had backed off to give her some serious space. He figured she needed to devote herself to her new relationship and he didn't want to encroach on her time and seem like some sort of needy twat. Whatever he felt for her, they were friends and nothing more. Ashton took a deep breath. It was like an illness, one without any cure, it seemed, but he needed to pull himself together and be mature about it. He straightened his bow tie and headed round the side of the château, knowing the party would be taking place in the main salon. He bumped into Max as he headed away from the gardens.

'Ash.' Max greeted him warmly, shaking his hand. 'I haven't seen you for ages.' Ashton looked immaculate in a well-worn but made-to-measure dinner suit and a white bow tie. Max frowned, thinking Ashton looked rather dejected.

Realising he probably looked miserable, Ashton plastered a smile on to his face. 'I've been tied up in Paris. How are things?'

Max looked shamefaced. 'Did you hear about us getting thrown out of college?'

'Ah, yes. Guy told me when I phoned to speak to him about the building.'

'Oh, right.' Max's eyes flashed bitterly. 'You must have heard the terrible version of the story then. Dad isn't exactly pleased with us at the moment. How come Leoni didn't tell you?'

Ashton walked alongside him into the château. 'We've . . . we've both been very busy,' he said, not wanting to say they'd barely spoken since she got together with Jerard. The only text he'd received from her in recent weeks was a formal one asking if he was coming to the party, followed by a cryptic one inquiring about a possible date he might bring. Ashton was baffled. Surely Leoni didn't think something was going on with Marianne, and why would she care anyway? Maybe she thought a relationship between himself and Marianne might jeopardise the building purchase. Ashton grimaced.

'Leoni's always busy,' Max mocked. 'What's changed?'

Ashton felt his heart lift. Was it possible Leoni wasn't with Jerard any more? Could it be that she was tied up with her home fragrance pitch and that her lack of contact was simply as a result of working flat out? Anything had to be better than the thought of her being whisked out on romantic dates and staying out all night. Ashton winced, hating the thought of it.

Max paused. 'She has got that new boyfriend, of course.'

Ashton's heart plummeted.

'Jerard. Some millionaire, I think, with his own company.' Max glanced at Ashton, wondering why he looked so tense. His bright blue eyes looked dim as though someone had turned out the switch behind them. 'Seems like a nice enough guy but I'm not sure he's right for Leoni.'

'Really?' Ashton tried his best to appear normal in front of Max. 'Why not?'

Max grinned. 'He's even more of a workaholic than she is. They'll never have time for sex or romance!'

One could only hope, Ashton thought ruefully. Jerard was clearly a more fitting a suitor for Leoni than an architect with only a prime-time Paris apartment to shout about. Just her type, he told himself, feeling surprisingly bitter.

Max decided Ashton needed a drink. 'Cocktails are that way. By the way, you didn't see Seraphina on your way in, did you? Maybe . . . with an older man?'

Pulling himself together, Ashton shook his head. 'I'll let her know you're looking for her if I do, shall I?'

Max nodded cheerfully, not letting the panic he felt inside show. 'Great, thanks. Catch up with you later on, Ash.'

Only after Max had gone did Ashton register what he'd said. What was Seraphina doing with an older man? She was only sixteen.

Ashton shook his head. He needed a drink.

Wearing a black vintage Chanel dress with a sequin-encrusted cardigan and a gold chain at her throat, Delphine greeted her guests self-importantly. She wished she could abandon her mahogany stick because it spoilt the regal image she had worked so hard to portray but unfortunately she needed it; her arthritic hip was stiff and painful.

'Cybille! How lovely to see you. Do help yourself to a champagne cocktail. Cosette . . . you look *divine*. Thank you so much for coming.'

Delphine mingled with her guests, delighted to be hosting such a glamorous, well-attended party. The château looked absolutely stunning, with gorgeous, heavily scented floral arrangements everywhere, their blooms echoing the Ducasse-Fleurie colour scheme exactly. White bags containing special, celebratory editions of Rose-Nymphea, rose-pink silk corsages and some beautiful vintage-style lipsticks Leoni had managed to obtain from an old friend who worked at one of France's biggest make-up companies sat on a table in the main salon. Tied up with curly reams of lilac ribbon, they were ready to be distributed at the end of the evening once the speeches had been made.

Delphine scrutinised the waiters and waitresses she had prepped with military precision over the past few days. Dressed in black and cream uniforms, they were circulating with trays of classic cocktails like dancers performing a Viennese waltz, their steps smooth and faultless. Small but delicious-looking canapés of foie gras on toast, salted quails eggs and lobster tartlets were being passed around and even the thinnest and most figure-conscious women were finding them hard to resist. Classical music was being provided by the same string quartet that had played at Leoni's party and the volume was just right.

Delphine glanced outside. Strings of muted white fairy lights were looped prettily around the pool area and a row of flamed torches studded the edge of neatly clipped pathways and flower beds. Tea lights in clear glasses hung from trees and the sturdier plants, giving the garden a magical glow as if fairies had descended with baskets of sparkle and glitter.

All the hard work was worth it because the overall effect was wonderful and everything was running like clockwork. Delphine checked her watch, feeling excitement rising in her stomach. And if everything else she had on the agenda went according to plan, there would be surprises all round later on, and not just in the form of the stunning, three-thousand-euro firework display she had organised. Making a quick phone call in the hallway, Delphine made sure the arrangements were in place for her big finale. Hearing the answer she was hoping for, she returned to the party, buoyed up and brimming with anticipation.

Delphine faltered slightly, gripping her cane. Was she doing the right thing? What would Xavier's reaction be? He wasn't the sort of man to take kindly to interference.

Delphine straightened her shoulders. It was too late to change anything now. She just had to hope she hadn't made a monumental mistake.

She nodded at the daughter of a former president and her American singer boyfriend. She'd given the boyfriend a slot after the string quartet had finished. It was a special favour to the former president, who was a personal friend, but Delphine did hope the singer wasn't too shouty or loud; that wouldn't fit well with the elegant evening she had planned.

Noticing Guy staring out of the window, deep in thought, she wondered what was on his mind. She wasn't sure if he was preoccupied or simply bored and the thought aggravated her. She joined him. 'Why aren't you talking to anyone?' she hissed at him disapprovingly.

Guy looked affronted. 'I'm not five years old, Mother,' he snapped crossly. 'I'm well aware you expect me to circulate. I just can't help thinking it all seems so . . . so false.'

'False?' Delphine rolled her eyes. She had put all her time and energy into organising this party – at Guy's insistence!

'Who *are* all these people?' he said tetchily. 'I hardly know anyone. They're all just here for the free goodie bags.' Guy did a double take as a famous model to his right burst into peals of laughter. Petal, as she was known, had the most exquisite face, but Guy couldn't help thinking she had painfully thin arms, and was a collar bone really supposed to stand out like a metal coat hanger? He shuddered. Why on earth did Seraphina want to be a model? He would rather die than allow her to look like that. 'Where are the kids, by the way? It makes me nervous when I can't see them.'

Delphine sighed. 'I have no idea, Guy. I'd rather not think about the twins. Who knows what they might be up to.' She preened as she surveyed the room. 'Have you ever seen a more wonderful turnout? Not only have all of my most important friends made the effort, but so have the celebrity contingent.' She inclined her head in the direction of one of

Hollywood's most well-paid actors. 'So pleased to make your acquaintance,' she gushed. 'He owns a vineyard in Bordeaux and he adores France,' she confided to Guy in an awed whisper. 'He came today because I promised his beautiful wife some free perfume – she's a scriptwriter. She might be around somewhere, in fact.' Guy didn't look impressed. 'She loves Xavier's trio of fragrances so I promised her a boxful. Isn't it lovely that people want to join us for this momentous event, Guy?'

'What, for the anniversary of Rose-Nymphea that only Cat noticed?' Guy snapped, losing patience. 'This family is so caught up in its own drama, Mother, that none of us are actually paying attention to anything that's going on right under our noses. Cat seems to be the only one around here that notices anything, and that speaks volumes.'

Delphine recoiled. 'Guy, what rubbish! Cat Hayes is of no consequence to any of us.' She straightened her dress and headed in the direction of a glossy celebrity with teeth as white as her own hair.

Guy gripped his glass of wine. Quite frankly, he couldn't give a shit about any of these celebrities and their vineyards. He couldn't shake off the feeling that the twins might be up to no good and until he'd tracked them down, he wasn't going to relax. Dumping his glass on to a tray as a waiter whirled past, Guy went in search of his youngest children.

Seraphina took another sneaky swig of champagne as she checked out her appearance in a full-length mirror in her bedroom. She was wearing a midnight-blue silk gown with spaghetti straps that made the most of her loose, platinum-blond hair and her alabaster skin. The previous day's tanning session with Cat hadn't changed her skin tone one bit but Seraphina wasn't bothered, her pale skin was something her boyfriend raved about. The sound of chatter and music drifted up from the party downstairs. The string quartet had finished and a solo, male voice could be heard singing something raspy and soulful. Seraphina approved but she was also surprised; this was hardly the sort of music her grandmother would normally lay on.

'I'll be out in a minute!' Cat called from the bathroom. 'Just . . . struggling with this zip . . .'

'Come on out and I'll do it,' Seraphina called back distractedly. She and Cat were getting ready together and they'd been ages. Cat had done her make-up for her, using lots of youthful pinks with a touch of grey and navy around the eyes. Seraphina felt really pretty for once.

Tonight's the night, she told herself, butterflies racing around her stomach. Finally, she was going to do it. She was going to drink as much champagne as she could for courage and then she was going to sleep with her boyfriend. After weeks – no, make that months – of holding him at arm's length, Seraphina had convinced herself that she was ready.

Did he care that she was a virgin? she wondered, stroking her hair into place with a shaky hand. Men like him were so worldly-wise, so confident. Seraphina felt like an inexperienced, gauche schoolgirl when she was with him. Tonight, though, she would shake off her childishness and immaturity and she would become the sophisticated, grown-up woman he wanted her to be. Seraphina felt both excited and scared at the same time . . . actually, very sick, now she came to think about it. She reached for her champagne flute again and drained it. Immediately, she topped it up and started again, enjoying the feeling of the champagne seeping through her system. She felt more confident already; she was sure of it.

'Are you sure this looks all right?' Cat said, emerging from the bathroom. She was wearing one of Seraphina's glamorous gowns, a black satin figure-hugging number that left her golden shoulders and arms bare and fell to the floor in an inky pool. Cat wasn't convinced it was a good fit, however. It was a simple design that clung to her figure flatteringly but it was a fraction too tight. Cat was worried she might burst out of it at any moment.

None of Seraphina's other gowns fitted her so she really didn't have any other option; Bella had sent on a pair of dowdy black trousers and an unsuitable basque, as well as a purple dress Cat hadn't worn in two years. Cat could only imagine Bella was distracted by Ben because if she'd been thinking straight, she would have known the clothes weren't suitable for a party Hollywood actors would be attending.

Seraphina stood back and viewed Cat critically, glad to take her mind off what she had planned for the night. Cat had taken care with her make-up, outlining her aquamarine eyes with smudged eyeliner and three coats of sooty black mascara, and her cheeks were brushed with peachy blusher.

'It's too tight, isn't it?' Cat asked, about to back into the bathroom. 'I'll just wear my black trousers and a top . . .'

'You'll do no such thing.' Seraphina spun her round and positioned her in front of the mirror. 'The dress looks gorgeous . . . it's your hair.' She scooped it up in her hands and twisted it until it was all piled on top of Cat's head like a beautiful, butterscotch whirl. 'You should wear it up. Otherwise it spoils the line of the dress. You have the shoulders to pull it off, so let's do it. I'm good with hair. Watch.'

Cat sat stiffly on the edge of the dressing-table chair while Seraphina deftly took locks of her hair and pinned it up in pretty loops and waves. She noticed Seraphina's flushed cheeks and the agitated movements of her fingers as she reached for clips.

'Have you been drinking?' she asked, worriedly.

Seraphina coloured. 'Only one glass,' she protested, avoiding Cat's eyes in the mirror.

'Just one? You look very flushed.'

Saying nothing, Seraphina finished pinning Cat's hair. She sat on the bed, looking apprehensive. 'Can I ask you something?'

'Anything,' Cat responded, standing up quickly for fear of splitting the dress. She checked her hair, not sure she could carry it off, but Seraphina had done a beautiful job and had added a simple diamond necklace to Cat's throat as a finishing touch.

'Your first time . . . what was it like?' Seraphina went even pinker and not bothering to hide her champagne glass any longer, she reached for it and almost downed the contents in one out of sheer nerves. 'Were you nervous?'

Cat watched the champagne disappearing. 'Why do you want to know?'

'Oh, I'm just asking.'

Cat wasn't convinced. In fact, she was fairly sure she knew exactly why Seraphina was asking her such a question. She perched gingerly on the end of the bed and thought carefully about what she was going to say. She wanted to be as honest as possible, without glorifying the idea of sex. Seraphina probably really needed her mum right now and Cat felt the responsibility of saying the right thing weighing down heavily on her shoulders.

Seraphina pleated the bottom of her dress with trembling fingers. 'I just want to know . . . well, what it feels like . . . when you were ready . . . who you did it with . . .'

Sighing, Cat thought back to her first boyfriend. 'My first proper boyfriend was called John and we were both about seventeen or eighteen, I think. He was this beach-bum type with blond, surfer-dude hair and those baggy shorts they all wear.' She paused, lost in memories for a moment. 'We'd been going out for, oh, about six months or more and we ended up staying out all night at the beach.'

'Was it romantic?'

'It was . . . messy.' Cat smiled. 'It's true what they say; sand gets *everywhere*. But if you want details, I suppose it was nice, rather than earth-shattering. I wasn't nervous because we were such good friends but it felt like a big moment in some ways.'

Seraphina nodded, her hair falling into her eyes. 'That's it . . . it feels like a big moment. So big and so scary, I don't know if I can go through with it.'

'So don't,' Cat asserted, concerned. 'What's the rush? I was one of the last out of my friends and I still felt unprepared for all the emotions I went through.'

'But . . . I have to do it sometime, don't I?'

'It doesn't have to be tonight.' Cat witnessed relief flooding through Seraphina's eyes but it was fleeting. She could tell the young girl had made up her mind, even though she was clearly terrified. Cat took Seraphina's hand. 'I really wouldn't recommend sleeping with your boyfriend just because you feel you should or . . . or because he's older than you and he tells you all sophisticated girls do it.'

Seraphina blinked and topped her champagne flute up clumsily. 'He's not . . . he hasn't . . .'

'Really?' Cat didn't believe her. 'Look, you should only do this if you want to . . . if it feels right.' She regarded Seraphina, admiring her luminous beauty. She was so beautiful and quirky, Cat couldn't bear the thought of her losing her virginity to someone who didn't appreciate it, especially some older man who was clearly pressing Seraphina to take their relationship a step further.

'If you're not ready, say no, Seraphina, please,' she urged. 'If you're worried he'll leave you because of it, you still say no, because that means he isn't worth it. Actually, it means he's a total shit.'

'But I love him!' Seraphina jumped to her feet, tears in her eyes. 'I don't want to lose him . . . I can't. He's all I've got.'

'What are you talking about?' Cat stood up. 'You have an entire family around you. You have Max and your father . . . and Xavier.' She felt strange saying his name out loud; she had been doing a good job of not thinking about him for the past ten minutes. 'All of these people care about you and, believe

294

me, that counts for a lot. I didn't have any family around me so I really *was* on my own, but you're not, Seraphina. You must know that.'

Seraphina tossed back her champagne recklessly and when she turned back to Cat, her eyes sparkled with defiance. 'My boyfriend is the only one who doesn't treat me like a stupid child around here, Cat. He's the only one who takes my modelling career seriously too – even Max told me he doesn't want me to model. He's always trying to discourage me . . . he never wants me to do anything . . . he's just as bad as my father.' She was slurring her words now.

Cat grabbed Seraphina's hand. 'He doesn't think that, he's just trying to protect you.'

'I don't need protecting!' Seraphina yelled, pulling herself away from Cat. 'I'm sixteen, I'm not a child. And I wish everyone would stop treating me like one!' Spinning round, she headed unsteadily out of the door.

Cat felt terrible. She hadn't done a very good job of dissuading Seraphina with her honest tale about John the surfer; if anything, she had fuelled Seraphina's already reckless mind. She seemed to think sex would solve all her problems and insecurities and she couldn't be more wrong.

'There you are.' Max poked his head round the door. He was wearing a suit for once, albeit it with a white T-shirt and red baseball boots. 'Wow. You look *really* hot.'

Cat raised her eyebrows. 'Thank you. You look pretty good yourself.'

Seeing that she was alone, Max frowned. 'Where's Seraphina?'

'Gone to meet her boyfriend, I think. Didn't you just bump into her?' Cat swished to the door in her gown, wondering what to do.

Max looked upset. 'No. Has she really gone to meet him?'

Cat dithered for a moment. She didn't want to betray

295

Seraphina's confidence but she couldn't help thinking the young girl was about to do something she might bitterly regret, especially since she was drunk. 'I need to talk to you,' she told Max, making a decision. 'Seraphina will probably hate me forever but I just can't let her do something she's been pressured into doing . . .'

Cat filled Max in, hoping to God she was doing the right thing.

Xavier burst into the main salon clutching a box, hardly aware that the party was in full flow. The male singer was taking a break so most people had drifted outside to the pool area. His father was missing, as were the twins; in fact, the only family member he could see was Leoni, who was standing outside with a man with brown hair. Xavier recognised him as Jerard Monville, the businessman Leoni had been seeing for a while. They certainly looked cosy enough together, if not deliriously happy.

Xavier had been in the lab until around ten minutes before. He had hastily thrown on a dinner suit with a black tie undone around his shirt collar. Delphine, making sure everything was ready for the speeches, smiled at Xavier's impromptu arrival. His dark hair was sticking up all over the place and his eyes were slightly bloodshot but he looked elated.

He had finally figured out the missing ingredient to his fragrance. It would mean a trip to Morocco but at least the elusive element that had been evading him had finally made itself known. Xavier's eyes darted around the room, searching for Cat. Still fuming about their altercation the other day, he had thought about it – and about her – constantly ever since. Xavier had finally acknowledged something he'd been in denial about since Grasse.

'Xavier. Is that what I think it is?' Delphine nodded at the box in his hands, wondering why his eyes were sparkling so vividly.

296

Xavier grinned. 'Not quite. I'm still working on the fragrance but I think I now know what the missing ingredient is. Hey, since when has *he* been one of our friends?' Amused, he stabbed his finger in the direction of the Hollywood movie star who was holding court out by the sun loungers.

Delphine smirked. 'Isn't it wonderful? We've been so lucky with our attendees this evening.' She gestured to the box again. 'So, if that's not the fragrance, what is it?'

Xavier rubbed his slightly stubbly chin, thinking he should probably have had a shave. 'It's the prototype bottle for the new fragrance.' He unfolded the crisp, white tissue paper from the box and drew the bottle out carefully. 'What do you think?'

Delphine cradled the bottle in her hands, turning it this way and that, watching as shafts of light splintered through it. 'It's beautiful,' she commented. 'I thought it might be modern and angular but . . . it's stunning. It almost has a vintage feel.'

'That's right,' Xavier agreed, pleased she liked it. The bottle, shaped like a ripe but elegant teardrop, begged to be handled. It fitted into the palm of the hand and it was made of thick, shimmering glass that would look sensational once the scent was inside it. The thinner end yielded an antique-style silver stopper with filigree detail around the neck and the overall effect was both stylish and eye-catching.

Xavier slipped it back into the box. He had a really good feeling about it. It felt right for the new fragrance and it was going to be the perfect way to really lift it into a more modern consumer band.

'Where's Cat?' he asked, thinking she'd probably like to see the prototype.

Delphine looked vexed. 'I do wish everyone would stop talking about that girl! I have no idea where she is, Xavier. I haven't seen her and I'm not in the least bit interested in what she's doing.' She stared at her favourite grandson, her hazel eyes watching him keenly. 'Why are you so desperate to see her?'

'I'm not desperate,' he said defensively. 'She had a hand in designing this bottle, that's all.'

'Really?' Delphine raised thin eyebrows. 'Is there no end to that girl's talents?' Quite frankly, she was sick and tired of hearing people gush about Cat Hayes. 'The sooner that girl goes back to England, the better,' she added, annoyed. 'And from what she tells me, it will be very soon.'

'What?' Xavier's head snapped up.

Delphine caught sight of an influential French politician and raised her glass at him politely. 'She told me the other day that she needs to get home after the party. I think her patience has run out and her new passport should arrive any day.'

Xavier experienced a moment of panic. Cat couldn't be leaving . . . not yet. Even though he had known she wouldn't be hanging around forever – at least, not without a good reason – he hadn't realised her departure was quite so imminent. There were things to say, feelings to confront . . . Xavier realised he'd better speak to Cat again – as soon as possible.

Wearing an emerald-green dress with long sleeves and an extremely low back that exposed her slender form, Leoni was feeling edgy. In a fit of vanity, she wasn't wearing her glasses and as she deplored contacts, she was squinting at people rather rudely because she couldn't quite make out their faces. For all she knew, she had been chatting warmly to a waiter and ignoring a president's daughter, but she had wanted to look her best for Jerard. It was worth it; he had been transfixed by her since his arrival.

'You look lovely,' he said, his eyes flirting with hers. 'That dress is really beautiful on you.'

'Thank you.' Leoni gripped her champagne flute. She had never been any good at accepting compliments; it stemmed from years of criticism from her parents who'd been disappointed that she hadn't inherited the dazzling Ducasse looks. Her grandmother in particular had a way of making her feel frumpy and not good enough, even now.

'I think it's customary to return the compliment,' Jerard joked, sweeping a hand downwards to indicate his expensive-looking dinner suit. It had satin lapels and monogrammed sleeves and it was certainly dashing.

Leoni smiled. Now that she knew about his wealth, it was obvious in so many details – the exquisite cufflinks, the handmade bow tie and even the heavy watch on his wrist. Still, having grown up around opulence, Leoni was unmoved by such things; they were commonplace in her world. 'You look very handsome,' she said, feeling bold as she slid her arm round his waist. 'Irresistibly so, in fact.'

'Really?' Jerard tucked her hair behind her ear and leant down to kiss her. 'I'm beginning to think you've got something planned for tonight. Or am I mistaken?'

Leoni blushed and shook her head. 'No. I mean . . . I'm not sure.' She wished Jerard wouldn't keep doing that thing with her hair; it wasn't flattering to her ears and it made her feel self-conscious. And rather child-like, Leoni thought with a frown. She didn't want to feel like a child, she wanted to feel like a woman.

He put an arm loosely round her shoulders. 'Shall we go outside for a while? It looks magical with all the lights.'

She nodded, her heart beating fast. This was it; she was finally going to find out if he was serious about her and, frankly, the revelation couldn't come soon enough. Ducking into the alcove Seraphina had hidden in all that time ago when Cat first arrived, Leoni took a seat.

'I'm so pleased we found each other,' Jerard said, taking a seat next to her. 'We're so well suited, aren't we?'

She nodded. 'I suppose we are.'

Jerard nodded, taking her hand. 'There is no "suppose" about it. I've never been with someone who understands my

299

commitment to business as well as you do. Every relationship I've had . . . women have just fallen by the wayside because they don't appreciate what it takes to keep a successful business afloat.' He shook his head, his blue eyes dismissive. 'But you do. You're in the same boat and you understand that business takes priority. I mean it, Leoni. You're the one.'

'I'm the what?' She was shocked. Was he saying what she thought he was saying? It sounded as though he was going to propose or something. Her heart gathered pace but she couldn't say exactly why. How would she feel if he did propose? Overjoyed? Petrified? Disappointed?

'The one who understands me,' he explained, giving her a smile. 'Whatever happens, I know you'll be fine about me putting business first because you work so hard yourself.'

Was she? Was she all right about Jerard always putting business first? Leoni frowned. She wasn't so sure. Business had always taken priority in her life but she now realised it had been to her detriment. She admired Jerard's business ethic and she could admit that they had a great deal in common.

It was just that . . . Leoni couldn't help feeling deflated by Jerard's comments. She wanted romance, she wanted that high people talked about when it came to love, that crazy, dizzy, inexplicable buzz in the stomach that was like nothing else. Even her grandmother, austere and cold, had been in love!

Leoni knew that she too had been in love, with Ashton, but that had been one sided. All the breathless, wonderful feelings had been there but, unreciprocated, they had died a death. A slow one, admittedly, but eventually she had seen sense. Leoni sighed, staring at Jerard. As much as she loved his commitment and focus, she wanted to be important in his life too. Didn't every woman want that? Didn't all women want to be adored and desired and put first, just once in a while? Remembering the cute old couple in Paris, Leoni knew she wanted that; she wanted to be married to someone until she was old, someone who loved her, despite what she looked like or what she did for a job, someone who thought she was special enough to be the most important thing in life – even if it was just now and again.

'You must know how I feel about you,' Jerard said softly, his thumb moving over her hand.

Leoni didn't but she felt her heart flutter slightly. She wished he would gather her up in his arms and kiss the life out of her, sink his hands into her hair and tell her he couldn't live without her. 'No, no, I don't,' she stammered, waiting.

'Then let me show you . . .'

Jerard bent his head and kissed her face all over, his eyelashes brushing her skin. It was romantic, achingly so, and Leoni's breath became laboured as she eagerly met his mouth with her own. But his hands were holding hers, which was somehow inhibiting. She didn't feel she could let herself go and passionately kiss him the way she wanted to. She willed him to ravish her. She wanted to be thrown on to a bed and kissed endlessly and she wanted her clothes to be torn from her body, her sheer, expensive stockings ripped off in the heat of the moment . . .

'You're so special to me,' Jerard murmured, smoothing her hair back again. Irritably, Leoni noticed Jerard's phone had fallen to the ground. He knelt down to retrieve it, still holding on to her hand. As he did so, Leoni looked up and thought she saw Ashton. She caught a glimpse of blond hair and a dinner suit, but without her glasses on, she couldn't say for definite that it was him. Then whoever it was disappeared into the darkness.

Still on his knees, Jerard was reading a text message. 'Oh, that's great news! That big deal I was telling you about? I got it, and it's even better than I thought it would be. An incredible order.'

'How wonderful,' Leoni said, watching his eyes light up and feeling herself shut down in response.

Jerard tucked his phone in his pocket, his expression apologetic as he stood up. 'It means I have to cut this lovely evening short, I'm afraid.'

'Oh no!' Leoni was crushed. Was he really going to walk out and leave her, just as things had been about to get interesting? What about her plans for them to sleep together? What about the way he had been about to ravish her? Or was that just in her head?

'I'm really sorry,' Jerard said, squeezing her hand. 'But I have to get to the office. I need to get in touch with all my overseas contacts, particularly in Japan.' He kissed Leoni again, touching the tip of her nose with his finger. 'I know you're the woman for me because you understand why it's so important for me to address all the details now.'

Leoni's shoulders drooped. 'Yes, of course. Of course I understand. Business is . . . everything.'

'Not everything,' Jerard admonished. 'There's plenty of time for us, isn't there? And I'll make it up to you, I promise.' Standing up, he looked down at her admiringly. 'You really do look beautiful tonight, Leoni. I can't wait for us to spend more time together.' With an effort, she hid her disappointment and watched Jerard disappear into the night. How silly she was being, how selfish. This deal had been taking up all of Jerard's time over the past few weeks; it was only natural that he would want to go into his office and sort everything out before morning. She'd do the same thing, wouldn't she?

Leoni got to her feet and straightened her emerald-green dress. It was just a blip, that was all. Jerard had made it very clear he was serious about her and she was sure he would make it up to her as promised. This was a grown-up, meaningful relationship, Leoni berated herself, so it was about time she stopped holding out for silly declarations of love and accepted that Jerard wasn't that way inclined.

*

Back inside the château, Ashton was feeling utterly destroyed. He helped himself to a large Scotch and did his best to cover his feelings when Xavier found him.

'Xav . . . good to see you.'

'You too, Ash.' Xavier glanced at him, wondering why his old friend looked as though he'd been punched in the chest. 'That looks good,' he added, nodding at the drink and grabbing one for himself as a waitress went to pirouette past him. 'Enjoying yourself?'

Ashton nodded, looking away. 'Delphine's done a wonderful job with the château.'

'Hasn't she?' Xavier pulled a face. 'Considering she didn't even want to host this party in the first place, she's certainly gone all out to invite flashy guests and lay on a lavish feast.' He glanced over his shoulder casually, wondering when he could dash off to find Cat.

Ashton said nothing.

'Have you seen Leoni?' Xavier asked.

'Yes, I've seen her. She was with her . . . her boyfriend.'

Xavier raised his eyebrows. 'Jerard Monville? He's even more work focused than Leoni. One of my old girlfriends dated him for a while, said he was sweet but more likely to make love to his laptop than her.'

'Really?' Ashton couldn't even manage a smile. 'They looked pretty loved up when I saw the pair of them in the garden just now. In fact, Jerard was down on one knee.'

Xavier was flabbergasted. 'Proposing? No way! I don't believe it, Ash. Jerard is not the settling type. Seriously, if you think I'm anti-commitment, Jerard is an absolute pro at it. He just likes to have a girlfriend to while away the hours with when Japan shuts down.'

Ashton looked unconvinced. He put his glass down on a nearby table. 'If you'll excuse me, Xav, I think I need some air.'

Xavier stared at him as he headed outside. So he was right.

He had suspected for many years that Ashton was in love with Leoni but he had never breathed a word about it to anyone. Olivier had mentioned it once in passing, saying the pair of them would never end up together, and Xavier had fleetingly wondered if Olivier had deliberately kept them apart because he couldn't stand the thought of his best friend and his sister hooking up. It would be just like Olivier to be so selfish; unless the world had revolved around him, he wasn't happy.

Thinking about Olivier made Xavier remember Cat. He still couldn't understand why someone as gorgeous and genuine as she was would have fallen for an egotistical idiot like Olivier but he reminded himself it was all in the past now. Olivier had hoodwinked many women who were intelligent and should have known better and Xavier realised how unfair he had been towards Cat about it.

Love at first sight . . . or perhaps at first kiss, Xavier told himself ruefully, clearly did happen. And lightning really did strike twice but this time . . . this time, he thought, going in search of Cat, it had well and truly pierced his heart.

Chapter Seventeen

Seraphina was feeling woozy as she waited in a deserted corner of the pool house. Her stomach was jumping around madly and even though she kept telling herself everything would be fine, she was finding it impossible to relax.

Why had she drunk so much? Instead of giving her courage, it was simply making her feel nauseous. Unlike Max, Seraphina wasn't used to drinking alcohol; having consumed more than a bottle of champagne now, she was feeling distinctly queasy and it wasn't helping the churning nerves in her stomach. She stood up and started pacing across the pool house in agitation, taking in deep breaths of fresh air.

Pull yourself together, Seraphina told herself sternly. It's sex, what's the big deal? Everyone does it. People younger than you have sex and don't lose any sleep over it, so stop being such a baby. Get it over with and stop whining. It was just . . . was it right to have such shaky hands? Was she supposed to want to 'get it over with'? Thinking of all the romantic films she'd seen, Seraphina wasn't sure that was the sentiment they promoted but maybe the rose petals, patient men and candlelight were just a fantasy.

At least she had moonlight, she thought rather hysterically. That was almost as good as candlelight, right? Who needed rose petals? The deserted pool house, shut off from guests due to refurbishment, was just as good. Romantic props were for silly little children, not a sophisticated girl . . . no, a *woman* like her, Seraphina corrected herself. And as for patient men, in reality, weren't they all full blooded and desperate for sex at any given minute of the day? Most magazines seemed to think so, which made even more of a mockery of the childish romance she'd been envisaging for her first time.

Drawing herself up to her full height and letting out a jerky breath, Seraphina made an effort to pull herself together. She had a gorgeous, older boyfriend who thought she was desirable and grown up. Everything was as it should be; she simply needed to find the courage to go through with something that was scaring her witless.

Looking up, she saw her boyfriend just outside the pool house. Wearing a suave but rather showy dinner suit, he looked sexy and mature. Seraphina's stomach flipped over again.

'Darling,' he said, kissing her cheeks slowly and deliberately. His mouth brushed hers as he moved from side to side and he linked his fingers through hers. 'You look . . . delectable,' he murmured, dropping a kiss on to her bare shoulder. The midnight-blue silk dress fitted her perfectly, highlighting her height and slender curves. Seraphina looked like a young girl attending her first prom but the blend of sexual innocence and womanly knowing she conveyed was utterly irresistible. To a certain type of man. And Seraphina's boyfriend was undoubtedly one of those men.

'Th-thanks,' she stammered, wishing once more that she hadn't touched a single drop of champagne. She sat down on a lounger abruptly and her boyfriend took a seat next to her. He nuzzled her neck, pushing her back on the lounger slightly. In the moonlight, her pale skin looked flawless, like creamy alabaster. He ran a finger down her arm seductively.

'Have you . . . thought any more about our conversation?' he asked.

Seraphina trembled but managed a nod in response.

'And?' He lifted his head, meeting her eyes. His mouth

curved up teasingly, expectantly, and Seraphina's heart skipped a beat.

'And . . . I'm . . . not sure.' Remembering Cat's words earlier, she tried to buy herself some time. Struggling to sit up, she pulled the strap of her dress back up and took a deep breath. 'The thing is, I really want to do this but I'm not sure I'm ready.' That was it in a nutshell; Seraphina really *did* want to do it. She wanted to get it over and done with so she never had to worry about it again and she was pretty sure she was in love with this man. It was just that . . .

He sat up with a look of regret. 'I see.' He shot his cuffs, somehow conveying his displeasure with the snappy gesture. 'So you're just a little girl after all.' The chilly, impatient statement was like a reprimand; he had lost patience with her.

Seraphina felt tears pricking her eyes. 'I'm not!' she cried hotly. Her stomach lurched again. 'I want to . . . I want you . . . I'm just . . . I'm sorry.' She felt distraught, everything was unravelling. She didn't want to lose him, not over something so stupid. Everyone did this! Still, Seraphina couldn't explain why she felt so uneasy about it or why it suddenly felt so wrong. A tear slid down her cheek and she brushed it away, embarrassed.

'It's up to you,' he told her, seemingly unmoved by her emotional outburst. 'There are any number of girls out there I could date, Seraphina. I chose you because I thought you were special.' His eyes met hers unrepentantly. 'I was wrong.'

Seraphina winced. Wasn't this how her father always made her feel? That she should have been special but that somehow she wasn't? Seraphina was sick and tired of being made to feel she wasn't good enough, that she was some silly little girl who didn't know what to do or how to behave. Impulsively grabbing her boyfriend's hand, she placed it on her thigh.

'You're not wrong about me,' she gulped. 'I want this . . . I want you.' Her eyes luminous in her face, she nodded. 'I'm ready.'

'Are you sure?' He looked sceptical but he left his hand on her thigh.

Say it doesn't matter, Seraphina pleaded with him silently. Say you don't care and that you'd never leave me. Tell me you love me anyway, and that I'm special even without that . . . please . . .

He did nothing of the sort. Instead, he smiled and pulled her down on to the lounger. 'This is going to be incredible,' he whispered in her ear. He slid his hand under her silky dress, his fingers sliding up her calf.

Seraphina squirmed, as ever, finding his touch both frightening and seductive. Her breath came in short, jerky pants; she willed her fizzing stomach not to let her down.

'You won't regret it, Seraphina, I promise you,' he murmured as he brushed his mouth against her exposed thigh.

Seraphina turned her head away as tears slid down her cheeks.

'Have you seen Seraphina?' Guy demanded as he bumped into Xavier in the garden.

Xavier started, taken aback by his father's uncharacteristically scruffy appearance. His silver hair was in disarray and his tie was askew. 'No, I haven't. I was looking for Cat, actually.' Noticing his father's stricken expression, he frowned. 'Why, is there a problem?'

Guy sighed. 'I don't know. No one's seen her for hours and I've got this gut feeling something is wrong, Xav. Max is looking for her too.'

Xavier felt distinctly ill at ease. He remembered Max mentioning the boyfriend Seraphina was dating, someone much older than her, and his jaw tightened. Was Seraphina in danger? 'I'll help you find her,' he said to his father.

Guy nodded. 'Would you? Maybe try the stables. There's Ashton. I'll get him to help me look up here.'

*

Unable to find Seraphina anywhere, Max was tearing his hair out. After what Cat had told him about Seraphina's plans with her boyfriend, all he could think was that he had to go after his twin and stop her. He knew Seraphina as well as he knew himself and deep down he was sure she wasn't ready for this. She might think she was and she might act as though she was but Max knew better. Seraphina was soft and vulnerable and he couldn't bear the thought of someone taking advantage of her. He could have kicked himself for ignoring the warning signs she had given him over the past few months.

It was all so glaringly obvious now. Seraphina had been in freefall for a long time now – ever since their mother's death, in fact. In Max's confused teenage brain, he couldn't help wondering if Seraphina had mistaken the attention her boyfriend had shown her for the love she so desperately craved elsewhere.

Max jumped as Madeleine appeared behind him.

'Sorry!' Madeleine apologised. She was wearing a long satin gown the colour of almond blossom and with her long, brown hair held up with a pretty, diamante comb, she was glowing. 'What's wrong?'

She looked nice, Max thought distractedly. Madeleine wasn't the prettiest girl he'd ever laid eyes on but she had a quiet, reliable quality he was drawn to. 'Listen, I can't find Seraphina anywhere and I'm worried sick. Cat reckons she might be with her boyfriend somewhere.'

Madeleine shuddered. 'Really? I saw him when he came to pick Seraphina up from college once. He's at least twice her age.' She looked apologetic. 'Sorry, I thought you knew.'

Max panicked. It was worse than he'd thought. He hadn't clapped eyes on the boyfriend and Seraphina had been so cagey about his age, he'd assumed the guy was only a few years older. Now he was absolutely sure Seraphina was making a mistake; no man over thirty should be messing about with a teenager – not unless he was only after one thing.

'I thought he looked like a creep,' Madeleine confessed honestly, seeing Max's eyes flash with anger. 'Do you think she's in trouble?'

Not wanting to talk about it, Max listed all the places he'd already checked, counting them off on his fingers. 'Any other ideas?'

Madeleine thought for a minute. 'Did you try the pool?'

Max frowned. 'No, but the place was full of guests earlier, so it's not exactly ideal if you want to be alone.' He snapped his fingers. 'The pool house!' he exclaimed. 'It's set back from the pool and Grandmother cordoned it off from guests because it's being redecorated.'

Without thinking, Madeleine grabbed his hand. 'Let's go.'

As they hurried up to the pool house, Max thought he saw movement inside. *Seraphina*, he thought, alarmed. Not sure what they were going to find, Max burst through the door.

Seraphina, her face streaked with tears, was lying on a sun lounger with her dress half off. Her boyfriend was standing over her, rubbing his chin and looking wounded.

'Fucking pervert!' Max yelled, clenching his fists. He wanted to hurl himself at the man and beat the shit out of him.

'Max, don't!' Seraphina screamed, holding her dress to her chest as she struggled to stand up.

'Don't stick up for him,' Max snarled. 'He's clearly old enough to look after himself.'

'Back off,' the man said, holding his hands up. 'What on earth is wrong with all of you? This family is insane.' His expression became sulky. 'I didn't do anything anyway,' he added, clearly feeling the need to defend himself.

Seraphina stood up and pulled her dress around her. Madeleine quickly helped her and Seraphina gave her a grateful smile.

Max noticed that a nasty bruise was appearing on the boyfriend's chin.

'You hit him?' Max asked Seraphina in astonishment. 'You've got the smallest fists in the world.'

Seraphina nodded. 'I used that, not my fists.' She gestured to a bottle of champagne which had rolled under the lounger.

'Wow,' Madeleine murmured, impressed. 'Talk about girl power.'

'I told him no but he didn't stop. Not even when I threw up.' She pointed to a towel in the corner. Seraphina was shaking slightly but she seemed surprisingly composed.

Max made for the boyfriend. 'You slimy bastard,' he hissed. 'You would have fucking raped her if she hadn't hit you with that bottle.' He gave him a withering look. 'Who are you, anyway?'

'Yves Giraud,' said a horrified voice behind them. Turning round, Max found his grandmother leaning heavily on her cane, as if she might fall down without it. She glanced at Seraphina's flushed cheeks then turned her appalled gaze to Yves. He met her eyes without flinching and Delphine felt her stomach plummet.

'You know him?' Max asked, puzzled. 'How?'

Delphine's cheeks coloured. 'That doesn't matter. What matters is that you all tell me what's—'

'Yes, Madame Ducasse,' Yves cut across her. 'Why don't you tell your family how you know me?'

Guy and Ashton appeared at that moment.

'What's going on?' Guy panted.

Ashton went and put his arm round Seraphina. 'Are you all right, darling?' She nodded and clung to him, clutching at the lapels of his dinner suit.

Guy pointed at Yves. 'Who's this?'

Seraphina hung her head. 'He's my boyfriend. Don't look at me like that, Dad! You have no idea what's going on in my life, so don't you dare judge me.'

Guy recoiled. Turning to Yves, he suddenly noticed how

311

old he was and exploded. 'How old are you? You better not have laid a finger on her, you bastard . . .'

Yves shoved his hands in his pockets and nodded at Delphine. 'She was about to tell you all something.'

Delphine swallowed, realising she had little choice but to confess. Otherwise, Yves would enlighten everyone himself and she would look even worse. 'I . . . hired Monsieur Giraud to do some work for me. Some . . . detective work,' she added.

Max glanced at Seraphina. Judging by her expression, she was just as surprised to hear this as he was.

Guy stared at his mother in confusion. Ashton looked totally baffled. The conversation was in rapid French and he was only just keeping up.

'Detective work?' Seraphina repeated, looking dazed. 'Please don't say it's something to do with Cat.'

Delphine went pink.

'You were trying to find something to use against her,' Guy realised, sickened.

'Grandmother!' Max said, forgetting any suspicions he'd had about Cat. 'This is ridiculous. Why can't you believe Cat married Olivier in good faith? She's said she's not interested in the Ducasse business or fortune. Why go to all this trouble to investigate her?'

'I was trying to protect the family,' Delphine said, her voice breaking slightly. 'It seems I have done the opposite.' She stared at Yves, suddenly realising something. 'No wonder you haven't been able to come up with anything, you've been far too busy chasing my granddaughter.'

Ashton tightened his grip on Seraphina protectively.

Yves shrugged. 'She's past the age of consent,' he said. All the men bristled; they were itching to get their hands on him, even Ashton. Yves backed away. 'All right, all right. I'm going.' Without even bothering to give Seraphina a second glance, Yves made a swift exit.

312

Seraphina realised everyone was staring at her. 'Don't worry,' she snapped, guessing what they were all thinking. 'I'm still intact. Hope that makes you all feel better!' Tearing away from Ashton with a sob, she ran out of the pool house.

Ashton cleared his throat and laid a restraining hand on Max's arm. 'I suspect she'll want to be left alone for a while.'

Delphine nodded, doing her best to compose herself. She was as pale as a ghost. 'I'm . . . I'm sure you're right, Ashton.'

Guy looked shell-shocked, as if he couldn't quite believe what had just happened. Ashton pushed his own distress over Leoni aside and took control. 'I think it's best if this is dealt with later. The party is still going on and the guests out there need attention. And aren't there some speeches planned?'

Delphine swallowed. 'Yes. Speeches and . . . and a surprise.'

Max rolled his eyes. 'God help us,' he said. He looked at Madeleine. 'Let's go and get a drink.' Dutifully, she followed him out.

Ashton headed for the door. 'Shall we?' he said, politely holding his arm out to Delphine. She took it gratefully, painfully aware that Ashton was able to be so forgiving because he wasn't family. Turning to Guy, she found him staring at her angrily. 'Are you coming, Guy?'

He shook his head. 'I'll give your speeches a miss, if you don't mind, Mother. That and your . . . *surprise.*'

Delphine flinched as though she'd been hit.

As Ashton and Delphine left, Guy almost lost it. He wanted to punch the wall, he wanted to smash everything up. He wanted it all to go away. How had this happened? And why hadn't he known what Seraphina was up to? Was it his fault? Guy threw himself into a chair, his jaw tight and his nerves crackling. No, this was all down to Seraphina's immaturity and recklessness and something needed to be done about it.

*

313

Tearing down to the stables, Xavier looked around for Seraphina. Where the hell was she? Yanking open each stable door in turn, he checked every corner and hidden square inch of the stables, feeling more panicked by the second. As he was about to head into the last, empty stable, Xavier started as Cat walked out. Wearing a tight, black dress that emphasised every deliciously toned curve, she took his breath away.

'What are you doing here?' he said more roughly than he meant to.

Cat looked taken aback at his aggressive tone. 'I was looking for Seraphina.' He looked drop-dead gorgeous in a dinner suit, she thought wryly. The man was built for made-to-measure couture. Cat pushed the thought aside. 'We're all really worried about her because—'

'I know, nobody can find her.' Xavier interrupted distractedly. He ran his hand through his dark hair, leaving it unruly. 'I was looking for you and then I bumped into Dad . . .'

'I've checked everywhere,' Cat told him, wondering where on earth Seraphina had got to. And, more to the point, what had happened to her. 'She's definitely not here.'

'Where in God's name is she?'

Xavier looked half crazed. Then his phone went off in his pocket. Putting it to his ear, he listened to a message and his anxious expression immediately changed. 'They've found her,' he told Cat, his voice flooded with relief. 'That was Ash. He said Seraphina is absolutely fine.'

Cat let out a shuddering breath, feeling unexpectedly emotional. 'Thank God. I was imagining all sorts of hideous things.' She shivered slightly and sat down on a nearby bench to pull herself together because she couldn't help thinking she might burst into tears at any second. 'Seraphina is so very innocent . . . I tried to tell her she didn't have to give in to this older man but I think she felt she had no choice.'

Xavier looked appalled. 'I feel so guilty . . . I'm her brother, I should have been there for her. Myself or Max, at the very least.' He'd been so caught up in himself recently – they all had.

'I wouldn't beat yourself up about it.' Cat rubbed her bare arms with her hands. 'I think some conversations can only be had with another female.' She smiled. 'I just happened to be there at the right time. If your mother had been around, she would have been the person Seraphina turned to, I'm sure.'

Xavier nodded, looking stricken. 'Of course.' He suddenly noticed how cold Cat looked. He took off his dinner jacket and wrapped it loosely round her shoulders. 'Better? I just need to grab my cigarettes . . .' He delved into one of the pockets.

Cat glanced at him. 'You . . . you said you were looking for me. Before you started to search for Seraphina.'

'Yes.' Xavier lit a cigarette and blew smoke out. 'I have a prototype of the bottle you designed in Grasse . . . I was going to show it to you.' He glanced down at his hands. 'God knows where I left it, it must be in the château somewhere. I kind of forgot about everything when Dad seemed so worried about Seraphina.'

Cat looked impressed. 'Wow, that was fast work. So how's it going with the new fragrance?'

'It's almost there, just a final ingredient needed from Morocco.' Xavier dropped the subject. 'That wasn't the only thing I wanted to speak to you about.' He paused. 'Grandmother said you were leaving as soon as your new passport arrives.'

Looking down at the ground, Cat wrapped Xavier's jacket more tightly around her shoulders. The sharp tang of his aftershave wafted off it and she closed her eyes, wondering if she really had the strength to leave La Fleurie . . . or rather Xavier. This wasn't supposed to happen, she told herself. How had she ended up here? She had come to Provence to meet Olivier's family; she had seen the trip as a way to let go of the past and move on. Instead, she had become embroiled in the

Ducasse family and had fallen hopelessly for her dead husband's cousin. Forget England; I'm going straight to hell, Cat thought despairingly.

Xavier stood up abruptly and starting pacing. 'Do you think that's . . . appropriate?' he said tightly. 'Leaving now, after . . . after everything that's happened?'

Cat gaped at him. Why was he angry with her? What had she done now? Maybe he meant because of Seraphina; perhaps Xavier thought she was abandoning the one person his sister could confide in. Cat sighed inwardly. The kiss in Grasse had changed everything. Someone she knew once said that when you kissed someone, you knew how you felt about them. It was true. She'd tried to deny it but she was lying to herself and the only way forward, as far as she could see, was to leave before she made a complete fool of herself.

'Look, I don't want to abandon Seraphina, especially not if she needs a friend. But if we're talking about "appropriate", I think we both know that's gone out of the window.'

Xavier's eyes flashed. 'I'm not talking about Seraphina. I'm talking about us . . . about me and you.'

'What about . . . us?' Cat faltered.

He dashed his cigarette to the ground. 'Do you really need to ask me that?' He pulled her to her feet by her shoulders, his jacket almost falling off. He stared down into her aquamarine eyes, daring her to disagree with him.

Cat gulped. So he felt something too. 'But . . . we row . . . constantly. We literally can't have a conversation without shouting at each other.' She could feel his hands burning into her shoulders. 'You drive me mad and I . . . I obviously infuriate you.'

Xavier rubbed his thumb across her mouth, removing all trace of her lipstick. 'Yes.'

Cat could feel her legs going wobbly. How did he *do* that? 'It's . . . it's wrong,' she said, trying again. 'I was married to your cousin, for heaven's sake . . . to Olivier.'

'Fuck Olivier,' Xavier growled, gathering her up in his arms and heading inside the stable. He didn't want to hear about his twat of a cousin, he didn't want to think about him anywhere near Cat's beautiful body. He kissed her, hard, and she kissed him back, wrapping her arms round his neck, clinging to him. She felt him move back until she was up against the wall. Her breath came in ragged gasps. She felt Xavier hike her skirt up, his hand running up the back of her leg. He lingered behind her knee for a moment, before she wrapped her leg round his waist and pulled his mouth down on to hers again. He ripped the pins out of her hair and it tumbled down around her shoulders. As he sank his hands into it, she unbuttoned his shirt with feverish fingers.

Impatiently, Xavier removed her hands and tore the shirt over his head. Faced with his tanned torso, Cat sucked in her breath and grappled with the zipper on her dress.

'I . . . I couldn't do it up myself,' she breathed, struggling. 'Seraphina had to do it . . .'

Reaching round, Xavier tugged the zip down with infinite slowness, allowing the black dress to fall to the floor in a pool of satin. He gazed at her standing there in a black lace bra and thong, then his mouth was searching for hers again. Xavier cleared a space on the floor and they fell down, tearing off the rest of their clothes.

As Xavier's hot tongue connected with her aching nipples, Cat groaned pleasurably. Suddenly, she stopped him and he looked down at her, his dark hair flopping into his eyes.

'I . . . I know you think I do this sort of thing all the time,' Cat stammered, going red. 'But I don't. This is . . . serious. More serious than anything I've ever done.'

Xavier nodded. 'Same here.' He ran a hand down her quivering body. 'I'm in . . . I think I . . .'

'Me too,' Cat said, pulling his body on top of hers urgently. 'Stop talking and show me.'

'My pleasure,' Xavier murmured, finding her mouth

again. Pushing her thighs apart with his, he lost himself completely.

Back at the château, Delphine was delivering the final speech of the night. She felt tired and frail but she was sure it was only because it had been such a dramatic evening. Leaning on her cane, she smiled at her audience.

'So it gives me great pleasure to ask you to join me in toasting the fiftieth anniversary of Rose-Nymphea,' she announced, motioning for the band she had hired to strike up. As they performed a jaunty version of 'Happy Birthday', Delphine searched the room for Guy. He was still missing and she was worried about him. He had looked so destroyed out there in the pool house and she felt responsible . . . well, partly responsible. Delphine chewed her lip. Xavier was nowhere to be seen either and Leoni looked preoccupied; she was standing in the corner, alone. Ashton was at the opposite end of the room, as far from Leoni as possible. Had they had a row? Delphine sincerely hoped not; she had high hopes for the pair of them. Jerard was a nice enough man, rich, if not exactly well appointed, but she had always thought Ashton and Leoni were meant to be together.

Her lips tightened as she noticed that Seraphina was missing too but she guessed her granddaughter was too embarrassed to show her face. At least Max was there, at the back of the room, even if he did seem more interested in talking to Madeleine Lombard than in the party. Still, there were worse girls for him to be mixing with. Delphine frowned in disappointment. Considering this was supposed to be a celebration of the family's best-selling perfume, her family were in scant attendance. Cat Hayes was also conspicuous by her absence, Delphine thought vaguely but she didn't care. The girl was hardly her concern.

She realised everyone was staring at her expectantly. She cleared her throat and spoke again. 'It also gives me great pleasure to announce that my grandson, Xavier, has created a brand new fragrance.'

A murmur of excitement fluttered round the room.

'And in honour of this, instead of our usual low-key campaigns which simply feature our bottle of scent, we thought such a significant event deserved something special.'

At the back of the room, Max rolled his eyes. 'Could this be any duller?' he murmured to Madeleine.

Grinning, she nudged him. 'Sshh, your grandmother will lynch you if she knows you're not being one hundred per cent supportive.'

Max yawned in response.

Delphine caught sight of him and narrowed her eyes. God, that child was disrespectful! Still, this should stop him – and everyone else – in their tracks. 'So I am delighted to be able to introduce you to the person who will be featuring in our new ad campaign to launch Xavier's fragrance . . .' As she paused for effect, a vision in a red Dior dress with acres of thigh showing swept into the room, a mane of shining blond hair hanging over one shoulder.

There was a collective gasp from the crowd, the biggest one from Max.

'Wow,' Madeleine breathed. 'Now that's an entrance . . .' She glanced at Max, suppressing the urge to close his gaping mouth. 'Get a grip, Max. She's stunningly beautiful but there's no need to look like an idiot.'

Max shook his head. 'It's not that,' he managed in a hoarse voice.

'Then what is it?' Madeleine frowned.

'I have to find Xavier,' Max murmured, wondering where the hell his brother might be.

'I think your father said he'd gone to the stables to look for Seraphina . . .' Madeleine shook her head as Max tore out of the room. What on earth was going on?

*

319

In the stables, Cat lay in Xavier's arms blissfully, wrapped up in his dinner jacket. She had never felt so wonderful in her life. Her chin was red-raw from his stubble, as were several other parts of her body, and she loved the fact that her skin was still throbbing from his touch.

Xavier traced his finger along her thigh, watching her squirm with pleasure. A horse whinnied in the stable next to them and he smiled. 'That's my palomino, Cassis,' he told Cat. 'She's probably jealous you've stolen my attention.'

'That beautiful, chocolate-coloured horse is yours?'

He nodded. 'I got her from Spain. They say the name probably comes from Juan de Palomino who received one of Queen Isabella of Spain's horses hundreds of years ago. Rumour has it palominos were named after a golden-coloured Spanish grape by the same name, so even though Cassis is a rare chocolate colour, she's named after my favourite Provençal wine.' Xavier rolled his eyes. 'You probably think that makes me sound like a total wine snob, the rich playboy all over again.'

Cat shook her head. 'I know I was wrong about that . . . I was wrong to compare you to Olivier. Look, me and Olivier . . . we only slept together a few times. It was more of a holiday romance than anything else – if we hadn't got married, if he hadn't died, who knows what might have happened to our relationship.'

Xavier immediately felt better. 'I need to tell you something, too.' He said, his eyes downcast.

'That sounds ominous,' Cat said, feeling her stomach tighten. She ran her hand across his broad chest, wondering when she had ever felt so happy.

'It's not,' Xavier assured her. 'It's just that you said in Grasse that I didn't want to open up to you because I was emotionally retarded and I want to explain.'

Cat blushed. 'God, the things that come out of my mouth. At least, I meant it at the time but—'

'There was someone,' Xavier interrupted, needing to be truthful with her. 'Someone I fell in love with and she . . . she changed everything.'

Cat felt a pang at his words. Of course he'd been in love before; she just wished the thought of it didn't make her feel nauseous.

Xavier stared past her. 'She made me do crazy things. I wasn't myself when I was with her but she had this hold over me, you know?'

Cat nodded. She did know; she had felt the same way about Olivier.

'It was serious between us, really serious. She found out she was pregnant and I was so happy. Then, within a few weeks, my mother died and the baby too . . . a miscarriage.'

Cat was too shocked to speak. Whatever she had imagined was behind Xavier's shutters, this wasn't it. She wanted to stop him because she could see how much it was hurting him to say it all out loud but now that Xavier had opened the floodgates, he couldn't seem to close them again.

'My girlfriend . . . she left, without a word,' he said in a flat tone. 'She wouldn't talk about it and I thought the worst of her. I had terrible suspicions that maybe she hadn't suffered a miscarriage . . . that she had never really wanted the baby in the first place.'

'So you stopped making perfumes,' Cat said, abruptly realising what had caused Xavier to turn his back on his passion.

'I felt dead inside. Probably the way you did when your parents passed away. Except that for me, I didn't want to live each second as if it was my last.' Xavier's mouth tightened and he met her eyes. 'I *wanted* to feel dead . . . I didn't want to feel anything. I couldn't find the enthusiasm to do what made me happy . . . I couldn't bear it.'

Cat stared at him. All at once, she understood Xavier; the casual girlfriends, the refusal to make perfumes, the desire to live life mindlessly and without regret. He was protecting himself. Like her, he had been broken; he had just responded to his pain and grief in a different way. Cat took his chin in her hand and kissed him, tenderly. Xavier kissed her back, grateful she had listened without judging him.

Pausing, he slipped his dinner jacket from her lightly tanned shoulder and kissed it. 'This is the first time I've trusted anyone enough to tell them about it. It's been years and the worst thing about it was that this woman is in the public eye. No one knew about us but still, I had to see her name, her face, everywhere.'

Cat tensed. An awful thought had just occurred to her but she couldn't be right . . . she *couldn't* be. 'Who . . . who was she?' she asked, her breath catching in her throat.

Xavier swallowed. Did he trust Cat enough? He decided he did. What had just happened between them had meant more to him than anything ever had before. 'She's an actress . . . only well known in France.' Hearing something outside, Xavier sat up suddenly. Throwing Cat's clothes at her, he hurriedly dressed. 'That sounded like Max. What on earth is he yelling about?'

Cat shimmied into the dress, feeling as though she could throw up. Catching Xavier's arm, she stopped him. 'The woman who broke your heart, what's her name?'

Xavier stared at her curiously. 'You won't even have heard of her. She's—' He turned as Max burst into the stable, his chest heaving.

'Xavier, you have to come up to the house,' he panted, leaning over to catch his breath. 'Grandmother . . . she arranged a surprise and you're going to be so angry.'

'What's going on?' Discreetly, Xavier tucked Cat's bra into his pocket but Max's words had sent a chill down his spine.

Max straightened up. 'Just follow me . . . you have to.' Shooting Cat a curious glance and noticing that her hair was loose and studded with straw, he said nothing. Instead, he headed out of the stable.

Xavier threw his dinner jacket round Cat's shoulders and grabbed her hand. She stalled, panicking. She had a horrible feeling she knew exactly what Delphine's surprise was and she had to warn him; she simply had to 'Xavier . . . Delphine's surprise . . . I can only apologise . . .'

'What? Let's go. Max must have come looking for me for a good reason.' Filled with apprehension, Xavier pulled Cat after him and they hurried towards the house. Cat breathlessly tried to explain the appalling mix-up but she knew she wasn't making any sense and he wasn't listening any way. Xavier's dinner jacket fell from her shoulders as they entered the main salon but Cat didn't even register the sudden chill she felt.

Xavier stopped dead when he saw Angelique. She looked stunning in her red dress. She was holding court in the room while photographers went crazy around her. Exuding star quality, she worked the room like a pro, shaking hands and murmuring greetings, politely accepting the gushing compliments of the star-struck crowd.

Delphine, accompanying Angelique on her gracious tour around the room, spotted Xavier and paused to gauge his reaction. She couldn't help noticing that his dark hair was all over the place and that his shirt was undone. Her eyes slid to Cat and, noting her loose hair and dishevelled appearance, Delphine felt a moment of disquiet. Surely not . . .

'Angelique,' Xavier croaked, unable to believe his eyes.

'It's her, isn't it?' Cat gulped, watching the blood drain from his face. 'She's the woman you were in love with.' His stricken expression said it all and Cat felt faint. 'I would never have approached her if I'd known,' she told him desperately. 'Please forgive me . . .'

'You?' Deathly white, Xavier spun round to face her. 'You did this?'

Cat shook her head dumbly. 'I didn't know . . . she's here for the ad campaign for your fragrance . . .'

Xavier's eyes turned dark with pain. 'Do you have any idea what you've done?' He shook her hand from his arm and turned to face Angelique as she sidled up to him.

'Xavier.' Seeing a hovering photographer she recognised from a gossip magazine, Angelique planted a juicy kiss on Xavier's mouth. 'Have you missed me?'

'Fuck off,' Xavier told her in a cold undertone, recoiling at the pungent waft of jasmine. He gave Cat a look of utter devastation before stalking out of the room.

Crumpling, Cat met Delphine's self-satisfied gaze. She really does hate me, Cat thought in shock.

Max put Xavier's dinner jacket around Cat's shivering shoulders. 'Shit. Cat, are you all right?'

Cat shook her head blindly. 'No, no, I'm not. Sorry, I have to go . . .'

Tearing away and not even able to look at Delphine again, she stumbled out of the room and ran up the stairs. Only when she was safely in her room did she fall on the bed and give in to her feelings. Burying her face in Xavier's dinner jacket and inhaling the evocative scent of his aftershave, Cat sobbed harder than she ever had in her life.

Chapter Eighteen

The following morning, Leoni found herself sitting in her office, listlessly sorting through her paperwork. Unusually, she hadn't put on one of her designer dresses; she was wearing a simple black tunic with a gold chain belt. Today, looking like a businesswoman who thrived on pressure and challenge seemed unimportant and inappropriate. Besides, who was she trying to impress?

Biting her nails, Leoni thought about last night. What a spectacle, what a drama! She didn't fully understand everything that had happened because she had been so caught up in her own issues, but the look on Xavier's face when Angelique had turned up . . . Leoni sighed.

Returning to her own turmoil, she thought about Jerard and the way she had presented herself to him. She accepted now that her work persona had been a shield to hide behind; a brittle, professional aura she had created to protect her emotional vulnerability. It was nothing more than an act, one she was tiring of. Couldn't she just be herself? Couldn't she just be allowed to be who she was and be accepted for it? It seemed that even Jerard, so perfect at first glance, seemed to want her to be something she wasn't.

No, Leoni corrected herself. Jerard wanted her to be the person she'd appeared to be: professional, committed to work and ultimately emotionless. She had given him the impression from the start that all she cared about was work and he had assumed she was a kindred spirit, a woman who didn't mind being left alone at a party just because a big deal had been finalised. A woman who didn't protest when a romantic moment was interrupted because, after all, business was everything, wasn't it? Leoni sighed. Ironically, it was Jerard, the only man she'd met who really liked the old Leoni, who had made her realise she wanted more out of life than work.

So, where did that leave them? Leoni wondered. Did she really want to be with a man who ditched her at the first sight of a deal? Because there would always be another deal, that much was obvious.

Leoni checked her phone. No messages.

And what about Ashton? He hadn't said a word to her all night, even after Jerard had gone. Ashton had arrived at the party without a date but he had seemed to be actively avoiding her and it felt horrible. Leoni was confused. Had she done something to upset him? She missed her best friend. Ever since Jerard had come on the scene, her friendship with Ashton seemed to have deteriorated. Was that the problem, perhaps? Did Ashton feel neglected? Surely not. He wasn't the type to be so self-absorbed. No, there must be some other reason.

Leoni looked up bleakly as the door opened.

'Sorry,' Cat mumbled, turning away. 'I-I was looking for Xavier.'

Leoni called her back. 'Wait. Come in. Please, come in.' She ushered Cat in, not sure why she was doing such a thing. But something in Cat's eyes told her that all was not well. 'What happened last night?'

Cat sat down in the stiff leather armchair Leoni offered her. She didn't want to be here; she didn't trust Leoni and Leoni couldn't stand her.

Leoni sat on the edge of her desk and stared at Cat. Usually so sparkling and warm, Cat's aquamarine eyes were dejected and sombre looking. There were violet shadows beneath them from lack of sleep and her long hair was pulled back in a messy bun. Her clothes had clearly been an afterthought that morning; she was wearing old jeans with a crumpled purple T-shirt that needed a wash.

'Talk to me,' Leoni said, concerned. 'You look like you need a friend. And I know I'm probably not your number one choice but I'm here and I'm listening.'

Cat looked up warily. What could she say? How could she explain? Leoni had warned her against getting involved with Xavier. 'One Ducasse is enough,' she had spat out nastily. Cat shifted uncomfortably. She had only just got her head around what her relationship with Olivier had been about – who he really was – and she had flung herself headlong into another ill-fated romance.

'This is to do with Angelique,' Leoni guessed accurately.

Cat rubbed a hand over her eyes, feeling exhausted. 'You could say that.'

'Xavier's ex-girlfriend. He was never the same after she left.'

Cat raised her eyebrows. 'Yes, he told me about it last night. I know . . . everything.'

'You know everything?' Leoni felt an irrational stab of jealousy. Xavier hadn't told her a single thing about it. In fact, as far as she knew, only the twins were in full possession of the facts and nothing would prise the truth out of those two when they'd been sworn to secrecy.

Cat, unaware of Leoni's thoughts, groaned. 'Why did I let Delphine talk me into speaking to Angelique? I thought maybe she was finally coming round to trusting me – liking me even, for fuck's sake!' She stopped, realising she'd let it slip about Delphine. What was she thinking? Leoni had claws, sharp ones, and she wasn't afraid to use them. Cat could have bitten her tongue off but it was too late now.

Leoni gawped. '*Grandmother* asked you to bring Angelique here?' She looked flabbergasted. 'Why would she do that?' Cat was silent and Leoni felt guilty. 'Look, I know I've given you a hard time and you don't trust me. I've been an absolute bitch and I think I've finally figured out why.' She met Cat's gaze head on. 'Ashton said something to me once that makes sense. I-I think I'm jealous of you. I mean, I was.'

Cat's jaw dropped. Why on earth would Leoni be jealous of her? Because she married someone she barely knew? Because she was a widow at the age of twenty-six?

'I know it sounds stupid but I think I was jealous that you were the person Olivier spent his last hours with,' Leoni confessed. 'We were so close – at least, I thought we were and yet I didn't even know he was married. And you didn't even know I existed! It hurt me, and with no Olivier here to blame, I took it out on you. It's horrible but I hope it makes some sort of sense.'

Cat nodded slowly. It did. 'I did love him; at least, I think I did.' She frowned, thinking about the way she felt about Xavier which made her feelings for Olivier fade into insignificance.

'It really doesn't matter any more,' Leoni told her, meaning it. 'I just wanted to get that off my chest.' She sat down in another armchair. 'Do you want to talk about what happened with Xavier? I won't be offended if you don't want to.'

Cat hesitated. She desperately needed to confide in someone but it was hard to spill her thoughts to Leoni. Realising that it had probably taken a lot for Leoni to own up to her jealousy over Olivier, Cat thought maybe she should give Leoni a chance but Leoni seemed to be in an offloading mood.

'All right, I'll tell you something about me, shall I? Something personal. Then maybe you'll be able to trust me.' She took a deep breath. 'I've fallen for Jerard, the guy I've been dating. But he . . . he puts business before me. We haven't slept together because his phone rings off the hook and, honestly, I think the only way we'll ever get it together is if I plaster an enticing deal all over my naked body to persuade him to pay attention to me for long enough.'

Cat smiled. She knew it must have killed Leoni to admit to that.

'And he buys me lilies and I can't bring myself to tell him I can't stand them and instead of telling me how he feels, he shows me . . . but he's always interrupted so I never really get to find out.' Spent, Leoni sat back in her chair. 'Is that enough sharing?'

Cat gave a short laugh. 'Yes.' Knowing she could trust Leoni with Xavier's secret past, she filled her in quickly, telling her the briefest facts of Xavier's relationship with Angelique. She didn't mention what had happened with Xavier in the stables; that was too personal . . . too intimate.

Leoni was perplexed. 'So she just left, without discussing losing the baby with him? That's a bit suspect, isn't it? And not a very nice thing to do, especially after Aunt Elizabeth had just died.' Leoni let out a slow breath. 'No wonder Xavier lost interest in the business . . . no wonder he howled at anyone who went near him.' Leoni felt mortified when she thought of the many jibes she had thrown at Xavier for not pulling his weight and creating more perfumes. How she had mocked him for walking away from the family business and not being as committed to it as she was. Leoni let out a strangled breath. She was learning an awful lot about herself lately. She wished she'd had a more open mind. Maybe she and her grandmother were more alike than she'd thought. Leoni frowned and suppressed that unpalatable thought for the time being.

She focused on Cat again. 'So, the bit we don't understand is what Grandmother is playing at, getting Angelique back here.'

'Exactly.'

'Well, she can't know about the baby situation or about Angelique just leaving Xavier like that,' Leoni pointed out reasonably. Seeing Cat's eyebrows lift doubtfully, she shook her head firmly. 'No, Grandmother is a tough old lady and we all know how she manipulates everybody but there's no way she'd hurt Xavier in that way. He's her favourite grandson, she adores him.' Leoni thought for a second. 'I can only imagine she thought Xavier was still in love with Angelique and that they'd had a silly row or something. I wonder if she thought she was playing Cupid?'

Cat bit her lip, realising Leoni was probably right.

'It was an honest mistake on your part,' Leoni pointed out. She could see how upset Cat was and she wondered why. Out of nowhere, the penny dropped. Cat had fallen for Xavier! Something had probably happened between them last night but Cat didn't want to talk about it. Leoni was surprised at herself for not being more bothered by the realisation.

'Aren't we in a mess?' she commented lightly, not letting on to Cat that she had guessed about Xavier. She gestured to her towering pile of paperwork. 'I've been working so hard on the home fragrance campaign, I've neglected everything else.' Leoni grimaced. 'And I don't even know if my proposal is any good.'

'Let me have a look at it,' Cat pleaded. 'Please, I need something to take my mind off all of this, at least until Xavier's calmed down and I can speak to him about everything.' Quite honestly, Cat still wanted to flee from La Fleurie and never set eyes on it again but she knew she owed it to Xavier to try and explain herself. According to Bella, her passport was on its way, so in all probability Cat would be leaving very soon. She needed to make her peace with Xavier before that.

Leoni was about to turn Cat's offer of assistance down automatically, the way she did whenever anyone offered help, but she caught herself. Why did she keep doing that? Hadn't she learnt yet that it wasn't a failure to admit she was struggling with something? Besides, with Cat's branding and advertising know-how, it would be madness to reject an offer of assistance when she so sorely needed it.

'Actually, yes. Do you mind?' Leoni dragged the paperwork towards her. 'I just can't get my head around how to pitch this to Guy. I thought I had it all worked out but now I can't even think of a reason to launch a home fragrance line. I've totally lost my way.'

Cat took the plans from Leoni. Mentally shelving her agonies over Xavier, she skim-read the proposal. Leoni watched anxiously from across the desk.

'It's good but it needs honing,' Cat assessed. She felt her imagination take hold and she was pleased. Anything to keep her from giving in to the appalling ache in her heart. 'Product placement is my speciality. I know exactly how you should pitch this to Guy. Hand me a pen and we'll get started.'

Throwing her a grateful smile, Leoni did as she was told for once.

Later that day, Guy was sitting in his office, barely holding it together. He was raging but he didn't know what to do with his rage or how to handle the situation. Seraphina's behaviour last night had appalled him. He hadn't thought she could possibly shock him more than she had the day she'd ridden round the college gardens naked but now she had done it again. And this time, it was far worse. This time, Seraphina's actions had taken a sinister turn, one that frightened the hell out of Guy.

He shook as he thought about what had happened. Seraphina was far too young for boyfriends, especially one who was old enough to be her father. Guy's mouth tightened. And he had been worried about perverts approaching Seraphina on the beach! It seemed he had far more to worry about closer to home. He cursed his mother for bringing that man into their home. What was she thinking, hiring a private detective? This obsession with Cat Hayes was completely out of hand.

Guy felt repulsed, both by his mother's actions and by Seraphina's. He was angrier with Seraphina because she was his daughter but, really, his mother was appalling these days. He laced his fingers together, wondering what he should do.

He wanted to speak to Elizabeth, to ask her advice because he was at a complete loss and it was making his head and his heart ache. But he couldn't, he could never ask Elizabeth anything ever again.

He saw his mother approaching and he shook his head at her in disgust.

Delphine flushed. Unlike the night before, Guy now looked to be fully in control of himself. He was wearing a spotless white shirt with a silver tie that matched the colour of his neat hair. He was pale beneath his tan and his brown eyes were aflame with anger but other than that, he looked scarily calm. Xavier often looked this way, Delphine mused, in the seconds before he erupted. She needed to have her wits about her.

'Now, I know you're cross,' she said in a soothing tone, fully aware it was an understatement, 'but I can explain.'

Guy gestured to a chair. 'Well, come on then, Mother. I can't wait to hear what you've got to say about all of this.'

She limped to a chair without her cane. Guy's aloof expression remained unchanged. If his mother was trying to get the sympathy vote, she'd have to do better than that, he thought harshly.

Delphine touched a hand to her snowy-white chignon shaking and, uncharitably, Guy was pleased to see it. His mother was always so in control, so restrained. She had always presented herself as a figurehead, someone to emulate and follow, but this time she had gone too far.

'You have every right to be disappointed in me,' she started.

'Disappointed!' Guy exploded. A vein throbbed in his head and Delphine stared at it worriedly. 'Disappointed doesn't even come close to how I'm feeling right now, Mother.'

Delphine inclined her head. 'I know you don't understand why I hired Yves – I mean, the private detective,' she said hurriedly, realising the use of Yves' name would be like a red rag to a bull for Guy. 'But I really thought I was doing the right thing. My friend Cybille—'

'Your friend Cybille is a poisonous old dragon,' Guy growled, slamming his hand down on his desk. 'She doesn't care about you or about this family. All she cares about is her place in society. She's nothing more than a social leech.'

Delphine was taken aback. 'I hardly think that's the case,' she protested, her brows knitting together. It wasn't true – was it? 'She recommended the private detective and I hired him because I was worried about Cat Hayes. I thought she might have a secret, something that might help us if she refused to go. Or that might damage the family in some way,' she added, thinking that sounded better.

Guy shot her a withering glance. 'Blackmail?' he asked, looking revolted. 'Surely we haven't stooped to that. Surely we haven't become people who resort to these sorts of tactics, Mother. Those are the kind of people who usually target wealthy families like us.'

'It's not blackmail, it's insurance,' Delphine protested automatically, using Cybille's words. 'Cybille says—'

'I don't want to hear another word about Cybille!' Guy roared, making her jump. 'This is about Seraphina. I'm furious with you for bringing that pervert into our house but I'm more concerned about my daughter thinking she can sleep with men twice her age. Does the girl have no morals?' He was ranting now and he couldn't stop. 'First she rides round her college naked and now this!'

'Guy!' Still stinging from Guy's comments about Cybille, Delphine wasn't going to let that one pass. 'Seraphina does have morals and, for the record, she didn't have sex with Yves.' Guy winced. 'I agree that we need to be concerned but have you thought about why she did this?'

Guy let out a hoarse laugh. 'I've thought about nothing else, Mother! Don't you think I've asked myself why my teenage daughter wants to become a model? Don't you think

I've asked myself over and over why on earth she wants to hurt me by sleeping with a man in his thirties?'

Delphine stared at him. 'You think Seraphina did this to hurt you?'

'Why else?'

Delphine lifted herself out of her chair with difficulty. Contrary to Guy's assumption that she had left her stick behind on purpose, she had actually taken a tumble that morning and broken her stick in two. Thankfully, nothing else was broken but it made getting around extremely difficult. Still, she wasn't about to admit to such a thing – she was in a weak enough position as it was without adding physical frailty to the list. Delphine gazed at her son sadly. He really couldn't see what was going on under his nose at the moment. Seraphina was acting up and doing things that were totally out of character all he could come up with by way of explanation was that she wanted to upset him.

Delphine limped to the door. Someone needed to tell Guy to wake up and smell the coffee but she wasn't sure the message should come from her and certainly not at this moment in time. He was too angry with her to take anything she had to say seriously and he was also playing the martyr, not that he knew it.

'I'll speak to you when you calm down,' she said quietly. 'And Guy, please take care of yourself. Think of your blood pressure. All this stress isn't good for you.'

Guy wondered when his mother had taken to stating the obvious. He didn't want to feel this stressed, for God's sake! He caught sight of Seraphina mooching around outside and felt furious all over again. He knew he needed to confront her and find out what she was playing at but he wasn't sure he trusted himself not to strike her. Best to wait it out and try to calm down first.

Gazing at the photograph of Elizabeth on his desk and feeling like a total failure, Guy put his head in his hands and wept.

Locked away in his lab once more, Xavier's emotions were all over the place and he was desperate for a cigarette. The last twenty-four hours had changed everything. Realising he had feelings for Cat . . . Angelique turning up out of the blue . . . Cat being behind the whole thing . . .

Xavier held up a phial of his fragrance. It was the unfinished article and without the missing ingredient it was pleasant, certainly, but not good enough. He wanted this fragrance to be the greatest achievement of his career to date – his comeback, if you like. He knew it was very close to being a bestseller and one of those fragrances that would last for years to come. It was young, sophisticated and sensual, a playful, sexy fragrance that had real staying power and an intoxicating, heady afterglow.

Xavier slotted the samples he'd created into a box. He'd created them so he could play around with the combinations and quantities once he had the missing element. Having got this far, he wanted this fragrance ready as soon as possible and he knew organising everything in advance would help.

Thoughts of the night before flooded back into his head. Xavier knew he couldn't be angry with Cat about it. She didn't know about Angelique because he hadn't told her. Even last night, he hadn't mentioned her name. He vaguely remembered Cat trying to tell him something as he'd dragged her back up to the house and he guessed her rambling words had been an attempt to warn him about what he was about to be confronted with.

The trouble was, even though Xavier knew it wasn't Cat's fault, he still couldn't go near her at the moment. She might have been oblivious of the fact that Angelique had been the woman who'd changed everything in his life a few years back but she had still brought the source of all his pain back to the forefront.

He pulled his fragrance notes towards him and stared at

them blindly. Xavier knew it was pointless trying to work but he didn't know what else to do. Last night in the stables, everything had seemed perfect . . . the chemistry between himself and Cat had been electric. Their mutual passion had astonished both of them. They had more or less confessed to falling head over heels in love with one another, which made Angelique's arrival all the more disruptive. Tearing off his lab coat, Xavier headed round the side of the lab for the much-needed cigarette. Drawing on it sharply in an attempt to steady his nerves, he sensed someone behind him and tensed. He smelt her before he saw her, the pungent aroma of jasmine seeping under his nostrils like creeping smoke.

'Angelique.'

She was wearing a black sundress that plunged almost down to her navel, revealing her luscious breasts. Angelique's mouth curved up bewitchingly. 'You lied last night,' she said, running her eyes down him in what could only be described as a possessive manner. God, but she had forgotten how sexy he was, Angelique thought, feeling her groin respond the way it always had around him. Those dark, dark eyes like melted chocolate, the almost black hair that looked particularly gorgeous when it was tousled the way it was now. That taut, toned body . . .

Why on earth had she left him back then? Pulling herself together, she put that thought aside. She knew exactly why she'd left him. It hadn't been guilt, exactly, so much as the realisation that she wasn't ready for what he had to offer. She had made mistakes – one notable one that would remain dead and buried forever – and she had allowed her life to spiral out of control.

Angelique flicked her hair over her shoulder. That was the past. Now she was back and she was more than ready for Xavier – Xavier and everything that came with him. She caught sight of the box of perfume phials, sure it must be the new fragrance. Was she the inspiration behind it? Angelique was sure she must be. She moved closer.

Xavier glared at her, furious that she was in his lab. He was moved by her presence and he hated himself for it. Angelique had always been a stunning woman, with her Brigitte Bardot-style blond hair and curves like a sex kitten. She was sex personified. She was nothing like Cat, who had a raw, natural beauty that was breathtaking. Angelique was like a fantasy woman . . . a sexual overdose. But who the fuck thought it would be a good idea for Angelique to feature in the ad campaign for his new fragrance? Xavier thought angrily. She was undoubtedly beautiful but she was too overtly sexy for what he had in mind; he would have chosen someone with a more restrained beauty.

'Admit it,' Angelique purred, moving closer. 'You lied to me last night. You said you didn't miss me but I don't believe you.'

Xavier wanted to shove her away from him but his brain and his groin were confused. Part of him wanted to tell Angelique to leave, to go back to her pornographic films and her glitzy, movie-star life, and part of him wanted to feel her again, to throw her into bed and revisit the place of so many dark but disturbingly sensual memories. He didn't trust her and he never would again but could he honestly say he hadn't missed her over the past two years? He'd be lying if he said her presence wasn't affecting him now.

As if sensing his weakness, Angelique moved even closer. Her heels scraped on the floor and the noise jarred on Xavier's already frazzled nerves. 'So you did miss me. You thought about me as much as I've thought about you.' She ran a scarlet-tipped fingernail along his shirt sleeve. The gesture seemed provocative, but then Angelique could make drinking a cup of coffee seem obscenely suggestive, Xavier thought wryly. He pushed past her, needing some air. Outside, he immediately lit a cigarette, inhaling gratefully.

'I've moved on,' he sniped at Angelique, who had followed him outside. It was true, even if it had only happened in the past few weeks. Remembering Cat's luminous, aquamarine eyes, Xavier felt a pain in his heart. He wanted to go to her, to feel her warm, sexy body against his . . . he wanted to block Angelique from his mind forever but he didn't know what to say to Cat, not yet.

'There's always room for a replay, isn't there?'

Xavier almost laughed. 'Is that what you think? That you can just come back here and pick up where we left off?'

She shrugged. 'Why not?' She smiled. 'Look, I know we had our problems but we had such a good time, didn't we, Xavier? Remember the sex.' She licked her lips suggestively. 'Remember how good it was?'

Xavier did. As he caught a waft of the jasmine oil she always wore, memories washed over him and he was blinded by vivid images of himself with Angelique. He shrugged them off because they made him feel sick.

'You're making fragrances again,' Angelique said, changing the subject abruptly. 'And I am the face of the ad campaign. What could be more perfect?'

'That was nothing to do with me,' Xavier snapped. 'Trust me, no one asked me if I thought you were the right person for the brand.' She wasn't. Xavier knew it would be a mistake to use her and he would do whatever it took to remove her from the campaign. But she had always had the ability to mess with his mind and she was doing it again.

'You still care.' Angelique taunted him hypnotically with her wide blue eyes. 'Why else would you have reacted the way you did last night?'

Xavier stared at her. He didn't know what he felt right now. Before he could sort out the maelstrom of emotions churning inside him, Angelique planted her mouth on his hungrily. Realising she had caught him unawares, she thrust her tongue into his mouth, toying with his urgently. Startled, Xavier found himself kissing her back, just for a moment. He felt her arms round his neck and her breasts against his chest and his groin almost let him down as Angelique ground herself against him deliberately. It felt . . . familiar. Not good, not bad . . . but familiar. And then it felt wrong, really, really wrong. Their relationship had been intense, like a honeymoon period. The brief happiness over the baby had been extinguished, and Angelique had packed up and headed back to her life and her career. Their relationship had never officially ended; it was unfinished business.

Hoping to clear the air with Xavier, Cat approached the lab. She stopped dead and her stomach lurched as she watched Xavier kissing Angelique, who was wound round him like a possessive octopus. She felt a shiver of pain go through her. She had thought Xavier really cared about her – loved her, even – but it seemed she was wrong.

Cat swallowed down a sob. What had happened between them last night obviously meant nothing to Xavier. Cat felt as worthless as the dirty glasses and half-eaten canapés left over from the party. With tears stinging her eyes, she hurried away before Xavier saw her.

Seconds later, Xavier abruptly stopped kissing Angelique. What the hell was he doing? He didn't want this – he didn't want Angelique. He had loved her once but she had hurt him too badly and he couldn't forgive her. He didn't want to dissect their relationship and figure out the truth any more than he wanted to resurrect it. A vision of Cat's beautiful, pure face swam in front of him and he felt tainted by Angelique's presence.

'Stay away from me,' he told Angelique curtly. 'I'm sure you think that kiss proves something and you're right. It proves that there's nothing between us any more.'

Angelique pouted. 'Oh, really? I thought I was the actress around here. The way you kissed me just then – that was real.'

Xavier shrugged. 'For a few seconds, maybe. And then I came to my senses, trust me.' He gave her a cold look. 'I'm leaving for Morocco in the morning and I'd be glad if you weren't here when I got back.'

Angelique stared after him thoughtfully. Xavier had clearly been affected by her arrival but whether it would lead to anything serious remained to be seen. For now, she would keep the pressure on and bide her time.

She slipped into Xavier's lab. Not really sure where to look, she was gratified to find that he had conveniently packed everything up for her. She took something she wanted – insurance, in case it all went wrong. She left the lab with a spring in her step.

Back in Paris, Ashton was making a monumental effort to put aside his broken heart and get on with his life. Seeing Leoni with Jerard – especially with Jerard down on one knee and Leoni looking as though all of her Christmases had come at once – had been more painful than he could have imagined. He didn't know for sure it was a proposal – maybe he was mistaken about that – but the two of them had looked very intimate and serious about one another.

He left his apartment and stepped out into hazy sunshine on the streets of Paris, telling himself to stop being such a wet. Leoni didn't think of him in that way and that was it. She never had done and she never would. It hurt like hell and he missed her like crazy now that she was with Jerard but he had to pull himself together. He had a building to buy and for the next few hours that was all he was going to think about. The public auction he was about to attend had been set up by the owner of the building. Such auctions were known in France as 'Audications Volontaires' – Sales of surplus property, mostly by private owners.

Focused on the task ahead Ashton hurried to the auction. In spite of everything that had happened, he was still going to do his best to secure the building for the Ducasse family. The property was intrinsically linked to Leoni; every aspect of his architectual plans, every corner of the store had been designed with her, and the idea for her home fragrance line, in mind. This made the whole procedure inordinately painful but Ashton was a man of his word and he was going to do everything in his power to get the building. He was wearing a dark suit, even though donning formal attire was unnecessary for auctions, because it made him feel more focused and more professional. On the outside, he looked very together; his hair was tidy and he'd shaved. On the inside, Ashton was falling apart but if he managed to carry on looking as composed as he thought he did right now, he was sure no one would guess.

Ashton was surprised to see so many people at the auction which was taking place in a large hall just on the edge of the ninth arrondissement, and he felt uneasy for a moment. He told himself his bid would be successful; after all, Guy had practically written him a blank cheque. There was half an hour or so to go before the auction was due to start, so after signing his bidding authorisation and proving his identity, Ashton ducked into the gents. He splashed cold water on his face and wiped it dry with a paper towel. He'd just finished when he heard someone come in. Turning, he was astonished to see Marianne standing before him, wearing her belted black trench coat and a pair of scarlet suede high heels.

'Er, Marianne, I think you've come through the wrong door.'

'I know.' Marianne smiled and came closer. Her red hair was loose again today, hanging around her shoulders in a fragrant cloud, the rich shade matching her glossy lips and shoes. Ashton caught a waft of her pungent perfume and recoiled. What the hell was she up to? He moved backwards as she advanced on him and found himself backing into one of the cubicles.

'The auction is going to start soon.' He frowned, watching Marianne toying with the belt of her coat.

'Not for another twenty minutes,' she purred, following him. She reached out and smoothed a lock of his blond hair behind his ears. 'You've shaved,' she pouted, allowing her fingers to trail down his strong, smooth jawline. 'What a shame. I prefer "the less polished Ashton".'

Ashton shook his head, feeling trapped.

Marianne let out a breathy sigh. 'Still, it's what's underneath that counts.' She deftly pushed the cubicle door shut behind her. They were chest to chest in the small space and Ashton couldn't help thinking he had accidentally been transported into a French farce.

He held her at arm's length. 'Marianne, stop this.'

'But I want you,' she said huskily.

Ashton shook his head. 'No, you don't. You want the property and if I've learnt anything about you since we've met, I'd say that this is all about Guy Ducasse.'

Marianne stared at him, her green eyes unflinching. She slowly undid the belt of her trench coat, then the buttons, one by one. When they were all undone she held the lapels of her coat and opened it. Beneath, she was completely naked, revealing a neat bush and voluptuous breasts topped by large, red-pink nipples.

'Is this about Guy Ducasse?' she asked in a throaty voice.

'Marianne!' Ashton quickly closed her coat.

'Are you . . . turning me down?' she asked, her eyes widening incredulously.

Ashton firmly did up the belt of her coat. 'In the nicest possible way,' he told her gently. He gestured to the door and reluctantly Marianne headed out of the cubicle.

'Let's see just how much Leoni Ducasse, and the rest of the family, mean to you,' she said in a sly voice, her eyes narrowing as she met his.

'Meaning?'

'Meaning that as you've turned down my first . . . offer, I will have to play dirty, as you English say.'

Ashton waited. He felt concerned but he was buggered if he was going to show it.

'I have the owner of the building we both want so badly in my back pocket. And whatever Guy Ducasse has sanctioned as a budget can easily be tripled by me,' Marianne stated airily. She looked Ashton in the eye. 'Trust me. If I want that building, it's mine. I have dealt with all other interested parties, so that only leaves . . . you.'

Ashton's heart sank. He believed Marianne. If she said she had the owner eating out of her hand, and that she had dealt with the competition she probably had. Given the way she'd propositioned him just now, Ashton had a fair idea how she'd managed it too.

'There is one thing that would change my mind,' Marianne said, inspecting her fingernails.

'Name it,' Ashton said immediately.

Marianne did. In one, short sentence, she told him exactly what she was after and what it would take for her to back off and allow Ashton to purchase the building.

He gaped at her. Whatever he had been expecting, it wasn't this. 'You can't be serious.'

'Oh, I never joke about business, you should know that by now,' she returned grimly. 'Business is about winning. And I hate to lose, Ashton, I really do.' She checked her watch. 'You have five minutes to decide. I'll wait for you in the auction room and we'll take it from there.'

Staring after her, Ashton gripped the edge of the counter in disbelief. Was she really asking him to do that? Of course she was. The question was, what was he going to do about it? Marianne was right, he had to think about how much he really loved Leoni. Was he willing to make this sacrifice for her, especially now that she was in love with Jerard? Could he give up the one thing that really meant something to him, even if he might never end up with Leoni?

He gazed at his reflection in the mirror. The fact that Leoni was besotted with Jerard made things easier in some ways: he now knew how he really felt about her. Marianne's ultimatum had given his confused feelings clarity, and now he had to prepare himself to make the biggest sacrifice of his life. Straightening his shoulders decisively, he left the gents and went in search of Marianne.

Chapter Nineteen

Guy strolled into a small salon at the back of the house, startled to find Cat curled up alone on one of the sofas. She was wearing jeans and a very crumpled purple T-shirt, her dark blonde hair loose around her shoulders and her nose looking slightly sunburnt.

On closer inspection, he realised Cat looked as if she'd been crying.

'What's wrong?' he asked, sitting on the arm of the sofa. 'What are you doing in here all alone?'

Cat looked up. She almost lost it at the sight of the concern in his eyes but she held herself together, just. 'I'm . . . I suppose I'm trying to figure out what the hell to do with my life.'

Guy headed to the sideboard and pulled a bottle of chilled white wine out of the fridge hidden in the unit. 'Would this help?'

She smiled briefly. 'It certainly won't hurt.' She watched him pour the straw-coloured wine into two glasses and accepted one when he brought it over.

'Cassis,' Guy informed her as she sipped the wine. 'Xavier's favourite.'

Cat buried her nose in it, almost coming undone. It was ridiculous, really, but even drinking Xavier's favourite wine made her feel sad now. She glanced at Guy again, wondering if it was his ability to appear so collected that made his children think he didn't care about them. Certainly, if she hadn't seen him weeping over his wife's grave with her own eyes, she never would have believed it. Guy had put a wall up around himself that was so impenetrable, he seemed robot-like at times. He was suave and friendly but he never really let his guard down.

Guy rubbed his eyes tiredly, leaning back against the sofa. 'So, do you feel your visit here has been a success?'

'Hardly!' Cat blurted out without thinking. 'At least . . . what do you mean?'

'I just wondered if you might have come here needing to exorcise a ghost,' Guy commented, wondering why she had reacted so strongly. 'I know it can't have been easy for you. Leoni and my mother are not exactly welcoming when it comes to outsiders but I was really thinking of you and what you might have been able to overcome since you'd been here.'

Cat toyed with her glass. 'I guess it's been good in that way,' she admitted. She didn't want to say out loud that learning about Olivier and all his misdemeanours had pretty much killed whatever she had felt for him. 'I've finally realised that being impetuous isn't always the way to go.' She said the last words bitterly, thinking about Xavier. As a vision of him with Angelique slobbering all over him came into her head, she felt the wine making its way back up into her throat, acidically.

Guy raised his eyebrows. 'You call it impetuous, I call it romantic. Xavier has always been considered to be the romantic in the family, you know.' Seeing her look of surprise, he continued. 'Oh, yes. He's creative and he's temperamental but he has always believed that marriage is something to be taken seriously. He saw the way Elizabeth and I were and he wanted the same thing, a soulmate, someone who was as passionate as he was.'

Cat sipped her wine. It made sense and it explained why Xavier had been so scathing about her marriage to Olivier; he assumed it had been hasty and reckless, rather than a real meeting of minds. He wasn't wrong, Cat thought soberly.

346

'Do you know why he changed?' she asked Guy curiously. She was sure he didn't know but she wondered if Guy realised Xavier had tried to tell him about it in the past.

Guy shook his head. 'No.' He leant forward. 'Do you?'

Cat nodded guiltily. 'But it's not for me to say. Maybe . . . maybe you should ask him about it one day.'

Guy looked perplexed. Changing the subject, he remembered he had been planning to ask her about branding. He did so, saying he'd be interested in her thoughts about Ducasse-Fleurie as a company. 'We've never really paid too much attention to advertising or branding,' he added. 'Maybe it's an arrogant thing but we always just relied on the family name to give us the profile we needed.'

'It's not arrogant, brand names count for a lot. I did a paper on this at college. They really are important. The name is the identity of a company, it conveys the personality behind it, the service it provides.' She warmed to her theme, glad of a distraction from thoughts of Xavier.

Guy wasn't sure he understood it all, but he was pleased to be focused on something other than Seraphina for a moment. 'I think we just created perfumes we wanted to and because people liked them, we became lazy and didn't try too hard.'

Cat nodded. 'It's understandable.'

'What would you change about our brand?' Guy asked.

Cat scratched her head. 'Well, you need some new products, as I mentioned before. Leoni's home fragrance line will be perfect, and the new fragrance of course.' It would hurt to say Xavier's name out loud, though she knew she was being stupid. 'Apart from that, the colour scheme . . . it's a little dated, if you don't mind me saying.'

Guy looked unconvinced. 'Our lilac and white colour scheme is so safe. If we changed it, people might feel confused about who we are.'

'Not if you tweaked it slightly. What if . . .' Cat thought for a moment. She glanced at a photograph of Guy and Delphine accepting an award in New York years ago. The annual FiFi event was thought to be the Oscars of the fragrance world and any award given by them was extremely prestigious. Cat frowned at the lilac ribbon in the photo, sure that this was the detail that jarred.

'What if you changed the lilac ribbon for a deep, rich purple?' she suggested. 'You could keep the classic white boxes and packaging, they're clean and sophisticated and they do make the Ducasse-Fleurie brand instantly recognisable. But the overall look would be more dynamic.'

Guy held his hands up; he just couldn't visualise it.

Cat grabbed the edge of her purple T-shirt and held it against a white box someone had left lying on the sofa. 'See? It's a lovely contrast. It's much bolder and younger but I don't think it would put the older generation off because it's such a classy combination. It's sophisticated rather than flowery.'

'All right, I can see how that might work,' Guy conceded, somewhat grudgingly. As open as he was being, he did find change difficult. 'But how do we go about doing something like that?'

'It's easy enough,' Cat said, her mind flipping through her mental encyclopaedia of advertising scenarios. 'I can think of a couple of companies who've done this over the years. The best example is Brash, the clothing company. They changed their logo from an exclamation mark to the name itself.'

Guy took the perfume box and turned it over in his hands. 'We can afford it but I just wonder if it's worth it.'

'Ducasse-Fleurie is a great brand,' Cat said earnestly, leaning forward, 'but with fresh ideas and a more modern look it could be an amazing one, something really exciting and vibrant. Wouldn't that be more fun? Wouldn't that make all of you want to go into the office every morning and get involved?'

Guy stared at her.

'I think you should take Leoni more seriously,' Cat ventured, settling back down on the sofa again. 'Leoni has her finger on the pulse. She knows what modern fragrance brands are doing and she wants to branch out and give the Ducasse-Fleurie brand a chance to really become a household name. The home fragrance line, the shop in Paris – she's right. In my opinion, her visions are just what this company needs.'

'Wow.' Guy sat back, his thoughts all over the place. He thought about the Paris building and felt guilty. He had pushed Ashton to acquire it but only because of Marianne, hardly the most sensible of reasons! Cat was making him realise he should have listened to his niece more carefully. Perhaps she really *did* know what was good for the business . . .

Cat watched him. Despite having told herself not to throw caution to the wind again, she did just that. 'It makes sense outside of business too.'

Guy drained his glass. 'Sorry, what?'

'That sometimes you have to take a fresh look at things, try a different approach. Don't you think?' Gently, Cat braved Guy's wrath. 'I . . . saw you the other day. In the graveyard.'

Guy's head snapped up. The blood drained from his face. 'Y-you what?'

Cat quickly carried on speaking. 'Please don't be embarrassed. I haven't said a word to anyone. And I've done the exact same thing. If you'd stumbled upon me when I first arrived, you would have seen me yelling and crying over Olivier's grave. It's cathartic.'

'I was just feeling emotional,' Guy said in a dismissive tone. However, his face contorted with agony at the memory of it. The thought that he'd been seen was excruciating and he thanked God it was Cat who had seen him and not a member of his family. 'It was a one-off,' he added, keen to gloss over the incident.

'Was it?' Cat saw his shoulders shaking slightly and, moving closer, she grasped his hands. 'Guy, my parents died in a skiing accident when I was a kid and it nearly killed me. I . . . I know what grief looks like.'

Guy stood up, shocked. He ran a hand through his silver hair, 'I'm not grieving! Elizabeth died over two years ago.'

'Grief can take years to manifest itself . . . I saw a counsellor when I was younger and he said I managed to suppress mine for around a year before I faced up to how terrible I was feeling.'

Guy paced the room, agitated. 'Fine, so I get upset about Elizabeth now and again. Isn't that natural? When something goes wrong, I wish she was here to help me out because I feel as though I don't know what to do.' He loosened his shirt collar, feeling light headed. 'That doesn't mean I'm grieving!'

Cat bit her lip. She'd seen people behave exactly the way Guy was now at her counselling group. It was ages ago now but there had been a man there who was exactly like Guy; he felt dreadful but he couldn't believe it could be down to his wife's death five years ago.

'Maybe you could see someone,' she suggested cautiously. 'It might help . . . you might find you can support Max and Seraphina more . . .'

Guy spun round. 'Oh, so I'm not supporting them?' he roared. 'Did they put you up to this? Because if they did, so help me God—'

'Of course not!' Cat rushed to correct him. 'The twins had nothing to do with this. I'm saying this because I can see the signs. I've been through this.'

'My children are fine. Why would you even bring them up?'

Cat shook her head, not sure what to say. 'Guy . . .' She paused, wanting him to know she was trying to help him. 'I'm saying all this because . . . because I care about you, all right? You're hurting and it's horrible and you don't have to do this on your own.'

Guy froze. His eyes filled with tears at her kind words and he turned away from her. 'My children are fine . . . and I'm fine. Do you understand?' Fiercely, he turned and pointed his finger at her. With that, he stormed from the room.

Cat was horrified at herself. What on earth had possessed her to push him so hard? Guy was clearly in a mess and she had pushed and pushed until he had almost cracked. She put her head in her hands, wishing she'd kept her mouth shut. Remembering Xavier, Cat found herself sobbing again.

The following day, Angelique was reclining on an ivory chaise longue wearing nothing but a lilac body stocking. Stretched out and posing from the tips of her toes to the top of her blond head, she was looking into the camera with a knowing smile.

'I can't see the perfume bottle,' the director that Delphine had hired called out.

Angelique rolled her eyes and held the bottle out in front of her.

'Not like that,' Stefan groaned. He threw a glance at Leoni who had stopped by to take a look at the campaign as it got underway. 'I thought she was supposed to be a professional,' he muttered under his breath.

'Professional pain in the backside,' she murmured back. Leoni had never really liked Angelique. When she had last been at La Fleurie, she had been charming and gracious but Angelique always expected to be the centre of attention and, as such, she was exhausting. The constant demands were tiresome and after a while her exotic presence palled. And now that she knew what Angelique had done to Xavier . . .

Leoni frowned. She had never really thought Angelique and Xavier made a very compatible couple. They looked sensational together, of course, but that was about it. They hadn't seemed to have much in common; in fact, Leoni had always had a sneaking suspicion Angelique had had the hots for Olivier. The pair of them were similar in personality – both were brash extroverts and both did whatever they wanted, regardless of the cost to others. Leoni had asked him about it once, but Olivier had vehemently denied any attraction to Angelique, claiming that he detested women who had a bigger ego than he did, and Leoni believed him. Olivier had always been a liar but his words had had a strong ring of truth about them.

Staring at the shot of Angelique holding the perfume bottle, Leoni wasn't sure the image was what she had envisaged. She had now read the brief Xavier had put together and on the face of it, Angelique fitted the bill. She was glamorous, sexy and aspirational, but something was missing. Angelique's body was flawless; she was in great shape and it was clear she spent an enormous amount of time looking after herself. Leoni would kill to have breasts like Angelique but, wryly, she decided they wouldn't suit her boyish frame and that they would probably make all her clothes hang strangely.

'Get me some water,' Angelique ordered her quivering assistant. 'And make sure it's iced.'

'Right away,' Celine said, rushing to do as she was told.

Leoni felt uncomfortable as she watched the exchange. How often had she snapped at staff like that when she was working? How often had she treated people with disdain just because she was busy? Her thoughts were a bit like being doused in the ice-cold water Celine was handing Angelique.

'Isn't she professional?' Celine commented to Leoni as she stood out of the way. 'I don't know how she does it.'

Leoni nodded, Celine was clearly in awe of her famous boss. 'She has incredible skin.' Leoni frowned, wondering how Angelique could look so good round the clock. 'It looks as though she polishes it or something.'

'Regular massages,' Celine confided behind her hand. 'She has this wonderful masseuse who looks after her because she's so famous for her glowing skin.' Leoni raised an eyebrow. If only she had time for such things. Still, whatever Angelique did to look after herself, it was working. Her skin was flawless and glowing and she looked years younger than she actually was.

Celine was goggling at the room and its paintings and ornaments. 'This château is so beautiful,' she said, turning shining eyes towards Leoni. 'I was all set to hate it because it wasn't Hollywood but now I'm here, I can see what all the fuss is about.'

'Hollywood?'

Celine's eyes flickered to Angelique but seeing that she was having a heated exchange with the director about the position of her breasts, Celine couldn't resist gossiping. 'Angelique was due to go to Los Angeles to discuss a Hollywood film,' she whispered in a conspiratorial tone. 'A really big one. Her agent, Mason, is absolutely livid about it.'

Leoni gave her a sideways glance. 'I don't blame him. Why would Angelique turn down such an exciting opportunity?'

'I don't know.' Celine shrugged. 'As soon as Delphine Ducasse phoned her about the campaign, she wasn't interested in anything else.'

This was all news to Leoni; according to Cat, *she* had been the one to approach Angelique with the idea – on Delphine's suggestion, admittedly, but still. Something wasn't right. The news made her feel better about one thing, however; Angelique's feelings for Xavier had to be real. Why else would she give up the chance to break America unless she was head over heels in love with him?

'Did you realise Angelique still had feelings for Xavier before she came back here?' Leoni asked Celine, watching Angelique as she turned on to her back and let her legs fall to one side. 'I mean, are you two close in that way?'

Celine looked vague. 'I don't know anything about Xavier,' she replied, not really paying attention. 'Angelique has never mentioned him before. And yes, I suppose we are rather close.' She flushed. 'I know she sounds rude sometimes but she does actually tell me quite a lot.'

Leoni was feeling more confused by the minute. 'But Xavier is the reason she's here, isn't it? She can't really have turned down a Hollywood part for a perfume campaign, it has nowhere near enough exposure.'

Celine shook her head. 'Not to my knowledge. Angelique says she's all about her career and I believe her. No, she's here for this ad campaign and nothing else, as far as I know. I think Angelique wants respect, you see, to be taken seriously. And that's something she thinks the ad campaign will bring her.' Celine looked impressed. 'My boss is the hardest working woman I've ever met. Men adore her, of course, but she really doesn't seem to care too much about them either way.'

Leoni stared at Angelique thoughtfully. Perhaps she kept up a professional attitude in front of her assistant, perhaps she made a point of not discussing her personal business. But Leoni couldn't ignore a niggling feeling of doubt. Something was wrong with this picture . . . something didn't ring true. It was what Celine had said about Angelique wanting respect and wanting to be taken seriously. Leoni could relate to that and she realised how fronting up a campaign for Ducasse-Fleurie would bring her the kudos and respectability she craved. She just wondered if Angelique had far bigger plans for raising her profile and ensuring she would never have to take her clothes off and prostitute herself any longer.

Relieved to have something other than Ashton to think about, Leoni decided to make it her business to find out exactly what Angelique was up to.

Still fuming about the party, Max was brushing his horse with rapid, jerky strokes. Wearing a smudged, duck-egg blue polo shirt and black jodhpurs, he stalked around Le Fantome, rubbing her grey coat more gently as she whinnied and nudged him. Seraphina, walking towards the stables with Cat, noticed how dark Max's mood was from ten feet away. 'Look at him, he's seething,' she commented, tearing open a can of Coke.

Undoing her plait with one hand, she shook her hair free until it lay in ripples around her shoulders. Wearing a white sundress over a khaki bikini, she cut a stylish figure, but her expression was one of exhausted misery. The business with Yves had hit her hard and she was struggling to cope with the public humiliation of it all.

Feeling equally dismal, Cat observed Max. His body language was aggressive and his anger was apparent in every movement. Cat glanced at the stable she and Xavier had found themselves in at the party but she tore her eyes away deliberately, refusing to dwell on what had happened. She had cried far too much lately and it was time to pull herself together.

She realised Seraphina was talking to her about Max's mood. Putting Xavier firmly out of her head, she turned to her. 'What's wrong with him? Why is he so angry?'

Seraphina sighed. Leaning over the fence, she surveyed the lavender fields. 'God knows. I think he's mostly annoyed with Dad but you know Max, he's not talking to anyone.'

'That's teenage boys for you,' Cat said, joining her at the fence. 'I really hope you've forgiven me for betraying your trust. I . . . I didn't do it lightly; I just wanted to protect you.' She stared straight ahead of her, hoping she'd get a chance to see the lavender flowers; they were supposed to look glorious before the harvest. Cat noticed a hangar beyond the fields and wondered what it was for but she didn't like to ask Seraphina when they were discussing the Yves issue.

Seraphina shook her head then rested her chin on her arms. 'There's nothing to forgive, honestly, Cat. You did the right thing. I mean, I came to my senses anyway and bashed him with the bottle but . . .' She closed her eyes, scrunching her face up. 'I can't be sure but I can't help thinking Yves still might not have taken no for an answer.'

'Don't, Seraphina.' Cat put her arm round the girl's shaking shoulders. 'What a bastard. Thank God Max arrived when he did.'

Seraphina opened her eyes and nodded. 'I think I knew deep down that Yves wasn't right for me, especially when he kept putting the pressure on, but I just wanted to please him. Isn't that sad?'

'Of course not. It's normal. It's Yves who was in the wrong. He took advantage of you, that's all.'

'It was terrifying, Cat. I'd drunk so much and I felt so woozy . . . I threw up and still he wouldn't stop.' She started to cry, suddenly looking very much like the sixteen year old she was. Her bottom lip quivered and tears slipped down her cheeks. 'What kind of person does that, Cat? I thought he cared about me, I really did. But he was just after what he could get.' She wiped her eyes. 'He just wanted all of this, I think.' She swept her arm wide, encompassing the grounds of the Ducasse estate. 'He talked about it constantly.' Seraphina glanced at Cat, realising she probably knew nothing about why Yves had been on the scene in the first place. She changed the subject, thinking about Angelique.

'And what about Angelique? What was Grandmother *thinking*? I mean, I know she hasn't a clue what happened and she was just doing what she thought was best for Xavier . . . but God, how wrong could she be?' Seraphina drained her can of Coke. 'I can't believe Grandmother asked you to invite Angelique here. Xavier can't stand Angelique.'

Cat felt her heart constrict. 'I wouldn't be too sure about that.' Loath to tell Seraphina about the kiss she'd witnessed, she kept quiet.

Seraphina didn't seem to hear. 'She's awful. She might be beautiful but it's definitely only skin deep. Underneath all that hair and those big blue eyes, she's a viper. And I'm sure she's had her ribs removed. No one has a waist that tiny, not even a child. And quite frankly I can't even understand what Xavier saw in her in the first place – apart from the obvious, of course, but even then, you're far prettier than she is, for a start.'

Cat couldn't even raise a smile.

'I saw you working with Leoni yesterday,' Seraphina commented. 'Are you two best buddies now?'

Cat stared straight ahead. 'Not best buddies but we've cleared the air. We sorted out her pitch for the home fragrance line and we talked a bit.' She looked up as Max strode over to them.

'Have you seen Dad?' Max asked Seraphina, his dark eyes moody and truculent.

Seraphina shook her head. 'I think he must be shut away in his office.'

'Of course, where else would he be?' Max's lip curled contemptuously. He kicked the fence with his riding boot, clearly needing to vent some frustration. The fence obediently buckled and gave a satisfying crack.

'Are you . . . are you angry with me?' Seraphina said, her brown eyes concerned. 'I know I was stupid but I honestly didn't realise Yves was such a creep until it was nearly too late . . .'

Max grabbed her shoulder. 'Of course I'm not annoyed with you!' he cried. 'It's Dad I'm furious with. I don't even know what to say to him but I want to have it out with him. At the very least to let him know how fucking useless he is.' Giving the innocent fence one more boot for good measure, Max headed back to the stables, his dark head bent.

Seraphina gulped. 'He means it, I can tell. I'm worried, Cat. They both have such terrible tempers, who knows what might happen if they confront each other properly?'

Cat took her arm. 'Let's go to the beach or something and take our minds off it. Or we can talk about it, if you want to.' She was desperate to get away from La Fleurie for a while; anything to avoid the agonising sight of Xavier and Angelique together. Unaware of Cat's inner turmoil, Seraphina smiled gratefully and took her arm.

*

357

Throwing clothes into a bag haphazardly, Xavier caught sight of Cat as she walked past his open window. She was wearing an aquamarine bikini under one of Seraphina's robes that he knew would match her eyes exactly. Her shoulders drooped dejectedly and for a moment Xavier had the urge to run out and gather her up in his arms. He resisted; they needed some time apart. It wasn't her fault, none of it was, but the fact that Angelique was here, screwing with his head again, was down to her. It occurred to him to wonder what had made her think of approaching Angelique, but he didn't pursue the line of thought. Right now he just wanted to get away.

Glancing out at Cat, he saw her chatting quietly to Seraphina and he was glad his sister had someone to talk to. His grandmother seemed to be keeping her head down for some reason – always a bad sign, in Xavier's opinion – and Max, with characteristic belligerence, had resorted to stomping around the château and riding all day long. Xavier would have expected his father to immerse himself in work in lieu of facing up to the magnitude of Seraphina's actions, but in fact, bewilderingly, Xavier had found him pacing his office in a state of pure rage about Seraphina's so-called horrendous behaviour. He appeared to be blaming everyone but himself.

Xavier tossed a pile of lightweight shirts into his bag and then threw himself into a chair. A moment later, he was surprised when Leoni knocked on the door. Beckoning her to come in, she took a seat opposite him, pushing her glasses more firmly up on to her nose.

'Hey.' She glanced at his bag. 'Where are you off to?'

'Morocco,' Xavier replied shortly.

Leoni frowned.

'It's work related,' he added, looking irritable. 'Did you need me for something?'

She leant forward. 'I . . . I just think there's something you have to know before you go. Well, a few things, in fact.'

'Go on,' Xavier said, rubbing his eyes wearily. He really

didn't think Leoni could tell him anything significant enough to change the way he was feeling but he was willing to hear her out.

Leoni counted on her fingers. 'All right, well, firstly, this Yves person Seraphina was seeing? He was Grandmother's private detective.'

Xavier looked stunned. 'Her *what*?'

'I know, crazy, right?' Leoni nodded, her brown eyes glittering. 'That awful friend of hers, Cybille, recommended him, said he helped her out with her divorce or something. Anyway, Grandmother hired him to investigate Cat.'

'You're not serious?' It was outrageous, even for his grandmother. Xavier frowned. 'So that's how Seraphina met him – she bumped into him here, I'm assuming.'

Leoni raised her eyebrows. 'Exactly. Grandmother must be feeling pretty guilty about that but if she does, she hasn't come out and said it yet. And the other thing I wanted to tell you was also about Cat. Angelique turning up here like that? Grandmother engineered the whole thing. She approached Angelique in the first place and then used Cat to sort out the ad campaign.'

Xavier put his head in his hands. It made sense. He had known Cat wouldn't have approached Angelique off her own back – why would she? But why would his grandmother do such a stupid thing in the first place?

'She was playing at matchmaker,' he realised. 'She doesn't know what happened when we split up and she thinks I wanted Angelique back.' Xavier groaned.

Leoni watched him. She wasn't about to let on that Cat had filled her in about Xavier's relationship so she stared back at him silently, pretending she was still in the dark. 'By the way, Cat only did what Grandmother asked her to do because she thought it might mean the old lady was finally accepting her. And she didn't want to say anything to you because Grandmother asked her to keep it a secret, though knowing you, you probably didn't give Cat a chance to say anything much. Frankly, I think she should have blown the whistle on Grandmother immediately but as you've probably seen, Cat isn't like that.'

Xavier sat back, trying to process all the information Leoni had given him. Everything made sense; it was just a case of rearranging perspectives in his head and getting his emotions sorted. He glanced at Leoni, not sure what she knew. He hadn't spoken to her about Angelique's pregnancy at the time so it was unlikely she had been aware of it, although . . . Xavier paused. Olivier had known. Somehow, Olivier had overheard something and he had seemed oddly keen to make sure Xavier wasn't about to top himself over the incident, although why he had been so concerned was beyond Xavier.

Had Olivier spoken to Leoni about it? Xavier wondered. It was possible but his gut feeling was that he hadn't. Leoni might not be the most emotional of women but he was certain she would have said something about Angelique's pregnancy if she'd known. Still, Xavier wondered why Leoni was fighting Cat's corner all of a sudden and he said as much.

Leoni smiled. 'She helped me out with my home fragrance campaign . . . we talked about . . . oh, girl's stuff mostly. She's not as bad as I thought she was,' she admitted, seeing Xavier's amused expression. 'In fact, she's lovely, all right? I just couldn't see past my own jealousy, that's all.'

Catching sight of the time, Xavier stood up and finished packing. 'That's a bit deep and meaningful, where did all that come from?'

'Ashton, actually,' Leoni said a shadow crossing her face. 'Back in the days when we were talking.'

'Why, what's up?'

Leoni sighed. 'I don't know. Since I met Jerard, I think I might have shut Ashton out a bit. I thought he might have been seeing this woman Marianne in Paris – long story, but she's totally wrong for him.'

Xavier met her eyes. 'That's his choice, though, isn't it? I mean, I'm not saying I think Jerard isn't the man for you, am I?'

'Is that what you think?' Leoni was astonished. She wasn't even aware that Xavier knew Jerard.

Xavier looked non-committal. 'I just want the best for you, that's all. Jerard is . . . he's very focused on work, to the exclusion of everything else.'

'How do you know all this?'

'An ex-girlfriend of mine dated him and she got thoroughly fed up with being cast aside in favour of his BlackBerry,' he explained, hoping he wasn't trampling all over Leoni's heart.

'Really?' Leoni looked dismayed. 'That sounds familiar. At least it's not just me. I was beginning to think there was something wrong with me because Jerard kept choosing work over spending time with me.'

Xavier zipped his bag up smartly and kissed her on the cheek. 'Don't be silly. And I hope I haven't hurt your feelings, L. I just want you to be happy. You deserve to be adored, you know? By someone who puts you first . . . who worships the ground you walk on.'

'I wish. Let me know if you know anyone who might do that, won't you?' Leoni wondered why Xavier had used Ashton's old nickname for her.

Xavier stared at her before be answered. 'Yes, yes, I will.'

Leoni frowned. What was eating him? 'Do you think I should get in touch with Ashton?' she asked as Xavier headed downstairs.

'Definitely.' Xavier paused and looked up. 'And I doubt very much he's dating that woman you mentioned.'

'How do you know?'

'Because he's been in love with the same woman for years.' Xavier fervently hoped he was doing the right thing. 'Ashton's definitely a one-woman man, and he cares more about romance than business, that's for sure.'

Seeing Leoni staring down at him in bewilderment, Xavier hurried to the pool but Cat was nowhere to be seen. Damn. Now he was going to have to go to Morocco without speaking to her. Xavier grimaced. He just hoped she stayed at La Fleurie until he had done what he needed to do in Morocco. He had to be sure of his feelings and then things needed to be sorted once and for all. Xavier made for the front of the house and slid into the car waiting to take him to the airport.

Sitting bolt upright in a rigid chair in her private quarters a few days later, Delphine felt absolutely wretched. She had started out with such good intentions but she had inadvertently caused a dreadful mess. Boundaries had become blurred and lines had definitely been crossed. Delphine felt uncomfortable as she recalled the almost triumphant way Leoni had informed her that Xavier knew she was behind Angelique's involvement in the ad campaign. She supposed it was bound to come out sooner or later but she had half expected Cat to spill the beans. The fact that she hadn't was to her credit; it had been Leoni who had finally informed Xavier.

Gripping the top of her new cane, Delphine wondered how she could have got it all so wrong. She still didn't know what had gone on between Xavier and Angelique but she got the impression from Leoni that Angelique had done something unforgivable, something that should have made her think of Xavier's hurt feelings before coming back here so deliberately. Yet, here she was at La Fleurie, behaving for all the world as though she belonged here, ordering the staff around, wafting around in next to nothing and generally making her presence very much felt.

Delphine chewed her lip. Had she been blind to Angelique's faults the first time round? Or had Angelique simply played her for an old fool, turning on the charm and acting the successful-but-misunderstood career woman for all she was worth? Delphine suspected it was the latter, as much as it pained her to admit it. Her thoughts turned to Seraphina and she was suffused with guilt, the acrid sensation leaving a bad taste in her mouth.

She, Delphine, was responsible for bringing Yves Giraud into their home. She had trusted him, in spite of her misgivings about his manner and his unhealthy interest in La Fleurie and everything that came with it. Delphine didn't know if Yves had started out with hopeful aspirations of ingratiating himself into the Ducasse fold via Seraphina or if he was simply an opportunist with a taste for young girls, but either way, her own involvement in the whole sorry affair was shameful.

Delphine had done her best to atone for her sins by making sure Yves would find it hard to work within their circle again. She had cancelled any cheques he hadn't already cashed – after all, he had hardly earned them – and she had put the word out amongst her friends that Yves was untrustworthy. Her good friend Cybille had been surprisingly sanguine in response to Delphine's tale of woe, which led Delphine to wonder how pure Cybille's relationship with Yves had been in the first place. She suspected Yves might have helped Cybille through her painful divorce in more ways than one but she knew better than to voice her opinion out loud. Cybille was far too powerful to offend.

Delphine got up and slowly walked across the room. Her hip was playing up badly – caused by stress, her doctor had told her. Apart from Seraphina's traumatic experience, the biggest thing Delphine had been forced to face up to was that she was a terrible judge of character. There was Yves, and now it seemed that Angelique was not the woman she had thought she was. And as for Cat . . .

Delphine stared at the package on her desk. Cat Hayes had undoubtedly triggered this bizarre chain of events but she herself had held the reins and orchestrated the whole debacle almost single-handedly and that was something she was going to have to live with. And she felt guilty – guiltier than she had ever felt in her life. She had ignored the misgivings she had felt about getting in touch with Angelique and she had allowed the situation to unfold without much thought to the consequences if her assumptions turned out to be wrong.

Suddenly feeling very old, Delphine picked up the parcel on the desk. She had a chance to buy some more time and she wasn't going to waste it. There were many things to put right and it wasn't going to be easy but she knew she had to do more than most to put everything back together again. Decisively ignoring the parcel, Delphine sat down again and let out a heavy sigh. She only hoped she wasn't too late.

Chapter Twenty

Having worked tirelessly with Cat on her proposal, Leoni was at last ready to pitch it to Guy. Feeling nervous but as well prepared as she thought she could possibly be, she set her laptop up in the boardroom and made sure there was a glossy brochure at the head of the table.

Leoni flicked through it, realising how glad she was that Cat had helped her at the end. Her product knowledge was exceptional and she certainly knew how to put a glitzy, well-thought-out proposal together. The brochure they'd created was so slick and convincing, it would surely persuade Guy to go ahead with the home fragrance idea. Cat had somehow found a way to make the whole idea seem utterly crucial to the advancement of the business yet achingly simple in its execution; a perfect idea presented in a fail-safe, businesslike manner.

If only she'd accepted Cat's offer in the first place, Leoni thought, she could have saved herself a huge amount of stress but she knew she hadn't been ready to take the olive branch Cat had been proffering until now. Maybe she was finally laying Olivier's ghost to rest, Leoni thought, feeling a moment-ary sense of peace. It was definitely time to stand on her own two feet; she had been hiding behind Olivier's business loyalty for far too long; she was now finally ready to be a lone, but confident, voice.

Toying with the brochure, Leoni thought about Ashton for a moment. She missed him, really missed him. If only as a friend, she knew she wanted him back in her life. She must call him as soon as the meeting was over, she decided. Hearing Guy approaching, she hurriedly closed the brochure and slid it back across the table. Looking up, she was surprised to see how ashen he looked. His silver hair was as smooth and tidy as usual and his pale blue shirt with monogrammed white cuffs was impeccable but his brown eyes had heavy bags beneath them. The drooped set of his shoulders added to his air of dejection but, by contrast, his mouth was tight, suggesting he was in no mood for idle chit-chat.

That suited Leoni down to the ground but she couldn't resist checking he wanted her to present her idea today. 'Are you all right, Uncle?' she asked, concerned. 'You look . . . tired.' She wanted to say 'terrible' but there seemed little point in kicking Guy when he was clearly down.

'I'm fine,' he snapped, glaring at her. 'Why wouldn't I be?'

Leoni started up the laptop without a word. She guessed Guy was upset over the drama with Seraphina at the party but she was taken aback to see anger flashing in his eyes. As her visual presentation began on the big screen on the wall, Leoni wondered why Guy seemed irate rather than regretful. Wouldn't most fathers be worried and desperate to protect their offspring in a situation like that? Perversely, Guy was bristling with rage, looking very much as if he would like to throttle Seraphina rather than give her a fatherly hug, should he clap eyes on her.

Leoni couldn't understand his reaction but she knew him well enough to know she wouldn't be thanked if she attempted to question him about it. No one had been able to reason with Guy since Elizabeth's death; he was blind to his own faults and hell-bent on lashing out at anyone who dared to question him.

Guy was aware of Leoni's scrutiny. He was also aware he was going to have to summon every ounce of concentration to give Leoni a fair hearing. He was so agitated about his children, he could barely see straight. Besides which, he was still very opposed to the home fragrance idea, partly because he knew his mother hated it with a passion and partly because he wasn't sure he could see the point of it either. But then, didn't he feel that about most aspects of the business right now? None of it seemed to matter, none of it seemed important in the scheme of things, and that feeling had been building for months now, maybe even years.

Guy's heart constricted but he couldn't bear to allow the desperate feeling that was spreading through his body like a cold, icy finger to take hold. He had no idea what might happen if it did but he feared he may well fall apart if he allowed his inner sorrow a voice. He had kept it at bay for so long now, it was almost a knee-jerk reaction, but every so often it caught him unawares, prickling at his conscience like a well-meaning and overly tenacious friend who was keen to force him into submission. Guy remembered what Cat had said to him about grief counselling and almost growled out loud as he dismissed the idea. What rubbish!

He sighed tiredly, knowing Leoni deserved her moment and knowing he owed it to her to put his own turmoil aside for the next fifteen minutes. He had delivered Leoni an ultimatum with a time limit in terms of putting her idea together and presenting it; the least he could do was hear her out. He pulled himself together and sat up, forcing himself to appear both alert and open, despite his misgivings and regardless of his relentlessly churning stomach.

'Please.' He gestured for Leoni to begin. 'I'm ready when you are.'

'Let me introduce you to the world of home fragrance,' Leoni started, feeling her nerves slide away now that her big moment had finally arrived. 'This is home fragrance the Ducasse-Fleurie way, which means luxury, style and, above all, quality.'

Getting into her stride as soon as she started speaking and

fully believing every word of her pitch, Leoni proceeded to present her idea coherently. She backed up each aspect of her presentation with facts about their target market and plenty of well-researched figures but she also appealed to Guy's creative side by describing her candles, her linen sprays and her room scents in detail. She outlined the luxurious design, the simple but effective packaging and the intended promotional plans with evocative wording. On Cat's insistence, she also kept it professional and informative. Guy detested flowery prose and Cat believed he would respond better to something slick, colourful and straightforward.

'I believe this line will be simple, elegant and a beautiful addition to our luxurious and much-loved products,' Leoni finished, allowing her laptop presentation to flash up images of the samples Jerard had created, as well as some other ones she'd had made in anticipation of her pitch. She carefully removed the sample products themselves from their boxes and allowed Guy to handle them, not even realising she was holding her breath as she waited for him to respond.

'It's . . .' Guy paused, not because he was intending to keep her dangling, but because he was searching for the right word. 'Impressive,' he said finally, meeting her eyes. He picked up the candle and turned it round in his hands. 'Really impressive,' he added with a nod.

'Really?' Forgetting to maintain a cool, detached exterior as Cat had suggested, Leoni's brown eyes lit up behind her glasses. 'I'm so pleased!'

Guy smiled briefly but warmly and just for a moment Leoni caught a fleeting glimpse of the uncle she had grown up with. She had missed him; he had been in hiding for the past few years.

'Look, it's not what I expected at all,' he informed her, his eyes regarding her keenly. 'I admit I envisaged this line as tacky and commercial but it's not at all. You've truly embodied the feel of Ducasse-Fleurie and you haven't compromised on the elegance or the wonderfully opulent aura of our fragrances. Well done, Leoni.'

She beamed, delighted by his reaction. For the first time, she felt important and relevant in the family business. She felt as if she'd finally proved herself.

'I can't take all the credit,' she garbled, her words jumbling up in her excitement. 'Cat helped me put this together.' Leoni flushed. 'I would have finished it a lot sooner if I'd just let her help me but it took some time. Olivier . . . you understand, it was all too hard for me to accept but I finally came to my senses.'

Guy raised his eyebrows. 'I suppose I understand what you mean about Olivier. Personally, I feel that he's finally done something good . . . something all of us can be grateful for.'

Leoni stiffened. Loyalty to her sibling was automatic but, in spite of herself, she was intrigued. 'Something good? What do you mean? By marrying Cat?'

'Maybe.' Guy shrugged. 'Olivier was such a troublemaker. He was always telling lies and creating havoc. It's just … doesn't it strike you as odd?'

'What?'

'How a perfect stranger can come into our world and make more sense of it than we, the family, can?' he responded, drumming his fingers on the table mindlessly. His expression became sombre. 'What does that say about us?'

Leoni stared at him, unable to think of an answer. She had never heard Guy talking so introspectively before and she had never thought of Cat as a saviour in any way. Glancing down at the glossy brochure, she knew she would never have been able to produce it alone. Maybe Guy had a point. Leoni also realised that Guy wasn't just talking about brochures and PowerPoint presentations when he mentioned Cat saving the family. It was a sobering thought.

'I'll review the figures and get a budget drawn up,' Guy

said, getting to his feet. 'I'll also speak to your grandmother about it, so don't worry about that.'

'Thank you,' Leoni said, feeling euphoric. She was aware that she couldn't wait to get out of the room and phone Ashton, when really she should be phoning Jerard to tell him the good news. What Xavier had said about Ashton and his feelings for someone were also niggling at her. She hurried out of the room and bumped into Cat.

'How did it go?' Cat asked. When Leoni failed to respond immediately, she shook her head. 'Oh no, did Guy reject the proposal? I can't believe it, not after all the work you did.' She looked troubled. 'I honestly don't see how he could say no to it, it's such a great—'

'He said yes,' Leoni interrupted, looking preoccupied.

Cat stopped. 'What? That's brilliant! So . . . why do you look like someone kicked your cat?'

Leoni stared at her nonplussed. 'Oh, it's nothing . . . no, I'm really happy, honestly. I just realised I've been neglecting Ashton shamelessly and that I need to put things right.'

Cat smiled, wondering if Leoni had finally worked out that Ashton was head over heels in love with her. Or that she was more than a little bit in love with Ashton.

'I just . . . miss my best friend, you know?' Leoni said, thinking Cat was looking at her very strangely. 'Are you all right? Yes, I was thinking I might actually pop up to Paris to see him. Now that I've pitched the campaign and have some good news to tell.'

'Sounds like a plan.' Cat nodded. 'You can tell him in person then.'

Leoni beamed. 'I know, he'll be so excited.'

Cat held out a small package. 'This arrived for you this morning. Looks like it's another gift from Jerard.'

'Thanks.' Leoni barely glanced at it. 'I'll open it later.'

Cat wondered why she wasn't tearing the paper off like a five year old. Considering the fact that most of Jerard's gifts seemed to be beautiful and shockingly expensive, she wasn't sure why Leoni was so indifferent to the arrival of another. Cat shrugged to herself. Leoni had grown up in a privileged environment; perhaps she was harder to impress than the average girl.

Leoni actually seemed to have other things on her mind. 'I spoke to Xavier, by the way. I hope you don't mind.'

Cat felt a flash of trepidation. Whenever anyone said anything to Xavier or any other member of this family, everyone seemed to get the wrong end of the stick. Her stomach sank.

'Er . . . what did he say?'

'Not a great deal, actually, but I think he was a bit shocked about Grandmother's involvement in everything that has happened. He's gone to Morocco now . . . something to do with the fragrance.'

Cat felt poleaxed. So Xavier knew everything now and he still hadn't wanted to speak to her before he'd left for Morocco. She hated herself for missing him so much but she couldn't help it. Realising Leoni was still chuntering on about Paris, Cat plastered a smile on to her face.

'Well, I'm really glad your presentation went so well,' she said, meaning it. 'And have fun in Paris, all right?'

Watching Cat slope off sadly, Leoni wished she could give Xavier a resounding slap. Didn't he realise how perfect Cat was for him?

'I hope Seraphina is all right now. What a horrible way to find out her boyfriend isn't the nice guy she thought he was.'

Hurrying alongside Max who was striding through the lavender fields purposefully, Madeleine flicked her hair over her shoulders with a nervous hand. Max, a brooding character at the best of times, seemed caught up in his own thoughts. His dark hair fell into his eyes as he strode along and his brow was furrowed with concentration. Wearing a pair of black shorts and a T-shirt as the sun was warm, Max's tanned body was as lean as a jockey's. As good looking as Xavier, his broad shoulders and height made him seem older than he was but his glowering expression made him seem like an immature teenager.

Doing her best not to stare at his bronzed back as he stormed ahead of her, Madeleine knew Max was cut up about what had happened to Seraphina at the party but she wasn't sure what to say or do for the best. Being an only child, she had no real concept of sibling loyalty but she knew enough about Max to know he cared deeply about his sister and that what had happened was playing on his mind.

Madeleine sighed and thrust her hands into the pockets of her cut-off jeans. She had teamed them with some silver gladiator sandals and a pretty white bodice, not that Max ever noticed what she was wearing.

Struggling to keep up with Max's rage-fuelled strides, Madeleine considered him. She wasn't sure it was prudent to say it out loud but she couldn't help feeling that Max was far angrier than he should be after the event. Seraphina was upset for obvious reasons but Max was pent up and fuming, rather like a bubbling volcano on the brink of exploding, molten lava mere inches beneath the surface.

'What?' he barked, suddenly aware that Madeleine had said something to him. He threw her an impatient sideways glance. 'Yves, he's a bastard, yes. A pervert too, if you ask me. His type always think they can get away with murder and take advantage of people.'

'Seraphina's not a child,' Madeleine pointed out mildly, aware she was taking her life into her hands as she uttered the words. Seeing Max's eyes darken with fury, she rushed to explain. 'I didn't mean Yves isn't a creep or that he might not have taken no for an answer. It's just . . . your family seems to treat Seraphina like she's a little girl rather than a grown woman.' Sensing his scowl, Madeleine stood her ground. She cared about Max but she wasn't going to allow him to browbeat her into agreeing with him just because he was angry. 'And I don't mean you, specifically, Max; your entire family wrap Seraphina up in cotton wool.'

Max stopped abruptly, turning to face her. His jaw was rigid and his arrogant stance suggested he saw Madeleine's comment as absurd. 'Is it any wonder? Look what a mess she got herself into. If we hadn't arrived, who knows what might have happened.'

Madeleine shook her head. 'I think Seraphina had the situation under control. And if you don't mind me saying, you seem far more worked up about this than she does. I'm sure she thinks Yves is an idiot but she's not raging a war against the world the way you are.'

Max grimaced. 'I'm not raging against the world, thank you very much.' He kicked the grass with the toe of his baseball boot. 'Just my father, if you must know.'

'Is he really to blame for all of this?'

He stared past her. 'Yes, he is. He's been a useless father for more than two years and I'm sick of it.' Max practically spat the words out.

Madeleine wanted to help him but she didn't know how. 'Maybe you should have it out with him . . . say all this to him, face to face.' She felt strongly that Max needed to be honest and voice his feelings aloud, calmly and clearly, but she knew he wouldn't agree. She braced herself for the acerbic retort she was sure Max would throw back at her so she was unprepared for his flat agreement.

'You're right,' he said in a level tone. 'I intend to have it out with him. I tried the other day but he'd gone off to some meeting.' He raked back his dark hair. 'Someone needs to tell him what a terrible father he is.'

Madeleine felt a momentary panic. 'I didn't really mean that . . .'

Max wasn't listening.

'No time like the present,' he murmured. Suddenly, he

couldn't wait to seize the moment and get everything off his chest. 'See you later,' he said tersely, turning and heading back towards La Fleurie.

Madeleine stared after him numbly, wishing she could take her words back. She had a feeling Max had something very different in mind than the composed, adult discussion she had been hinting at and she couldn't see it ending any other way but nastily. Wondering what to do, Madeleine headed home worriedly.

'This is my best light,' Angelique snarled, snapping her fingers at the poor man fiddling with the lighting. 'Are you some sort of imbecile?' Rolling her eyes as he scurried away like a goblin, she shook her blond waves out and composed herself.

'Action,' she called, holding the perfume bottle up and leaning her ample cleavage into the camera.

Stefan, the director, bristled. He detested it when people stole his line. Motioning for filming to begin (his staff knew better than to listen to a model yelling directions), he watched through the lens as Angelique performed her lines. Holed up in one of the upstairs bedrooms which was decked out in shades of lilac and vanilla, the setting was perfect. May sunshine shone through the windows, providing gorgeous natural lighting, in addition to the lights that had been set up at various points in the room. Angelique looked at her very best, her flowing curves covered by a sheath of lilac silk that made the most of her tiny waist and the shapely edge of her hip.

Stefan frowned. This was the fourth setting they'd attempted and he'd told Angelique it was just for variety of shots and the different scenarios they had in mind for the campaign but he wasn't being truthful. What he was really trying to do was get just a few shots he would actually want to put his name to because, right now, he didn't have any. Stefan wished he could put his finger on what was wrong with the seemingly flawless image he could see through the camera but he couldn't. He had shot many of these perfume campaigns before and they had all been jaw-droppingly beautiful. He had worked with uglier models and actresses in far shabbier surroundings but he had always managed to create breathtaking photographs with some indefinable quality.

Stefan wasn't happy with what he was seeing. He didn't know if the brief was wrong or if Angelique wasn't the right choice, however delectable she looked in her semi-naked state, but he had serious doubts about making the campaign believable.

'How's it going?' Cat asked, poking her head round the door and immediately wishing she hadn't as she found herself staring at Angelique's taut stomach, the stomach that had once held Xavier's baby. A searing, white-hot stab of envy shot through her. Cat wished she could stop feeling the way she did about Xavier. She couldn't allow herself to do this, it hurt too much. She had to go home – where the hell was her passport, for God's sake? Bella and Ben thought she'd relocated to France for good – they kept teasing her that she was never coming back and that she'd taken root amongst the Provençal lavender, but they weren't able to speed up the process any more efficiently in England either. The job at the rival firm was still hers for the taking, apparently, but Cat couldn't imagine them hanging on forever. And what about the elusive legal papers she was supposed to sign? Cat was thoroughly fed up with it all. It was almost June now – she could hardly believe it.

'What's the problem?' she asked Stefan who was clearly unhappy with the rushes he was looking at.

She peered over his shoulder and took a peek. Angelique's skin looked luminescent and her body was toned in all the right places, just the way it looked in real life, only better. Cat felt sick as unwanted images of Angelique's sensual form wrapped round Xavier's tanned body forced their way into her mind.

'She is a very good-looking girl,' Stefan assessed coolly, 'but maybe not on the inside, eh?'

Cat shrugged. What did it matter? Confronted with Angelique's enviable face and body left Cat in no doubt as to how she might compare. And judging by the lingering, smoking-hot kiss she had witnessed, Angelique was well on her way to winning Xavier back, regardless of what had gone on before.

'I think she looks wonderful,' Cat said dully, meaning it.

'She's looked better,' said a brash American voice.

Glancing over her shoulder, Cat recognised Mason, Angelique's agent. He was wearing a genial smile but it didn't reach his eyes. He threw Angelique a look which seemed fuelled with dislike.

'She looks tired,' he followed up, critically.

'Really? I only wish I looked that good when I need more sleep. I tend to look like I've got two black eyes.'

'Good make-up,' Mason snarled.

Angelique turned on to her back and caught sight of Mason. Her blue eyes widened in surprise and her expression became truculent. Clearly she wasn't expecting him and as the lilac material slithered down her body and revealed a perky pink nipple, she stretched an arm up provocatively and stared back at him with some defiance.

Mason's mouth tightened. He muttered something under his breath that sounded very much like 'slut' to Cat but she couldn't be sure. He checked his watch with obvious irritation. 'How much longer is this going to take?'

Stefan frowned. 'This should have been wrapped up ages ago but I'm not happy with the results. I can superimpose the name of the perfume when Xavier has made his decision but it's not that . . .' He checked the angle again and instructed the cameraman to try another shot in the corner of the room. Huffily, Angelique stood up, tugging the lilac material loosely around her body, and sashayed to the corner of the room.

'I can't believe she turned down a meeting with Hollywood for this,' Mason growled, throwing his heavy frame into a delicate-looking period chair that creaked beneath his weight. 'It's only a fucking perfume, for Christ's sake.' He glanced at Cat in vague apology. 'No offence.'

'None taken. It's not really anything to do with me, anyway. I'm just . . . a guest.'

Cat sat on the edge of a satin-covered sofa. It was true; she was just a guest and it was better that she thought of herself that way. She had allowed herself to get far too close to the Ducasse family. The thought of leaving Seraphina and Max and Guy tore at her, let alone leaving Xavier. She cursed herself for getting so involved. Even when she signed everything back over to the Ducasse family, even when her marriage to Olivier was nothing more than a distant memory, she knew her life was irrevocably linked to the Ducasse family. As far as her heart was concerned, at any rate, Cat thought, remembering the feel of Xavier's skilful hands all over her body.

'What's the attraction with this stuff, anyway?' Mason picked up one of the perfume bottles and sniffed it dubiously. Realising it was only filled with coloured liquid for the purposes of the advert, he tossed it back into its box. 'I can't for the life of me understand why Angelique wants to do this advert.'

'Perfume is an extension of someone's personality,' Cat intoned automatically, observing Angelique contorting herself into a position that could only be described as sexual. 'It's a glamorous, sexy product. I suppose any actress would love the publicity that comes with such an advert. Having your own perfume would be even better, of course, as it means you're a brand, that you have an identity people recognise and want to be associated with.'

Mason looked unconvinced. 'This', he gestured to the perfume bottles, 'doesn't fit with her master plan, believe me – at least, not the one I thought she had in mind. This is a

377

woman who wants to conquer the fucking world so why she would turn down Hollywood for perfume beyond me. Her own perfume, *that* I can believe because she's such a fucking egomaniac, but not representing someone else's. That's just lame.'

Cat glanced at him, not sure how much Mason knew about Angelique's private life. It was apparent he didn't know about Xavier or Angelique's desire to hook up with him again. 'Maybe it's not just about the perfume, maybe there's something else Angelique wants.'

Mason's eyes narrowed. For a moment, a strange expression flitted across his face. Jealousy? Cat wondered. It disappeared a second later so she decided she was mistaken. Far from lusting after Angelique, Mason looked as though he detested her, which was odd as he was clearly a red-blooded male.

'You're suggesting that she might be here because of a *man*?' Mason let out a coarse, dismissive laugh. 'No way, baby. Angelique doesn't have a heart. A groin, maybe, but she doesn't even let that rule her life. No man could get her to change her career plans, not in a million years.'

Cat's brow furrowed in confusion. 'I think you're wrong,' she asserted, remembering the way Angelique had publicly laid claim to Xavier the night of the perfume party – and since then. To her mind, it was patently obvious why Angelique was here and it had little to do with the launch of Xavier's new fragrance and everything to do with Xavier himself.

'That's a wrap!' Stefan called out wearily. He came over to Cat and Mason, looking beaten. 'I'm still not a hundred per cent happy but I'm calling it a day. I'll check out the shots in the office later and see what I can do.'

Mason looked displeased. Stefan left the room and Cat followed him out.

'What are you doing here?' Angelique asked Mason, feeling his eyes running over her body, albeit with no interest. She glanced at the broad width of his shoulders and found him repugnant and sexual in equal measure, as usual. 'I didn't say I needed you here.'

'I'm checking up on you,' he snapped rudely. 'Seeing as you've fucked all my Hollywood plans up.'

Angelique waved a hand. 'Hollywood will wait. This is what I want to do right now.'

Mason looked fit to explode. 'Hollywood will wait? You're too arrogant for your own good, Angelique. Opportunities like that don't come along every day.' He narrowed his eyes at her. 'What's this all about, Angelique? Is it about a man? That girl Cat seems to think it is.'

'Really?' Angelique preened, clearly pleased. 'Good.'

Mason grabbed her arm, his chunky fingers biting into the flesh. 'Why? What are you playing at?' His eyes seemed to be pleading with her to be honest and Angelique was taken aback.

'What the hell does it have to do with you?'

'Everything,' he snarled at her. His lips were inches from her face and he stared down at her semi-naked body for a moment. Tearing his eyes away, he met hers unflinchingly. 'And you know it.'

Angelique tore her arm free from his grasp, her cheeks stained red. 'Fuck off, Mason,' she hissed. 'Don't you dare ruin what I've set up here! There's more at stake than just Xavier Ducasse. You have no idea what I have planned.'

With that, she stalked back to her room, leaving Mason clenching his fists impotently.

Arriving breathlessly at the building in Paris, Leoni was disappointed not to find Ashton there. She had already tried his apartment but no one was home so she had assumed he might be at the property. She glanced down at herself, feeling foolish – for once, she had abandoned her black dresses and had donned a pretty green one that made the most of her slender figure and boyish cleavage. She suddenly felt incon-

379

gruous and vulnerable without her usual uniform. Also, she had no idea why she'd made such an effort. Ashton wasn't around and the building looked to be under renovation with dust flying everywhere. Work was clearly underway – inside, builders were banging and crashing and there was plastic sheeting and scaffolding wrapped round the front. On the ground was a large sign covered with bubble wrap and, holding her breath, Leoni lifted the wrap to look underneath.

'Ducasse-Fleurie Perfumes', the sign said in distinctive, flowing writing. Leoni's heart skipped a beat. Ashton had acquired the property! Why hadn't he told her about it? She flushed. Maybe because they were barely speaking any more.

Feeling upset, Leoni wondered how things had got to this stage. How had they let such a good friendship fall by the wayside? Too much focus on work, for a start, and also her relationship with Jerard, Leoni admitted guiltily. Jerard was now in Japan, finalising the details of the deal that had interrupted him at the party and no doubt looking for even more business. They had spoken several times on the phone and Jerard had sent flowers, chocolates and even a stunning diamond bracelet – the packet that had arrived before her departure to Paris. Leoni glanced at it on her wrist. It was stunning but it was no substitute for the real thing.

She still couldn't believe they hadn't slept together. How had there not been enough time for such an important event to take place? Shouldn't they be desperate to rip one another's clothes off and tumble into bed? They were young, they had their own apartments and they should fancy the pants off each other at this early stage in their relationship. Leoni knew this was something they needed to talk about when Jerard returned from Japan. She needed him to know what she wanted from the relationship, that however much she cared about business and work, she wanted more than that.

Stepping inside the building, Leoni asked one of the builders about Ashton's whereabouts. She added that it was a personal visit, lest they think she was some sort of building official, but no one seemed to know anything. Not sure what to do next and beginning to think she had been hasty turning up in Paris without letting Ashton know first, Leoni turned to find a glamorous redhead watching her.

'Is Ashton around?' the woman asked, her keen green eyes running over Leoni with interest.

'No, I was looking for him myself.' Leoni stared at the woman, realising she was Marianne Peroux.

'I am Marianne Peroux,' the woman confirmed, smiling as she held out a hand with scarlet-tipped fingernails. She winced as some concrete fell next to them. 'We don't have hard hats – let's go outside.'

Leoni followed Marianne, taking in her sleek appearance. Wearing a red dress with narrow shoulder straps and a full skirt, her figure was womanly and curvaceous. In spite of her green outfit and heels, Leoni felt rather drab and unfeminine by comparison. She could see exactly why Guy – and even Ashton – might have been captivated by her. Marianne was difficult to ignore; even in a shop full of building work and noise, she stood out like a colourful butterfly. Leoni had no idea why but the thought of Marianne and Ashton together suddenly seemed like a horrible idea. And not just because Marianne had been after the building.

'Leoni Ducasse,' Leoni said, remembering her manners and holding her hand out.

So this is the infamous Leoni Ducasse, Marianne thought to herself in surprise. She inspected Leoni from head to toe, not bothering to hide her stare. Goodness, but she was plain! The glasses she wore did nothing to enhance her looks and the chin-length bob emphasised rather than hid the strong jawline. Her petite, slender figure no doubt lent itself to French fashion, which seemed to be designed for small children, Marianne thought disparagingly, thinking of her own ample hips, but Leoni was certainly not what she was expecting.

It must be sickening for her that the rest of her family were so startlingly attractive, Marianne decided, slightly affronted that Ashton had rejected her in favour of this plain child. He was a gentleman, of course, but still, he must love this girl very much to turn down free sex with her.

Did she love him back? Marianne wondered. She wasn't sure. Ashton had mentioned a boyfriend but there was something in Leoni's eyes, a yearning, that suggested maybe she felt something for Ashton. Or maybe she didn't know it yet, Marianne guessed astutely. She shrugged; each to their own. Still, thoughts of Ashton's rejection, as well as Guy's all those years ago, flooded into her mind and she couldn't resist meddling. Just a little.

'I was hoping to find Ashton here so I could thank him,' Marianne explained to Leoni chummily, her green eyes alight with mischief. 'I really hoped to purchase this building, you see, but we managed to find a way to accommodate one another.'

'Really? That's . . . er . . . that's great.' Leoni's stomach shifted uneasily.

Marianne smiled at Leoni, unable to help toying with her the way a cat did with a bird caught in its paw. 'He made a *huge* sacrifice, and I appreciated it so much, I let him have the building.'

'I see.' Leoni was beginning to feel a little sick. She really should have had more than a black coffee on her flight to Paris.

Marianne ran an idle hand down the skirt of her dress, the gesture somehow suggestive. 'I wanted something he had and he gave it to me.'

What did she mean? Leoni swallowed.

'It was a very satisfactory arrangement all round,' Marianne added for good measure. 'Satisfying and very, very enjoyable.'

Her meaning was clear, leaving Leoni in no doubt as to the kind of transaction that had taken place. 'Did you . . . did you sleep with Ashton?' Leoni was taken aback to find her voice croaking slightly.

'I think it would be tacky of me to discuss the details,' Marianne murmured. 'But suffice to say, we came to an arrangement and it worked out very well.'

She was surprised when Leoni backed away, muttering something about needing to get back to Provence. Marianne had assumed Leoni would be like Guy; tough, unapologetic and totally in control. Even Ashton had painted a picture of Leoni as a ballsy businesswoman with an emotional deficit, yet here she was, looking as though someone had put her bunny in the furnace.

Marianne watched Leoni stumble away in her high heels, feeling oddly uncomfortable. Had she done a terrible thing? Surely not! Leoni had a boyfriend, and Ashton had said Leoni didn't even know he existed. But something about the way Leoni had recoiled suggested she might have feelings somewhere deep down inside, which would explain her reaction just now.

'Marianne.' Seconds too late, Ashton arrived, looking none too pleased to see her. 'What can I do for you?'

About to confess all, Marianne thought better of it. If Ashton and Leoni were meant to be together, they would find a way. She had told herself that when Guy left. Marianne inwardly shrugged. That was love for you; it was a cruel bitch that ate up some poor mortals and spat them out. Leoni needed to toughen up and sort her life out.

'I have the paperwork here,' Marianne stated, pulling it out of her handbag.

'Right.' Ashton sniffed the air and frowned. That scent smelt just like Leoni's! But how could that be? She was in Provence, no doubt in Jerard's bed. Feeling a pain in his heart, he turned back to Marianne. 'Let's get this over and done with,' he said in a muted voice, holding his hand out to take the papers.

Wondering if she'd gone soft, Marianne nodded wordlessly and followed him inside the building.

Wandering through the medina in Marrakech wearing a loose linen shirt and trousers, Xavier felt his senses reeling. The trip reminded him so tangibly of his mother. They'd taken the trip several times together before her death in the pursuit of exotic oils and the trip felt both sad and cathartic. Xavier was also aware that he had decisions to make back home, and his mind was all over the place as thoughts of Cat's aquamarine eyes and Angelique's knowing blue ones swam across one another.

A haze of heat sat around the medina which was characterised by low, terracotta houses and tall palm trees, and the honeyed smell of cedarwood hung in the air, along with the rich, sensual aromas of cinnamon, nutmeg and cloves. Sacks of herbs and spices lined the alleys, wafting their aromas to passers-by, mixing with the familiar smell of hash smoked by students in furtive corners.

Aware the many sellers procured their fragrances from Grasse and passed them off as their own, Xavier knew he had to go into the very depths of the souk to find the real perfume sellers. Morocco was one of the biggest producers of essential oils and the raw materials of scent but actual perfume itself was hard to come by – original versions, at any rate. Serge Lutens, the famous *senteur*, lived in Marrakech and Xavier could understand why. The exotic smells couldn't fail to inspire and the earthy scents were so complex and erotic, it was impossible not to imagine them blended and wafting off warm, bare skin.

Xavier refocused his mind on what he had come to Marrakech for: neroli, one of the four essential oils that came from the orange. The other three were bergamot, which was extracted from the rind and was rich and aromatic; orange flower absolute which was floral; and petit grain, distilled from the leaves and unripe fruit, which had bittersweet, woody qualities. The process of distilling orange blossoms to produce neroli was a complicated one: the blossoms needed to be picked dry, not wet, and the leaves had to be removed. The flowers would be spread out and turned overnight, and then boiled in water to yield both orange flower water and, eventually, neroli oil which was skimmed from the top of the water.

Xavier continued through the maze of alleyways that told him he must be close to the souk El Attarin, where all the perfume-sellers were located. They sat behind white curtains that protected their precious perfumes from heat and sunlight and Xavier ducked into each one, stating his interest in petit grain and neroli. Refusing to be anointed with oily scents, Xavier stuck to his guns and sampled only the aromas he was interested in.

Passing on a bergamot petit grain which was too strong and a citrusy one that was too sharp and a dozen others that were too sweet or woody, he was drawn to one that was distilled from orange flowers and petit grain oil. It was delicate and floral, with a deliciously bittersweet heart note. Xavier couldn't stop breathing it in. He knew he needed something rounded to complete the fragrance, a scent that wouldn't overpower the other components but would complement it and give it an elegant edge.

Xavier found himself lost in thought as he remembered the brief he had put together a few years ago, the one he'd tailored with something – someone – very specific in mind. He hadn't known what her face looked like or what her name would be but he had known the sort of woman he had in mind, the sort of woman who would wear a fragrance such as this. His mind flitting between Angelique and Cat, Xavier forced himself to be truthful with himself about which woman truly represented the inspiration behind his new fragrance.

Was it based on a lingering memory of something heady

and sexual, something he might now rediscover should he choose to, or was it based on a romantic fantasy, set out in the brief he drawn up in a moment of sheer hopefulness, long before that woman had presented herself to him? He and Angelique had history, they had shared something so personal and intimate it was difficult not to feel drawn to her because of it. Seeing her again had brought up both good and bad memories, and even without the added complication of Cat, Xavier knew he would be in a mess because of Angelique's sudden reappearance in his life.

But Cat . . . Cat was something else entirely. She was Olivier's widow, but so much more than that now – almost part of the family, Xavier thought, stunned. With a flash of insight, Xavier knew without doubt where his heart lay. Suddenly he couldn't wait to get back to La Fleurie so he could make his feelings known. It had taken this journey to clear his head but now he knew exactly where he wanted to be and, more importantly, who with.

Knowing he had tracked down the perfect final ingredient for his fragrance, he made the perfume seller's day by informing him of his identity and the quantity of the order he required. Fully aware of the need for tough negotiation, Xavier bartered expertly, having watched his mother doing exactly the same thing over the years. Securing a deal he knew his father would approve of – and his mother, if she were still alive – Xavier emerged from the souk feeling calm and triumphant. He could fax the details back to the factory tonight and be on the first plane home. He also had something else for the fragrance that always eluded him – the name. He'd been battling with himself for ages but as the realisation about who he was meant to be with slotted into place in his head, so did the name for the fragrance.

Tiredly heading back into La Sultana, the five-star hotel his family always used, Xavier was surprised when he was stopped on the stairs by Rene, the owner. He was a small man with a rotund stomach and eyebrows like the scarab beetles found in the Moroccan desert.

'Monsieur Ducasse,' Rene said, shaking his hand warmly. 'We haven't seen you here for a long time. Is your cousin with you?'

Xavier raised his eyebrows. 'Olivier? You obviously haven't heard.' He quickly updated the owner who looked shaken at the news of Olivier's death.

'I am so sorry,' Rene said, shaking his head sadly. 'He was here often but when he didn't visit for a while, I did wonder what had happened to him.'

'I didn't know he visited Marrakech regularly,' Xavier confessed, realising he hadn't known Olivier as well as he'd thought. But then, had any of them?

'Oh yes. He stayed here a few times with his beautiful girlfriend.' Rene nodded sagely. 'The one he was serious about.'

Xavier was momentarily jolted. Who did Rene mean? Cat? Surely not. They'd only just met each other in the south of France – hadn't they? Xavier began to feel rather queasy. Something wasn't right here. Suddenly he remembered Matthieu, his climbing companion, talking about Olivier a few months ago. Hadn't he mentioned something about a woman Olivier was serious about – one he regularly took to Morocco?

Rene frowned. 'Maybe I am mistaken. Monsieur Olivier brought many women here. And he talked about many others. But there was one in particular. He never told me her name but he was smitten, oh yes! Said he was going to marry her one day.'

Xavier thought it was odd, even for Olivier, to bring a serious girlfriend to Morocco before marrying a perfect stranger in St Tropez, but with Matthieu and Rene saying the same thing, he realised it couldn't be a coincidence.

Rene raised his eyebrows. 'Did he ever marry her? He talked

about her a lot, this one he was serious about.' His mouth twisted as he tried to remember. 'Last summer, it must have been. Yes, that was the most recent time he told me about her.'

Xavier felt relieved. Perhaps Olivier had popped to Morocco during the time he'd been in St Tropez. He was most likely talking about Cat. 'Yes, he married her,' he said, wincing slightly as he did so. He hated discussing Cat's marriage to Olivier, however short lived and false it had been.

Rene asked him a few more questions and Xavier wasn't sure if he had got his wires crossed. Rene was rambling on about Paris and about Olivier's intentions to get married there but he must be confused. Xavier quickly corrected him.

Rene looked embarrassed. 'St Tropez, you say? Ah, my mistake, Monsieur Ducasse. Young Olivier was such a playboy, was he not? So many women . . . I must have misunderstood. St Tropez, how funny, that's not what he told me about the wedding he had planned. Oh, well.' Ducking his head respectfully, Rene left.

About to take a hot shower before catching a flight back to La Fleurie, a thought occurred to Xavier. It wasn't a pleasant one but as soon as it had taken hold, he couldn't let go of it. He did some investigating online but it didn't really get him anywhere and he realised he might need to go back to Provence before heading off to Paris. Suddenly, things made sense and even though the final picture the hastily assembled jigsaw presented was awful, it all fitted together perfectly.

Tight lipped after his shower, Xavier snapped his battered Louis Vuitton suitcase shut and stepped out onto the balcony of his room. He stared out across the colourful vista of Marrakech, the busy streets lit up by torches and candles and the sky slowly turning from rose-pink to a seductively dusky terracotta. He caught a waft of orange blossom in the air and felt his senses collide. He battled against what his gut was telling him could be the truth, a truth he really didn't want to face.

Xavier gripped the edge of the balcony with white knuckles. If the jigsaw he'd put together in his mind was the right one, the truth was going to come out. And it would change everything.

Chapter Twenty-One

Waking up in the flat above the newly acquired store in Paris on a partially deflated air bed, Ashton felt as though he had a blinding hangover. He knew he hadn't, as he'd touched nothing but black coffee in twenty-four hours. He'd been working like a demon to get everything done in time for the proposed launch of Xavier's new fragrance and he was absolutely shattered. Xavier was still in Morocco and Guy was in the process of drawing up a budget for Leoni's home fragrance line, but there was so much to do. The building had been stripped down to a shell so a new floor and ceiling could be added, amongst other things, but frankly, Ashton was glad of the distraction.

Sitting up, he rubbed his eyes blearily and glanced around at the tiny room that had become his home since the renovation had started. Living there was so much easier in some ways, as he could supervise the works, but it wasn't exactly luxurious. It was cosy, he'd give it that, but it was also cramped, chilly and badly in need of a lick of paint. That job was going to have to wait, however, because he had no time to waste picking out fetching shades of paint for a room no one else would see for a while.

Downstairs, he heard the builders arrive, their raucous banter and noisy equipment interrupting his rare moment of early morning solitude. Glancing at a dusty calendar on the kitchen counter, Ashton was vaguely aware that his parents had promised to visit but he couldn't remember the exact date.

He hoped it wasn't today; he was expecting several deliveries and he needed his mind to be sharp and focused on the job if he had any chance of meeting his deadline. Tugging a crumpled black T-shirt over his head and standing up in the jeans he'd slept in, Ashton rubbed his stubbly chin and wondered when he'd last shaved. Or when he'd last had a haircut, he thought, raking his fingers through his dusty blond fringe. Renovating the building had taken over his life, not because it was a difficult job but because the time constraint was so tight. Ashton was used to working under pressure but this had been the worst project he'd ever undertaken and one that he'd become overly involved in, more so than he had any other job. He had practically taken on the role of project manager, not just architect. The builders were working like Trojans but deliveries had been late, furnishings had arrived damaged and to the wrong specifications and his carefully thought-out technical drawings had been reworked so many times, the paper was beginning to resemble a discarded fish and chip wrapper.

Irritably, Ashton realised he was out of coffee and he headed downstairs, the noise hitting him as soon as he entered the store area. He greeted the builders with a cheeriness he didn't feel. At least the complicated renovation was taking his mind off dwelling on thoughts of Leoni, he reflected ruefully. He assumed Guy had told her about the store and he acknowledged to himself that he had been secretly hoping it would at the very least cause her to text him or call. The fact that she hadn't proved that either she didn't have time for him any more or that her relationship with Jerard was as serious as he'd feared.

Ashton felt sick. Obviously Leoni had no idea what he had sacrificed to acquire the building for her and he would never tell her – it had been his decision and he was an adult; he had made his choice, and that was the end of it. How he would explain things later on was something he hadn't quite figured out but he was sure he would think of something. Not that it made things any easier to bear on a daily basis, Ashton thought, rubbing his chest. He missed her, in every way possible. His head ached, his stomach churned and his heart hurt so painfully, it felt as if he was bleeding on the inside. Or perhaps he just had terrible heartburn from all the coffee, Ashton thought with a flash of humour, hating the thought that he was turning into some whinging idiot.

'Who's for coffee?' he asked his team of builders in English. He didn't bother to speak French to them, which he knew they found hilarious. They got by: that was all that mattered.

'*Café leger*,' Bernard, the head builder called, not looking up from the counter he was cutting with minute precision. He was extremely competent and he ruled his team of workers with a rod of iron; idle chit-chat was not his style. He seemed to remember something suddenly and he flicked his jigsaw off and lifted his goggles. He reverted to pigeon English, knowing it would be quicker in the long run. 'Monsieur Lyfield, Madame Peroux, did she speak you? There was a girl here for you on Tuesday . . . no, sorry, Wednesday.'

Halfway out of the door, Ashton ducked back in. 'Sorry?'

'There was a girl here,' Bernard insisted. 'She was looking for you.'

Ashton's heart skipped a beat. Could it have been Leoni? 'Did she say who she was?'

Bernard shook his head blankly. He rather wished he hadn't mentioned it; now he would be interrogated and his memory was shocking, especially when it came to this sort of thing.

'What did she look like?' Ashton tried another tack. He gestured vaguely to his face. 'Hair colour? Eyes? Height?'

Bernard gave a broad shrug, his expression vague. 'Er . . . tall. Green thing . . . a dress, maybe.' Details were clearly not his forte; his brow was furrowed with the effort of it all.

Ashton sighed, feeling despondent. Hearing 'tall' had made him feel hopeful but a green dress didn't sound like Leoni at all. If Bernard had said a black dress, that might have convinced him.

'Never mind, Bernard. It's probably just something work related. I'm sure whoever it was will call again.'

He made to leave again, halting as Bernard shook his head. '*Non*, Monsieur Lyfield, not work. It was personal, she said.'

Ashton's heart was in his mouth again. For the first time, he really wished he spoke better French.

'Glasses!' Bernard provided triumphantly. 'She wore glasses. And the hair, it was black. *Non*, brown. Like this.' He put his hands to his chin to show he meant a bob.

Ashton gripped the door. It was Leoni, it had to be! She had come to Paris, to the shop. She had asked to see him, which meant she still wanted to be friends, at least. Pleased with himself, Bernard nodded. He pulled his goggles back on, unaware he was doing a sterling impression of Danger Mouse's Penfold.

Something occurred to Ashton. 'Hang on, Bernard. Did you say Madame Peroux was here as well?'

Bernard nodded impatiently, keen to get back to work. 'They talk . . . then the girl in the green dress, she runs away.' He mimicked the movement with his fingers. 'Coffee?' he said hopefully.

'Yes, of course.' Ashton nodded, backing out of the store. He felt something cold trickle down his back. Marianne had been here, talking to Leoni? Knowing Marianne as he did, Ashton knew that might be very bad indeed. And the fact that Bernard had said Leoni had 'run away' after her chat with Marianne suggested that something had been said to upset her.

Had Marianne told Leoni about the sacrifice he'd made? Surely not, it wasn't her news to tell, and could she really be that proud of what she'd asked him to do? Ashton couldn't believe it. Not even Marianne could be that arrogant and insensitive, could she?

Had she – God forbid – embellished what had happened between them in the toilets? Ashton shivered. It didn't bear thinking about. Nothing had happened but Marianne was so mischievous, would she think it amusing to tell Leoni something more had gone on? Ashton groaned, wishing he'd never got tangled up with Marianne in the first place. She had given him nothing but headaches ever since he first clapped eyes on her. Longing more than anything to dash back to La Fleurie to find out what had upset Leoni, Ashton knew he couldn't leave the building project, even for a day.

Taking out his phone, he almost sent Leoni a text but shorthand colloquialisms seemed wholly inadequate in the current situation so he left a voicemail instead. He said he was very sorry to have missed her and that he hoped she would be in touch soon. He also left a heated message for Marianne, tersely asking her to call him back. Stalking up and down the road as he made the call, he crashed straight into his parents who were carrying their suitcases.

'Darling, is everything all right?'

Joyce Lyfield knew in an instant that her son wasn't himself. He had three-day-old stubble on his chin, his hair was in disarray and his clothes were unwashed. But, actually, it was nothing to do with that; it was the look of utter anguish in his eyes that told his mother he was suffering badly.

'We went to the apartment,' Arthur said, clasping his son's free hand and shaking it heartily. 'They wouldn't let us in so we came here.'

Ashton apologised to them. What a mess! Feeling about twelve again, as his mother gathered him up in a hug and her perfumed cheeks connected with his, he clung to her for a second.

'Leoni?' she said gently, accurately guessing the reason behind his torment.

He nodded, only slightly taken aback that his mother seemed to know exactly what was going on in his head. She had developed the knack in his teens and always seemed able to get to the heart of the matter without any faff or nonsense.

'Sort things out with her, son,' Arthur urged, joining in. 'Life's too short and all that.'

Ashton shrugged helplessly, his blue eyes clouded with distress. He gestured to the building. 'I have to sort this out . . . there's no time. And Leoni, we're barely speaking these days. She has a new, rich boyfriend,' he said dismally. 'French, of course,' he added.

Joyce gripped his arm and gave him a confident smile. 'It's not over yet, Ash. Don't give up before you've really put your heart on the line.'

Arthur nodded encouragingly. 'Your mother's right.'

'Are you saying I haven't done that already?' In spite of himself, Ashton pulled a face of mock dismay. 'Seriously, you have no idea! I'll tell you all about it in a minute.'

Joyce picked her suitcase up. 'First things first. Where can we dump our luggage and where's the kettle?'

Feeling ridiculously grateful for their presence and completely forgetting his builders were waiting for coffee, Ashton handed his parents hard hats and led the way into the building.

Back at La Fleurie, Leoni was in the breakfast salon, sifting through some photographs Stefan the photographer had sent over. She was preoccupied. The thought of Ashton and Marianne together, and of Ashton 'sacrificing' himself in order to secure the building, was quite simply nauseating. It changed Leoni's entire perspective of Ashton and unnerved her completely. He had always been such a rock, a very proper, reliable rock that she could always turn to, especially after Olivier died. But now, after Marianne's revelations, Ashton seemed like a different person and not the sweet, honourable person Leoni had always believed him to be. He was obviously a liar, something she would never have believed possible of him, in spite of all the time he had spent with Olivier, and he now seemed to have a sinister edge which didn't suit him at all.

Leoni swallowed. It really bothered her. It had been grim enough to find out that her little brother had been more of a liar and a cheat than she had imagined, but somehow this was worse. She had always known Olivier had bad habits, but where Ashton was concerned, Leoni would never have believed him capable of behaving in such a way. It was so unlike the Ashton she thought she knew.

Leoni glanced outside. The air was sultry, and dark clouds were gathering, threatening a storm. She prayed for it to break; it was suffocatingly humid and the atmosphere was crackling with tension, mirroring the mood of the family perfectly. Tearing her attention back to a photograph of Angelique reclining on a chaise-longue, Leoni frowned. It left her cold. Angelique's pouty mouth, covered in gooey lip gloss, looked almost obscene and her body, as desirable as it was, seemed overly sexual. The image jarred. Leoni knew it did not convey what Xavier had in mind for his perfume at all.

Her phone buzzed into life and she listened to a voicemail from Ashton. He sounded achingly familiar, the Ashton she remembered as her best friend, not the one Marianne had described. Leoni felt stricken but she slowly deleted the message. She couldn't stop thinking of Ashton as a cheap gigolo, sleeping with Marianne just to secure the purchase of a building. Why had he done it? Surely he hadn't believed he needed to stoop to such levels? Leoni shook her head. It would be easier to think Ashton had slept with Marianne simply because he'd been attracted to her but if so, surely Marianne would have said as much.

Telling herself not to bother caring so much about Ashton, especially since he couldn't see fit to talk to her in person about any of it, Leoni forced herself to look at the photographs of

Angelique again. Trying to be objective – Angelique had never been her favourite person – she tried to get a handle on exactly why the photographs didn't work. Thinking back to Xavier's short brief of glamorous, young and sexy and the extended one that contained all the other words pertaining to his new scent, Leoni could fit them all to the images but they didn't ring true someone. Part of the problem with Angelique's photographs was the lack of intimacy and warmth. They did not fit the Ducasse-Fleurie brand. It was obvious Stefan thought the same because he'd attached a Post-it note with 'Best of a bad bunch, re-do?' scribbled across it. Leoni frowned. There were any number of models out there but did they have time to source another?

Leoni looked up as Delphine entered the room. Her snowy-white hair was caught up in its usual neat chignon and her cream suit was as spotless as ever but Leoni couldn't help thinking her grandmother seemed somehow older – fragile even. It was an unsettling thought. Delphine was the figurehead of the family and someone they all relied upon for strength and resilience. However bossy and cutting she could be, Delphine was a force to be reckoned with. The idea that she might be less than robust was something Leoni didn't care to linger on but she fervently hoped Delphine's health wasn't suffering with all the drama going on.

'Have you seen Guy?' Delphine asked, gripping her cane with more dependency than normal. She looked troubled and her shoulders were sloped as though she was carrying an enormous weight on them. 'He's usually surgically attached to his office but every time I try and speak to him, he's nowhere to be found.'

Leoni shook her head. 'Max was looking for him earlier too.' An idea occurred to her as she glanced down at the photographs again. Was it a crazy thought? It would require an awful lot of work in a very short time. Delphine was waiting for an explanation.

'Er, sorry. Max was charging around like a man possessed looking for Guy this morning, said he had something to talk to him about. I'm hoping he didn't find him, actually, because he looked as though he was about to explode.' Leoni frowned. Where did Uncle Guy keep disappearing to? He had been difficult to track down ever since the incident with Seraphina back in the spring. Leoni wondered if he was having a breakdown.

'Teenagers.' Delphine sniffed, reverting to her snippy self for a moment and not appearing to be overly concerned with Guy's odd absence. She noticed the pile of glossy photographs and nodded at them.

'What do you have there?'

Leoni gathered them up and held them to her chest. 'Just something to do with the ad campaign. I'm thinking of something a bit different. These photos of Angelique don't seem quite right.' She lifted her eyes to meet her grandmother's, almost daring her to disagree. 'Do you have any objection if I play around with another idea?'

Delphine sighed. Ever since Angelique had set foot in La Fleurie – no, before that – Delphine had been feeling uncomfortable about her meddling. She regretted her decision to draw Angelique back into the fold, not least because Xavier seemed so incensed. He had disappeared to Morocco and no one had heard from him in days, even though he should have been back by now. Angelique was swanning around as if she owned the place, upsetting the housekeeper and several of the maids with her rude and unreasonable requests. How could she have been so wrong about the girl? Delphine fretted. Far from being a positive influence and the love of Xavier's life, it was obvious Angelique was unhealthily ambitious. And the fact that Xavier felt antagonistic towards her spoke volumes because Delphine knew that despite his tempestuous temper, he was very sure of his feelings when it came to the people close to him.

'Do whatever you think best, Leoni,' Delphine uttered finally, sinking into a chair. So much had gone on over the past year or so since Olivier's death and for the first time in her life, she felt terribly *old*.

'Thank you,' Leoni said, feeling a rush of gratitude. Not quite sure why, she dropped a kiss on Delphine's powdery cheek as she headed to the door. Leoni would have been astonished – and greatly moved – had she seen the tear trickling down her grandmother's cheek at the tender gesture.

Embarrassed, Delphine wiped the tear away quickly. Anxiously, she wondered where Guy was. Something bad was about to happen, she could sense it. Like a row of wobbling dominoes, Delphine felt as though her family were about to topple and fall.

Having been spoiling for a confrontation for the past few weeks now, Max finally tracked his father down near the stables, staring out across the valley that had claimed Elizabeth's life. Max marched up to him, grabbed him by the shoulder and spun him round.

'What the hell do you think you're doing?' Guy demanded, his brown eyes darkening with rage.

Momentarily distracted, Max noticed threatening clouds circling overhead like ghouls sensing a twisted party they wanted to gatecrash. He refocused his gaze on his father. 'I'm doing something I should have done ages ago,' he roared, angered by his father's reaction. It was his fault everything was so screwed up at the moment and Max was sick and tired of pussyfooting around and letting him get away with it.

His eyes roamed over his father. The impeccable white shirt he wore and the silver-grey hair that was combed carefully into place enraged Max even more. He wanted to see his father look ravaged with guilt, he wanted to see him ruffled and crumpled and losing control, for once. What the hell was wrong with him? Didn't he have any sense of remorse whatsoever?

Bristling at the contemptuous scrutiny his son was subjecting him to, Guy glared at Max, his nostrils flaring. How dare he be so aggressive! Who did he think he was, charging up to him like that? Guy, already on the defensive, immediately went on the offensive, knowing he was in for a fight.

Neither of them noticed Cat emerging from one of the nearby stables wearing white shorts and a torn yellow vest top. She had been looking for an earring she had lost that night with Xavier. She stood rooted to the spot, not sure whether to duck back into the stable or discreetly slip off to the château. Pulling her T-shirt away from her sticky skin, Cat wished the muggy weather would make its mind up and either subject them to a thunderous downpour or allow the sun to work its way through. She couldn't believe it was June already . . . the weeks at La Fleurie seemed to merge into one another, slipping past blissfully, yet uneventfully with nothing resolved from her perspective.

'Do you even care about Seraphina?' Max yelled, his fists clenched by his sides. He was dressed in a red polo shirt that matched the high spots in his cheeks and dirty beige jodhpurs with boots. 'She fucking idolises you and you've done nothing but let her down!'

'Seraphina?' Guy made an impatient sound. 'Of course I care about her! I want to throttle her for what she's done and I can't bear to look at her right now but do I care about her. What a stupid question.'

Max snorted. 'It's not stupid, and how dare you say you can't bear to look at her? What right do you have – what has she done wrong here?' He was becoming increasingly inarticulate as he struggled to get his point across. 'Oh, don't tell me, Dad; she's a massive disappointment because she almost slept with some bloke old enough to be, well, you?'

Guy stared at Max. Feelings he'd done his best to suppress sprang to the surface and he couldn't push them down again.

400

He wanted to stop Max's torrent of abuse but he felt powerless.

In the shadows by the stables, Cat shifted awkwardly, realising she had no choice but to stand still. She felt voyeuristic – she really didn't want to witness the confrontation between Max and his father.

'Do you know how . . . how *useless* you've been since Mum died?' Max howled, feeling a pain in his chest. 'Do you know how abandoned we've been feeling? Sending us away to college like that, was that the best you could do?'

Guy recoiled. Useless? Abandoned? Where was all this coming from?

'Did you think you were the only one who missed Mum?' Max's voice broke. 'Did you think we didn't want to talk about her . . . to remember her? Why did you stop us from doing that? Why did you act as though we weren't allowed to be as devastated as you were?'

'I didn't . . . I was . . .' Guy's voice was hoarse and his hands flapped helplessly.

'Oh, save it,' Max spat.

Cat's heart lurched. She knew Guy had an awful lot to answer for but it was like watching a firing squad hit him repeatedly whilst he scrabbled around on the floor in agony. She willed Max to ease up but deep down she knew he had every right to vent his anger and let his true emotions out.

'Why do you think I've been doing all the stupid stuff I've been doing? Have you even bothered to think why Seraphina might have lapped up attention from some old guy she didn't even know very well?'

Guy looked horror-struck and bewildered. As if to punctuate the moment, thunder cracked overhead.

Max hadn't finished. In fact, he was on a roll. 'Did you ever stop to think how it would make us feel to send us off to some stupid college miles away? Did you ever think we both might need you, that Seraphina needed you?' He lifted his

401

chin, scorn burning in his eyes. 'She wants your attention, your – I don't know – maybe your approval.' Max faltered. 'And . . . and what about Xavier? You pushed him away too. You have no idea what he was going through after Angelique left.'

'What are you talking about?' Guy struggled to take everything in. It was as if his worst nightmare had come to life. All the feelings he'd pushed down again and again had reared up without warning and grabbed him by the throat. It was as though someone – his own son, in fact – was pumping him full of reality, tearing down the previously tough and efficient walls of self-delusion he had built up over time to avoid responsibility and blame.

Guy's head was swirling but he latched on to Max's comment about Xavier. What did he mean? What had happened with Angelique? Something had gone on, obviously; one minute the pair of them had been inseparable, as though they would spend eternity together, and the next they were two separate beings once more, alone, wounded and apart.

Guy guiltily recalled at least three occasions over the past two years when Xavier had attempted to have a heart-to-heart with him. Guy, unable to deal with emotion on any level, even someone else's, had batted Xavier away, using work as a convenient shield. Eventually, Xavier had given up, pulling down his own emotional shutters and refusing to work in the family business.

Guy felt terrible. And he felt ashamed, horribly so. He wanted to tell Max he was sorry . . . he wanted to explain to Xavier that he hadn't meant to let him down and that he had all the time in the world to hear what had happened with Angelique. He wanted to pull Seraphina into his arms and tell her she would always be his baby and that he would always protect her.

But he hadn't, had he? Seraphina had ended up in the

slippery arms of Yves. Was Max right? Had Seraphina really ended up with a man twice her age because she'd been craving her own father's attention and approval? Guy thought he might throw up on the spot.

Cat watched, agonised. Max sorely needed to get everything off his chest but Guy couldn't take much more. He looked so pale, so aghast; Cat was worried he might have a heart attack. She was aware that Guy had been wandering off on his own since the party; several times she had discovered him silently weeping by Elizabeth's grave. He seemed incapable of coping with day to day life right now.

Feeling a drop of rain on her bare shoulder, Cat looked up at the darkening sky fearfully, guessing a huge storm was on its way. Rather like the one being played out in front of her, she thought worriedly.

Inflamed that his father was saying nothing and determined to stick the knife in once and for all, Max spoke again, his voice now scarily calm. 'That slimy bastard Seraphina ended up with took *your* place, Dad. He did all the things you were supposed to do. That and a whole lot more, eh?'

'Stop,' Guy gasped, stumbling backwards as if he'd been struck. 'Don't say that. You can't mean it, you can't.' He clawed at his throat as if he'd been deprived of air. 'You can't mean that . . . you can't think I rejected her . . . both of you, like that.' As he said the words, Guy knew that was exactly what he had done. Everything Max said was true. When Elizabeth died, he had been so caught up in his own grief, he hadn't considered their feelings.

Guy leant against a nearby fence for support, appalled at the realisation he had been avoiding for the past two years or more. He was a terrible father. He had sidelined his children when they needed him the most, just because he was inconsolable after his wife's death. He had mourned her loss so deeply, he had punished everyone around him by cutting them off and making himself unavailable.

Rain began to pelt down and a terrifying fork of lightning pierced the sky.

'I think he's heard enough,' Cat said, unable to hold back any longer. She stepped forward, wishing she was wearing more than shorts and a T-shirt. Max spun round, his mouth twisted in a snarl, but Cat stood her ground. 'I'm sorry, Max. I'm sure everything you've said is true but your father just didn't realise. He's devastated by what you've said.'

'I don't give a FUCK!' Max bellowed. 'He's a father, he's not supposed to screw everything up and get away with it.'

'I don't think he is getting away with it,' Cat stated gently, catching sight of Guy sliding down the fence. He ended up awkwardly on the ground and stared at them sightlessly. He was soaked but seemed oblivious of it.

Cat was about to go to him when she caught sight of Angelique sauntering towards them. Wearing a smart pair of beige jodhpurs with a cream silk sleeveless vest, she was carrying a clear umbrella over her head and her blond hair was tied up in a smooth bun. She looked as though she was off for a photo shoot rather than ride and, unlike the rest of them, she was bone dry and immaculate.

'I can't believe it's raining,' she pouted, seemingly unaware that Guy was looking utterly destroyed in a crumpled heap by the fence. 'I was about to go for a ride. I'm an excellent rider. Is the horse I used to ride still here?' she asked for Cat's benefit.

Max shot her a withering glance. 'That horse died over a year ago,' he snapped. 'Something you'd know if you hadn't fucked off and left Xavier to pick up the pieces.'

Angelique flushed. Little upstart, talking to her as if she was nothing! And what did he know about what had happened with Xavier? Forgetting the Ducasse family were extremely close, Angelique dismissed any possibility that Xavier had confided in his younger siblings.

'Fuck this,' Max said, losing patience with everyone. Charging towards the stables, he pulled Le Fantome out. The horse's eyes rolled crazily as thunder rumbled around them. Not bothering to saddle up, Max leapt on bareback and cantered into the field, his red shirt the only bright speck in the curtain of rain.

Cat watched him worriedly. Max was an extremely competent rider but the conditions were going to be treacherous in no time at all. Throw his uncontrollable anger into the mix and disaster beckoned. She looked at Angelique desperately. 'What are we going to do?'

Angelique pulled a face. 'Don't look at me, I'm not riding in this weather!' She gestured to her clothes. 'Do I look as though I'm about to charge off in thunder and lightning?' She looked at Cat's scruffy wet shorts and T-shirt disparagingly.

'You said you were an excellent rider,' Cat retorted heatedly. She pointed to Max's disappearing form. 'He's out there alone in this fucking storm and he's angry and hurt. We have to do something!'

Angelique shrugged. 'Count me out. Family domestics aren't my thing. And stroppy teenagers aren't really my forte either.' She strolled off and Cat gaped at her. Didn't she have any feelings whatsoever? Cat went to Guy's side and helped him up.

'Go to the house,' she told him in a loud, clear voice. 'Get help. It doesn't matter who. Just tell them Max is out riding and he's in danger.' She blinked as rain streamed down her face. Guy was looking back at her helplessly. 'Do you understand? Guy, do you understand what I'm saying?'

Guy nodded blankly. 'It's all my fault but I didn't know . . .' His voice trailed away. 'I didn't mean to shut them out . . . I didn't mean for Seraphina to replace me with that . . . that awful man. Oh God, Cat, what have I done?'

'I know,' Cat soothed, speaking to him as though he were a

405

child. 'It will be all right, Guy, I promise. But right now, we need to get Max. Go and get help. Now, please!'

Shoving him towards the château, she dashed through the rain to one of the stables. Finding a horse that didn't look too put out by the storm, Cat hurriedly saddled it up, her fingers struggling with the buckles. It had been years since she'd ridden, even longer since she'd put a saddle on. Hoping to God the saddle was secure, Cat leapt on the horse's back and kicked off her flip-flops.

She headed in the same direction as Max, clutching the reins for dear life. She felt the horse skid around beneath her on the sodden grass and she forced her knees into the saddle, leaning down low over the horse's neck as his wet mane flipped up and slapped her across the face. She scrabbled to stay mounted, winding the reins round her wrists.

She could see Max in the distance. She yelled at him but her voice was snatched away by the wind. Cat cantered after him, grappling to keep control of the now petrified horse. Wind howled around them and thunder crashed and thumped, making the ground itself feel as if it was shaking in its boots . . . or melting with fear.

Shrieking to Max to slow down, Cat saw his dark head turn for a second. Suddenly, he disappeared from sight and Cat shouted out in terror. She pushed the horse harder, her eyes searching for him. He was nowhere to be seen. Scared stiff the valley that had claimed Elizabeth had just claimed Max, Cat kept going, determined to find him. Her limbs ached with the effort of keeping her seat and she was soaked to the skin and shivering. She realised Max's horse had slipped on one of the treacherous ledges in the valley and that he must be lying in the grass, and she called out to him in the rain. She heard something behind her; it sounded like the pounding of another horse's hooves, and her concentration lapsed for a second. As the sky turned white with another jagged shaft of light, she was blinded. Her wrist slipped free of the reins, and her horse threw her. She crashed to the ground with a sickening thud and felt herself slide into darkness as she rolled over and over. She came to a halt beside a rock.

Over the next few minutes, Cat swam in and out of consciousness, aware of a horse near her, then strong arms gathering her up. She heard voices yelling at one another in French, the words unintelligible through the pouring rain and thunder. Hazily, Cat felt hot breath on her cheek and, in the distance, she thought she heard someone telling her not to think about dying, and something about her being the one rescued for once. Not sure if she had imagined a mouth meeting hers fiercely and a waft of orange blossom scenting the air, Cat passed out cold.

Staggering back to La Fleurie with Cat in his arms, Xavier gritted his teeth. He had been horrified when he'd seen her flung from her horse at such speed – she had hit the ground like a broken doll and he hadn't been able to do anything. He prayed he hadn't put her in more danger by scooping her up from the undergrowth the way he had but he couldn't leave her there. He needed her alive and kicking . . .

'Don't you dare die on me,' he murmured, looking down at her. Xavier rubbed his fingers across Cat's lips again, worried they were turning blue. He saw the ambulance services his father had called carry a pallid-looking Max towards the château on a stretcher and as the rain hammered down on his head, forcing his dark hair into his eyes, Xavier yelled for a doctor to follow him upstairs. He waited with bated breath as the doctor assessed Cat and instructed a nurse to get her into some dry clothes.

'She'll be fine,' the doctor informed him. 'She's hurt her ankle and she'll have a sore head in the morning but apart from that, there isn't too much to worry about.' He cheerfully collected up his things. 'Unless she loses her memory, of course, but probably not much chance of that.'

Standing in the doorway, Xavier leant his head against the frame and stared at Cat. What a mess. There were so many loose ends to tie up, so many things to say. Unable to resist, he went back to the bed and kissed her full, still mouth. Xavier knew he had to sort things out with both Cat – and Angelique, but for now, he was going to stay by Cat's side.

Chapter Twenty-Two

Blearily opening one eye, Cat turned her head. She was in bed; her curtains were open but she was half lying, half sitting under a sheet, her neck and head propped up by a number of pillows. Staring out of the window, she was almost blinded by the sight of some unapologetically bright lavender she could see bursting into life in the distance. Glistening with droplets of overnight rain and dazzling the eye with indigo, magenta, lilac and violet, the fields stretched proudly out across the Provençal countryside, no doubt providing a glorious scent. Dazed, Cat opened the other eye, wincing as she felt the cracking pain in her head. Whimpering, she struggled to push herself up from the pillows but she couldn't.

'Just relax,' said a voice that seemed to be far away. Bit by bit, Seraphina's luminous brown eyes and pale skin swam into view. Wearing a white sun dress with her hair held back by a red band, she resembled a rather glamorous nurse.

'W-what happened?' Cat managed, moving a tongue around a mouth as dry as Ghandi's flip-flop. Her head hurt, her eyes were stinging and she ached all over. It was like having the most awful hangover – but much, much worse.

'You can still speak French. Good.' Seraphina held a cup of water to her mouth. 'Here, take a sip.' Tipping it slightly, she fed a straw into Cat's mouth and helped her drink it. Afterwards, Cat flopped back against the pillows, looking frail. Her hair was tangled from the rain and without a scrap of make-up on, she looked about twelve. If she'd been able to look in the mirror, Cat would have found her skin to be unnaturally waxy-looking and her normally sparkly eyes dull and bloodshot but thankfully she wasn't able to do more than lift her head a fraction.

Seraphina was taking her role of nursemaid seriously. Her expression was grave as she glanced at some notes on the bedside table. 'Can you remember your name, your date of birth and what the day is?'

Cat gazed at her. 'Yes, yes and not sure on the last one. Depends how long I've been here.' Mystified, she inhaled, sure she must be imagining the aroma of raw meat in the air. Cat felt panicked. Just how hard had she hit her head? It couldn't be normal to be getting wafts of bloody meat under the nose after a head injury, could it?

Seraphina looked relieved to hear Cat speaking so succinctly. 'Just overnight. Good, so you're not seriously concussed, then. Do you remember anything at all?'

Cat put a shaky hand to her head and wondered why her ankle felt as if it had been bludgeoned with a hammer. 'I don't know.' She closed her eyes and tried to concentrate. Images flitted in and out of her head. 'Hang on, things are coming back. It was raining, I remember that.' She glanced outside, seeing the brilliant sunshine flooding down and engulfing everything and for a moment she was unsure her memory was as clear as she'd first thought.

Seraphina nodded. 'You're right, there was a huge storm yesterday. The rain only stopped a few hours ago.'

'All right, so I'm not mad, after all.' Cat thought hard, her brow wrinkling with the effort. 'Yes, I remember. I was on a horse! It was a huge great thing and I couldn't control it. Max was there and Guy . . .' Her eyes snapped open. 'Oh my God, the row! Oh, Seraphina, it was awful. Max . . . the things he said to your father . . . poor Guy looked as though he was about to have a heart attack. Is he all right?'

Seraphina nodded. 'He's fine. Honestly, I think this is the

best thing that could have happened.' She glanced at her hands. 'I mean, there's still a lot of talking to do but things are better, I think. Max is fine too — at least, he will be. Anyway, go on. What else do you remember?'

Cat thought hard. 'Max went charging off on his horse . . . he was so angry and it was pouring down with rain and all I could think was that he was going to kill himself out there. So I went after him.' Looking rueful, she pleated the sheet. 'Not one of my best decisions. I haven't been on a horse for years, and I've never ridden in such terrible conditions. It was one of those spur of the moment things.'

Cat grimaced. When would she learn? She felt so foolish.

'Good. At least your memory is intact.' Seraphina laid a damp flannel on Cat's head. 'You fell off your horse and got a nasty bump to the head.' She lifted the flannel and peered at it. 'It's pretty big, actually, and it's going to be really colourful.'

'I'm an absolute idiot,' Cat stated as she touched her head gingerly.

'An idiot? Why? Because you went after Max like that? He could have died out there. He came flying off Le Fantome and really hurt himself. He was knocked out instantly . . . it's so frightening.' A sob caught in Seraphina's throat. 'If you hadn't gone after him, he could have died out there in the cold, just like our mother did, because you woke up briefly and garbled something about Max's location. I can't bear the thought of how things could have been if you hadn't done that.'

'Max is . . . he's all right, though, isn't he?'

Seraphina nodded, dashing the tears away from her eyes. 'He had to go to hospital and have a brain scan but they think he's fine.'

Cat was shaken. A brain scan?

'A doctor examined you here,' Seraphina continued efficiently, clearly needing to keep herself busy with nurse-type duties to take her mind off Max. 'He left those questions for

411

you so I could check you didn't need to go to hospital this morning.'

'I see.' Cat shifted under the sheet and caught an overpowering waft of raw meat again. 'So what the hell is wrong with my ankle?'

'You twisted it badly when you fell. I put some frozen filet mignon on it last night. Does it hurt?'

Cat burst out laughing. Only Seraphina would put frozen filet mignon on a twisted ankle. What was wrong with peas? Perhaps the French frowned on frozen veg. Either way, Cat felt relieved. At least it explained the odd smell of raw meat in the room; she'd been worried it was a sign of damaged brain cells.

'The ankle hurts like hell,' she admitted, shifting in bed and trying not to brush it against the sheet too much. 'Where were you yesterday, by the way?'

Seraphina suddenly seemed very interested in tidying Cat's bedside table. 'Oh, I was around,' she replied vaguely. 'I was just a bit . . . busy. I had no idea Max was going to go for Father the way he did, otherwise I would have stopped him. I mean, I'm angry too . . . at least, I was, but there was no need to lay into him like that.'

'You obviously have more compassion than your brother,' Cat commented. Max's onslaught had obviously been the result of more than two years of mounting resentment and Cat couldn't really blame Max for finally letting rip, but it had been devastating to watch. She couldn't help feeling sorry for Guy. He had been good to her since she arrived. Especially having witnessed his breakdown at Elizabeth's grave, something no one else had seen.

'Do you remember anything else about yesterday?' Seraphina asked curiously, her brown eyes keen as they scrutinised Cat's face.

Cat frowned. 'No. Should I?'

Seraphina shrugged and her eyes slid away shiftily.

A memory of being lifted up in strong arms swam into Cat's mind but, just as quickly, it swam out again. She had thought Max had scooped her up after her fall but that couldn't be right because Seraphina said he had been knocked out cold. There was another reason it couldn't have been Max but, Cat couldn't recall what it was. The details of her rescue lay tantalisingly out of reach.

She groaned. 'God knows why I thought I was the best person to go after Max but there was no one else there.' She frowned. 'Hang on, that's not right. Angelique was there but she refused to go.'

'Are you serious?' Seraphina said angrily. 'Angelique was there?' This was clearly news to her. 'She probably didn't want to mess her hair up or something. She's such a strong rider too. How could she have refused to go after Max?'

'If I remember rightly, it was her clothes she was more worried about.' Cat had been shocked by Angelique's indifference. If she cared about Xavier as much as she claimed to, wouldn't she want to look after his family and do whatever she could to help?

Out of the blue, another memory surfaced, this time a smell. Oranges? Orange blossom? What a strange thing to remember. She was sure she must be mistaken about it, though. The raw meat aroma might have been explained away but there was no earthly reason why she should have been smelling oranges.

'Leoni sends her love,' Seraphina said suddenly. 'She wanted you to know that she'll come and see you as soon as she's finished working on something.'

Touched, Cat reached up to feel the bump on her head. It felt as though she was growing an ostrich egg on her forehead. 'What's Leoni working on?' she asked with interest. 'Something to do with the home fragrance pitch?

Seraphina bit her lip. 'She's . . . I couldn't possibly talk about it,' she said in a guarded tone.

Cat lay back tiredly, wondering why Seraphina was being so cagey. She looked up as Guy poked his head round the door and then glanced at Seraphina apprehensively. She wasn't up to witnessing another row. Her head was pounding painfully.

'All right if I come in?' he asked.

'Of course, Dad,' Seraphina replied, looking amazingly serene. 'I'm just off to get Cat something to eat.' She strolled past her father and closed the door quietly behind her.

Cat smiled at Guy weakly.

'How are you feeling?' he asked, sitting on the edge of the bed. Reassuringly, his appearance was as suave and well groomed as ever; his silver-grey shirt matched his pristine, smoothed-back hair and he was wearing a tie again, a sure sign that things were back to normal.

Whatever that meant, Cat thought woozily as her eyes started to close. 'Normality' had become an elusive concept lately. After all, she should be at home, in England, working in an advertising firm, not holed up in a French château with unfinished business all over the place.

'I'm fine . . . I think,' she answered.

'That's great,' Guy told her, with a warm smile. 'I can't thank you enough,' he added. His brown eyes clouded over with shame. 'Not just for dashing after Max like that but for trying to alert me to how much I was hurting the twins. And Xavier,' he added as an afterthought.

Cat opened her eyes with difficulty. 'That's all right. I thought you might think I was interfering.'

Guy laughed. 'That's not interfering, and my mother has that corner of the market all sewn up anyway.'

Cat smiled and closed her eyes again. She felt Guy take her hand.

'I miss her so much still,' Guy said, smoothing a lock of hair out of Cat's eyes. 'Elizabeth was my life . . . I felt so lost without her.' He gazed at Cat tenderly. 'Sleep, darling. You need to rest.'

Cat tried to shake her head. She wondered if it had been Guy who had plucked her from the undergrowth but she didn't think so somehow. She remembered the rain and the rich, earthy smell of the sodden ground . . . she remembered shouting and voices and horses whinnying. She just couldn't recall the face of her rescuer.

'Must go home,' she said randomly, not sure where the thought had come from. But it was true. She had more than outstayed her welcome and there was nothing for her here; not any more. 'Xavier loves Angelique and Delphine hates me. Nothing for me here.'

Guy squeezed her hand. 'Don't say that. We all love you, even my mother. We want you to stay. And don't be too sure about Xavier.'

Cat felt tears sliding down her cheeks. 'So sweet . . . but you're wrong . . .'

'Cat.' Guy gripped her arm. 'Cat, listen to me. You must come to the launch party in Paris. Please? For me,' he insisted, resorting to emotional blackmail. It made him smile; he had clearly picked up a few tips from his mother.

Cat shrugged feebly, not even sure what she was agreeing to.

'Good.' Guy tucked her in as though she were a child and stared down at her thoughtfully. Something had to be done to tie up all the loose ends and he knew exactly who needed to do it. He left the room without a sound.

An emotionally spent Cat didn't even notice and within seconds she was fast asleep.

Reviewing the perfume with a critical eye – or rather, nose – Xavier was extremely pleased. More truthfully, he was over the moon. Finally able to sit in his lab and put everything together as he had visualised it (dummy phials transported between countries never yielded the same result), he knew it was the best thing he'd ever created. It was sexy, sultry, romantic and glamorous, all the things he'd hoped it would be. It was youthful but not exclusively so and it had a beautiful, lasting quality that he knew would be a hit with women the world over.

Xavier inhaled it again, almost unable to believe what he had managed to create after all this time, but suddenly he knew exactly how and why he'd been able to create it. Finally, sitting alone in his lab, the significance that had been slowly building over the past few months hit him square between the eyes.

He knew he had to get moving. Emailing follow-up instructions to the team at the warehouse to add to all the emails he'd fired off in Morocco, Xavier quickly made sure everything was in place for the launch of the new fragrance. He'd sent details of the name on in advance so the team could get working on the packaging. All that remained now was for the fragrance itself to be blended, bottled up and sent out. He had already hired more staff and a veritable army had been sent to the warehouse to help out, as well as to another empty warehouse Xavier had rented on the outskirts of Grasse. He had promised his family everything would be ready for a July launch and he was going to achieve it, however challenging the deadline.

He viewed a pile of photographs Stefan the photographer had left for him and he frowned as he viewed Angelique in various provocative poses. Regardless of his personal feelings towards her, he wasn't happy with what he was seeing, for a number of reasons. This wasn't down to Stefan. He was a master of his art and his photographs were famous the world over. No, this was down to the content of the photographs, not any lack of skill with which they'd been taken.

Xavier drummed his fingers on the photographs, wondering what to do about them. Could anything be done at this late stage? And what were the legal implications? Angelique must have signed a contract but maybe Pascal, with his knowledge of the law, might find a loophole. Xavier didn't have a clue how it could all be untangled, but something had to be done, even if it damaged the sales of the fragrance for a while when it was launched.

Working into the night, Xavier finally finished everything he'd come back to La Fleurie to do. Well, not everything; there were a number of things he still needed to sort out but Xavier knew he could only tackle one thing at a time. Satisfied there was nothing more he could do to with regard to the perfume, he turned his attention to his much-neglected personal life.

He still needed to fly to Paris and with the launch due in a few weeks' time, he knew he should go early and track down the information he was after. He hated the thought of leaving so soon after he had arrived, especially when both Angelique and Cat were in residence, but he didn't see what else he could do.

Xavier banged a fist on the counter impatiently. Was he right to be as suspicious as he was? The very thought of what he was imagining appalled him and he knew once he discovered the truth, it could result in Cat or Angelique, or both, leaving La Fleurie and never returning. It was up to him to ensure that the right person was vindicated and that the other was exposed as a cheat and a fraud.

Xavier threw off his lab coat to reveal a pair of loose jeans and a pale blue shirt. Breathing in gulps of fresh Provençal air, he reached for his cigarettes out of habit. The blanket of flourishing lavender fields looked stunning and the air felt still and tranquil – the calm after the storm, as it were. He hoped Max, too, would find some peace after his storm of rage. It had been long overdue. The consequences of all that anger finally being voiced had been frightening and potentially fatal, but hopefully some good would come of it. At least no one had been seriously hurt, and he was grateful for that.

Deciding to check something, he headed inside the château.

Making sure he wasn't being watched, Xavier went into one of the upstairs bedrooms. He quickly flipped through wardrobes and drawers before he found what he was looking for. Gripping it in his hands, Xavier felt sick. So he had been right – about this, at least. Slipping the incriminating piece of evidence back where he found it, he left, feeling thoroughly shaken.

He bumped into Leoni downstairs in the kitchen. She seemed very busy which surprised him. As far as he was aware, she had delivered her home fragrance proposal to Guy and she was at a loose end. And yet she was bustling around with her phone in one hand and a batch of notes in the other.

'What are you doing?' Xavier asked, helping himself to a black coffee and almost giving his throat third-degree burns as he knocked it back too quickly. He needed something to kick-start his adrenaline but he hadn't intended to scar himself. Xavier noticed that Leoni was exceptionally thin, even for her, and her clothes were hanging off her frame unattractively. Her cheekbones looked even more prominent than usual and it didn't suit her.

'I'm working on something,' Leoni responded evasively. She pushed her glasses up her nose, not giving anything away.

Xavier felt exasperated. 'What, exactly?' Was everyone hiding something around here?

Leoni held her phone and notes close to her chest as if she feared he might snatch them from her. 'Do you trust me?'

Xavier checked his watch. He was due to catch a flight to Paris shortly. 'Yes, of course.'

'Then just know that I'm doing something that's in everyone's best interests.' Leoni nodded firmly. Her eyes shone behind her glasses. 'I think I'm doing the right thing – no, I *know* I am. And I'm confident you'll agree with me when you see the final result.'

Xavier gave up. He had no idea what Leoni was talking about and he didn't have time to guess. He wished he had time to go and visit Cat in her room but he guessed she was probably sleeping and he didn't want to disturb her.

'Have you spoken to Cat?' Leoni asked, reading his mind. 'I think you should . . . before it's too late.'

Xavier shook his dark head, his heart flipping over at Leoni's words. 'I want to, I really do, but I don't have time. That sounds callous but you have to understand, this other thing I'm working on is crucial. Something that is in everyone's best interests, as you would say.' God only knew what Cat must make of him running off every five minutes. He realised Leoni was speaking and he forced himself to listen.

'So I bought her a dress as a thank you,' Leoni was saying. 'Cat was so pleased, it made me realise how nice it is to do something for someone.' She caught his glance and half smiled. 'I know, I know, at last I've figured out that being selfish isn't all it's cracked up to be.'

Xavier grinned. 'I'm just glad you and Cat are finally getting on. I wasn't sure you'd ever forgive her for marrying Olivier.'

Leoni nodded. 'Me neither. I was so angry . . . so jealous. Hey, we all make mistakes, don't we? I honestly think she's one of the nicest people I've ever met. And she's got a backbone too.'

Xavier said nothing. It was his turn to be evasive.

Leoni didn't notice. 'She was so brave, wasn't she? Imagine how different it could have been for Max out there in that valley if she hadn't been able to tell us where Mak was . . . I don't know if I could have survived another tragedy.'

Xavier reached an arm out and pulled her into a hug. 'I know. Thank God Cat had the guts to charge after Max like that. Madness, of course; she hasn't ridden for years, by all accounts.'

Leoni nodded. She changed the subject as they headed outside. 'Grandmother is desperate to speak to you. I think she feels guilty about meddling so much.'

'So she should,' Xavier replied moodily. 'Hiring Yves,

inviting Angelique back here – what was she playing at?'

Leoni surprised herself by defending her grandmother. 'She thought she knew what everyone wanted . . . she thought she was doing the best for the family.'

Xavier let out a short laugh. 'She shouldn't make decisions on behalf of the family. We might all be related but we're individuals too, she can't possibly know what's best for each of us.'

Leoni nodded in agreement. 'I think she realises that now. She hasn't said anything but I'm sure it's how she's feeling.'

'Hmmm.' Xavier wasn't convinced. As far as he was concerned, his grandmother had come out of the womb interfering and getting her fingers burnt a couple of times wasn't going to put her off. She had done untold damage with her prying and high-handedness and Xavier was finding it difficult to shrug off the impact it had had on his life. His grandmother couldn't have known about the potential time bomb he was certain he was going to find proof of in Paris, but still, she should have stayed out of everyone's business.

'Have you been to see Max?' Xavier asked. He shuddered, thinking how differently things could have turned out.

Leoni rolled her eyes. 'Silly boy. He's messed his face up a bit and his head is going to be scarred for life but apart from that, he's lucky to escape with some cuts and bruises.' She gave him a sly glance. 'A bit like Cat. Lucky you managed to get there in the blink of an eye.'

'Wasn't it?' Xavier met her eyes and raised his eyebrows. 'Dad called the emergency services about Max but it was only after he'd had a stiff drink that he remembered about Cat going after him.'

'Didn't Angelique tell you?' Leoni was taken aback. Seraphina had given her to understand that it must have been Angelique who alerted Xavier to the fact that Cat was out in the rain on their most temperamental horse.

Xavier shook his head. 'Angelique? No. I didn't even know

she knew.' He scowled. 'Are you saying Angelique could have gone after Max but that she chose not to?'

Leoni shrugged. 'I have no idea. You'd have to ask her.'

Xavier frowned. 'I don't have time.' He glanced at his watch. 'I have to go or I'll be late for my flight to Paris. I seem to be living out of a suitcase at the moment. I hope Ashton doesn't mind me crashing at his place – I must call him on the way.'

Leoni's eyes flickered for a moment.

Xavier watched her. 'Any message for Ashton, by the way?'

'No, thank you.' Leoni didn't even know how she was going to face him at the launch. Her heart ached at the thought of losing Ashton's friendship forever but she didn't know how she was going to get past what he'd done. 'Actually . . . ask him how he got the building,' she said.

Xavier looked bemused. 'How he got the building? Er, all right. I'll ask him. Would you like me to tell you what he says?'

Leoni looked away. 'No. I don't think there's anything he can say that will make me think differently of him.'

'Right.' Xavier had no idea what was going on. Maybe Ashton would be able to enlighten him when he arrived.

Bewildered, Xavier stepped out on to the gravel driveway. He was beginning to think they'd all done far too much in the name of the family recently. They all deserved to be happy so it was about time they started living and doing what they wanted, not what they felt they *should* do.

Grimly, Xavier strode to the car waiting for him in the driveway and got in. As the car pulled away, he turned and took a glance at La Fleurie. He had a feeling things were going to be very different for everyone after Paris.

'Please be all right,' Madeleine pleaded as she swept Max's dark hair back from the bandage wrapped round his head. He was asleep and in spite of the fact that she was neglecting her studies, she hadn't left his side once since she'd heard the news about his accident.

Madeleine sighed. That wasn't completely truthful; she'd been forced to sit outside on a number of a occasions as a stream of visitors had filed in and out, including Seraphina, Guy and Delphine. Seraphina had been practically inconsolable in the beginning and she had only calmed down when she had been fully assured that Max was going to be fine, with no lasting damage. Finally convinced her twin was in safe hands, she had left him to heal, popping in each morning and then going back to La Fleurie to look after Cat, who was also battered but thankfully not hospital-bound.

Guy had been equally distressed and when Max had come round, they had spent hours talking to one another. Madeleine had kept her distance, hovering outside the door with her hands clasped round a cup of coffee. She knew the discussions taking place were serious and it was only when she saw Max crumple and Guy hold him tightly that she knew everything was all right between them. Leoni had also made an appearance, bringing Max's favourite chocolates as well as some rude magazines Xavier had sent on inside some other, more innocuous-looking journals. Leoni had scolded Max like a child, before giving him a warm hug that showed just how pleased she was that he had survived the terrible accident.

Enjoying a rare moment of solitude with Max again before any visitors were due, Madeleine gently stroked his face. Neither Vero nor the boys had been to visit Max, which summed up how little they cared about him. They knew about the accident because Madeleine, unsure of the best thing to do, had sent them a text to let them know. She needn't have bothered; the boys hadn't responded and Vero had sent a jaunty text back to say she might visit when she'd finished partying in Marseilles.

Madeleine felt tears approaching as she examined Max's

injuries. A large bruise stained Max's left cheek where his perfect cheekbone had been shattered and his lip was torn. His head was tightly covered in a bandage with a large, padded section over the gash he'd received from the jagged rock he'd fallen on. The doctors, delighted to have someone as glamorous as Max Ducasse in their wards, claimed he had nearly died and would have done if the ambulance services hadn't reached him as quickly as they had.

Madeleine didn't know what to believe but the thought that Max might have died was too much for her so she chose to think the doctors were being dramatic. She did know he was covered in bruises and that he had stitches on almost every limb but Madeleine wasn't prone to dwelling on the negatives; she'd rather think he was over the worst. She sat up as Max's eyelashes flickered and whipped her hand back. She had no idea if Max was slipping in and out of consciousness or if he was just sleeping and she felt self-conscious at the thought of him hearing her banging on about how worried she'd been.

'Madeleine,' he murmured, his eyes fixed on hers.

Madeleine thought he sounded pleased to see her but she wasn't sure. 'How are you feeling?'

'Like shit,' he responded, pushing himself up on one elbow. 'I could murder a coffee.'

'I'll get you one.' Madeleine started to get to her feet.

'Stay,' Max said, grabbing her hand. She sat down again. 'Have you been here every day?' he asked, reaching out to touch her soft brown hair. Wearing a white peasant blouse dotted with red cherries and cut-off denim shorts, she was a sight for sore eyes. 'Remind me if I forget – I need to ask you about Paris.'

Madeleine blushed. 'Er, yes, I have been here every day. I know that makes me look like a stalker but I wanted to make sure you were all right.' She took out her phone. 'I sent a text to Vero and the boys but they . . .' Just then Vero poked her head round the door. Wearing black leather from head to toe

423

and flipping her long, black hair out as she removed her motorcycle helmet, she cut a vampy figure.

Madeleine stood up, feeling redundant. How could she, the epitome of the girl next door, compete with Vero?

'I heard you had an accident,' Vero mentioned coyly as she came into the room. 'Thought you might like some company.'

'I would, actually,' Max said.

Madeleine stepped back, crushed.

'I meant Madeleine's, not yours,' Max told Vero coldly, enjoying her startled expression. 'You only want to hang out with me when I'm doing something stupid, which makes me think you don't exactly have my best interests at heart.'

Vero flushed.

'I thought so. Go away, please. I'm busy.'

He held his hand out to Madeleine. As Vero flounced out of the room, Madeleine took his hand, her heart beating frantically. She felt euphoric that Max had chosen her over Vero.

'What were you saying about Paris?'

'Oh yes.' He nodded then thought better of it. His head hurt like hell. 'When I was lying here with nothing to do but let the doctors sew me back up, all I could think about was you.' He smiled at her in the most heartbreaking manner, stopping as his split lip hurt. 'Ouch! I realised you were the one who'd stood by me all through the idiotic stuff I did at college and being there when no one else was. That means a lot to me. *You* mean a lot to me.'

Madeleine melted. However mean he'd been to her in the past, none of it mattered. Not now.

Staring at her, Max realised she had very pretty eyes. 'How do you fancy coming to Paris with me? To the launch, I mean.'

'Oh, just try and stop me.' Madeleine laughed, squeezing his hand.

*

Guy went in search of Delphine and found her in her quarters. Outwardly, she seemed composed but when she turned to face him, Guy was troubled by her appearance. For the first time, he realised she was old, something he hadn't really thought about before. She was in her early seventies, hardly a spring chicken, but she had always seemed so sprightly before. There was a pile of unopened post in front of her, which was most unlike Delphine; she was efficiency personified. It was another detail that jarred.

He was worried about her. He couldn't help thinking she might be heading for a stroke or something. He couldn't possibly say such a thing to her; Delphine was known for being openly dismissive about illness which, rather like displays of emotion, she saw as a deplorable weakness. Taking the seat opposite her by the window she seemed reluctant to leave, Guy was shaken at the thought of something happening to his mother.

'I'm going to see a grief counsellor,' he blurted out, anxious to divert attention away from his concerns for her. He'd promised Max and Seraphina he would get some help and he was going ahead with it, regardless of what his mother had to say. 'I'm sure you'll think I've lost my mind and that the group will be full of weak-willed losers who should stop banging on about their emotions and just get on with it but I promised the twins. Or rather, I promised myself I would do this for them.'

Delphine inclined her snowy-white head but said nothing.

'What, no cutting comments?' Guy regarded her, feeling unnerved. As much as he detested his mother's coldness, there was a familiarity about it, a predictability that let him know he was in the critical but nonetheless close-knit bosom of his family. Without it, he felt rather like a raft abandoned by its mother ship: adrift, with no direction and no security. Guy had craved her affection pretty much all his life but he had always found reassurance in her sang-froid and practicality.

Delphine cleared her throat and sat up. 'You know how I feel about counselling, Guy.' Her querulous tone gave Guy a stab of encouragement. 'But if you feel it will help you, who am I to object?'

Guy shook his head in bemusement. 'Who are you to object? Mother, you haven't once, in all of my life, felt the need *not* to comment or object about anything. What's changed?'

Delphine glanced out of the window again. 'So many things have happened . . . so many terrible things,' she murmured, seeming distracted. 'Olivier's death was the catalyst but things have spiralled from there.' She laced her finely veined hands together. 'And I am to blame for much of it.'

Guy frowned. He wasn't used to hearing his mother take the blame for any of her actions and even though it was the right thing for her to do, again he felt unnerved by the change in her.

'I was the one who invited Yves here,' Delphine said, visibly shaking at the memory of what the man had nearly done to Seraphina. 'And what about Angelique?' Her eyes were bitter. 'I was so wrong. I thought Xavier would be pleased, that he wanted her back here. I thought he and Cat were getting too close and I wanted to put a stop to it. Why would I do such a thing, Guy? Why would I assume that I know better than my own grandson about his love life?'

Quick to reassure her, Guy did his best to sound reasonable. 'Well, we all make mistakes. Look at me. Which is why I'm trying to do something about it.'

Delphine lifted her delicate white eyebrows. 'And what shall I do about my sins, Guy? What can I do to atone for the mess I've made? Xavier is barely speaking to me. I know he returned from Morocco but he hasn't been to see me, not even for five minutes.'

426

'He's busy working on the fragrance,' Guy protested. 'I only saw him briefly myself. He said he had some business to deal with in Paris . . .'

Delphine waved a hand. 'Don't bother, Guy. I only hope he'll forgive me for inviting Angelique here. And who is that brute of a manager of hers? Mason something-or-other. He looks like a mafia boss.' She shuddered.

Guy laughed. 'I know. He says he detests Angelique but I have a feeling he's protesting too much.' His expression became more sober. 'I have a confession to make, actually.'

Delphine raised her eyebrows.

'The legal papers that would have severed all ties with Cat?' Guy's mouth twisted uneasily. 'The ones that disappeared? I . . . I shredded them.'

Expecting his mother to fire a tirade of abuse at him, he was astonished when she blinked at him before bursting into peals of laughter. She laughed so hard, she started crying and all Guy could do was sit and stare at her. He hadn't seen her laugh like this for years and even though he didn't know the reason for her mirth, he found himself joining in.

'Oh, Guy, you have no idea how funny that is.' Delphine wiped her eyes. 'You are literally the last person I would have suspected of doing that. But it all makes sense.' Her expression softened. 'She reminds you of Elizabeth?'

Guy swallowed. 'Yes, but not in the way you might think. She's beautiful, yes, but I have no feelings for her in that way. It's . . . it's more complicated than that.' He tried to put it into words. 'There's something about her, something special, and I know you don't agree but I really feel that she's changed our family for the better, that she's *saved* us, if that doesn't sound silly. The twins adore her and even Leoni is now her biggest fan.'

'And Xavier?'

Guy looked concerned. 'I'm pretty sure he's in love with her but I don't know if he's figured that out yet. What with

Angelique wafting around all over the place and no doubt enticing him into bed . . .'

'Don't.' Delphine looked crestfallen. 'What an error of judgement. I liked her so much the first time round; I thought she was a wonderful example of womanhood because she seemed so ambitious but so family oriented at the same time.' She made an impatient sound. 'Angelique reminded me of myself at her age – how egotistical! Now I realise she was simply putting on a front, playing up to my sense of family loyalty. I forgot what a talented actress she was.'

'As I said, we all make mistakes.' Guy looked sympathetic. 'I just hope it's not too late for Xavier and that he realises how amazing Cat is.'

Delphine nodded.

Guy became wistful. 'As for me, Cat was the only one who recognised I was grieving for Elizabeth, the only one, Mother. No one else noticed . . . because we're all too caught up in our own problems to be the intensely loyal, committed family we should be. The family we mistakenly thought we were.'

Delphine nodded sagely. 'I agree with you.' She saw Guy's eyes snap up in surprise. 'Oh yes, Guy, I admit I haven't been the best judge of character of late but even I have been . . . charmed by Cat and what she's done for the family.' A mischievous smile played at her lips. 'Pascal drew up a third set of papers, you know.'

'He did? Well, if they've gone missing, it wasn't me.'

Delphine smiled. 'Well, not missing exactly.' Delphine reached into the drawer of her desk and pulled out the stiff set of documents. 'I told Cat the papers hadn't arrived yet . . . I lied.'

She went pink. Hiding the legal papers hadn't been her only crime; Delphine hadn't told anyone she had taken Cat's passport for a while to bide some time. The fact that the replacement was taking so long to materialise was simply a stroke of luck, but Delphine was keeping quiet for now. 'Needs must, Guy. At least she's still here. We just need to make sure Xavier doesn't do anything silly and choose Angelique instead.' She frowned at Guy. 'He won't do that, will he?'

Guy considered. 'I don't know. Angelique is beautiful but she's so self-absorbed. I can't imagine why Xavier was attracted to her in the first place. Perhaps he really did love her once, though – which is unfortunate because it can create a very strong bond, can't it? Even years later.' Disconcertingly, Marianne Peroux flashed into his mind. Did he and Marianne have a bond? Perhaps they did. Not that it mattered; their paths were unlikely to cross now.

Delphine looked uncomfortable again. 'I wish I knew what went on between Xavier and Angelique, what secret they are hiding. I don't suppose I would have meddled if I'd known more.'

Guy swallowed, knowing he had probably pushed Xavier away when he had tried to talk about what had happened. 'I really need to go and get my head sorted out,' he sighed.

'Yes, well.' Delphine's tone became brisk and bossy once more. 'I have plenty of things to be getting on with before the Paris launch.' She flapped her hands at Guy. 'Go and do your little grief counselling thing.'

Feeling at least that some semblance of normality had been restored, Guy did as he was told and finally plucked up the courage to call a counsellor.

Chapter Twenty-Three

A few weeks later Angelique fumed as she reclined on a sun lounger. Xavier had returned from Morocco, locked himself in his lab to add the final stages to his precious fragrance and now he was off again to Paris. The launch wasn't for another few days, so what was the hurry? Angelique considered her next move as she rubbed factor fifty into her body with vigorous strokes. She never allowed herself to tan but sunbathing allowed her to flaunt her flawless body so she indulged every so often. And the June sunshine was too glorious to resist. Wearing a tiny red bikini with her blonde hair pinned up in a seemingly careless bun that Celine had spent an hour teasing into place, Angelique knew she appeared serene on the outside. On the inside, however, her mind was whirring. She had to pull off what she had set out to achieve. She had bided her time for long enough, as well as turning down many good opportunities; falling at this final hurdle just wasn't an option.

Running a hand idly down her jasmine-scented thigh, Angelique bit her full bottom lip so hard it hurt. What was Xavier playing at? Why hadn't he spoken to her when he returned from Morocco. Surely he wasn't interested in that English girl? Cat, or whatever her absurd name was, was his cousin's widow, hardly the most suitable girlfriend. Turning as she sensed someone behind her, she tutted when she saw that it was Mason. Wearing a striped brown suit despite the sweltering weather, with one of the loudest ties she'd ever seen, he looked incongruous in the grounds of La Fleurie; hot, uncomfortable and ridiculously American. Recoiling as she noticed the beads of sweat sliding off his big nose, Angelique glowered at him. His shoulders blocked out the sun.

'I could get one of those restraining orders out against you,' she snapped in English, thrusting her sunglasses up on to her nose, mostly to dim the brightness of his horrible tie. God, it was ugly! Just like Mason, she thought to herself uncharitably. He was a brute of a man and his orange and brown tie summed him up perfectly.

Mason let out a harsh laugh, his big hands making fists at his sides. 'I'm your manager, Angelique. I don't think anyone would take you seriously if you attempted something so foolish.'

'Why are you here?' Angelique hissed, sitting up suddenly, her breasts almost bursting free from her scarlet bikini top. 'This isn't just a career move; this is my personal life, and you have no business in it.'

'I should have,' Mason hit back with equal force. One of his huge hands grabbed her slender thigh and his dark eyes glittered. 'You and me, we're very alike, do you know that?'

Angelique scoffed. As if she and Mason were alike! What a hilarious notion.

'Oh yes,' Mason insisted, 'we are very much alike. You just don't want to admit it to yourself.' He tightened his grip on her thigh. 'Do you know what your problem is, *chérie*? Your problem is that you're too busy trying to be something you're not. You've got ideas above your station, you think you should be some international brand. For some reason, Angelique, you seem to be under the impression that you are a superstar others might wish to emulate.'

Angelique was so angry, she couldn't speak. How dare he speak to her like this, how *dare* he!

Undeterred by Angelique's obvious fury, Mason wasn't finished. 'You're not that person and you never will be. You're a talented actress who's been blessed with a decent face and body but you don't have the likeability factor.'

'The likeability factor?' Raging, Angelique struggled to break free of his grasp but his iron fingers had her thigh in a vice-like grip. 'Who do you think you are? Simon Cowell, or whatever his name is?' she spluttered. She glanced down at the big fingers gripping her thigh and hazily found herself wondering what it would feel like to have them touch her in a more intimate way. Disgusted with herself, she tried to prise Mason's fingers off but she wasn't strong enough.

Out of the blue, Mason grinned. 'No, I don't think I'm Simon Cowell. I'm fully aware of who I am and what I'm capable of. It's you who is delusiona, Angelique.' He let go of her thigh, his eyes staring thoughtfully at the red finger marks he'd left on her flesh. 'You're making a big mistake,' he added quietly, his softer tone somehow more disturbing than his callous one.

Angelique found she couldn't tear her eyes away from his. 'What do you mean?' She hated herself for asking but something in Mason's eyes told her he knew something. It was as if he was staring into her soul and she didn't like it one bit.

'Panting after Xavier Ducasse,' Mason spat distastefully. 'Especially when you have so much to hide.'

Angelique flushed. What did he mean? 'Xavier feels the same way about me as I do about him.' She felt a moment of disquiet deep in her stomach. Mason couldn't know . . . he couldn't possibly. Angelique felt a little faint but she blamed the heat.

Mason's expression darkened. 'You're fooling yourself if you think he feels the same way. You don't belong here, Angelique.' He gestured to the stunning grounds of La Fleurie, encompassing the lavender fields, the pool and the stables. 'You want to, desperately, but you just don't fit in. Beautiful you might be but, honey, classy and respectable you ain't.'

His words pierced her like a knife. Her jaw tightened. 'I could be.'

Wiping his sweaty brow with a gaudy handkerchief that clashed with his tie, Mason looked regretful. 'No, baby, you couldn't. You've spent years building yourself up and trying so hard to be taken seriously. You've taken roles in films you didn't want to do because you knew it would raise your profile. Your intention has always been to step away from those sorts of films at some point and be respectable. How am I doing so far?'

She stared at him with hatred in her eyes.

'Spot on, I reckon, judging by your expression,' Mason continued. 'So you've put up with the naked scenes and the dirty old men who interview you because your long-term plans have always been to come back here and finish what you started.'

Angelique couldn't speak.

Mason pointed to the beautifully shaped swimming pool and its lush surroundings. 'You think this, and the Ducasse name, will bring you the respectability you crave so badly. You think Xavier, with his "old money" and his highly regarded perfume conglomerate will put you up there with the big players. I'm right, aren't I?'

'Xavier loves me,' she muttered, wanting to strike Mason, needing to obliterate him and his cruel honesty from her life. 'The fact that he has all these other positive qualities is just . . . fortunate.'

'I think not. And by the way, you seem to have forgotten about Cat Hayes,' Mason added in a conversational tone, smoothing his expensive, pinstriped suit trousers with the flat of his hand. Having spent some considerable time at La Fleurie while Angelique shot and re-shot her photographs for the ad campaign, he had done some serious digging and he was sure he now know the score. Mason also knew how to push Angelique's buttons. 'In fact, you're so arrogant, you haven't even considered her, or how appealing she is on so many levels. But she has something you'll never have.'

'What's that? A flat chest?' Cat Hayes? What did she matter? And why did Mason saying he thought Cat was appealing feel as though he was being disloyal to her?

Mason waggled his finger at her. 'Naughty, naughty. What Cat Hayes has is that elusive likeability factor, Angelique. I've seen enough here to work out that the Ducasse family love her – all of them. Some more than others, even if they haven't figured that out yet,' he said pointedly. 'Cat fits, and you don't. It's as simple as that. And I feel for you. I've been there. You and me, we waste time thinking we're classier than we are but in the end we have to face facts.'

Looking up, Angelique flinched, expecting to see derision in his eyes. But she was wrong. What she saw in his heavy, hooded eyes was empathy. She shrank back from him, shaking. Were they really as similar as he said they were? Angelique couldn't stomach the thought. She wrapped her arms round her legs, knocked sideways by Mason's insight and accuracy. What he said made sense and yet, somehow, Angelique couldn't bring herself to let go. She had worked so hard for this, it had been her dream to shrug off her sordid past – some of which had never been made public – and be the kind of figure people would look up to and envy.

She was so close, too; she was sure Xavier had feelings for her. Angelique knew she had messed up last time but she was convinced she could win him over. She bristled. If Cat Hayes was the only thing standing in her way, she would just make damned sure she was removed from the equation, even if it meant crushing her underfoot. If not, it would be on to plan B, but Angelique would prefer to walk off with all the prizes, if she could.

Mason stood up and straightened his garish tie. 'Remember what I said, Angelique. You and me, we're the same. I know it, even if you haven't worked it out yet. And when all this,' he gestured casually at La Fleurie and its grounds, 'is snatched away from you and your dream is shattered, come and find me. I'll be waiting.' He hesitated then appeared to make a decision. 'And just in case it affects anything, I know everything there is to know about you.' Mason met her eyes unflinchingly, as if to prove he was telling the truth. 'And I mean *everything*. Your secrets are safe with me but . . .' He shrugged. 'I'll be waiting for you. Like I said.'

Angelique watched open mouthed as he strolled away. What the hell did he mean about knowing everything about her? She went cold all over. How could he? How could he know everything? Her hands were shaking and to steady them she gripped her thighs where Mason's hands had just been. No one knew all her secrets – no one living, at any rate. Her heart thumped while she tried to collect her thoughts. What to do, what to do?

Angelique faltered, straddling the line between right and wrong. In light of Mason's revelations, she knew what she should do but could she turn her back on everything she had worked so hard for? Ever since she had split up with Xavier, coming back to La Fleurie, back to respectability, had never been far from her mind or from her plans, however it might have appeared to the outside world. And if that failed, she'd be able to set up on her own and have a whole line of products with her name plastered all over them – Angelique clothes, Angelique make-up, Angelique perfume . . .

Strangely, she trusted Mason. Whatever he knew about her, she believed he wouldn't spill the beans. But what had he been trying to say to her? That even if the terrible truth came out, he would be there for her? Angelique frowned. 'I'll be waiting for you.' That's what he'd said. It was almost as if he was offering himself to her on a personal level, almost as if he had been saying that he wanted her, even if Xavier didn't.

Making a decision about which side of the metaphorical fence she sat on, Angelique stood up. Angrily throwing on a see-through black kimono, she stormed into the château with one thing in mind. She was going to find Cat Hayes and she was going to make sure the girl knew her time was up. Angelique wanted Xavier, and everything he could give her, and she wasn't giving up without a fight. If Mason thought Cat Hayes was one of the obstacles in her way, she was going to dispense with her once and for all.

Heading upstairs, she burst into Cat's room, finding her with her butterscotch-coloured hair tied up in a ponytail with a big plaster on her forehead which made her look adorably vulnerable. Mason's words rang in Angelique's ears and she fought hard not to launch herself at Cat and scratch her eyes out.

'Angelique!' Cat put a hand to her chest and wobbled on her still sore ankle. 'You frightened the life out of me.' Angelique was probably the last person she had expected to pay her a visit. Cat watched warily as Angelique strolled around the room in a predatory manner, the diaphanous kimono and tiny bikini doing little to cover her toned body.

'You're packing,' Angelique said with some satisfaction, noting that the bed was covered with clothes. A half-packed bag sat on a chair and another sat by the door, bulging and zipped up.

'Yes, for Paris,' Cat said, carefully sliding a dress into a suit bag. The silky, turquoise sheath Leoni had presented her with as a thank you for helping with the pitch carried an impressive designer label and, no doubt, an enormous price tag, but to Cat it was worth more than its monetary value. It meant Leoni had finally accepted her and Cat felt as though she'd climbed a mountain and made it down the other side. Leoni didn't allow herself to care easily so her friendship meant a great deal.

'Just for Paris?' Angelique asked sweetly, moving closer like a deadly spider sidling across its web.

Cat shrugged. 'Well, actually, my replacement passport has

finally arrived, so I guess I'll be leaving for good soon.' It hurt to think about leaving La Fleurie and the Ducasse family, but what else could she do? As soon as the legal papers turned up, she would have no reason to stay here, especially now that she had a glossy new passport. Cat knew that whatever she felt for Seraphina and Guy and Leoni, let alone for Xavier, wouldn't matter once she had formally severed ties with the family. She felt a wrench in her heart at the mere thought of it.

Angelique perched on the end of the bed, squashing a pair of Cat's shoes carelessly. 'I just mean that after Paris, there won't be much point in your coming back here. Isn't it time you went home? You are only Olivier's widow, after all. Not so important, really. He is dead and buried which makes you rather redundant.'

Feeling sick, Cat picked up the bunch of dried lavender Xavier had bought for her in Grasse. It was very faded now, just a parched bundle of herbs to anyone else. Cat gulped as she gripped them in her hand. She had finally worked out that it was Xavier who had saved her that day in the valley; it had been his strong, capable arms that had scooped her up and rescued her and his hot mouth that had claimed hers as she drifted in and out of consciousness.

In a rush, Cat remembered the words he had murmured in her ear . . . something about her being rescued for once. She had no idea what he meant. Her feelings for him were strong, as strong as they had been when they had first kissed in Grasse and after what had happened in the stables. Cat closed her eyes at the memory. It had simply proved what she had known for a long time now; she was in love with Xavier. It was inconvenient and it was inappropriate but it was the truth. She wanted him to feel the same way more than anything – and before Angelique's arrival, she had almost been convinced he did – but she had no idea what Xavier was thinking now. They had hardly spoken and the last time she had properly seen him, he had been wrapped around Angelique, kissing her. Feeling disillusioned, Cat slowly placed the bundle of lavender in her bag.

Irritated by Cat's distractedness, Angelique went in for the kill. 'You must be glad I managed to send Xavier out to save you that day,' she said, picking up one of Cat's crumpled T-shirts between her finger and thumb, then dropping it as though it was dog excrement. She lifted her large, blue eyes to Cat's. 'I told him about you dashing off after Max and he was so angry with you.'

'Angry?' Cat turned to face Angelique, feeling her stomach plummet a fraction. 'What do you mean?'

'He thought you were foolish,' Angelique continued airily, wandering round the bedroom, poking her nose into Cat's belongings. 'He said it was the most stupid idea for you to ride off in that weather when you were such an inexperienced rider. I tried to convince him that perhaps you were brave, but he wouldn't listen.'

Cat turned scarlet. Was Angelique telling the truth? Was that really what Xavier had thought? Sitting down on the bed with a bump, she wondered if she had misheard what he had said to her. Maybe he had been cross with her, maybe he had been saying that he had needed to rescue her, or something.

But the kiss? Cat put her hand to her lips. She had imagined it, she must have done. Dully, she realised Angelique was still talking but rather like the way she had heard things after the accident, it sounded as though she was underwater. Drowning, even.

'So, really, you should know you have no right to be here – not like me,' Angelique finished in a smug, confident voice. Mason's stinging words rang in her ears, giving her the impetus to crush Cat underfoot. 'I won't be packing. I belong here, with Xavier – with the Ducasse family. In fact, I am fairly certain Xavier will be making a big announcement about us at the launch.' She shot Cat a pitying stare, noting the devastation in her eyes.

'An . . . an announcement?

Angelique checked her reflection in the mirror, rearranging her Brigitte Bardot waves. 'Oh yes. And I cannot *wait* to smell this new fragrance. It was inspired by me, you know. He started to create it before I had left and now I'm back, he was able to finish it.' She turned to Cat, her eyes gleaming. 'Very romantic, don't you think?'

Cat stared at her, her heart plummeting like an out of control lift. Of course she wasn't arrogant enough to think Xavier's new-found passion or the fragrance itself had anything to do with her but to hear Angelique talking about it so confidently made her feel totally inconsequential. As Angelique had said, she was only Olivier's widow, she wasn't very important, not really . . .

Cat jumped, realising Angelique was almost in her face.

'You have outstayed your welcome. Time to leave before it becomes embarrassing, little English girl.' With that, she swept out of the room.

Aghast, Cat stared after her. Angelique was right, she didn't belong at La Fleurie. Aside from her short-lived marriage to Olivier, which would be signed away very soon, she had no reason to stay and not one claim to the Ducasse family. Feeling defeated, Cat threw everything she owned into her bag.

As hot tears pricked at her eyelids, Cat reached into the bag she had been packing for Paris. Pulling out the bunch of dried lavender, she inhaled its sweet, dusty aroma one last time before dropping the whole thing into the bin. She closed her eyes, feeling the loss of Xavier acutely. But she knew she needed to be strong. After Paris, she was going to have to go home and forget about Xavier and the Ducasse family. So it was about time she started cutting ties, Cat thought shakily, wishing the thought didn't make her feel so destroyed.

*

In her nearby apartment, Leoni, too, was packing for Paris. Hearing the doorbell ring, she hurried to the door and signed for the special delivery from Stefan. Leoni opened the package with fumbling fingers and drew the photographs out nervously. Holding them up to the light, she gasped.

They were spectacular, better than she had expected. Checking each one in detail, her excitement mounting as she did so, Leoni knew she had created something incredible. Each photograph showed a slightly different angle or subtle change in position but they were all sensational. The new location, the natural light – everything about the photographs was right this time. They showcased the new fragrance beautifully and the images personified Xavier's brief, bringing his vision to life with heart-stopping vividness.

Xavier was going to be delighted, Leoni thought tremulously, slipping the photographs back into the envelope. She was sure she had done the right thing. Xavier hadn't said much but she knew he hadn't been happy about the photographs of Angelique. She assumed he would have instructed them to be changed if he'd had the time but he was far too busy finalising the perfume and sorting out whatever else he felt needed his urgent attention.

Leoni paused for a moment, wondering what Xavier was up to in Paris. And what would happen when he spoke to Ashton? Ignoring the stab of pain in her heart, she told herself not to think about Ashton any more. The trouble was, every time she closed her eyes, a vision of Marianne in Ashton's arms and Ashton's hands all over her voluptuous body crept into view. Leoni couldn't bear it.

Leoni looked up as the doorbell rang again. Frowning, she opened the door. Jerard stood there, his arms full of brightly coloured packages. He had a slight tan and he was wearing a new, well-cut suit which emphasised his shoulders and his lean physique.

'Long time no see,' he said in a cheerful voice, leaning in for a kiss. Somehow, Leoni moved her head slightly and he got a mouthful of hair.

'Er, come in,' Leoni said, standing aside.

'Thanks.' Jerard placed his parcels on a nearby table. 'Just a few things from Japan,' he explained. 'To make up for not being here for so long.' He glanced at her wrist. 'I see you're wearing your bracelet. I picked that out especially.'

Leoni gave him a brief smile. She had no doubt the gifts he'd bought her would be extravagant as well as thoughtful but she had no desire to tear the paper off and investigate. 'I'd rather we just spent some time together,' she said, feeling foolish for sounding so needy.

'Oh, me too,' Jerard said, gathering her up into his arms. 'I've missed you, more than you can imagine. Mmmm, you smell so good.'

Leoni lifted her face to his. He had a knack of saying all the right things, but she felt unmoved. 'My home fragrance pitch went really well,' she said, feeling the need to keep the conversation business-focused now that her slightly emotional comment had slipped out.

Jerard smiled down at her. 'You said in your text. I'm so happy for you, you must be elated.'

'I am … I was.' She felt his hands moving up and down her back and wondered why the gesture was leaving her cold. 'I just … it would have been nice to celebrate it together at the time.'

'I know. But we can still do that,' Jerard said, flipping open his new iPhone. 'Let me check my diary.'

Leoni sighed and extricted herself from his grasp.

'Something wrong?' he asked, noting her pained expression.

She nodded. 'I'm afraid so. I think I owe you an apology.'

'An apology? Why?'

'Because I think I've given you the wrong impression,' Leoni confessed honestly. She gestured to the sofa and sat down, waiting until Jerard took a seat next to her. 'When we first met, I was totally focused on business and so were you. I think that was why we were attracted to one another.'

Jerard's brow knitted together. 'Well, it was one of the reasons,' he commented jokily.

'Yes, of course.' Leoni felt uncomfortable. 'But I've realised as the weeks have passed that other things are important to me too – relationships, romance.' She felt herself blushing. She wasn't used to talking about such things.

Jerard nodded, seemingly unperturbed.

Leoni pushed ahead. 'It's just that . . . I love your business ethic, Jerard, don't get me wrong. But I need some of your time, too.'

'Quite right. And in three weeks' time, my diary is looking free, so we can arrange something for then.' He gave her a bright smile.

Three weeks' time? Was he serious? 'What about the launch of the new store in Paris?' she asked in confusion. 'I invited you . . . you said you were coming.'

Jerard looked awkward. 'Ah, yes, Paris. Look, Leoni, I'm really sorry but an opportunity has come up in the States and I really can't turn my back on it. I need to leave tonight, unfortunately, but we'll meet up as soon as I'm back. Or you can join me?' he suggested suddenly. 'I'll be in meetings most of the time but I might have the odd evening off.'

Leoni stood up sadly. 'Jerard, that's not good enough. I want more ...'

He gave her a genial smile. 'Of course you do. And you'll get it, I promise. It's just that this deal is so important . . .'

'They're all important!' Leoni interrupted. 'Rightly so; it's your company.' She slid the diamond bracelet off and placed it gently in Jerard's hands. 'But I can't do this any more. I need a one-woman man who worships the ground I walk on . . . or at least puts me first.' She realised with a start that she was echoing Xavier's recent words, which reminded her of something else he'd said, the comment about Ashton being in love with someone for ages. Leoni brought her mind back to Jerard. 'I'm so sorry. I was having doubts before, but now . . .' She shook her head. 'It's made it easier for me to do this, that's all.'

'Why is Paris such a big deal?' Jerard asked, getting to his feet and pacing the room. 'I know I said I'd come but things come up where business is involved; you know that as well as I do.'

She nodded sadly. 'That's true. But sometimes, sacrifices have to be made.' An ugly image of Ashton and Marianne flashed into her head and Leoni pushed it away. 'This launch in Paris is really important to me, to my family. I really wanted you to be there and you know that.' She reached up and kissed his cheek.

Jerard let out a sigh. 'What a shame,' he said heavily. 'I really thought we had something special.'

'Me too.' Leoni bowed her head. 'And you're lovely, you really are. You're just . . . not for me.'

'Is there someone else?' he asked roughly. 'I hate to ask but you seem so detached.'

Leoni's mouth twitched at the irony of it all. 'No. You were the only person I ever made time for.' She hadn't even given Ashton as much courtesy and he was her best friend. Was, being the operative word, Leoni told herself sadly.

Jerard looked disbelieving. 'I think you're fooling yourself,' he told her not unkindly. Seeing her eyes widen, he smiled. 'You don't even realise it yourself but think about it. There's someone you talk about constantly, whether it's to say you spent time with him or to say you miss him.' Jerard pressed the diamond bracelet into her hands. 'Keep it, please. I bought it for you and I want you to have it. But if you really want to sort out your personal life, you need to face up to what you've been avoiding. I'm so sorry it didn't work out between us.' With that, Jerard gave her one last kiss and left.

Leoni stared after him. What on earth was he on about? Who did she talk about constantly? Ashton, at one time, maybe, but that was to be expected, they had been close friends. Jerard had it all wrong if he thought her feelings for him ran deeper than that, Leoni thought.

Grabbing her phone, she remembered that she had a million and one things to do before she left for Paris. She'd think about Jerard's bizarre ramblings when she got there.

Sitting in his hotel room in Paris with a photocopy in his hand, Xavier was trembling with anger. Even though he had feared he knew the truth, it was totally different when he had the actual facts in his hands. Tracking down the information he had been after had been a thankless task and had involved sifting through endless paperwork with no idea of specific timescales. But he had got there in the end. Every fibre of his being had been hoping Matthieu and Rene, the Moroccan hotel owner, had been mistaken. But here it was, in stark black and white. The evidence was in front of him and it was truly sickening. With a heavy heart, Xavier realised how wrong he'd been about certain people. Not only was the evidence he held in his hand damning on a personal level, it was going to impact on the family greatly. Just as they all thought their problems concerning inheritance and claims to the family perfume business were over, it was about to start all over again. And Xavier had a feeling that this time around, it wouldn't be anywhere near as easy to resolve.

Xavier walked and smoked, needing to clear his head. He had decided to stay at the Four Season's George V Hotel rather than imposing on Ashton. He was heading for Ashton's apartment on the off chance he might be there but decided to go straight to the store instead. When he arrived, he found sheets hanging over the front, keeping it hidden from nosy onlookers. Inside, builders were shouting at each other as they banged and crashed loudly. Ashton was outside on the phone, speaking in painfully slow French. He was bright red in the face and about to blow a gasket.

'What's the problem?' Xavier asked, shaking his hand quickly. Ashton didn't look his usual happy self. His cornflower-blue eyes were dull and listless and his hair was all over the place. He was wearing a grubby polo shirt that had seen better days and judging by the paint spatters all over his jeans, he had been helping out with the painting in the store, as well as everything else. Xavier was fairly certain architects didn't usually do such things but he guessed Ashton had become more personally involved in developing the Ducasse perfume store than he would in other projects.

'Thank *God*,' Ashton cried in relief as soon as he saw Xavier. He knew he was being dramatic but he couldn't help it. 'What are you doing here so early? Fuck, I don't care. Can you help me? Please?'

He'd been trying to speak to the caterers about the launch party for the past thirty minutes and the joker on the phone seemed to think it was highly amusing to misunderstand everything he said in his atrocious French. Ashton didn't have time to deal with caterers; if the builders didn't get a move on, the launch wasn't even going to happen. Having worked his nuts off on this building, he was buggered if he was going to let a cocky catering assistant mess him around. Explaining the issue to Xavier briefly, Ashton handed his phone over and clutched his hair in genuine frustration.

'This is Xavier Ducasse,' Xavier said smoothly, his eyes meeting Ashton's in amusement as the idiot on the other end of the phone quaked in his boots. He sorted out all the catering woes in a few minutes and handed Ashton's phone back. 'The power of the Ducasse name,' he said wryly.

'Some people are so xenophobic.' Ashton grinned in relief.

'Some people need to learn to speak French properly,' Xavier retorted with an equally wide grin. How Ashton could survive in Paris with his excruciatingly slow French was beyond him. For a moment he had forgotten what he'd just discovered but as it all came flooding back, Xavier also remembered what Leoni had said to him before he had left for Paris.

'Hey, I have a message from Leoni for you.'

'You do?' Ashton looked both fearful and full of hope at the same time.

'She asked me to ask you how you acquired the building,' Xavier said. He held his hands up. 'I haven't a clue what she was getting at.'

Ashton groaned. 'Xavier, you have no idea what's been going on.' Quickly he outlined what had happened since he'd last seen him.

Xavier whistled. 'You did that . . . you did all that, for Leoni? That's serious, Ash.'

Ashton nodded, miserably picking at the paint splodges on his jeans. 'You don't have to tell me, I know I'm a mug. An idiot,' he added, seeing Xavier's frown of confusion. 'A plonker, a moron . . . *un cretin fini*, as you would say.'

'Don't be daft; that's not what I meant at all. I mean, have you told her you did that for her?'

Ashton shook his head. 'I didn't get a chance to. She came here to see me apparently, but she spoke to Marianne and that was it; she was off.' He scowled. 'I don't know if Marianne said something awful because she's been avoiding my calls but, whatever, Leoni doesn't want to speak to me. And what does it matter, Xav? She doesn't care about me.'

Xavier felt sorry for him. He knew exactly how Ashton felt – the feeling of happiness, both present and future, being crushed underfoot was pretty demoralising.

'What you've done is the most romantic thing in the world,' he told Ashton honestly. 'No woman could resist it, not even Leoni. Be honest with her, Ash. Go after the woman you love. If you feel that strongly about her, what have you got to lose? Are you really sure she doesn't want to speak to you?'

Ashton rubbed his hands across his eyes. 'It hurts like hell but what can I do? I haven't a hope with her – Olivier told me that much.'

Xavier took his cigarettes out again. 'Are you sure Olivier was telling the truth when he put you off Leoni all those years ago?'

Ashton stared at him. 'What do you mean?'

'Just that Olivier could be an absolute shit when he thought he might not be the most important person in the world to the people he was close to.' Xavier shrugged. 'I've often wondered if he kept both of you apart all those years ago. A word in your ear, a word in Leoni's – that's all it would have taken.'

Ashton turned white. 'Don't even . . . Are you saying Leoni had feelings for me back then?'

Xavier lit a cigarette. Was he meddling? Or was he simply undoing a great wrong that Olivier had committed? 'Leoni was head over heels for you at one time,' he admitted. 'She was so in love with you, she barely knew what to do with herself and Olivier told her you wouldn't fancy her in a million years. He said . . . oh, I can barely remember now . . . that you preferred leggy redheads or something.'

'He . . . he did *what*?' Ashton was horrified. 'But he . . . he told me Leoni wouldn't fancy *me* in a million years. He said I wasn't her type because she only dated rich Frenchmen.'

Xavier shook his head. 'That's rubbish, Ash. See, I was right. Olivier was just jealous that the two of you might end up together. He was worried he wouldn't be number one to either of you any more.'

Ashton put his hand over his mouth. He felt sick, physically sick. 'I can't believe it. He was my best friend! How could he do that to me? To Leoni?' He raked his hand through his dusty hair. 'It's too late now, though. It's all gone tits up. It's all gone wrong.'

Xavier frowned. 'Listen, you're not the only one in a mess,' he said, to make Ashton feel better. 'Olivier was a bastard keeping you and Leoni apart, I grant you, but wait until you

447

hear this.' Baldly stating the facts to save time, he outlined what he was doing in Paris and what he'd discovered.

Ashton looked flabbergasted. He rubbed his stubbly chin. 'Fucking hell, Xav. That's going to . . .'

'Cause a whole set of new problems?' Xavier sucked on his cigarette. 'Tell me about it.' His expression was dour. 'And I still haven't spoken to Cat yet. Or Angelique.'

'Everything will be all right, won't it?' Ashton asked worriedly. His own situation was dire enough; he hated the thought of Xavier ending up a miserable, whinging git as well. If Olivier was here right now, Ashton knew he'd punch him square in the face but as he was never going to have that satisfaction, he'd just have to figure out if he could salvage anything.

Xavier blew smoke into the air anxiously, his head in just as much of a spin as Ashton's. Quite honestly, he had no idea how any of it was going to pan out. Right now, he was pissing in the wind and he knew it.

Feeling thoroughly uncomfortable, Guy knocked on the door of the house. He was certain he'd got the wrong address; he'd been expecting a grief counselling centre, not a pretty little cottage on the outskirts of Mougins.

The door opened and a grey-haired lady with a motherly smile greeted him. 'I'm Elena. Do come in.'

'I'm Guy Du—'

'No surnames needed,' she interrupted him with twinkling eyes. If she recognised him, she wasn't letting on. 'Just Guy is fine.' She led him through to a sun-drenched salon, which was set up as a sitting room, with chairs and tables and refreshments on a simple, bare-wood dresser. A glass conservatory was attached to the side of the room.

Guy watched Elena as she bustled through the room, nodding at couples chatting and saying the odd word. Wearing a long green sundress with bejewelled flip-flops, Elena looked to be around fifty. It was only her grey hair that gave away that she might be older but she clearly wasn't bothered about such things as hair dye. She was attractive but not self-consciously so and she looked more like a teacher than a grief counsellor.

Not that he had met many of those, Guy acknowledged to himself. Nervously, he ran a hand through his silver hair, not sure if he might look as though he had tried too hard with his appearance.

'Coffee?' Elena offered, holding a pot up.

Guy nodded and looked round the room. To his surprise, it wasn't full of sad bastards crying into their cups, nor was anyone expected to stand up and talk about themselves, by the looks of things. That wasn't to say there was a party atmosphere; some serious conversations were taking place and there were a few scrunched-up, soggy tissues in evidence. But the overwhelming sense Guy had was one of calm. The room, the garden it overlooked, Elena herself, everything was warm and comforting. He was relieved to find that he wasn't remotely attracted to Elena; he didn't want to get emotionally attached to her, he just wanted her help.

'Not what were you expecting?' Elena asked astutely, handing him a cup of coffee and gesturing to the milk and sugar. 'Some sort of Alcoholics Anonymous set-up, where we all make you stand in the middle of the room and say "I'm Guy and I'm upset because so-and-so died"?'

Taken aback, Guy raised his eyebrows. 'Well, yes.' He met Elena's eyes, seeing wisdom in them – that and a whole lot of living.

'Ah, well, hopefully you'll see that making people perform isn't what counselling is all about.' Helping herself to a coffee before leading him to a sunny corner and curling up on a chair, Elena fixed her eyes on him. 'So, who did you lose? Your wife?'

Smiling at her directness, Guy gave her a brief outline. Maybe it was because he had made peace with himself about coming here or perhaps it was because he had almost lost Max, but talking about Elizabeth suddenly didn't seem so painful. He spent the next thirty minutes talking about her, without even noticing how much time had slid past. Reaching the part where he was about to talk about letting his children down and realising he had been totally dominating the conversation, Guy came to an abrupt halt.

'Sorry, I can't believe I've been talking for so long!' He felt faintly embarrassed, even though he had enjoyed reminiscing. He only usually waxed lyrical about business; discussing Elizabeth and his relationship was something he had avoided since her death.

'Don't stop,' Elena urged him gently. 'You were saying about your children . . .'

Guy hesitated. How could he own up to his appalling behaviour? What would Elena think of him if he told her what he'd put his children through over the past few years? About to tell Elena coming here had been a big mistake, he felt her hand gently patting his arm.

'No judgements here,' she assured him. Her expression became sombre. 'When my beloved husband died ten years ago, I had a nervous breakdown and walked out on my job and my children while I went on a grief-stricken, self-destructive ride to hell. It's not something I'm proud of but it's something I'm now able to use to help others because I know how it feels to be swimming around in anguish, utterly unable to do anything but get through a day until blessed sleep comes around again.' She eyed Guy with understanding. 'I loved him so much, you see. So, so much.'

Guy nodded, biting his lip as tears threatened to fall. Thinking about Elizabeth again and how much he had loved her, he was almost undone. He felt so guilty about his children too, so thoroughly ashamed.

'You should know that we . . . my family . . . are all back together,' Elena went on. 'It's taken some time and I know you think they won't forgive you but they will. Trust me, in my experience, almost anything that's broken can be mended and put back together. You'd be surprised.'

Deeply affected by her honesty and courage, Guy stared down into his empty coffee cup. Forcing himself, he started to talk again in a halting whisper, lifting his eyes as he recounted his life After Elizabeth, the capital letters very much in evidence as he said it out loud. Continuing with brutal frankness, Guy began to realise that owning up to what he was feeling was half the battle. And frankly, he thought, if Elena could do it after what she had been through, then so could he.

It was early evening, an hour before they were due to leave. Seraphina found Cat listlessly staring out across the lavender fields.

'I just had a text from my friend Bella,' Cat said, sounding flat.

Seraphina frowned. 'And?'

'And I think she might be moving to Australia with her boyfriend Ben.'

'Sounds like fun.'

Cat nodded. 'I'm going to miss her, that's all. I haven't seen her for ages and now she's leaving.' Her voice caught in her throat.

Seraphina gave her a sympathetic smile. 'Are you all packed and ready for Paris?' Dressed in a pretty pink strapless dress and heels, Seraphina seemed strangely fidgety and Cat glanced at her, suddenly noticing how smart she looked.

'Paris?' She shrugged, glancing back at the view. Apart from a slight breeze, it was a perfect day – weather-wise, at any rate. It was sunny, warm and the air was dry and still. She wanted to remember La Fleurie this way forever when she'd left . . . drenched in July sunshine, the lavender fields were a dazzling display of violet, purple and lilac. Cat swallowed and spoke again. 'I've always wanted to see the Eiffel Tower. I know it sounds touristy but it's one of those things you want to do before you die, isn't it? Well, it is for me, anyway.'

Deep down, Cat was absolutely gutted. She'd always wanted to go to Paris but not like this. The trouble was, she couldn't think of a valid reason to back out. Saying she felt the whole experience would be too hurtful wasn't going to cut it. Not unless she admitted how she felt about Xavier, and that wasn't going to happen.

'The Eiffel Tower is all right.' Seraphina wrinkled her nose. 'Personally, I think it's a bit phallic.'

Not in the mood for jokes, Cat didn't laugh. 'It's just one of those iconic, romantic places you see in movies and want to see close up.'

'So why aren't you doing a jig, then?' Seraphina frowned at Cat's outfit. She wasn't sure cut-off trousers and a vest top were appropriate attire for what they were about to do.

'Well, I'm pleased for Leoni, she's been dreaming about this shop for years. And Xavier . . . the new fragrance will be a triumph, I'm sure.'

'You'll be around to see it, won't you? After Paris, I mean?' Seraphina was confused. 'You're coming back to La Fleurie – you must be.'

Cat shook her head. 'I don't think so. What's here for me now? I need to go back home and stop outstaying my welcome.' Unconsciously echoing Angelique's words, Cat felt no bitterness about it; she just felt sad. Inexplicably, painfully sad.

Seraphina spun her round. 'Er, me, Max, Father, Leoni. And, most importantly, Xavier. You must know how he feels about you!'

'Apparently, he thinks I'm an idiot for dashing after Max the way I did,' Cat responded crabbily. 'Foolish, I think the word was.'

'Really? He said that?' Seraphina's brown eyes were puzzled.

'I can't believe he would have said such a thing. Who told you that? Did Xavier tell you?'

Cat couldn't be bothered to explain that it was Angelique. She stared out at the gorgeous view she wouldn't be seeing ever again after they left for Paris.

'You do know Xavier hasn't been on a horse since our mother died?' Seraphina announced, knowing she had to do something drastic to change Cat's mind about leaving. Cat slowly turned to face Seraphina, her aquamarine eyes lighting up just a fraction.

'That's right,' Seraphina continued emphatically. 'He swore blind he'd never get on a horse's back again after our mother's death but as soon as he heard you were in danger, he tore down to the stables and didn't even think twice about it.'

'He was probably going after Max,' Cat said, refusing to feel hopeful. After the chat with Angelique, there seemed little point. 'It probably had nothing to do with me at all.'

Seraphina shook her head. 'No, sorry. He was going after you. The emergency services had already been called by my father and they were heading towards Max. Xavier came after you, honestly.'

'Why did Angelique tell Xavier I was out there?'

'Angelique?' Seraphina scoffed. 'She didn't tell him! My father told him after he'd had a stiff drink. He suddenly remembered you'd chased after Max and Xavier dropped everything and left.'

'But Angelique said . . . she said . . .' Cat was reeling. Her heart leapt but she didn't want it to. It felt too bruised to be put through the wringer again.

'Oh, don't believe anything that nasty old witch told you!' Seraphina said, checking her watch. 'I think you have time to change so we'd better get a move on.'

'Change? Why?' Cat glanced down at her outfit. 'I want to be comfy on the plane. I was going to change when I got there.'

Seraphina burst out laughing. 'We're not going on easyJet, you know! You can change when we get there but you can't wear that on the private jet. Well, you can but you might feel a bit silly.'

Cat's mouth fell open. 'The what?'

Seraphina took her arm. 'You know we're rich, right? Well, over there in that hangar is a private jet.'

Cat couldn't help smiling. Of course they had a private jet! 'Is . . . Angelique coming with us?' she asked, feeling the need to prepare herself.

Seraphina scoffed. 'Of course not! She's making her own way there because she's a total diva. Anyway, you'll want to look smart because we're staying in the George V,' she finished, grinning as Cat's mouth fell open again.

Allowing Seraphina to drag her upstairs to get changed, Cat's mind was working overtime. What else had Angelique lied about? Were any of her spiteful statements true? What about the 'big announcement' she said Xavier was going to make?

Cat gazed at her reflection as Seraphina hurriedly pulled out dresses for her to try. She had no idea what was true and what wasn't any more but suddenly, all that mattered was seeing Xavier face to face and talking about it, whatever the outcome.

'Hair up, I think,' Seraphina suggested helpfully as she eased a white linen dress over Cat's head. She quickly pinned up her tresses and covered Cat's head in swirls of hairspray, hoping the simple but elegant chignon would last the night.

Cat shivered in anticipation. This was it; everything was riding on this trip to Paris.

The rest of the family were already aboard the private jet as Cat and Seraphina hurried past the lavender fields to join them.

Chapter Twenty-Four

On the short flight, Max and Madeleine sat together, chatting and listening to music. Max was still sporting an impressive bruise on his head, but a besotted Madeleine seemed oblivious. Seraphina sat across from them, drumming her fingers restlessly on the arms of her seat and leaning over to stare out of the window every so often. She clearly had something on her mind but whatever it was she was keeping it to herself, even though it looked as though it was killing her not to spill the beans.

Watching her, Cat had felt a moment of disquiet. Was Seraphina back in touch with Yves? Surely not; Cat was certain Seraphina had learnt her lesson. No, whatever was causing her to wriggle against her seat belt like a puppy straining at its leash had nothing to do with smarmy older men.

Anxiously, Cat glanced at Guy. Seemingly lost in his own world, he sat beside Delphine, staring into space but with a peaceful expression on his face. He was wearing a debonair silver-grey suit with a white shirt and baby-pink tie, and the black smudges beneath his eyes seemed to be fading and the taut line of his shoulders seemed more relaxed. He'd confided in her that he was attending grief counselling and she thought it was brave of him to finally confront his demons. Cat hoped it worked for him.

Guy was preoccupied but he was also calm for the first time in over two years. He had seen Elena on several occasions now and his head felt clear and focused. It was amazing how talking about his grief made it seem manageable somehow; how openly admitting how shitty he'd been feeling had made him feel so much lighter.

Glancing out of the window as the jet circled Charles de Gaulle airport, Guy remembered the most significant thing Elena had told him. Fixing her wise, kindly eyes on him, she'd told him that when he was ready to love again, he'd know. And she had said that when he did, he should also prepare himself for something new, instead of trying to replace Elizabeth. And even though Guy was sure he wouldn't be ready to date anyone for a long time, the relief at hearing that he shouldn't measure any other woman against Elizabeth had been huge. For some reason, Guy had assumed that if he could even bring himself to be with anyone else, the woman would seem a poor second to his beloved wife. He hadn't realised that part of his healing process was letting go of the perfect memory he had created of Elizabeth. And that when he was ready, it was all right to allow someone totally different into his life.

Not that this was about meeting someone new, Guy told himself. He had a long way to go before he was ready for that. Giving Cat a heartfelt smile, he hoped his gratitude towards her was obvious because without her suggestion that counselling might work for him, he was sure he wouldn't be on the road to recovery. Cat returned Guy's smile and nodded to Delphine. She was taken aback to detect the ghost of a smile on the old lady's face. My God, Delphine had looked almost friendly for a second! The smile slipped away but her eyes remained friendly. Effortlessly elegant, Delphine looked the epitome of the stylish older woman in a sparkling, oyster-coloured suit with a floor-length skirt and a fitted jacket with a stand-up collar that made the most of her fabulous diamond earrings and pretty make-up.

Perplexed but secretly delighted by the warmth in Delphine's eyes, Cat stole a glance at Leoni and realised she was clutching the armrests and biting all her red lipstick off.

'It'll be all right,' Cat assured her, reaching out to squeeze her hand. Cat didn't know what had gone on in Paris with Ashton but Leoni seemed very upset by it. She had also mumbled that she had finished with Jerard, but oddly she didn't seem overly bothered about that. She seemed far more distraught about her trip to Paris and Cat couldn't help wondering if Leoni had finally figured out she felt more for Ashton than just friendship.

Thinking about Xavier briefly, Cat felt her stomach flip over. Angelique's venomous words were still clear in her head but the woman clearly had her own agenda – basically, getting Xavier back – so Cat realised she shouldn't trust her. But Xavier had made no effort to clear the air with her when he had returned from Morocco and Paris – at least, not that Cat was aware of.

But he had ridden after her and he had kissed her. Or had he? Cat gave up. She wouldn't know what the situation was until she saw Xavier again and had a chance to talk to him.

Paris looked gorgeous in the early evening sunshine as the private jet touched down on the concourse. Unclipping her seat belt, Cat followed the Ducasse family out and they all ducked into waiting limos. At the George V, Cat gaped at her stunning room, charmingly named the 'Suite Anglaise'. It was large enough for six and came with elegant columns and a four-poster bed. It was on the seventh floor and it had a balcony overlooking the Marble Courtyard.

Cat quickly changed into the beautiful turquoise dress Leoni had treated her to and touched up her make-up. She caught sight of an envelope on the bed. It was addressed to her and when she opened it, she found a stiff card inside with the hotel motif at the top. In handwriting she recognised as Xavier's, she read: 'Not everything is as it seems. Trust me. Xavier.'

Cat stared at it. What on earth did that mean? Wishing Xavier would sometimes just talk to her, she grabbed her handbag. She stuffed the card inside it as an afterthought and went downstairs to meet the family. They were driven to the shop in the limos. Cat tried to take in the sights as they whisked past the window but she only really got a good look at the Champs-Élysées, which was lit up majestically.

At the shop, Cat and the Ducasse family gasped in unison as they climbed out of their limos. The front was lit up with discreet spotlights that played on bottles of perfume positioned on white columns of different heights. The beams of light picked out the silvery glass and ornate stoppers, and swathes of rich, deep purple satin were draped luxuriantly around the base of the perfume bottles. Cat tried to get a glimpse of the name of the fragrance but it was out of view and the perfume bottles were too far away to see. A matching dark purple carpet reached from the open door to the pavement edge, which was lined with photographers. Behind barriers and security men a crowd of fans jostled to hold up phones and cameras to get shots of the celebrities.

As Cat joined the guests in their dinner jackets and brightly coloured couture gowns, she was suddenly very grateful for the shimmering turquoise sheath dress Leoni had bought her and that Seraphina had worked her magic with her hair. She could see the Hollywood actor Delphine had invited to the party at the château to her left, his arm loosely round his gorgeous wife's shoulders (he in Armani Privé and diamonds, she head to toe in Chanel and sapphires) as well as a former president and a bunch of young, trendy French, American and English celebrities recognisable from films, pop groups and billboards.

Not for the first time, Cat realised how well connected the Ducasse family were. This was essentially the opening of a new perfume store, yet the purple carpet outside resembled Leicester Square at a major box office premiere.

The shop was jaw-droppingly gorgeous inside, classy and upmarket. It felt both spacious and intimate at the same time.

The finish was superb and it felt like an Aladdin's cave, full of must-have fragrance and goodies. Billboards, covered with yet more purple fabric, hung from the high ceilings and sat propped up on different surfaces. A screen had been set up at the back, presumably to play the new advert for Xavier's fragrance and the air was thick with expectation.

Max immediately grabbed glasses of champagne for himself and Madeleine. Guy and Delphine pretended not to notice. They were fairly sure Max had calmed down sufficiently enough not to have to be monitored like a child and it was only a glass of champagne, after all. As far as Guy was concerned, and on Elena's advice, Max would obviously benefit from some fatherly guidance but he could also do with some freedom as an adult. Guy planned to ask him what he wanted to do about college and careers later on, and he fully intended to listen to whatever Max had to say. Seraphina, looking more serene than she had in a long time, was resolutely ignoring the champagne and the mouth-watering canapés that were doing the rounds. Instead, she simply stood at the back of the shop and watched everything that was going on.

Cat glanced at Leoni. She was dressed in a navy silk dress with a plunging neckline and a long skirt and she looked pale and thin. She was wearing contact lenses, which seemed to make her brown eyes look huge, but she looked fragile, as though she could faint at any moment.

'Leoni, do you think you should eat something? You look awfully pale,' Cat commented worriedly.

Leoni shook her head, her shiny brown bob grazing her chin. 'I'm fine,' she said, sounding anything but.

'Is it how you imagined it?' Cat asked, knowing this must be momentous for her. After all, this store had been her dream.

Leoni smiled sadly, noting Jerard's exquisite candles sitting stacked up on a curved shelf. 'Better,' she asserted. 'The light in here, it's wonderful. And the way the counters have been designed, well, they are just perfect for the products. It's as though Ashton knows me inside out . . .' Her voice faded.

About to ask Leoni about Ashton, Cat caught sight of the name of the fragrance as a celebrity moved out of the way and exposed an enormous billboard by the till area. 'La Spontanéité', it said, in purple, swirly writing. And underneath: 'L'Amour . . . Le Risque . . . La Spontanéité . . .' Love, risk, spontaneity. Cat sucked in her breath. Romantic spontaneity, a notion Cat had cited as a way to live life and one Xavier had defensively rejected, at the time. Cat didn't dare hope that the name of the new fragrance meant anything.

Ashton appeared in the store from the flat above. Cat saw Leoni swallow and meet his blue eyes. They stared at each other in agonised silence. Breaking the tension, Leoni moved out of his line of vision and slipped behind a group of anorexic models. Hearing a commotion at the door, Cat turned to see what was happening.

Xavier had arrived. Resembling one of the many celebrities milling around, he looked devastatingly handsome in a discreetly expensive black dinner suit with a snow-white shirt and an undone black silk tie around his neck. The light played on his tanned face for a moment as he stood in the doorway, highlighting his arrogant nose and the wide, sexy mouth that was curved into a polite smile. His sleepy-looking, chocolate-brown eyes slid around the store as though he was looking for someone and then they came to rest on Cat. She almost felt he was trying to say something to her but then she saw something that made any hope she might be feeling dissolve.

Behind Xavier but very clearly with him was Angelique, wearing a racy dress in her favourite shade of scarlet, killer heels and an extremely smug smile. From the way she was clutching him possessively, Cat was pretty sure they'd been glued together in the limo all the way from the hotel to the store.

Feeling very much as though she was going to be sick, Cat

realised the tag line on the billboard meant nothing. Or maybe Xavier did feel that way about life now, but very evidently he didn't feel that way about *her*. Cat bit her lip, forcing back the tears. She must have imagined the kiss after he had rescued her and any hopes she had been harbouring about him were clearly foolish, just an embarrassing fantasy. Forgetting about the message Xavier had given her on the card in her handbag and unable to stomach the sight of Angelique smirking and cosying up to Xavier any longer, Cat looked round for the nearest exit.

'Ashton.' Marianne slid her arms round him and made him jump.

'Marianne!' Ashton frowned and extricated himself from her grasp. Glancing over his shoulder, he wondered if Leoni had witnessed Marianne's overly flirtatious greeting. He sincerely hoped not, although it probably didn't matter anyway as Leoni obviously wasn't speaking to him. Ashton sighed. He was consumed with regret; it was probably far too late for him and Leoni now. What a mess, he thought. Talk about bad timing. It was like that film, *Sliding Doors*. Except that the main characters in the film hadn't been manipulated by a spoilt, self-indulgent idiot like Olivier, Ashton thought angrily.

'You're not even invited,' he told Marianne when he'd pulled himself together.

She smirked. 'I know, isn't it delicious? But, chéri, I had to come, you must know that.' Wearing an emerald-green suit with a knee-length skirt and a jacket with a nipped-in waist and peplum edge, Marianne looked every inch the successful businesswoman she was. The colour complemented her long russet hair which was loose except for a pretty comb to one side. The well-cut suit made the most of her full curves, leaving little to the imagination. She eyed Ashton hungrily, regretting that things hadn't become more intimate between them. He really was quite a catch.

Ashton courteously handed Marianne a glass of champagne. 'Guy Ducasse. That's why you're here.'

She pulled a face. 'Some people get under your skin, don't they?'

Ashton stared at Leoni. 'Don't I know it,' he murmured. He wanted to go to her, to talk to her. She looked so thin and pale, he wanted to gather her up protectively and never let her go again. He wondered if she had broke up with Jerard but refused to feel hopeful about the prospect. If it had caused her to look so horribly ill, he would rather that wasn't the reason, even if it meant his love for her going unrequited indefinitely.

Ashton downed his glass of champagne in one go, wishing things were different.

Marianne's teeth gnawed at her bottom lip. Feeling uncharacteristically uncomfortable, she battled with herself. God, is this what it's like to have a conscience? she thought irritably. She came to a decision. 'I . . . have a confession to make,' she informed Ashton rather grandly, feeling cross with herself. Did she really have to do this?

Ashton wasn't listening. All he could think about was how achingly vulnerable Leoni looked with her fragile collarbone exposed in the deep V of the navy dress. Marianne, however, had made an unprecedented decision to be truthful, so she insisted on being heard. 'There was a day some while back when Leoni Ducasse visited you here at the shop.'

'I know. What do you think all the texts you've ignored have been about?' Ashton glanced at her impatiently.

'Yes, well. I need to tell you something about it.' Marianne squirmed as she felt his cornflower-blue eyes boring into her intently. 'I may have . . . misled Leoni somewhat.'

Ashton felt his stomach lurch. 'What have you done?' He knew that whatever Marianne had said, it would be part, if not all, of the reason Leoni was no longer speaking to him. Christ, wasn't it bad enough that Olivier had destroyed any chance they had of being together?

Marianne coughed. 'I may have mentioned that we came to a special agreement about the shop.'

He frowned. 'We did. I wasn't intending to tell Leoni that but if she knows, she knows.' What did it matter any more? he thought to himself.

'I didn't tell her the actual details of the deal,' Marianne confessed. 'In fact, I do believe I made her think you and I had slept together. That the sacrifice you made was your . . . body.'

Ashton gaped at her. 'You did what?' Recoiling, he shook his head. 'You didn't . . . you wouldn't. Marianne, you know how I feel about her! Why would you make her think I did something like that?'

Marianne flipped her russet hair over her shoulder, shifting from one foot to the other. Damn this conscience! 'I don't know what came over me. I'm sorry, I really am. But Leoni looked like Bambi standing there with her big eyes and that … that Ducasse nose.' She refrained from saying she thought Leoni was plain and drab looking; she knew Ashton's feelings ran deeper than that.

Ashton stopped short. 'She reminded you of Guy. That's it, isn't it? You looked at her, and she reminded you of Guy and you couldn't help yourself. God, Marianne, you really should be ashamed of yourself.' His temper was mounting and he couldn't hide it. 'Just because you once lost the one person you loved, you have no right to destroy Leoni's opinion of me. We were friends. Do you even care about that?'

Marianne was shocked. Ashton was so mild mannered, so British. It was unnerving to see him so angry.

Furiously, he stabbed a finger in Guy's direction. 'If you love the man, go and fucking well tell him! It's not a bloody crime to have feelings, you know.' Ashton paused. 'Isn't this more about the fact that you let Guy down all those years ago?' he added softly. 'You feel guilty about that and about your feelings, but you'll never know for sure if he's forgiven you if you don't speak to him.'

Marianne flinched as if he'd slapped her. About to retort that Ashton was wrong, she caught sight of Guy for the first time in years. Standing by the front of the store, chatting to the Hollywood actor everyone was gawping at, Guy looked relaxed and debonair. He looked older, of course; he had more lines and his dark hair had turned silver, but it suited him. Always suave and always impeccably dressed, time and age had simply given Guy an added air of charm and experience that made him seem utterly irresistible.

Marianne hated herself as she felt her heart shift. Was Ashton right? Was that why she had deliberately destroyed Leoni's faith in Ashton, because deep down she felt so overwhelmed with guilt about the way she had treated Guy? Marianne realised she had never fallen out of love with him, even after all this time. Turning to Ashton, she put her hand on his arm. 'I'm truly sorry, Ashton. You have always been a perfect gentleman and I have let you down appallingly.'

Taken aback at her heartfelt apology, Ashton calmed down fractionally. 'It's fine. It's done . . . it's just . . . I know what Leoni must think of me now.'

Marianne glanced in Leoni's direction, a smile playing at her lips. 'As for you being friends, I think there is far more than that going on . . . on both sides.' Registering the astonishment on his face, she nodded wryly. 'And while we're on the subject, take your own advice, eh? Tell her you love her. Before it's too late. Life is too short, as they say. Go on, Ashton. You may well be surprised by her response.'

As she swished away in her expensive suit, Ashton digested her words. Marianne was right about one thing: life was too short. Enough time had been wasted and he had one last chance to make things right. His heart thumping in his chest, Ashton headed straight for Leoni.

Angelique smirked as wafts of Xavier's new fragrance were pumped into the store. It was a runaway success, beautiful, sophisticated and sexy. She caught sight of Cat Hayes and threw her a triumphant smile. The girl looked pretty enough, Angelique sniffed; the expensive turquoise dress brought out the startling aquamarine of her eyes and complemented the golden tan she had acquired at La Fleurie but that was about it. She was no match for a real woman like herself; it was like comparing a magnificent tigress to a cute kitten, she purred to herself. The tigress, powerful and strong, would always win out in the end.

As everyone exclaimed and tried to capture the scent in their fingers as it bewitchingly evaporated, the smile faded from Angelique's face. She sniffed the air as a fresh bout of perfume was spritzed into the store. The fragrance smelt different to how she remembered it. It was richer, rounder and there were tones to it that hadn't existed before. Its new component was something sensual and earthy, with citrus undertones.

But how could that be? Angelique frowned as she sniffed the bare skin of her arm, inhaling the gorgeous scent as it settled there. Had Xavier added something else to the formula? And if so, when?

The penny dropped at the same time as Angelique's stomach. Xavier's visit to Morocco – it had been to get more ingredients for the fragrance. She hadn't made the connection; her previous visits to Morocco had been for pleasure, not for work, and any treks through the souk had most assuredly not been fragrance-related. But Morocco was famous for perfume ingredients and Xavier knew the country well. Angelique felt her world shift imperceptibly. The fragrance was different and this changed everything; suddenly, the strong, secure hold she assumed she had over her life and her future felt as flimsy as paper. All her back-up plans had just gone up in smoke and the one thing she had taken as security to set herself up for life had changed. Her own perfume, based on the incredible scent Xavier had created, had been her back-up plan if it didn't work out with Xavier. But now that he had changed it and the formula was different, it would be impossible for her to replicate it.

Trying to control her breathing, Angelique's blue eyes frantically searched for Xavier in the crowds. He was nowhere to be seen and neither was the English girl, Cat. Panicked, Angelique tried to tell herself she had nothing to worry about. Posing for a photograph with an American singer young enough to be her son, she plastered a smile on her face and willed everything to go her way. If she no longer had her back-up plan, Angelique knew she had to make damned sure Xavier proposed to her by the end of the evening.

Seeing Ashton and Marianne talking chummily in the corner, Leoni was desperate to get away. Joyce Lyfield was making a beeline for her and Leoni wasn't sure she could cope with her brand of friendly, well-meant chatter, not when Joyce reminded her so desperately of Ashton. But why did that matter so much? Leoni asked herself, wondering why she felt so profoundly distressed about Marianne's revelation about him. Was she . . . dear God, was she *jealous*? Shaking the odd thought off, Leoni found Joyce Lyfield by her side.

Used to seeing Ashton's mother in practical gardening clothes, she smiled as she checked out Joyce's classy black cocktail gown. High at the neck and falling below the knee, it was surprisingly stylish and her faded blond hair was neatly brushed and held back with a black satin bow.

'Leoni, darling. Wonderful dress you've got on . . . couldn't wear it with my matronly chest, of course.' Gathering Leoni into a hug, Joyce was startled to feel the younger girl's hip bones against her plump middle. She was literally skin and bones and the cutaway dress, stunning as it was, didn't do much to hide her protruding collarbone and visible ribs.

'Now, have you spoken to Ashton yet?'

Leoni shook her head, her mouth quivering. 'N-no, I haven't. We . . . we don't have much to say to one another at the moment, I'm afraid.'

'Nonsense,' Joyce said firmly. She took Leoni's cold hand in her own rather weathered one. Year-round gardening wasn't conducive to silky-smooth fingertips but Joyce knew where her priorities lay. Arthur didn't care one jot about her rough hands and that was all that mattered. 'Darling, whatever anyone else says, the one thing you should always trust is your heart. Don't believe everything you hear, just focus on what you *know*.'

Leoni blinked at her. 'I don't have a clue what my heart is saying. And I'm pretty sure I don't know what I *know*, as you put it.'

'Yes you do,' Joyce told her cheerfully. 'Just speak to him and everything will be all right.'

Leoni let out a small laugh which turned into a gulp. 'You would say that, you're his mother. He can do no wrong in your eyes.'

'Of course he can!' Joyce tipped Leoni's chin up and looked her in the eye. 'I was furious with Ashton when he booted a football through my kitchen window at the age of fourteen and I was just as angry when he got drunk and threw up all over my favourite sofa. But ultimately I know he's trustworthy and so do you. He's a good man. And you need to ask yourself why you're so upset about what you've heard.' She winked at Leoni. 'Why is that, Leoni? Now do excuse me, I rather fancy another glass of the bubbly stuff.'

Leoni faltered as Joyce swished away in her dress. Why *was* she so upset about what she'd heard from Marianne? Why did it matter so much? Turning, she found Ashton at her elbow. He looked . . . just like Ashton always did. But suddenly, Leoni felt as though she was looking at him through new eyes. His preppy blond hair was smoothed back, apart from a lock that had fallen across his forehead. His cornflower-blue eyes were clear and he had shaved recently because there was a tiny nick on his neck. Leoni stared at his mouth, wondering how she had forgotten how sexy it was.

'We need to talk,' Ashton said, unnerved by her scrutiny. 'Marianne just told me what she said to you.'

'It doesn't matter.' Leoni shrugged, turning away. She couldn't bear to look him in the eye, not if he was going to talk to her about Marianne.

'This is important, Leoni. Really important.' Ashton forced her to look at him and almost caved when he saw how vulnerable she looked. Her beautiful lips quivered and her brown eyes, not hidden behind glasses for once, looked wide and scared. 'I didn't sleep with Marianne.'

His words filled Leoni with relief. 'You . . . you didn't?'

'No.' Ashton shook his head. 'I didn't sleep with her and I have never wanted to. Listen, Olivier mucked things up for both of us.'

Leoni frowned. 'What do you mean? What does Olivier have to do with this?'

'Everything . . . nothing. Listen, Xavier told me you had feelings for me once.' Ashton's blue eyes pleaded with Leoni's. 'Please be honest, L. It's important.'

Blushing furiously and making a mental note to slap Xavier hard later, she cast her eyes down. 'All right, I did. A long time ago – for quite a long time, actually. It was lucky Olivier told me you wouldn't ever see me as anything other than his sister, otherwise I would have gone on trotting after you like a lapdog, as he put it.'

Ashton let out an angry exclamation. 'Leoni, I had no idea! Olivier had no right to say those things to you. To say them to me.'

'To you?'

He nodded. 'Olivier knew I was in love with you and he put paid to it by telling me a whole pack of lies. Like a fool, I

468

believed him. But it hasn't really changed anything. It stopped me from telling you how I felt but my feelings have stayed the same.' Ashton looked embarrassed. 'Even after all this time.'

Leoni looked up at him. 'W-what feelings are they?'

Ashton took her hands. 'I have only ever truly been in love with one woman. You. It's always been you.'

So Xavier was right, Leoni thought, her knees going wobbly. She felt overwhelmed but euphoric; Ashton's declaration was startling yet at the same time it was everything she wanted to hear. And she was angry, livid, at what Olivier had done. It was so selfish, so unnecessary. Had he really been so insecure that he felt the need to keep his best friend and his sister apart, even though he knew they had deep, genuine feelings for each other?

Leoni felt so disappointed in her younger brother, she could barely think straight. But about one thing she was absolutely clear: she loved Ashton. That's why she'd been so upset to hear Marianne talking about sleeping with Ashton, why she had never fully invested in her relationship with Jerard, why she wasn't more cut up about the relationship coming to an end. She was about to tell Ashton what she'd taken so long to work out when something occurred to her.

'What did you sacrifice?'

Ashton started. 'My apartment,' he answered flatly. 'I sacrificed my apartment to get this store. Marianne wanted it and I . . .' He paused, wincing as he finally uttered the words out loud. 'And I gave it to her.'

'No,' Leoni whispered in horror. 'But you love that place . . . it was the one thing you loved most in the world.'

Ashton shook his head, looking down at her earnestly. 'No, that's you. I did it for you, because even if you're still with Jerard and you don't feel anything for me at all, I wanted you to have the store.' He smiled at her. 'It's an apartment, L. I loved it, but I love you more. I love your ambition and your dedication but I love your sensitivity too, however well hidden it is.' Ashton stroked her arm. 'You're beautiful . . . and I want you, all of you.'

Leoni closed her eyes and tears slid down her cheeks. It was too romantic for words. No one had ever done something like this for her and she could hardly believe she deserved it. Ashton . . . her Ashton, had done this for her and she alone knew what an enormous sacrifice it was. And he wanted her; he didn't just love her, he wanted her. After Jerard's indifference, it mattered to be desired . . . it mattered that Ashton desired her. Leoni opened her eyes and linked her fingers through his. His blue eyes widened and she gulped, doing her best to be brave. She wasn't used to talking about her feelings but she knew this was the right time to start. 'I love you,' she said, smiling through her tears. 'Not because you gave up your beloved apartment for me, although it is so achingly romantic, I can barely stand it. I just . . . love you.' She reached up and touched his mouth. 'I can't believe it's taken us this long to be honest about our feelings.'

Ashton wrapped his arms around her. 'Yes, well, we have Olivier to thank for that, the bastard.'

'Screw Olivier,' Leoni said, reaching up and kissing him. Curling her arms round his neck, she pulled his mouth to hers and kissed him again, urgently. Kissing her back, Ashton gathered her up in his arms until her shoes lifted off the floor. Grinning with delight, he spun her round.

'You do know you're kissing a homeless guy? I've been living in that crappy little apartment above the store for weeks now and it's a mess.'

Leoni kissed him again. 'I could live there with you,' she offered, kissing him again. God, he was sexy. She wished they could dash off to bed right now and in a panic she wondered if he felt the same way. It was wonderful to be loved but she really needed to be desired too.

'No, Leoni, you really couldn't.' Seeing her eyes fill with uncertainty, Ashton laughed. 'It's dirty and small and horrible.

But we could find somewhere together, if you're serious. Would you really move to Paris?' He longed to take her to bed.

Surprising herself, Leoni nodded, her brown eyes sparkling. 'If that's where you're going to be, then so am I. Besides, someone needs to oversee the new shop, don't they?' She pushed his blond hair back with her fingers, her eyes roaming hungrily over him. 'We'll find a love nest together. I'll run the shop and you can find more buildings to renovate.' Leoni's mind raced ahead with possibilities. 'My home fragrance line will be up and running soon and I haven't spoken to Guy about it yet, but I have this idea for expanding into skin and body care . . .'

Ashton put a finger to her lips. 'Leoni, do me a favour?' As she nodded, he pulled her closer. 'Stop talking business for two seconds. Some things are more important . . .'

'Oh, you're so right,' she murmured, finding his mouth again.

Guy met Marianne's eyes across the store. For a moment, he was hit by a multitude of emotions. Regret, passion, guilt all sprung up at once. Guy gave himself a good talking to because he knew he had nothing to feel guilty about. As ruthless and ambitious as she was, Marianne had once meant a great deal to him; he wasn't cheating on Elizabeth just because he had clapped eyes on an ex. Guy remembered something Elena had said to him about forgiveness – she said it was the most important thing he needed to learn in order to let go of the past.

Guy glanced at Marianne, assailed by memories of her stealing his ideas and putting him out of work, but suddenly, he felt calm. It was all so long ago now; what did any of it really matter? Knowing Elena would be proud of him, Guy strode across the store and clasped Marianne's hand before he had a chance to talk himself out of it. 'Marianne, lovely to see you,' he said, meaning it. His brown eyes ran over her emerald suit, noting how beautifully it contained her abundant curves. She hadn't changed much. Her red hair was rich and full of autumnal shades and even if she helped it along a little, Marianne was still a very attractive woman who exuded success and confidence. 'I didn't know you'd be here tonight,' he added.

Marianne shook his hand, taken aback. She had been trying to think of a way to talk to him for the past half hour and now here he was, shaking her hand and smiling down at her as if the past hadn't happened.

'Guy,' she managed. 'How are you?'

'I'm very well,' he answered, knowing he was speaking the truth at last. 'But it's taken me a while to get here. Sorry, I don't mean to get to Paris . . .'

Marianne nodded. 'I heard about Elizabeth.'

Guy's eyes clouded over. He wasn't ready to talk about Elizabeth, not outside of his counselling. 'It's been . . . hard,' he said inadequately. 'I've made mistakes.'

'Haven't we all?' Marianne said lightly, feeling his pain.

'Still as unscrupulous as ever?' Guy asked, changing tack.

She smiled. 'Actually, I'm trying to change! But I only really made that decision tonight. From now on, I'm going to be nice to everybody.'

Guy grinned. 'You? Nice? Don't be ridiculous, Marianne! It's not in your blood to be nice.'

Marianne mocked outrage. 'Guy! I'm trying to be a better person and now you're telling me I can't change. It's too bad.'

Guy couldn't help thinking it felt good to see Marianne again. She was so mischievous and her sense of humour was lifting his spirits.

'We should . . . meet up again,' Marianne said, her eyes meeting his. 'For coffee or something.'

Guy considered. He had to get through his counselling and

472

he'd promised himself he would mend relationships with his children before he even thought about his own love life. Max and Seraphina needed a father and even Xavier could probably benefit from some father-son bonding time. Guy knew he had been selfish for far too long and that he needed to put his kids first for a while.

'Maybe,' he said non-committally. He noticed the light in Marianne's eyes dim slightly at his words and for some reason and in the nicest possible way, it gave him a warm feeling inside. She wanted to see him again and that felt good. And perhaps one day in the future, he would feel like seeing Marianne again too, not that he was about to tell her that.

'I'm astonished you're here, actually,' he commented, his brown eyes twinkling at hers. 'After you lost out on buying the building and all that.'

Marianne gave him a slow, seductive smile. 'I didn't exactly "lose" the store, Guy. But . . . I'll tell you about that another time. When we meet up again. You know, maybe.' She leant over to give him a lingering kiss on the cheek. She squeezed his arm and walked away.

Almost intoxicated by her pungent perfume, Guy couldn't help laughing out loud. Marianne really was one hell of a woman.

As he moved amongst guests efficiently and professionally, Xavier's eyes kept flickering towards Cat. He had to speak to her. But there was so much to sort out first. Checking his watch, he realised it was time to give a speech to launch his new fragrance; his chat with Cat was going to have to wait. Moving towards the back of the room, he turned to face the crowds, clearing his throat to get everyone's attention. Expectantly, celebrities and business representatives started clapping and whooping in anticipation. Several extremely well-known perfume creators nodded respectfully at Xavier in acknowledgement of both his achievement and his return to the world of fragrance.

'Thank you,' he said, when they'd finished. 'Firstly, I'd like to thank you all for coming tonight. This is a momentous event – our first store, in Paris, no less, which is very fitting and a wonderful, historic backdrop to our new venture.' Xavier waited until the applause had died down. 'I would also like to introduce the first exciting new product from my cousin Leoni's home fragrance line.' He gestured to the area showcasing the candles. 'Many other items will be added to this incredible line which will bring the luxury and decadence of Ducasse-Fleurie into your homes.'

Leoni was practically bursting with pride at this point, as was Ashton who couldn't stop kissing her. Watching the crowd's exultant reaction to Xavier's announcement about the home fragrance line, Delphine ruefully acknowledged how wrong she'd been to scorn Leoni's innovative idea. Clearly, owning candles and room sprays scented with Ducasse-Fleurie fragrances was a desirable notion, one she had known nothing about. Delphine sighed, realising she was going to have to move with the times. Or at very least, trust the younger members of her family when it came to what would and wouldn't sell.

Glancing at Leoni, Delphine felt immensely proud of her. It was about time she took her granddaughter seriously and made a distinction between Leoni and her hapless, deceased brother. Just because Olivier had been a loose cannon didn't mean Leoni was cut from the same cloth, Delphine told herself guiltily, realising she had accidentally tarred them with the same brush, as it were.

Xavier resumed his speech. 'And last but not least, tonight is about the launch of my new fragrance. La Spontanéité.' He took a deep breath. 'This fragrance has been . . . a long time coming. Most of you know that I hung up my lab coat after my mother's death and for a number of reasons I couldn't ever see myself returning to the perfume business.'

Everyone was watching and listening with rapt attention.

Xavier looked up, his eyes intense with emotion. 'But something . . . someone . . . reignited my passion. In more ways than one.'

Certain Xavier was talking about her, Angelique preened and threw a smirk in Cat's direction. Cat felt a wave of nausea. All she wanted to do was escape. Receiving Angelique's arrogant glances and hearing Xavier waxing lyrical about how his ex-girlfriend had inspired him was too much. Cat gripped the edge of a nearby counter.

'I had a vision some years ago,' Xavier continued, staring at Cat. 'It was a vision of the perfect fragrance, inspired by the perfect woman. I had most of the components already prepared, both the ingredients and the qualities of the woman I had in mind. I have to say at this point that the woman I am talking about didn't exist – at least, she wasn't present in my life at the time.'

Angelique stopped smirking and frowned at Xavier. What was he talking about? She and Xavier had been together when he'd started to create this fragrance. Cat also looked up, puzzled by Xavier's words.

'But it took meeting her to actually tell me what was missing,' Xavier continued. 'Meeting her told me everything I needed to know about this new fragrance, this scent that would hopefully captivate women across the world.' He nodded. 'All of a sudden, I knew what I needed to make this fragrance the best thing I had ever created and something I would always know was inspired by the woman I love.'

Murmurs and whispers began rippling through the crowds of people as they gossiped and speculated. Xavier Ducasse – in love? He was a notorious playboy like his cousin, Olivier. He waded through women the way farmers waded through blooming lavender. Everyone had always assumed Xavier Ducasse would remain the eternal playboy; devastatingly handsome, dangerously sexy and most assuredly unable to commit himself to one woman.

People glanced at Angelique, sure she must be the woman Xavier was referring to. Why else was she here tonight? Although she was reeling inside, Angelique was doing little to dispel the speculation as she caressed Xavier with intimate glances. Turning, she posed for the professional and private cameras she knew were angled in her direction.

Cat, spellbound by Xavier's words and intense gaze, realised she was holding her breath. Letting it out jerkily, she swallowed. He wasn't talking about her . . . he couldn't be.

'I had a brief for this fragrance,' Xavier said, his eyes never leaving Cat's. 'This woman, this fragrance, had to be glamorous but in a relatable way. I wanted it to be sexy and sensual and, most of all, warm, beautiful and aspirational. This fragrance is what and who all women want to be. It's luxurious and it's decadent too because that is what Ducasse-Fleurie is all about.' He paused for a moment. 'Someone once told me that branding is about knowing who you are and what connects emotionally with your target audience.'

Cat felt giddy. She longed to dash to Xavier's side and kiss him but she was so confused. It had been so long since they'd even spoken. Xavier took his eyes away from Cat for a moment to connect with his audience.

'Well, this fragrance, more than any others I have ever created, defines who I am, who this perfect woman is and, above all, what Ducasse-Fleurie stands for. It's alluring, it's sexy and it's memorable. It's about an unforgettable romantic encounter, one that changes your life, and it's a unique blend of notes that are both elegant and stylish.' He nodded for samples bottles to be passed around. 'Enjoy the initial glow of sweet rose, orchid and white lily. See if you can spot the creamy amber and the hint of freesias.' The air was suddenly full of exquisite scent as everyone enthusiastically tried the fragrance out on their pulse points.

Xavier smiled as he watched a ripple of excitement course through the crowds. 'Experience the rich plummy heart notes and the playful tropical accord. Hours later, you will be able to inhale the honeyed cedarwood, ambergris and the pure, earthy tones of sweet orange.'

His eyes slid back to Cat's. 'Many creators of fragrance speak of the spontaneous elements within the perfumes they have created. But this, this embodies the idea of taking risks in both life and in love. Everyone, I present to you La Spontanéité!'

Motioning for the billboards to be exposed at last, Xavier watched, along with everyone else, as the purple material billowed dramatically down to the floor. There were gasps from the crowd of onlookers, Xavier included. Not because the photographs weren't incredible but because instead of featuring Angelique, as everyone had expected, each and every one of the shots showed Seraphina Ducasse.

Chapter Twenty-Five

Angelique's mouth fell open. What had happened? Where were *her* shots? *She* was the face of La Spontanéité, not Seraphina! Angelique spun round and stared at another billboard, along with everyone else. Seraphina looked spectacular in the photographs. The scenes had been shot in the grounds of La Fleurie and the natural beauty of the place lent itself perfectly to the photographs. The biggest of the photographs had been shot in black and white in a series, with Seraphina lying on the beach, her long platinum-blond hair wet and straggly and her face and body half covered in sand. She wore a bikini and she lay staring moodily out towards the sea, her mouth slightly pouty, her brown, feline eyes narrowed. It summed up the brief for Xavier's perfume to a T. It was as though Seraphina had decided to stroll along the beach and roll around in the sand for the sheer hell of it. In one photograph, she clasped a bottle of the fragrance in her sandy fingers, a playful smile on her lips.

Cat gaped. The shot nearest to her was a colour photograph, with Seraphina wearing a simple white dress as she strode through La Fleurie's abundant lavender fields, swinging a bottle of perfume casually in one hand. Her blond hair was blowing in the wind and her white dress showed an expanse of golden thigh. The sensational backdrop of lavender fields provided a riot of colour with shades of lilac, violet and amethyst and the overall effect was wholesome yet sensual and glamorous. Another shot depicted Seraphina in a purple polo shirt with spotless white jodhpurs and dark boots. Riding a glossy black stallion bareback, she looked utterly gorgeous, carefree and sexy and for all the world as though she had decided to throw herself on the back of the horse then and there. A handsome male model stood watching nearby, holding the bottle of fragrance out to her.

Cat glanced from photo to photo in disbelief. In each one, the hunky male figure stood in the background looking on, providing the romantic element but not detracting from Seraphina as the main embodiment of the fragrance. The tagline for the perfume was repeated along the bottom of the ads in silver lettering.

Clever, clever Leoni, Cat thought, deeply impressed with the results. She'd spotted the flaw in the photos of Angelique and she'd identified the perfect solution. Not only that, she'd pulled it off in an absurdly short space of time. And now that Cat could see the improved version, the problem with Angelique's original photographs became painfully apparent. They had been too obvious. The sexual angle had been too forceful, it felt like a physical onslaught, and the photographs had been all about Angelique. But Seraphina captured the youthful appeal of the fragrance although it was difficult to pinpoint her age in the pictures, which made it seem fitting for anyone. The photographs were stunning in their entirety; Seraphina didn't take centre stage over the fragrance. And the backdrop of La Fleurie drew attention to the Ducasse family and their history, as well as hinting at their sought-after lifestyle.

Meeting Xavier's eyes across the shop, Cat felt as though they were the only people in the room. A faint smile played at his lips. She wanted to rush to him, to tell him how she felt, but she couldn't, not until he gave her some indication of his own feelings. It was too risky and she felt she had put herself on the line too much already. 'Remember the card,' Xavier mouthed at her. Cat took it out of her handbag but before she

479

could read it again, the lights dimmed and an advert was projected on to the screen at the back of the store. It showed Seraphina dancing along the beach, laughing and whispering the tag-line to the camera. At the end, the film froze with a shot of Seraphina staring straight down the lens of the camera as though it were the barrel of a gun. It was simple, breathtaking and very sexy, and it left the crowd literally gasping for more.

Seraphina, turning beetroot with pleasure at the riotous reaction from everyone, immediately glanced at her father. Her eyes searched his out anxiously because his approval was so important to her. He had been so against the idea of her modelling, he had been so adamant that she should 'grow up' and focus on her studies, Seraphina was petrified he would react badly. She needn't have worried; as Guy turned to face his daughter, the tears of pride streaming down his face were there for all to see.

'My darling,' he said proudly and held his arms out. 'You look so beautiful . . . I can't tell you how . . .' His voice choked. He hugged her tightly, feeling her cling to him. 'I'm so sorry I didn't believe in you,' he whispered in her ear.

'It doesn't matter . . . it doesn't matter!' Seraphina sobbed into his shoulder. Nothing mattered if her father approved of what she'd done.

Guy smiled down at her. 'Your mother would have been very proud,' he said, kissing Seraphina's cheek. 'If this is what you want to do, I support you. I really do.'

Seraphina looked delighted. 'That's great, Dad. But I want to finish my studies first.'

Guy was impressed. 'Whatever you want to do is fine with me.'

'But . . . maybe I can still model a bit here and there,' she said, taking his arm. 'Just for the family?'

Guy laughed. 'That you can definitely do!'

Grinning from ear to ear and unashamedly emotional, Max

started clapping and soon everyone was joining in. 'That's my sister,' he told the person nearest to him, bursting with pride. Max threw Seraphina a look of approval, which almost had Guy in tears. They were all going to be all right; he just knew it.

Marianne found the whole thing extremely touching and, worried she really had gone soft, she made a swift exit, hoping against hope that Guy would contact her in the future. Stefan, the photographer, was beaming. This was the kind of reaction he liked when his photographs were seen for the first time! He had been stressed to breaking point after working with Angelique but when he received the call from Leoni about using Seraphina instead, he had jumped at the chance. Angelique might be a big star but she simply wasn't capable of the subtlety needed in shots designed for a fragrance.

Angelique appeared to be the only person who wasn't delighted and impressed with the photographs. Her face was as red as her dress and her fists were clenched at her sides. 'What the hell is going on?' she screeched, her face turning ugly as she let rip. 'Where are my photographs? Who said they could be changed? Was it you?' she demanded, stabbing a finger in Xavier's direction.

'Angelique, I'm as surprised as you are,' he stated truthfully.

'I don't believe you,' Angelique hissed back. Remembering herself as several flashbulbs went off in her face, she plastered a fake smile on and made sure her best side was on show. Inside, she felt as though she was falling apart. And where the hell was Mason when she needed him?

Leoni stepped forward smoothly to do some damage control and took up the spot Xavier had vacated at the back of the store. 'If I can have everyone's attention, please? Thank you. My cousin Xavier knew nothing about this. This was my decision and mine alone.' She cleared her throat and did her best to usher Angelique to one side to avoid her making a

481

scene. 'As everyone can see, there has been a change of plan. Angelique Bodart was originally intended as the face of the ad campaign but due to creative differences, we decided to make use of a member of our family instead. I think you'll all agree that the shots are incredible and that they encapsulate Xavier's brief superbly.'

The crowd cheered in agreement. They didn't care that Angelique wasn't in the photographs; she wasn't that popular, anyway. Women detested her and even some men found her arrogant and brittle.

Leoni shot a worried glance at Xavier but when he smiled back at her, she relaxed. It had been a bold move but Seraphina was a natural in front of the camera. She had pulled the shots off effortlessly and had managed in a short time to do what Angelique had failed to achieve during several days of wasted film.

'We'll be using the beach shots as the main ad campaign,' Leoni added, keen to get the crowd focused on the photographs again and away from Angelique who looked fit to burst. 'The other shots will be used in selected outlets all over the world, with the short advert being played worldwide also. Please feel free to help yourself to as many samples as you can carry and please accept a goody bag each as a gift from the Ducasse family.'

Angelique was seething as she realised how many millions of people would see Seraphina in the ad campaign instead of her. And what the hell did Leoni mean about creative differences? No one had spoken to her about it. Angelique felt as though she'd been horribly outmanoeuvred by the Ducasse family. Keen not to cause a scene and damage her reputation, Angelique nonetheless wanted an explanation and she wanted it how. The Ducasses were going to regret messing her around, Angelique raged to herself. They had no idea what she had up her sleeve; no idea whatsoever.

Xavier began to quietly usher each member of the family

towards the room at the back of the store. Delphine exchanged a glance with Guy who looked equally baffled.

'Cat, can you join us?' Xavier asked.

'Er . . . it looks like a family meeting . . .' Not sure what was going on, Cat did as she was told when she saw that Xavier was including Angelique in the gathering.

Angelique pulled a face, furious at being pushed out of the campaign and outraged that Cat was being treated like a member of the family. She, for one, couldn't wait to go somewhere private and talk. Compensation would be a good starting point and if Xavier came quietly, there would be no reason to play dirty. But if need be, she was prepared to get her hands well and truly filthy.

The celebrities and distinguished guests continued to chat and drink champagne, hardly noticing as the Ducasse family withdrew.

'Max and Seraphina, do you think you can keep everyone happy out here?' Xavier asked. 'I'll fill you in later, but for now, I really need you to make sure our guests are happy and that they know everything they want know about the new fragrance.'

Seraphina nodded, buoyed up by the positive reaction to her first foray as a model. Max looked sulky for a minute but when Madeleine nudged him, he grinned. 'I suppose I can talk business for a while.'

Leoni pulled Ashton with her into the tiny office at the back of the store and Xavier closed the door.

'What the fuck is going on?' Angelique screeched before she could help herself.

Leoni shot her a poisonous glance. 'Calm down, Angelique! I made the decision to remove you from the ad campaign because the shots we took of you didn't fulfil the brief. We took vast quantities of photographs – you know that yourself – and none of them was right.'

Angelique scorned Leoni's words. 'This is nothing more

than nepotism! Using Seraphina is just the Ducasse family closing ranks for their own gratification.'

'It's nothing of the sort, Angelique,' Delphine interjected calmly. 'I gave my permission for Leoni to explore other avenues with the ad campaign and I happen to think she made the right decision. Seraphina did a superb job with the modelling and, unlike you, she embodies Xavier's new fragrance to perfection.'

Leoni felt warm and fuzzy inside at her grandmother's words. It felt good to be taken seriously at last. She glanced at Angelique, feeling a flash of sympathy for her. Angelique had been hired in good faith and she had worked hard to get the shots, even if they had been slightly vulgar and verging on pornographic at times.

'You can't just kick me off the campaign and not compensate me,' Angelique stuttered angrily, her face contorting. 'You asked me to come to La Fleurie and do the shots. I missed out on work because of it. Important work.' Her eyes flashed at the thought of what she had given up to go to Provence. She had turned down a Hollywood film, probably the biggest opportunity she had ever been presented with. Angelique conveniently forgot the reason behind her distaste for the Hollywood film – that she would, once more, be asked to strip off and perform like some kind of naked go-go dancer.

Leoni drew a document out of her handbag. 'You're absolutely right and I've put together a very favourable package to make sure you're not out of pocket for the time you spent at La Fleurie.'

Guy shook his head in amazement. Having ducked out of the business to focus on his grief counselling, he had known nothing about any of this but he couldn't help being impressed with Leoni's professionalism.

Angelique scanned the document sourly. 'How very generous of you,' she sneered. The sum of money she was being paid was astronomical but probably just a drop in the ocean to the Ducasse family. Livid, Angelique turned to Xavier.

'You say you knew nothing about this. Are you happy for me not to be involved?'

Cat, standing near Guy for moral support, felt her heart fluttering as she watched Xavier stride to Angelique's side. Terrified he was going to kiss her for a moment, Cat almost exclaimed out loud when he stopped in front of her, his eyes consumed with regret.

'I didn't like the photographs,' he admitted. 'When I saw them, I knew they weren't right for the new fragrance, but I didn't have time to do anything about them. And I didn't know Leoni had decided to get Seraphina to do some shots.' He took a document of his own out of his pocket. 'But that's not why I called everyone in here.' Xavier turned to face his family. 'Something came to my attention when I was in Morocco and I did some investigating. I had to come back to Paris to find the information I needed and here it is.' He glanced at Cat and when he spoke again, his voice softened. 'Sorry I haven't been around. I have my reasons and this was very important to me and you'll see why in a moment. In fact, this concerns you too.'

Cat stared at him then nodded. She trusted Xavier. She didn't know why, especially in view of his recent behaviour, but something about the look in his eye told her he had her best interests at heart.

Xavier unfolded the piece of paper he held in his hands and showed it to Angelique. 'Recognise this?' he said softly.

She snatched it from him and blanched. 'Where did you get this?' she whispered.

Xavier met her eyes unflinchingly. 'Here, in Paris. Where else?'

Angelique swallowed but she rolled her shoulders in a brazen manner. 'So you know. What of it?'

'Know what?' Leoni frowned. 'What's this about?'

'It's a marriage certificate,' Xavier answered. He shot Leoni an apologetic look before doing the same to Cat, who started to tremble. She had no idea what was going on but from the look in Xavier's eyes, something was about to change.

Xavier cleared his throat. 'It's a marriage certificate between Angelique Bodart and Olivier Ducasse, dated two and a half years ago.'

A heavy silence hung in the air.

'What?' Leoni grabbed the certificate disbelievingly. Reading the evidence with her own eyes, her mouth fell open. Wordlessly, she handed it to Delphine. Angelique and *Olivier*? It didn't make sense. Cat let out a gasp and almost lost her footing, grateful when Guy steadied her.

'Rene, the Moroccan hotel owner, alerted me,' Xavier explained in a cold voice. 'He remembered you from all your visits there with Olivier, Angelique – and why wouldn't he? He told me how happy you both were and how you planned to marry in Paris. It didn't take too long for me to put two and two together and figure out what you'd done.'

Cat's head was spinning. She had never been legally married to Olivier! He was already married . . . to Angelique. But Angelique had been Xavier's girlfriend back then – hadn't she? Olivier had not only been a liar, he had been a bigamist as well. She had no right to be staying at La Fleurie with the Ducasse family at all. Meeting Xavier's eyes in agony, Cat didn't know what to say.

Angelique turned on her and scoffed. 'I said you had no right to be there, didn't I?'

Still holding on to Guy, Cat felt tears pricking at her eyes. 'You did. And I guess you knew that better than anyone.' She glanced at Delphine, not sure whether to laugh or cry. 'At least you don't need to worry about me inheriting a chunk of the family business any more,' she said with a wobbly smile.

Delphine smiled back. If anything, she looked as though she wanted to rush over and give Cat a hug.

'It's not her you need to worry about, though, is it?' Angelique purred. 'My marriage to Olivier was legal, you've seen the documentation. But it doesn't matter, either way.' She slid a hand round Xavier's waist. 'If you marry me, everything will be as it should be. I made a mistake with Olivier.' Angelique shrugged carelessly. 'It's you I love, Xavier.'

Cat could barely watch. Her heart was thumping crazily in her chest but she knew she had no claim to Xavier, or to any member of the Ducasse family. Once again, she felt a desperate need to escape. Feeling suffocated, Cat glanced at the door, wondering if anyone would notice if she legged it. Easing herself out of Guy's grasp, she gave him a shaky but reassuring smile to let him know she was all right.

Xavier moved away from Angelique. 'If you love me so much, why did you marry my cousin? The date on that marriage certificate says you were together when we were still an item – just before my mother's death, in fact. I'd love to hear your thoughts on that.'

Angelique realised she was going to have to call on her acting skills. 'Olivier came on to me,' she said, deciding it was the best course of action to blame the dead person who couldn't defend himself. 'I did my best to resist him but one night we got carried away. We met up in Paris later and did a foolish thing – we got married. It's not a crime.' She gestured dismissively in Cat's direction. '*She* married Olivier on a whim and you all act as though she's part of the family because of it.'

'She wasn't sleeping with his cousin at the same time,' Leoni spat back nastily. 'Cat married Olivier in good faith, she didn't know he was a liar and a . . . a bigamist.' She glanced at Cat. 'I'm so sorry. I promise you I had no idea.'

Cat couldn't speak she was so choked.

'Oh my God!' Ashton smacked his hand against his head. 'I remember Olivier hinting to me back then that he'd done something really bad. He said he couldn't tell me what it was but it was terrible enough to cause a huge rift in the family.' He threw Xavier a sympathetic glance. 'I'm so sorry, Xav. Olivier was flying out to Morocco every few weeks back then but I had no idea he was with Angelique.'

Xavier gave him a brief nod. 'You have nothing to be sorry for, Ash.' He turned to Angelique almost casually. 'So what about the baby? Is that why you and Olivier got married?'

'W-what?' Angelique was caught unawares and before she could cover it up, her expression showed pure guilt.

'What baby?' Delphine asked in confusion.

Xavier said nothing, his eyes still focused on Angelique. 'It was never mine, was it?' His voice was dangerously quiet. 'It was Olivier's.'

Angelique hesitated but realised the game was up. 'Oh, all right! The baby was Olivier's. He didn't want it and neither did I.'

Xavier flinched but said nothing.

Angelique didn't notice. 'We got married in secret then realised we'd been stupid and we agreed to sort out the divorce later on. Time went on and we forgot about it and then Olivier died,' she added rather unnecessarily. 'He died and the first I knew about him marrying someone else was when I read about it in the papers.'

Leoni couldn't believe what she was hearing. Olivier had got Angelique pregnant? The story was getting more incredible by the minute. Leoni glanced at Ashton, who was looking as shell-shocked as she felt.

'What happened to the baby, Angelique?' Delphine suddenly asked. Her hazel eyes were frosty and she demanded an answer.

Angelique cast her eyes to the ground. 'I got rid of it,' she muttered.

Xavier let out a jerky breath. 'I thought so. You didn't "lose" our baby. It was never mine in the first place and you lied about having a miscarriage.' He gritted his teeth. 'That was one of the saddest times in my life, Angelique. How could you fucking do that to me?'

Angelique shrank back.

Xavier roared. 'You're a disgrace. You made me believe I'd lost a child when you were screwing my cousin behind my back and plotting abortions. You make me sick, Angelique, sick to the stomach.'

Guy was speechless. All at once, he understood why Xavier had been so utterly destroyed back then.

Delphine looked equally horrified, not least because she was responsible for Angelique's return to La Fleurie. She would never, ever intervene in her family's personal lives again.

Unable to hear any more, Cat slipped unnoticed out of the office.

Xavier folded his arms and stared at Angelique. 'So, what are you really doing here, Angelique? It has nothing to do with me and I've known that for a while. No, it's because of the family perfume business, isn't it?'

'So what if it is?' Angelique returned rudely. 'As much as it pains me to admit it, you, the Ducasse family, are respected. Your business is known throughout the world, you are a brand. That's what I want.'

'Respect!' Leoni burst into peals of laughter. 'You've got to be kidding. No one's going to respect you when they hear about everything you've done.'

Xavier shook his head. 'No one is going to hear about any of this,' he stated firmly. 'All ties to the family will be legally severed, with immediate effect. You will not contest that decision, nor will you ever try to claim any interest in the Ducasse family business, Angelique. Do you understand?'

It was Angelique's turn to laugh and the harsh sound grated on everyone's already shredded nerves. 'And why on earth would I agree to that?' she exclaimed.

'Because otherwise I'll tell the press that you tried to steal the formula for my latest perfume,' Xavier said impassively. 'Because you did, didn't you? It was a sort of insurance, wasn't it? You thought you could use it for your own perfume line if I didn't marry you or after you'd divorced me or some such nonsense.'

Angelique flushed, clashing wildly with her dress.

Xavier looked disappointed. 'What a shame. I was hoping I was wrong about that part. Get out, can you? Legal papers will be sent to you and none of us ever want to see you again.'

About to argue, Angelique backed down. As soon as she'd left the room, everyone heaved a sigh of relief.

'Unbelievable!' said Leoni, feeling tearful. 'Xavier, I'm so sorry about Olivier. I didn't realise he was capable of such awful behaviour.'

'It's not your fault.' Xavier put the marriage certificate back into his pocket for safekeeping. 'It's no one's fault.' He looked around suddenly. 'Fuck, where's Cat?'

Guy glanced to his left in surprise. 'She was right here! I was holding her up because I thought she was about to faint and then you said about the baby . . .'

Delphine tutted. 'Silly girl! Where on earth has she gone? And why would she leave like that?'

'Perhaps she thought she had no right to be here,' Leoni offered. 'She's just found out my stupid brother was a bigamist and she was probably embarrassed. I know I am.'

Xavier clutched his dark hair. 'Where would she have gone? Anyone … any ideas?'

Leoni thought for a second. 'Seraphina said she was going on about one of Paris's most famous landmarks before we left.' Filling him in, she pushed him out of the door but Xavier didn't need to be told twice.

As guests began to trickle out of the door, Leoni leant her head on Ashton's shoulder. 'The shop is so beautiful. I can't thank you enough.'

'I actually built that shelf myself.' Ashton pointed to the curved shelf that showcased Leoni's home fragrance line. He shrugged. 'Hey, I had nothing better to do and I quite enjoyed getting my hands dirty, for once.' He glanced down at her, tipping her chin up towards him. Loving the sight of her mouth without a scrap of red lipstick on it, he kissed her. 'I can't believe we're finally together.'

'Me neither,' Leoni said, snuggling into him. She breathed in the tang of his aftershave. Dunhill London, crisp apple, rose and patchouli, so very Ashton. 'So, show me where you've been living.'

Ashton laughed and took her upstairs. He watched her as she did her best to look unperturbed by the lack of space and the cold chill that crept in from the cracks in the windows.

'Oh no,' she said, shaking her head. 'This will never do.'

'I did say . . .'

Leoni smiled. 'I just meant, as a long-term solution. But for what I have in mind, it'll do just fine.'

Ashton looked at her. 'What do you have in mind?'

She blushed prettily.

'Aah.' As gently as he could, Ashton threw her on the inflatable bed. 'Just to warn you, clothes might get ripped in a minute and I can tell this dress is very expensive but I know I won't be able to help myself . . .'

Leoni grinned as her stomach did a flip-flop. This was it, this was the way she wanted to feel. 'Is that a promise?'

Ashton nudged her legs apart with his thigh. 'Seriously, L, haven't you learnt by now that the one thing you can say about me is that I never, ever lie . . .' Pushing her back against the bed, they both laughed at the sound of material ripping.

Shoving some notes into the taxi driver's hand as he pulled up alongside the Eiffel Tower, Xavier leapt out, nearly colliding with a group of Japanese tourists. The place was teeming with people; crowds were milling around the four great feet of the

491

tower, taking photographs and queuing to take a ride up to the top floor.

La dame de fer, the Iron Lady, as it was nicknamed, looked magnificent. Close up, it was immense and its base stretched out widely, encompassing a vast concreted area. It was lit up beautifully, rising majestically into the sky like a beacon and at 1,063 feet it unquestionably provided the best view of the city, especially at night.

This was madness. Xavier looked around in frustration. Cat could be anywhere in the city and, frankly, he thought it more likely she had gone back to the hotel to book an early flight to England. Just because she had mentioned to Seraphina that the Eiffel Tower was one of the places she'd always wanted to visit, didn't mean Cat was going to head towards it right at this minute. And if she had, how the hell was he going to find her?

Xavier tore up to the bridge for a better look, scanning the area with eagle eyes.

'Excuse me, mister . . . you take picture?' Someone was tugging at the sleeve of his suit.

Xavier was about to tell whoever it was to go away in no uncertain terms when he saw that it was a small Japanese girl with bunches and gappy front teeth.

'You very handsome,' she told him earnestly. She was holding up a funky little pink camera, no doubt the latest in forward-thinking Japanese technology. He didn't have the heart to turn her down.

Xavier sighed. 'Of course. How do I work this thing?'

After a quick lesson on pointing and pressing, he waited as the girl ran to stand with her family. Xavier held the camera up and pressed the focus button, accidentally panning back and sending the image of the family hurtling into the distance. About to correct the focus, Xavier gasped. There she was! In the background of the shot, he could see Cat. She was standing by the southern foot of the tower and through the powerful lens of the camera, her turquoise dress stood out brightly against the dark grey steel, as did her butterscotch-coloured hair.

He quickly took a photo of the Japanese family, thrust the camera into the girl's hands and tore after Cat before she moved and he lost her again. Zipping in and out of the crowds and doing his best not to knock anyone over, he kept his eye on Cat's turquoise dress, never letting it out of his sight. Seeing that she was starting to walk away, Xavier cupped his hands around his mouth and yelled her name at the top of his voice. Cat turned in surprise and when she caught sight of him, she gasped.

'What are you doing here?' Xavier panted as he caught up with her, his loose bow tie ends flapping. His dark hair was all over the place and he looked uncharacteristically dishevelled.

And ridiculously sexy, Cat thought. Standing there, looking like a glamorous French model in his dinner suit with his chiselled chin and kissable mouth, Cat knew she would never, ever feel the same way about another man again. It wasn't just his looks, it was his humour and his passionate nature that made him heart-stoppingly irresistible. Realising he'd asked her a question, she stumbled to answer it.

'I just wanted to see the Eiffel Tower before I go home.'

'Go home?' Xavier clutched her hands. She looked gorgeous, even though her cheeks were tear stained and flushed and her eyes were full of anguish. Xavier didn't think she had ever looked more vulnerable or more beautiful. 'Your home is La Fleurie.'

'No, it's not, Xavier!' She tugged her hands back. 'And it never was. I had no right to be there . . . I was never married to Olivier.' Cat hoped he couldn't see her tears. 'I feel so stupid, so embarrassed. I've spent months living with you all and I never should have been there in the first place.'

Leading her to the grassy stretch behind the Eiffel Tower and pushing her down on to the closest bench, Xavier took her hands again. 'I meant everything I said back there in the store,' he told her honestly. 'You were . . . you *are* the inspiration behind La Spontanéité. You're that perfect woman I had in mind. I just hadn't met you when I put that formula together. But you're everything I knew I wanted in a woman. You're beautiful – on the inside too, which matters more than anything.' Xavier stroked her fingers with his, aching to kiss her. 'You're genuine and you're brave.' He laughed. 'You must have been, to take on my family.'

Cat started to smile as she stared into his gorgeous eyes and focused on the gold flecks.

Xavier continued. 'Look, Cat, I didn't want to fall for you. You were Olivier's widow, at least, I thought you were, and I thought you were crazy to fall in love with him when you didn't really know him.'

'I don't think I was ever really—'

'It's doesn't matter,' he interrupted her. 'I was wrong to think that because it's exactly what happened to me with you. I had all these ideas about you but as soon as we went to Grasse, I knew I'd made a mistake and then I did the very thing I was mocking you for.' Xavier's expression was rueful. 'I fell head over heels for someone I barely knew.'

Cat's heart leapt.

He took a deep breath. 'And trust me, I didn't want to fall in love with anyone because the last time I did that, I got hurt. As you know. Although, obviously, I was very wrong about Angelique . . . she had other things on her mind.' Loath to talk about his ex-girlfriend for a second longer, Xavier looked at Cat with intent. 'But you showed me that life is about taking risks and being spontaneous, that even if something seems to be crazy, if it feels right, then it *is* right. That's how I felt about you in Grasse . . . and it's definitely how I felt about you that night in the stables.'

Cat blushed. 'It was amazing, wasn't it? I didn't imagine it . . .'

'You didn't imagine it,' he told her firmly. Leaning down, he kissed her. Taking her face in his hands, he kissed her again. Gently at first and then with increasing urgency. Feeling her heart flip over, Cat wound her arms round his neck and kissed him back as though her life depended on it. God, she had missed him! Loving the feel of his warm hands in her hair and feeling her body respond as he kissed her, Cat tingled all over.

'Did you . . . did you kiss me when you saved me that day,' she asked as they broke free for a second. 'The day of the riding accident?' She had to know the truth.

Xavier nodded. 'Not really the done thing, as Ashton would say, but I couldn't help myself. I was so relieved you were alive and I couldn't believe I'd nearly lost you.' He traced a finger over her mouth. 'I'm so sorry,' he said. 'About everything. For being angry with you about Angelique when you didn't even know her name . . . for not speaking to you before I kept dashing off everywhere. It's just that . . . making the fragrance, it was something I had to do . . . I had to finish it and you were in my mind the whole time.'

Cat grinned; that actually made her feel much better.

'You have . . . brought me back to life,' he told her in a jerky voice. 'Not just me, my whole family.' Xavier looked down at her hands, bringing her fingers to his mouth to kiss them. 'When my mother died, everything changed, all of us changed, and not for the better. And after Olivier's death, I don't think any of us knew how to function, not even Grandmother. And then you came along.' He smiled as Cat slipped her arms round his waist. 'You came along and you turned all of us upside down, and now I can't imagine La Fleurie – or life – without you. The way you went after Max like that . . . you're so brave. You . . . you grab life with both hands and it's taken me ages to realise it's the best way.'

Cat felt overwhelmed with happiness. She wanted to say something but she couldn't. Anything she could think of felt inadequate; besides, after all the confusion, she didn't want to jinx anything.

Xavier thought her silence meant she needed more convincing. 'Look, you've saved all of us . . . my father, Leoni, the twins. Me. I was a mess . . . after my mother's death, after Angelique, I didn't know how to feel any more. And you have to know that what I feel for you is more powerful and more real than anything I ever felt about Angelique. Trust me, I've had long enough to figure it out.'

'But you never said anything . . .'

He looked stricken. 'I know. I'm so sorry I shut you out when Angelique arrived. I was so confused . . . she kissed me once and I thought for a second that I wanted her back. Just for a second. And then I knew it was all just in the past . . . and deep down, I knew it was you I wanted.' He smoothed a lock of hair out of her eyes. 'It hit me like a thunderbolt in the stables that night and then it hit me all over again in Morocco.'

Cat reached up and kissed him. She was glad he'd told her about the embrace with Angelique; it meant there was nothing hanging between them that was unsaid.

Xavier pulled back. 'You changed me, you've breathed life into all of us. And don't you dare say you have no right to be at La Fleurie again. Because if you do, I swear I will take you to the top of the Eiffel Tower and I will do a Tom Cruise . . .'

'Oh my God, was that some sort of proposal?' Cat punched his arm. 'Because if it was, it was *rubbish*.'

'No.' Xavier stood up. Leaning down, he scooped her up in his arms, carrying her easily. 'When I propose, I'm going to do it when you least expect it. But I warn you, it'll be soon.'

'Really?' Cat clung to his neck, feeling absurdly happy.

'Yes.' He glanced over his shoulder. 'But right now, we need a taxi.'

'Why?'

Xavier pretended to look innocent. 'Because we need to get to the hotel.'

Cat sank her hands into his dark hair and pulled his mouth down to hers. 'Well, in the absence of a stable . . .'

'Exactly.' Xavier yelled for a taxi.

Hurrying away from the new Ducasse-Fleurie store in disgrace, Angelique kept her head down to avoid the camera flashes that recorded her early departure. She knew there would be a story about her in the papers tomorrow, about how her ad campaign had been scrapped and about her swift exit but there was nothing she could do about it.

Would Xavier really go to the press about what she'd been up to? Angelique wondered as she tried to catch her breath. If it was any other member of the Ducasse family who'd made the threat, she would take it with a pinch of salt, but one thing everyone said about Xavier was that he was as good as his word. And he was furious, which would make him even more determined to stop her from getting what she wanted.

Letting out a frustrated cry, Angelique realised she had been defeated. After biding her time and missing out on a Hollywood opportunity, she had ended up with nothing. Turning a corner without looking where she was going, she crashed into someone. She was gripped by two enormous hands and found herself staring up at Mason.

'W-what are you doing here?' she stammered. Her eyes were dazzled by another loud tie; this time, a bright pink one with white flecks. God, he's so *brash*, Angelique thought crossly.

'Has your dream been shattered?' he demanded, his nasal tones sounding guttural in the cool, Parisian air.

Angelique swallowed, her eyes travelling from his hooded eyes to his hooked nose before settling on his wide mouth. 'My . . . my dream?'

Mason shook her slightly. 'The Ducasse family. Have they sent you packing?'

She went limp in his arms and turned her head away. 'Yes. How did you know?'

Mason gathered her up, wrapping his big arms round her waist. 'Because I knew they'd want nothing to do with you in the long run.' He stared down at her. 'You're not one of them, you don't belong there. Didn't I tell you that?'

Tears ran down Angelique's face. 'I've been so stupid. I wanted this perfume thing and the Ducasse family because I thought it would bring me respect. I wanted to be taken seriously, Mason!' She beat her fists on his broad shoulders but the blows were puny against his vast size. 'I've done some terrible things . . . you wouldn't want to know me if you knew.'

Mason ran a finger over her ripe red mouth, enjoying the way she fought against him. 'I do know. I know about the marriage and about the abortion.' Feeling her start in his arms, he held on to her. 'I always investigate my clients, Angelique. Always. I've known about you for a long time. And the press have been sniffing round you for years. I've been protecting you . . . it's cost me a fortune.'

Angelique gasped. 'Why . . . why didn't you tell anyone?'

Mason stared at her. 'Don't you know?' He rolled his eyes. 'Christ, for a smart broad, you're so dumb at times.' He tightened his grip.

She shook her head.

'Look, you've just got to know who you are, baby,' he said in an exasperated tone. 'Who gives a shit about perfumes and respectability? You're going to be the biggest export France has ever seen in Hollywood soon.'

'Hollywood?' Angelique's head snapped up. 'Is the deal still on the table?'

'Of course it is! What do you take me for? I told them you were messing about with some ad campaign but that you'd rip your right arm off for the part once you were done.'

Angelique was overjoyed. 'So . . . so why have you been

protecting me from the press for all these years?' she pressed, for some reason needing to know the answer.

Mason stroked her hair away from her face. 'Take a guess.'

'Because you're a good agent?' she offered, not really believing it.

He laughed. 'I'm the best, but no, that's not it. You're different, you're . . . special.' Mason looked uncharacteristically emotional for a moment. 'You mean everything to me, Angelique. That's why I've spent years protecting your secrets from the press. And why I've put up with your shitty attitude when I should have kicked your ass into touch a long time ago.' He grinned.

Angelique's eyes widened. She had no idea why she felt this way and it wasn't just because of what he'd just said, but she wanted to kiss Mason. She actually wanted to kiss the man, to kiss him and not let him go again. 'But I hate you,' she said in a low voice. She felt genuinely confused by the fact that she was attracted to him. 'You're . . . you're repulsive.'

'Thanks,' Mason said without an ounce of hurt. He growled. 'I told you, you and me are the same, built from the same mould. We go after the things we want and we don't apologise for it.'

'And what is it you want?' Angelique asked Mason, although she thought she already knew. All thoughts of Xavier, Olivier and the Ducasse family were slipping away and suddenly she no longer cared about any of them.

'You, you dumb bitch,' Mason said, crushing his mouth to hers. Kissing her hard, he ran a hand down her quivering body and thrust his groin against hers. 'And don't you ever forget it.'

Clinging to Mason's enormous shoulders, Angelique realised they were indeed made of the same mould. In fact, as he scooped her up like a rag doll and headed towards their hotel, she had a feeling they were going to fit together perfectly.

*

In Xavier's seventh-floor suite in the George V, a room which apparently had artwork dedicated to Napoleon and Josephine, Cat shivered as Xavier's mouth brushed her neck. Leaving the curtains open so the jaw-dropping view of Paris by night was still visible outside, he reached up and undid her dress. She bit her lip in ecstasy as he left a trail of kisses down her bare back. The wait had been excruciating but now that she and Xavier were finally together, Cat wanted to linger on every, sensual moment.

By the time he'd reached the cleft of her spine at the bottom, she was a quivering wreck. As she felt her dress slither to the floor and she stood in front of him in a black lace bra and thong, Cat slowly eased his dinner jacket off. Tossing his phone on to a nearby table, he allowed her to undress him, his eyes fixed on hers. Standing in a pair of very tight, black boxer shorts, his tanned torso looming over her, Xavier pushed Cat up against the wall and they were both transported back to that erotic night in the stables. They both jumped as a text arrived on Xavier's phone, sending it twirling all over the table.

'What . . . what does it say?' Cat said as Xavier groped for it.

He glanced at it briefly, then tossed it out of sight. 'It's from Max. He said that Dad destroyed the second set of legal papers but, get this, Grandmother hid the third set.'

'Really?' Cat gasped as Xavier's tongue tickled her in a very rude place. 'Oooh, that's . . . that's really . . .' She hooked her thumbs into his boxer shorts and slid them to the floor.

Xavier groaned. 'I know . . . it's . . .' His eyes glazed over with lust as Cat's hands wandered. 'Don't stop . . .'

'Amazing,' Cat murmured as he dispensed with her underwear with agonising slowness. 'And there I was think-ing . . . thinking . . . that Delphine didn't . . . like me.' She really couldn't concentrate when he was touching her there, she thought, her head spinning.

'She's adores you, trust me.' Xavier threw Cat on to the bed and flung himself after her. 'And she can't wait to host a wedding at La Fleurie.'

Cat sank her hands into Xavier's hair. 'Was that . . . ?'

Xavier nodded. 'Yes, that was a proper proposal, Cat. Now, could you possibly shut up while we get down to something a bit more spontaneous?'

Cat smiled and pulled Xavier closer. 'Definitely,' she murmured happily.

Acknowledgements

So many people to thank! As ever, general thanks to my family and friends for being so supportive and excited about my novels. A big thank you to all the fabulous people who have contacted me to tell me how much you love my books … it's great for my ego, obviously, but on a more serious note, it really spurs me on and makes the tougher writing days easier to bear.

I must thank my brother, Paul, for his assistance with the French language parts of the novel, even though much of it disappeared in the edit! Richard and Julie Crompton at Monster Creative, for all their help with the advertising and branding information – your enthusiasm and time was much appreciated, and all the fascinating details made a difficult part of the novel much easier to illustrate. As always, thanks to my best friend Jeni, for being there with positive words and laughter, no matter where she is in the world.

Very special thanks must go to my lovely mum, who looked after Phoebe when she had chicken pox during deadline week, as well as plenty of other times when I needed to get my head down. And a big kiss to Phoebe for sleeping so well during the day and allowing me to get precious writing time in.

Thanks to my fantastic agent, Diane Banks, for her continued enthusiasm, encouragement and support, and to the wonderful

Sherise Hobbs at Headline, who patiently wades through my manuscripts and makes sense of them. Thanks to both of you for being so genuinely delighted about pregnancy news, even when it might affect writing deadlines. And to the lovely team at Headline who make the whole experience such a pleasure.

There's a theme here, but the biggest thanks must go to Ant. For putting up with me when I'm under pressure and probably a screaming banshee, for always believing in me and for our gorgeous daughter . . . and the one on its way. Much love.

69

The day is dry and bright and icy-cold, trees bare under a cloudless December sky, the high street busy with shoppers making the most of the good weather in the last few days before Christmas. Mia sits in her pushchair, chewing enthusiastically on a bright yellow teething ring with bunny ears. She's dressed in a white padded romper suit, with a blanket across her lap and a knitted bobble hat pulled down over her ears, wrapped up and cosy, her cheeks ruby red.

I smile as I see her, making my way over to a table by the window of the café.

'She's getting big,' I say to Dominic.

'Sitting upright,' he says. 'She'll be crawling soon.'

Mia is in her pushchair, with Dominic at her side. On her other side is Barbara, her great aunt, who's been helping to take care of Mia while Angela follows the long road of rehabilitation from her injuries. A sprightly sixty-something with an uncanny resemblance to her older sister, Barbara holds out her hand and I shake it.

'Nice to meet you at last, Ms Devlin.'

Dominic pushes a cup towards me as I sit down. 'It's good to see you again, Ellen. How are you feeling?'

'Much better, thank you.' I unzip my jacket, the warmth of the café a welcome contrast to the crisp winter cold outside. 'Feel like I'm pretty much back to normal. The physio has been good and the doctors seem to think I'm doing OK.'

It's true, but luck was on my side too: Gilbourne's bullet missed an artery by half an inch – clipping my lung instead. A fraction higher and I would have bled out long before help could arrive. Instead, the wound had left blood leaking into my lung as I lost consciousness, DS Holt arriving minutes later with other officers and paramedics. Gilbourne was already dead, the shotgun lethal at point-blank range as I knew it would be.

A storm of publicity about the rogue policeman-turned-killer has still not abated, the official inquiry only recently announced. Leon Markovitz finally got the big scoop he'd been chasing, the huge story to prove the doubters wrong, a worldwide exclusive that I agreed to help him with.

I give Mia a wave. 'So nice to see this little one again.'

She continues to chew on her teething ring, giving me a gummy smile.

I take a sip of my drink, the hot chocolate warming me, and Dominic tells me more about Mia and all the things she's been learning to do in these past few months. He's not a blood relative but he's keen to spend as much time as he can with her, to be part of her life. He's made peace with Angela and started to put his life back together again, the cloud of suspicion that had hung over him for a year finally lifted – his supposed criminal record, I know now, was just another part of Gilbourne's tapestry of lies. Dominic, Angela and Barbara will all be together for Mia's first Christmas and I can tell it means a great deal to him as he starts to rebuild and look to the future.

Barbara goes to the counter to ask about heating Mia's bottle of formula milk. I lean forward, lowering my voice a little.

'Why didn't you tell me, Dominic, when we first met? Tell me what was really going on?'

'Because I knew that sooner or later you were going to end up talking to the police, and I wanted them to have as little information as possible.'

'So you kept me in the dark.'

'I did what I had to do, to keep her safe. Both her parents are gone now, only her grandma left. And me.'

'She has her mother. She has Zoe.'

'You know what I mean. She needs someone who can look out for her as she grows up. I can do that.'

I nod slowly, catching his eye for a moment before looking away. I've been wondering whether to tell him, whether it would feel right, but now we're face to face I know I can't keep it a secret.

'What?' he says finally.

'There's something I wanted you to see.'

I've been carrying it around with me for the last few days, taking it out and looking at it every hour or so. Studying it last thing at night, and first thing in the morning. I take it out of my purse now and slide it across the table. A single sheet of A4 paper, folded over twice, already starting to crumple at the corners. A new world opening up in six short paragraphs.

Dominic unfolds the paper and reads the text. When he looks up at me, there is a broad smile on his face.

'Is this . . .' He trails off.

'Yes,' I say. 'It's the first stage, anyway. But I thought it was time to move on, get on with my life, do what I needed to do.'

'That's brilliant, Ellen, I'm so pleased for you.'

'According to the agency there are more hurdles to jump, but they say I'm potentially a good fit for adoption and they have kids they're looking to place. Maybe as soon as summer next year, if I'm lucky.'

'Boy or girl?'

'I don't mind. Either would be amazing.'

He reaches a hand across the table, gently touches my arm. 'And how do you feel about it?'

'Excited,' I say. 'Still not really believing it's true. Scared, too.'

'You, scared?' He gives me a grin. 'I didn't think you were scared of anything.'

I shrug, take another sip of my hot chocolate. 'Worried that I'll mess it up, I suppose.'

The few times I've been pregnant, I had always been terrified I would lose the baby. And now, buried beneath the joy and excitement and expectation of finally having my own little family, there is still a tingle of concern about whether I'll make the grade when that dream finally comes true.

'I think you'll make a fantastic mother,' he says. 'A tiger mother, in a good way.'

'How do you know?'

Dominic touches a hand to the fading scar on his cheekbone. 'Because I've seen you in action, Ellen Devlin. I know.' He smiles. 'Trust me.'

Acknowledgements

As I write these words, I've just discovered that my books have sold more than one million copies in the UK. This feels like an astonishing, unimaginable number and I still haven't really got my head around it, if I'm completely honest. I still remember very clearly being a debut author in January 2017, not sure how my first thriller would be received, wondering whether it might be a one-off. A fluke. To find myself three novels later with one million copies sold is basically a dream come true.

And so to *you*, for reading this book and hopefully some of my others, I just want to say a huge thank you for being a part of the last four years.

Of course, another key part of the journey has been having a brilliant publisher and I consider myself very lucky to have found a home at Bonnier Books. A big thank you to my editor, Sophie Orme, for her insight and expertise and for always asking the right questions. Thanks also to Kate Parkin, Katie Lumsden, Felice McKeown and Francesca Russell, for all their hard work on this and previous books.

I wrote *Trust Me* during the spring and summer of 2020, before and during the first national lockdown. With my wife working from home, my daughter returned from university and my son having school lessons delivered online, the house was a lot more lively (in a good way) than during an average pre-lockdown writing day. But it also meant they were always on hand when I needed to talk things through on the story that they first knew – before I even wrote the first chapter – as *The Baby*. So thanks as ever to Sally, Sophie and Tom for their thoughts, ideas and input into the process.

I'm very grateful to Chris Wall of Cartwright King Solicitors, for his legal advice (if I ever get arrested, I will definitely be giving him a call). And to Chief Superintendent Rob Griffin of Nottinghamshire Police for answering all my questions, even the really weird ones. Thanks also to Dr Gillian Sare, for advice on medical matters and the use and abuse of drugs like dexamphetamine. Naturally, any errors or omissions in the areas of law, policing or medicine are down to me.

I found a non-fiction book by Kate Bendelow – *The Real CSI, a Forensic Handbook for Crime Writers* – very useful, with details of this story that touch on crime scenes and evidence collection. I drew inspiration from another book, *Living the Life Unexpected* by Jody Day, who writes with extraordinary insight into childlessness in a way that helped to inform aspects of Ellen's story. I was also inspired by a podcast on Audible, *Evil Has a Name*, which explored a series of notorious crimes that went unsolved for years until a breakthrough using DNA.

Last but certainly not least, a heartfelt thank you to the stellar team at the Darley Anderson Agency, Mary, Sheila, Kristina, Rosanna, Jade and Georgia. This book is dedicated to my agent, Camilla Bolton, who took a chance on me when I was unpublished, and whose skill, knowledge and instincts for a good story have made me a better writer ever since. I'm glad you're in my corner.